The
TWELVE-MILE STRAIGHT

The
TWELVE-MILE
STRAIGHT

ELEANOR HENDERSON

4th ESTATE • London

4th Estate
An imprint of HarperCollins*Publishers*
1 London Bridge Street
London SE19GF
www.4thEstate.co.uk

First published in Great Britain by 4th Estate in 2017
First published in the United States by Ecco, an imprint of
HarperCollins*Publishers*, in 2017

1

Designed by Suet Yee Chong

Title page photography © JNix/Shutterstock, Inc.

A catalogue record of this book is
available from the British Library

ISBN 978-0-00-815868-2 (hardback)
ISBN 978-0-00-815869-9 (trade paperback)

Grateful acknowledgment is made to the Franklin D. Roosevelt Presidential Library
and Museum in Hyde Park, New York, for reprinted excerpts on pages 403–4 of
Franklin D. Roosevelt's November 28, 1930, Warm Springs, Georgia, radio address,
http://www.fdrlibrary.marist.edu/_resources/images/msf/msf00416

This novel is entirely a work of fiction. The names, characters and
incidents portrayed are the work of the author's imagination.
Any resemblance to actual persons, living or dead, events
or localities is entirely coincidental.

Printed and bound by
CPI Group (UK) Ltd, Croydon, CR0 4YY

MIX
Paper from
responsible sources
FSC
www.fsc.org
FSC C007454

This book is produced from independently certified FSC paper
to ensure responsible forest management.

For more information visit www.harpercollins.co.uk/green

For my father, Billy

And the children struggled within her; and she said, If it be so, why am I thus? And she went to inquire of the Lord. And the Lord said unto her, Two nations are in thy womb.

—GENESIS 25:22–23

The
TWELVE-MILE STRAIGHT

I

ONE

GENUS JACKSON WAS KILLED IN COTTON COUNTY, GEORGIA, on a summer midnight in 1930, when the newborn twins were fast asleep. They lay head to toe in a cradle meant for one, Winnafred on one side and Wilson on the other. In their over-stuffed nest, with the delicate claws of their fingers intertwined and their eyelids trembling with blue veins, they looked like a pair of baby chicks, their white skullcaps like two halves of the single eggshell from which they'd hatched. Only if you looked closely—and people did—could you see that the girl was pink as a piglet, and the boy was brown.

"He's just complected dark," Elma had told her fiancé, Freddie Wilson, that afternoon, when he'd peeked into the cradle for the first time. "It's my great-great-granddaddy's Indian blood."

"He don't look like no Indian," said Freddie, who was as freckled as Elma, with hair as pale and straight as straw.

It was Elma's father, Juke—who'd nearly killed Freddie himself for failing to make her his proper wife—who first accused Genus Jackson. Nine months back was harvest. There were plenty of colored men who worked as Juke's field hands in October, boys Juke picked up every morning in the Fourth Ward and piled in the bed of his Ford—civilized, God-fearing, Cotton County Negroes. But Genus was the one Juke had hired year-round, who'd moved into the tar paper shack behind their house after he showed up on the Twelve-Mile Straight looking for work, his clothes still black with the soot of the boxcar he'd leapt from. Juke had pitied him, folks said, for that was the kind of man Juke Jesup was. He'd give his last cow to the devil if the devil was hungry. He had a soft spot for colored folks, had liked to drink and dance with them since he was a boy—why else was he called Juke? So he kept Genus on even after he was discovered with a stolen pint of Juke's gin, even after he was discovered last fall in the barn with Elma. He should have run him off the farm then. George Wilson, who was Freddie's grandfather and the landlord, had told him as much. But instead Juke had given him another chance and a beating to remember. "You old enough to know better than to be found with no darky," he told his daughter, who was eighteen.

Late on Saturday night, coming up on Sunday, Juke and Freddie and three other trucks full of men left the mill village, drove to the farm, and walked the twenty paces across the scrubgrass yard from the house to the shack. Genus was asleep on his cot when the men came in without knocking, hauled him up by the collar, and threw him out onto his knees. He was wearing shoes on his feet, a pair of alligator boots. What kind of man but a guilty one slept in his shoes? Juke had never liked those boots. He shouldn't have trusted a man in those boots. The man took off down the dirt road like a swamp rabbit out of a briar patch, as though he'd already been running in his dreams.

A storm had passed that evening. That was the year drought had seized the state in its bone-dry jaws, but that night the Twelve-Mile Straight was pocked with puddles, the night air moist with the copper smell of rain on stone. Down the washboard road, into its white clay ditches, over the rabbit tobacco and wiregrass that grew along it, through the turkey oaks and hip-high cornfields, the men's torches lit after Genus's boot prints. At Tom Henry's farm, Tom joined them with his rifle; at Mancie Neville's, Mancie joined them with his hound. The Jesup girl's been raped! Find your daughters! Lock your doors! The men hopped in and out of the beds of their pickups; their headlights crept along the road. The Sloane brothers came on their horses. Lettuce Jones came on foot, his wife in her nightdress behind him. It was no night for a woman, but hell if he was going to leave her home alone with a mad brute roaming the country. Someone had seen him in Mancie Neville's peanuts; someone had heard him in Jeb Simmons's barn. The whole McArdle family streamed out of their house, the boys clutching slingshots, the girls armed with shovels, the baby in its mother's arms howling at the moon. Someone shut that kid up, a voice said through the dark, and the mother put the baby to her breast right there, another child's hand in hers as she rushed them along the edge of the road, hissing into the night as though looking for a lost cat. It must have been an hour the hunt went on; some said it might have been three. It must have been a mile they spread out, or it might have been ten. But it was in the creek not a stone's throw from Jesup's barn where they found him, only his mouth above the surface, gulping water and air, and Lord if those weren't baby Wilson's lips.

He was so wet he might as well have been naked, his union suit slicked to his skin, when Juke and Freddie thrust him into the front room where Elma sat nursing the twins in her rocker, one curled in each arm, helpless to cover herself. Both straps of her overalls were undone, her shirt unbuttoned to the world. The other men stood behind him in the doorway, trailing out onto the porch. At the window just over her shoulder, two little boys pressed their faces to the glass, watching her through their dirty fingerprints.

"Go ahead," Juke said to her. "Tell us what he done."

Elma stopped rocking.

"Go ahead," he said to Genus, wrestling his arms behind his back. "Tell us that ain't your kin."

Genus looked away from Elma's white breasts.

"This girl and her child ain't done no sin," said Juke. "They'll be spared by the Lord. But the Bible says when a man lies with a girl in the field, his neighbors must rise up and do what's called for."

Genus's boots, still on his feet, squeaked with creek water. The only other sound in the room was the babies' suckling.

"Boss," Genus said, struggling to catch his breath, "I'd lie with your mule before I'd lie with that girl."

Elma gasped, as though bitten by one of her babies. Freddie lunged after Genus, but Juke held him back. She looked from Genus to Freddie to her father, and just for a moment, her eyes filled with tears. Only then, lowering her eyes to the floor, did she offer the smallest of nods.

That was enough for Freddie and Juke. Some of the men waiting outside said they should send for Sheriff Cleave. Some of them didn't. All of them followed Juke with their torches and guns as he ordered Genus onto his swayback mule. They held his hands behind his back while Freddie tied them with a short length of rope. The mule's name was Mamie, and the colored man had been seen atop her back before, ambling up and down the Twelve-Mile Straight when the day's work was done. Now Juke led Mamie and the mob through the yard, over the charred remains of another shack, to the edge of the field. There were plenty of trees to choose from. There were black gum and cottonwood, pecan and pine, oak trees trimmed with silver tinsel, weeping over the road. But it was the gourd tree they settled on—not a real tree at all but a post shooting up over the sorghum cane, four strong wooden beams crisscrossed at the top like the telephone poles in town. From the beams hung a dozen gourds, bleached white from the sun—birdhouses for the purple martins, who were said to keep the mosquitoes away. Elma had carved and dried and hung the gourds herself, close enough to each other to make a dull kind of music, like wind chimes, though there was no wind tonight.

"It's all right, old girl," Genus could be heard to say. "The Lord will take me. The Lord will have me."

Freddie looped another rope over one of the crossbeams and the noose around Genus's neck. Genus didn't struggle, and Mamie didn't have to wait for Juke's tap. Spooked by the dark, or the crowd, she dashed out as soon as she was free of their hands. Genus dropped, his neck snapping like a chicken's, his body falling limp. The martins shot out of the gourds, black as bats, and for a moment formed a single shadow above them.

From the tin in the chest pocket of his overalls, Juke took a grab of loose-leaf chaw and arranged it along his gums. He did this while cradling a shotgun, a Winchester twelve gauge, as easily as the mother on the road had held the baby to her breast. Genus swung in the July night, the moon near full above him. He was tall, and Mamie was not. The toes of his boots hovered but a foot from the ground.

Then one boot, heavy with water, dropped into the dirt. Freddie let go of his rifle and picked up the boot and inspected it. "That real alley-gator?" He slipped the other one off, carefully, as though not to wake a sleeping lover, and then he unlaced his own shoes. They fit the dead man snugly. The boots were loose on Freddie, but they looked fine. "Now we square!" he said, doing a little dance, and the people cheered.

The children threw the first stones. Then some drunk fool with a twenty-two started unloading bullets. It was Tom Henry, or it was Willie Cousins, or it was Willie Cousins's cousin Bill, or it was all three shooting wildly, into the sky, into the empty sockets of the gourds, the post and the body receiving the bullets with the same soft thud. "Ain't no nigger lover now, ain't you, Juke?" The next day, and for weeks afterward, boys would come to the gourd tree to run their fingers over its scars, to collect the stray bullets at its feet.

"Enough!" Juke said now, spitting the tobacco into the dirt. He'd walked to the barn for his sickle and now he cut down Genus before he'd been dead ten minutes. "I can't stand to see a man hang all night."

That might have been the end of it, but Freddie thought folks in town should get a look at the body. Juke had gone back to the house by the time Freddie tied Genus's bound wrists to the rear of his Chevrolet truck and drove back down the Twelve-Mile Straight, continued into Florence where the road became Main Street, then, at the far edge of town, left him in the middle of the street in the mill village. In fact, everyone had gone home by then. No men had jumped into the back of the truck, and no joyful shots were heard as the vehicle made its way into town; Mancie Neville's hound had not chased the body down the road, tearing an ear from his head; the mill workers had not rushed from their homes to claim a finger; Tom Henry had not fallen from the truck and broken his left arm—if you asked him later, he'd tell you he'd fallen from his hayloft. If you asked folks the next morning, as the sheriff did, where they were at midnight, you'd learn that they were home in their beds, every last one of them, sleeping like babies.

TWO

COTTON COUNTY WAS IN THE SOUTH-CENTRAL PART OF THE state, an anvil-shaped box at the edge of what they called the Wiregrass Region. There were acres and pale acres of sorghum and cotton and peanuts and corn, piney woods spotted with sandhills and cut through with the blades of rivers and swamps that made the sky seem even bigger, reflecting it like the back of a spoon. The rivers that ran north past the fall line ran rusty with red clay, but most of the clay in Cotton County was white as chalk. The Creek River was grand enough to power the Florence Cotton Mill in town, though six miles west, at the Wilson farm, it was no bigger than your biggest cow, tongue to tail. That year the drought had dried it to little more than a creek carved into the shoulder of the Twelve-Mile Straight, which ran alongside the river like a twin. It was known to most as the crossroads farm, since it was where the Straight crossed what was now called String Wilson Road. On the southeast corner of the crossroads sat the Creek Baptist Missionary Church, and catty-corner to it was the crossroads general store, where after church on a Sunday folks could be seen milling about on the porch, the Jesups among them. The Jesups had been the principal sharecropping family at the crossroads farm since the turn of the century, when the Wilsons built the mill and moved from the farm to the county seat, and the Jesups moved from the tar paper shack into the big house.

They called it the big house, but it wasn't big. It was one of those single-story dogtrots you saw in the country in those days, built high off the ground, split in two, with the kitchen and front room on one side and the two bedrooms on the other. Down the middle of the house was a hallway open to the outdoors, so the breeze could come and go and keep the rooms cool. A front porch faced the creek and then, over a plank bridge, the road, and a back porch faced the outhouse and smokehouse and sugarhouse and barn, which had a little cotton house attached to it, and the garden and the shack, with stump-strewn fields to the north and to the west and the edge of the acres dense with pines along the road. There were four mules and four cows in the barn, and four or five hogs that preferred the cool clay refuge under the house. The hallway was so wide the house almost seemed to be two houses. But a single tin roof covered both halves. On windy autumn nights, pecans blasted the roof like rain.

Since the spring of 1912, when in a single week he lost his father to consumption and his wife, Jessa, to childbirth, the farm had been in Juke Jesup's care. He returned from burying his father with his people in Carolina to find two hundred acres and a baby girl waiting for him. His mother had died the same way. Juke told Elma he'd have buried his own arm to have her resemble her mother, but it was Juke she favored.

It was Ketty, the colored maid, who delivered the baby. She'd been a granny midwife since she was old enough to tie a knot, and she'd lost mothers before—"Midwives is just delivering the Lord's wishes," she said. But she wore Jessa's loss hard. She washed her friend and prayed over her and dressed her in her wedding gown and took care of the baby until Juke came home, carrying Elma out to the barn to suckle from the cows. She refused Maggie's milk but loved Ida's (it was just the two cows then); until Ida quit milking, it was only hers Elma would drink. Juke kept Ketty on to cook and clean and look after Elma while he worked the fields with Ketty's man, Sterling. Ketty and Sterling lived in what used to be the Jesups' shack, behind the big house, the two buildings strung together with the dull flags of their shared laundry. It was the shack Genus Jackson would live in years later.

Elma was four when Ketty had her own daughter, Nan, and five when Ketty cut out the baby's tongue with her scalpel so she wouldn't die like her great-grandmother and her grandmother and, when Nan was twelve years old, Ketty herself, cancer eating their tongues like a weevil through a cotton boll. The baby was old enough then to wean, and Elma helped the poor child learn to eat milky grits with a spoon. When Elma asked Juke what had become of Nan's tongue, he told her, laughing, that Ketty had eaten it, for that's what coloreds did— didn't she see what unsavory parts they took of the pigs each winter? Ketty ate tobacco and Ketty ate dirt, so Elma believed her father. After she cut out her tongue, Ketty fed Nan dirt too, white clumps of clay she found between the road and the creek. She ate real food, but it took her a long while and she made a good mess. The white clay was creamy and it was free and it gave her something to chew.

Used to be George Wilson would pay Sterling and Juke the same, for their work was the same, but after the boll weevil came, they were glad if they broke even. If there was anything left, it went to Juke. When Nan was little more than a baby, Sterling left on a freight train, saying he was headed for the steel mill in Baltimore, that men were needed now that the country was taking up with the war, that he'd send for Nan and Ketty when he was settled. The war ended. He didn't return. But he sent money when he could, and a Buffalo nickel every birthday. When Ketty died, he sent two, and Nan moved into the big house, into the pantry off the kitchen, and began doing the housework her mother used to do. Juke said, "No use having your pretty head get wet in the rain." He would give her a nickel too when she was good, and with her mother gone she began to take over her midwife work, delivering the younger brothers and sisters of the babies Ketty had brought into the world. The money she earned that way came back to the big house, for they were meant to share. As for the shack, George Wilson came to allow Juke to put who he pleased in it, and to share how he pleased as well. And because he was the kind of man he was, Juke divided the fruits of their crops when there was fruit to divide. If he told the field hands he was overseer, and maybe he did from time to time, it was only because that was the closest word for what he was.

The girls grew up working side by side on the farm, Nan after her chores and Elma after school. (Why couldn't Nan go to the colored school in town? Elma asked her father, and he said, What tongue's she gone use to learn her letters?) At picking time, Elma stayed home from school to help. She picked and she chopped and she plowed and she tilled, riding in her father's lap over the harrow while Clarence and Mamie pulled them, thrilling at the thrum of the disks spinning the earth beneath their feet. Nan did the listening—she was good at listening—and Elma did the talking and the telling and the singing. Elma sang on the porch and in the kitchen and in the fields, to the guineas and chickens and cows and mules, "Amazing Grace" and "Down in the Valley" and "Down by the Riverside." She sang while she picked cotton and while she shelled peas, while she washed her hair in the creek and while she brushed it. She sang in church, though she didn't need church to sing, or even to praise God, since God lived in the sky and in the trees, Ketty had liked to say, in the dirt and the seeds they scattered over it.

Elma worked so hard her daddy didn't notice he had no sons. She was her father's daughter because she couldn't be anything else. She had the same mineral-red hair as Juke and the same glass-bottle-green eyes. She had the same widow's peak over the same high, sunburnt forehead. She had the same swift, steady way of walking, picking up her feet as though the ground were hot through her shoes, and always straight, even when she wasn't in the field, as though there were corn growing up to her elbows on either side. And she was tall, Elma was, near as tall as Juke. She wore three different dresses to school and to church, but on the farm she seemed mostly to wear her daddy's old Sears, Roebuck overalls, the sleeves of her flannel shirt rolled to her elbows, a bird's nest of a straw hat perched on her head, worn clean through at the crown. From the road, looking out across the acres with the sun in your eyes, used to be it was hard to tell whether the body in the field was father or daughter.

Nan wore dresses, though now she looked like a boy herself. She'd cut her hair short when she was thirteen, the way Negro men wore it, almost no hair at all. She was as skinny and dark as a shadow. That was the way Elma's daddy put it. Elma's daddy said Nan was so skinny because she ate so much dirt.

There were times, growing up, when Elma wished she were as dark as a shadow. She liked the way the sun warmed the skin of the men in the fields, their arms and necks and cheeks glowing the color of sorghum syrup by summer's end. She hated her freckles, hated the way the sun turned her pink, how it burned her skin like paper. When she got a bad burn, Ketty mixed up a bowl of aloe and black tea and slathered her with it, which wasn't so bad, because the inky jelly was cool on her skin and made it look darker, darker even than little Nan, whose skin was the woody brown of the paper-shell pecans that fell in the yard.

It gave her an idea. One morning when she was seven, when her father had gone to town, she found a jar of syrup in the pantry, made from their own sweet sorghum. She stripped down to her britches and painted herself with it, using the brush they used for basting. She covered every exposed inch, from her widow's peak to her toes. When Ketty came into the kitchen carrying Nan on her hip, she let out a holler.

Elma said, "Look, Ketty! I'm Nan's sister."

The sorghum wasn't as soothing as the aloe and black tea, nor was the kerosene that Ketty used to scrub it off. She poured it right into the water in the tub on the porch, and it stung worse than any sunburn. "You like playing around like a colored child, do you? Lucky your daddy ain't here," she said, holding Elma's face and scrubbing her chin. "I won't be telling him, and I suggest you don't, either."

"He won't be mad, Ketty. He done the same thing hisself when he was a boy." Elma told the story of when her father and his friend String, George Wilson's son, had painted themselves with tar to play like colored folks. That was the first time George had told String not to play with Juke, but it wasn't the last. It was true that it was Juke's idea. He'd found the tar in a pail in the shed. It was the tar they used to paper the shack. The shack smelled of it, and as a child living there Juke had loved the smell and later he loved it because it smelled like that day with String, and now Elma loved it too.

Ketty shook her head and scrubbed some more and said, "You both crazier than a rat trapped in a tin shithouse. Ain't enough kerosene on God's earth for you fools." Then, her voice softening, she said, "I reckon I should be glad this ain't tar." Ketty sent her to the creek to wash off the kerosene.

Now Ketty was gone, the only mother Elma knew. It was the three of them, Juke, Elma, and Nan, living in the big house, and though it all belonged to George Wilson—the house, the mules, the seeds in the ground—it was easy to think it was theirs, that they weren't true sharecroppers, since other than the Wilsons the only ones they shared with were each other. They didn't struggle the way of the other halvers-hands down the Straight, farmers with eight, ten, twelve mouths to feed, who wandered from county to county each harvest, who even before the hard times came were on hard times. The big house had glass in the windows and rugs on the floors. The Lord had blessed them.

("Nigger lover think he mighty, three a them in that big house," a neighbor might be heard to say. And then the wife would remind him, "You ain't talk like that come slaying time, when you needed him to do for the hogs." And the husband wouldn't remind her, because she didn't like to be reminded, how much he did like Juke Jesup's gin.)

So the three of them worked the same fields, ate at the same table, shared the same Bible, Elma reading to Juke and Nan each night. And now that Nan slept in the big house—well, if they weren't sisters, what were they?

———

Every Sunday morning since she was a girl (except for the winter ones, when she would heat water for the tub on the porch), Elma would follow the clay footpath through the pines behind the big house to bathe in the creek. A hundred years before, the Creek River had been called the Muskogee, for the people who had lived on its shores, but after the tribe was forced west and the land surveyed and mapped and distributed to whites, the town's founder had renamed it the Creek, the tribe's more civilized name, and a more suitable one for modern Florence. (It was the age when Georgia named her towns after the craggy city-states of ancient Europe—Athens, Sparta, Rome—though Florence was the name of the founder's mother, who went by Flo.) That made the creek, when the river trickled into one, Creek Creek. George Wilson's grandfather had been one of the men distributed two hundred acres of land along the road they called the Twelve-Mile Straight, for that was the age when they named a thing for what it was and no more. The Straight was straight, no kinks or curves, just a rise here or there, barely a hill.

Nobody called Creek Creek by its name. Some—the few Black Dutch left in the Indian village east of town—still called it the Muskogee. Most just called it the creek. Elma called it Lizard Creek, for the lizards that darted at her ankles and also because from the sandhill bank, it was shaped like a lizard looking over its shoulder, and the surface was as green and scaly as a lizard's back. Sunday mornings she'd string up her clothes on the lowest branch of the catalpa tree—

the overalls she'd stepped out of, and the clean dress she'd change into—slipping the branch through the sleeves like an arm, so the clothes hung from the tree side by side, two friends keeping her company while she bathed with a soap cake in the creek. It was the place where her father had taught her to fish, plucking a fat catalpa worm from a leaf and threading the hook through its leopard hide. In the fall, Elma and Nan would gather the catalpa's pods from the bank, long as their arms and rattling with seeds, and they would make music with them and weave them into wreaths.

Nan did not go to church with the family (what did she need with the Lord, Juke said, when He had already withheld his blessings?), and so she did not go to the creek with Elma on Sundays. It wasn't proper to bathe with coloreds, Juke said, though Elma had washed Nan in the tub when she was small, though they went to the privy together, and though Elma had shown Nan how to fold a rag when her bleeding came last year, just as Ketty had shown her. Nan bathed on Tuesdays, the day they did the wash, and Elma's father bathed in town at the mill when he made deliveries, in a shower stall with heated water.

So late one September night in 1929, when Elma went to the privy and heard footsteps on the path to the creek, she thought it must be the new field hand. The footsteps were slow, careful. Branches snapped. Genus Jackson had lived in the tar paper shack for little more than a month. Other than the field hand they called Long John, he was as tall a man as she'd seen, but he made his way through the cotton field hunched over on his long, cornstalk legs, his back sickle shaped, his gait tight, as though hiding some pain in his gut. He'd said barely ten words since he'd come to the crossroads. He didn't join in the songs while he picked. He kept his distance from Elma and Nan, from Ezra and Long John and Al and, when they were there, Al's three sons. He hid his face under his hat. But the other day, when the gate to the chicken yard had come off its hinge, he'd helped her lift it back into place, and when he'd smiled she saw that one of his front teeth was missing, and when she looked again she saw that it wasn't missing but gray as a fossil. He told her his name. He asked for hers, and nodding at the house, Nan's. The tooth made him look like a little child and an old man at the same time. He was, she noticed, not much older than she was, which was seventeen. On his head was a corn-shuck hat and on his feet were a pair of boots made from what looked like alligator hide.

Now he walked without shoes, and without a lantern. There was a slice of moon to see by, and under its white glow, through the privy window, Elma watched him disappear in his union suit through the pines.

It was Saturday—maybe Sunday already. In a few hours, she would wake to do her milking and her feeding and then she would go down to the creek herself. And in fact the next morning, the cake of lye soap she'd left in the crook of the catalpa tree wasn't yet dry. She had made it herself, with bits of cornmeal and lavender leaf, in the same tub where she washed the laundry and cooked the lard. She held the soap to her nose, then ran it roughly between her legs, then dried and dressed and went to church with her father.

That evening, after a day of picking, after supper, she knocked on the door of Genus Jackson's shack with a slice of blackberry pie. He wasn't there. She looked in the fields, in the yard, the barn. She found him in the hayloft. He tossed a bale of hay down the ladder and almost knocked her over with it, knocked the plate out of her hands instead, sent the fork flying. He raced down the ladder fast as he could in those boots, swearing under his breath. "Miss Elma! I could a crushed you flat!"

Under the bale, the pie was smashed to muck. Elma laughed, and then Genus laughed at her laughing, and then seeing the tooth's dull shine made her stop laughing and filled her chest with an icy heat. She shook the hay from her apron. "Well, there goes one delicious slice of blackberry pie," she said.

She could see he was pained by this. She wondered if he was sorry for her trouble or just hungry. He took breakfast and supper alone in his shack, and dinner with the other hands, under the cottonwood tree. Nan delivered it to him in a straw basket.

"I'm powerful sorry, miss," he said. The barn cat appeared and began to lick the plate, and Elma let her. "And you just trying to do me a kindness."

"What happened to your tooth?" she asked him, pointing to her own incisor. He touched the tooth. He had large hands and long fingers and fingernails the shape and color of the inside of an almond. She could smell the sweat on him, and her soap, lavender and lye.

"My auntie called it my shark tooth."

"You were born with it?"

"Naw. I got kicked by a horse name of Baby."

Elma laughed again. "Did it hurt?"

"Like the devil. She had the devil in her, that one. Horse the same color as the tooth. I reckon she didn't want me to forget her."

"It don't look like that," Elma said. "It's pretty as a silver tooth."

He smiled, showing it again.

"How come you walk bent over that way? Was that the devil horse too?"

"You ain't afeared of asking questions, are you, miss?"

"My daddy says I got a loose tongue."

"You ever carry a cotton bag over your shoulder?"

"Since I was a tot."

"Well, you tall as I am, it's inclined to bend you in half too."

Then it was Genus's tongue that got loose. He had questions for Elma, about the house, the farm, about Nan. With her mind Elma followed the sweat traveling down his temples. She traced the curve of his nostrils. They stayed out in the barn until the yard was in shadow.

"Stay here." She held up a finger. "I'll get you another slice of pie."

But from the porch, Elma's father saw her coming through the yard looking dazed, saw her smoothing her apron, pulling hay from her hair. He stood up from his chair. Where had she been? What was she doing in the barn? She was to bring no one no kind of pie, get in that house. And Elma went inside and Juke went to the barn, where he found Genus Jackson sitting on a hay bale, sweaty and satisfied, licking blackberry juice from the tines of a fork. When Juke returned to the house, he said to Elma, "Learned that boy not to come near you again. Don't make me take the hoe to you too."

He had never taken a hoe or a hand to her. She had not known him to take a hand to anyone. So she had said nothing. She had not protested. She had not explained. She did not know how bad a beating it had been. Later, when she suspected how bad, when she began to learn to protest, she would wonder why her father had kept Genus on the farm when he could have had a new man in the shack by dark. If only he had run him off the farm! But Genus woke up same as always and carried on, and so she did too. She believed she must have done wrong, that she had invited Genus's punishment, and that she must be very careful.

The following Saturday, there was rain. They were all glad. Genus did not go down to the creek in the middle of the night, or Elma didn't hear him.

But the Saturday after that, Elma heard his door open and close. She counted to one hundred, crept into the kitchen, and took the whole blackberry pie from the windowsill, where she'd left it to cool that afternoon. It would be her way of making amends for the hot water she'd put him in. There was no way to talk in the daytime, not with her father's eyes on them. The moon was brighter tonight, near full, but her bare feet didn't need it to find their way down the path. She knew which branches to move aside to avoid snapping, which roots and rocks to step over.

He was humming. She heard it as she came to the edge of the sandhill, before the land sloped down to the shore. Under the lowest-hanging turkey oak, she placed the pie on a flat rock and lay down, pressing her chest to the ground. She watched as Genus shed his union suit, took her soap from the catalpa, and waded into the water.

She had never seen a man the way the Lord intended. There had been men around her all her life, her father, Nan's father, the landlord, the field hands from town, the last hired man who had lived in the shack—a scrappy, white-whiskered white man named Jeroboam who as far as Elma could tell didn't bathe at all. She had seen nothing of them but their sunburnt backs. Now there was her beau Freddie Wilson, the landlord's grandson, who liked to press his manhood upon her while he taught her to drive his Chevy. "Less go ride," he'd say, and he'd sit her between his blue-jeaned legs, nearly in his lap, the jar of her daddy's gin in his hand cool against her thigh through her dress, his left arm hanging a cigarette out the window, and he'd show her how to ease the engine into motion, how to work the pedals and turn the wheel without jerking the truck into next week. "That's it, that's it," he'd say, his arms around hers on the wheel, the heat coming off his body like a sun-warmed shirt straight off the line, his pecker hard as a tree trunk against her tailbone. "Less go park in them trees," he'd say, kissing behind her ear, his liquor breath thick as a swamp fog, and she'd say, "Freddie, quit," and he'd say, "Gotdamn, Elma," and she'd climb out of his reach and he'd drive her home. *Goddamn*, she allowed herself to say in her head. Goddamn if she didn't like the way she felt in Freddie Wilson's lap.

Under the moon, knee-deep in Lizard Creek, Genus Jackson stood humming. A slim brown branch hung between his legs. He lathered her soap between his hands. He washed his chest, his neck, under his arms. The cricket frogs called to each other from the bank. Gentle as a teapot, Genus poured a stream of piss into the water. She felt her body flush, the blood rushing between her legs.

It took all her will not to join him in his song, to join him in the water. But then what? She might spook him. He might call out. They might be heard. If her father found them, he'd take a hoe to both their hind sides. She looked at the pie, dark and dumb on its rock. What was she thinking, bringing a pie to a stranger in the middle of the night? Was he meant to eat it there, standing in the creek with his manhood hanging between them?

Besides, he would know that she'd followed him. What she needed was for him to come upon her. She lifted the pie, crawled out from under the branches, and tiptoed back up the path.

All week, at school, in the fields, in her bed, she counted the days to Saturday, when she would go down to the creek and wait for him. She imagined floating on her back in the creek, her hair swimming around her face like copper fish. Or she would sit on a rock on the bank, brushing it over her shoulder like a mermaid. Or she would be standing in the water where he had been, washing herself with her soap (that square of soap, the goose bumps of cornmeal, how they would brush against her skin), and he would come upon her. A vision. In her vision, she said, "Genus Jackson, have you been using my soap?"

Come Saturday, she listened to the sounds of the house settling down. As soon as she was sure her father was asleep, she slipped outside in her nightdress. It was October, and the clay path was cool under her feet. The light of day still paled the edge of the west field. The mules snuffed and snored in the barn.

Elma knew the sound of Mamie's snoring, and of Archie's shitting. She knew the sound a hog made just before it was slain, and the sound a stallion made when it was upon a jenny, and the sound the jenny made, which often as not was no sound at all. This was the sound she heard as she made her way down the path—the sound of one animal and the silence of another. The sound changed as she walked, a grunt, then a moan, and then nearly a hum. By the time Elma reached the end of the path, and the creek came into view, she did not want to look, but she did. She found her place on the sandhill under the skirt of the oak. It was so dark that at first the two silhouettes looked like round rocks in the creek. Then she made out the shoulders and heads above the water—the same shape, shorn of hair. If it hadn't been for the sounds,

Elma might have found beauty in their symmetry, two busts carved of black stone.

Above, a cloud drifted past the moon, and then the light caught the ripples of the creek and their open mouths, and both mouths now made a certain sound, a tongueless sound, one unlike any Elma had heard on the farm. The sound would stay in her ears for a long time, and later she would have to reckon that it was what the Lord intended, though at that moment it seemed that the two figures in the creek had invented it themselves.

———————

The next Saturday, when Freddie Wilson directed Elma to drive his Chevy into the canopy of pines twelve miles west of town, she did. It was the place where the Straight dead-ended into scrubgrass, where no passing eyes could find them. Freddie looked as though he could hardly believe his luck, but he didn't wait for her to change her mind. He shifted her off his lap and unbuckled his belt. Only if he would marry her, Elma said. Would he really marry her? Of course, he said. Of course what? she said, hand on his chest. He said, Of course I'll marry you. And then Elma heard the sound again, though Freddie sounded more like a horse in a barn. Two months later, in the truck, when she told him her bleeding hadn't come, he punched the window with his fist. It scared her so much she waited another month to tell her daddy, but her daddy wasn't even mad, just nodded solemnly over his plate. He's got to marry you now, he said. Long as he'll do you right.

It wasn't until she was far along, when the newspapers started using the word "Depression," that Elma thought back to that fall and saw that the Crash had come then, not long after the night she first saw Genus Jackson disappear down the path to Lizard Creek. It was hard not to draw a line between the two, her following him, and what followed. Pregnant as a potbellied pig, she read the newspapers front

to back—it was the one luxury her father allowed in those months—
and she could feel the hot, inextinguishable flame of her badness,
spreading beyond the horizon like fire on a field. Was it her watching,
her wanting, that called the devil down to the creek? It seemed that
way, even before the babies came. And after they did, and after Genus
disappeared for good, it was hard not to feel that she'd caused the
whole world to crash.

THREE

GENUS JACKSON HAD BEEN DEAD TWO HOURS WHEN A POWER-ful knock came at Sheriff Cleave's door. He lived in the quarters below the jailhouse in the Third Ward, and he thought the ruckus was his fool guardsman, reporting a problem with a prisoner. Best he could recall the only one up there was Wolfie Brunswick, the raggedy-bearded drunk of a vet who was drying out in the bullpen. Last night Sheriff and the guard had rolled their chairs into the cell to play Georgia Skins with him, Sheriff and the guard drinking Cotton Gin in the office between hands, drinking it in the teacups that had belonged to Sheriff's grandmother, clinking the cups daintily together, growing more and more boisterous, until they were drunker than the drunk himself and the drunk was beating them soundly, a fact that threw them into greater and greater hilarity, and more and more teacups of gin. They were playing for peanuts, real peanuts, and the dust of them was still caked in Sheriff's teeth.

It wasn't the fool guardsman at the door. It was George Wilson, a coat over his nightclothes, his silver head bare. Rarely had Sheriff seen him out of his pearl white suit. At the curb, his Buick idled. There was no driver waiting.

Sheriff, still in nightclothes himself, covered his own head with the hat hanging by the door. His first thought was the mill. A quarrel between two drunk lintheads on the graveyard shift. Maybe a quarrel with Wilson himself. There had been unrest in the mill village, you could say, doffers and spinners complaining of too many hours and too little pay, as folks were given to. Folks not showing up for their shifts, or showing up drunk. If they were drunk, they were drunk on Juke Jesup's Cotton Gin, which Wilson ran himself, if "run" was the word for it, for it didn't run far beyond the county, and mostly ran his own help into the ground. But he did not suggest this to George Wilson. It was Sheriff's job to look away, and besides, Sheriff too was drunk on it. Years before, Sheriff's father and Wilson's brothers had all followed their fortunes north, and Sheriff and Wilson had stayed behind in the little county seat that no one beyond twenty miles could find on a map, and so their loyalty to each other was a tonic for their shame—that together they might make themselves worthy.

"It's Jesup," George Wilson said, standing at the door. So it wasn't the mill—it was the gin. And then Sheriff thought of himself, of his own badge. Things had gone sour between Wilson and Jesup. Sour as they'd gone in the mill. Sheriff didn't know why, but he could smell it. When Wilson said, "He's gone and killed my man on the farm," Sheriff had to hold himself up in the doorway. "He'll say it's Freddie, but it ain't Freddie. Well, Freddie was there—I saw him with my own eyes when he come back to the mill—but he's gone now."

"Gone where?"

"Hell if I know. Gone."

"Come in, George. Sit down."

"No, thank you kindly. The man is still there. He's there in the road at the mill, what's left of him. Freddie cut him from his truck."

"From his truck?"

"The men at the mill said he'd . . . he'd defiled Jesup's daughter." A thread of spit sprung from Wilson's mouth and caught in his mustache. "That's why he did it. I reckon Juke's the one tied him to my grandson's truck. But there's a whole mess of them come out from the Straight."

Sheriff had to look down at his feet. That a mob had gone through the county and lynched a man without so much as a courtesy whisper, that Sheriff had been having a tea party while it happened, that he hadn't been given a chance to at least provide the necessary performance of peacekeeping—it was an embarrassment.

But maybe it was for the best, that his hands should be clean. The guardsman and the prisoner would vouch for him, when the papers came around.

He said, "What is it I can do for you, George?"

George Wilson tugged on his earlobe and sucked his square white teeth. "Quiet it down, honey, for pity's sake."

So Sheriff mounted his motorcycle and followed Wilson's car back to the mill village. Through the bars of the bullpen, Wolfie Brunswick watched him buzz down the road like a tiny king, kicking up dust. He was no taller than a mule, Sheriff was, with a slick, mule-colored mustache, and a Homburg hat that looked ready to topple him. If he'd ever had a name other than Sheriff, a name his mother had sing-songed over the cradle, it was long lost.

In the headlights of the motorbike, the men scattered over the mill village, back to their shacks. From George Wilson's house Sheriff rang up the undertaker and waited for him to arrive and load the body into the Negro ambulance. On Monday, the local doctor would help arrange for the autopsy at the colored hospital in Americus. When no one claimed the body, it would be transported back to Florence and buried, what was left of it, in the cemetery behind the colored church, no marker but a dried gourd. By then Sheriff had gone knocking on doors throughout the village. Not one of the mill hands had seen it, they said, but all of them knew it was Freddie Wilson. "How do you know," Sheriff asked them, "if you ain't seen it?" And they all said that Freddie had it in him, that he was madder than a blind bull, that he was not the sort of man to be cuckold to no darky. The men didn't say they'd had a grievance toward Freddie since he started as foreman, that he liked to knock them with his broom when they were too slow, and flick his cigarette butts in their looms, and put his hands under the dresses of their daughters and wives, and then disappear into the office and drink his grandfather's gin and pass out on his leather couch. If Sheriff didn't know better, he'd ask the lintheads if they had any prejudice against the Wilsons, or any allegiance to Juke Jesup, who when asked, when Wilson wasn't looking, might sell a case or two straight to a thirsty mill hand for a song.

There was one more errand he had to make. It was still the middle of the night—that first July night—when Sheriff drove his motorcycle from the mill out to the crossroads farm, but there was a lamp on in a window of the big house. A colored maid answered Sheriff's knock, no more than a girl, though at first, with her short hair, Sheriff took her for a boy. It was so dark in the doorway he collided with her as he stepped through it.

"Beg your pardon, child." Sheriff took off his hat and placed it over his heart.

"Sheriff," Juke said by way of a greeting, coming in from the breezeway carrying a lamp. He was still in the overalls he'd worn that day. He looked tired or drunk or both. He may have been in deep with George Wilson, he may have brewed the gin that flowed through the county, but up close Sheriff saw he was just a rednecked farmer, his sunburnt face lined with creeks and crags, spotted as a pine snake. He set his kerosene lamp down on the kitchen table. "I told that boy to mind his ire. They weren't no stopping him. Lord knows I tried."

Juke pulled out a chair. Sheriff sat while the girl made coffee. The daughter, poor child, was nowhere to be seen. Juke told him about the mill men who'd arrived in their cars, how he stayed indoors to protect his daughter from the mob, how the farmhand was swinging from the gourd tree before he knew what had happened. "Just younguns," Juke said, shaking his head. "Younguns full of fire."

"You saying Freddie led the whole thing?"

"Why else would he run? Other than he couldn't abide being no father?"

Sheriff shrugged. "Spect you put the idea in his head."

"The idea of stringing the man up, or the idea of running?"

"Both."

"Freddie ain't need no help. He got ideas of his own."

Sheriff knew how these things happened. It might not have happened in Cotton County, but it happened in every county it touched. A hill of men, too many to count, too many to haul in, too many most times for a sheriff to do anything about except throw up his arms. But in all his years he'd never seen a mob finger one of its own.

"You sure you ain't out there, helping em, after what the nigger done to your child? It was me, I might a done the same."

Juke stood, walked to the pantry, and returned with a jar of gin, which he poured into Sheriff's black coffee, then his own.

"I might a done it." Up close, Sheriff could see that burns braided the man's right arm from his knuckles to his elbow, his skin a mess of scar tissue, hairless and pink as a pecker. "All us sinners is capable, I reckon."

Sheriff lifted his hands to the ceiling. "Spect we'll have to wait till he come back and tell us."

"If he come back."

"If?" He thought Jesup was betting, figuring it out as he went. He was counting on those men covering for him, fingering Freddie, and he was probably right. "Where's he gone go?"

"Where he ain't a wanted man, I reckon."

Sheriff laughed. "If you say so. Ain't the law that wants him back much as his pawpaw."

Then the house girl put a plate of corn pone on the table, each one cold and hard as a brick. Something was wrong with her. Her eyes were bloodshot, and they stared through the room as though they didn't see anything in it. Sheriff thought she might be touched, or empty in the head, but then he remembered. "She the one can't form words?" he asked Juke. All those years he'd allowed him and George Wilson to run their liquor and he'd never set foot in the big house. It was his job to look away.

"Show him," said Juke, and the girl, still dead in the eyes, rolled her head back and opened her mouth to reveal the pink stub veined with scars, a blind slug in the cave of her mouth. "She's the one delivered the twins. Her momma learned her good." And from there he told the story he'd tell the neighbors that visited in the days after, the reporters, the other lawmen bearing the badges of curious county seats. Wilson came first, Juke said, and Winnafred minutes later, their cords braided like streamers on a maypole, sister nearly taking hold of brother's heel, like Isaac's children. They were so surprised to know there were two babies in there that they hadn't noticed, at first, that one was darker than the other. Even Juke hadn't been sure. Babies looked all kinds of ways when they were born. But there was no denying it. Freddie saw that the baby boy wasn't his blood, and after that, well, it was a damn shame, all of it.

Before he left, Sheriff asked to look in on the babies. Something was tugging at him. He'd been caught up in George Wilson's grand aspirations and perhaps too in the deluded ones of his bootlegging tenant. He shared with the two men an affinity for gin and his belief that a workingman should have it if he wanted it. But unlike them he was a veteran and a servant of the law, with a soldier's eye and a detective's nose. He'd sniffed out a German spy in the pisser at a whorehouse in Paris, France. He'd identified the Wiregrass Killer in a barbershop, when the man was inside with half his face covered in cream and Sheriff was in the road, twenty yards away, on his horse. Now he smelled a skunk and he wanted to see it with his own eyes.

It was something about that maid. Her empty eyes. The way she froze up when they talked about the dead man, and again when they talked about the babies. And where was the daughter? If Sheriff had more than peanuts to bet, he'd put his money on that colored girl be-

ing mother to the dead man's child. Two Negroes doing as Negroes
did, carrying on in the woods. Who knew how the Jesups got tangled
up in it, but what other explanation was there? Sheriff was a humble
man but he'd been through as much school as church and he wasn't
one to believe in miraculous wombs.

The white one was asleep. The colored one was awake. The boy.
His eyes skated toward the light of the doorway. Then the daughter
emerged from the darkness of the room, crossing from her chair to
the cradle, shielding the light with her wrist. Before she did, he got a
good look at her pretty, outraged face. "I beg your pardon," said Sheriff, holding his hat to his heart. He stood between the door and the
cradle for close to a minute, the light falling over the boy. What he saw
was a colored baby with his white mother's face. She lifted him and
held him to her shoulder, and Sheriff put his hat back on. He shook
his head and gave a little laugh. Ain't a Fritz behind every pisser door,
he reminded himself.

Back in the kitchen, to Jesup, he said again, "I beg your pardon."

"Damn shame, ain't it," said Jesup. "Neither one of em's gone
know its daddy."

That was how it came to be that Juke Jesup went free. Sheriff left
him with a handshake and a warning. "I don't care how friendly Wilson been to you. He ain't gone let his boy take the fall so easy. You best
walk with the sun at your back and keep your shadow in front of you."

———————

It was the day that belonged to the Lord. If you hung your wash on a
Sunday, everyone in church would know it, and you might have your
sins prayed for. When the first reporter showed up that afternoon,
before Genus's body was even cold, Juke sent him away, saying, "Let
the dead have a day's rest."

But Monday morning, the knocks came quick—a reporter from
the *Florence Messenger*, the *Albany Herald*, the *Valdosta Daily Times*. They
all ran a photograph of the gourd tree, a short length of rope hanging

from a beam. They seemed disappointed that there was no picture of
Genus hanging. There was no picture of Genus at all. In the front-
page article in the *Messenger,* they spelled his name "Genius."

> FLORENCE, Ga., Jul. 7—At approximately 12:30 A.M.,
> Genius Jackson, a Negro youth of unknown origins, was alleg-
> edly killed by George Frederick "Freddie" Wilson III, 19, on the
> property of his grandfather George Frederick Wilson, known
> as the crossroads farm, near the intersection of String Wilson
> and Twelve-Mile Roads. Although the deceased's body suffered
> multiple gunshot wounds, an autopsy revealed the cause of
> death to be a fracture of the cervical spine.
>
> According to witness John "Juke" Jesup, the sharecropper
> who hired Jackson as a wage hand, Jackson was hanged from a
> gourd tree in retaliation for the rape of his daughter, Elma Jesup,
> 18, Wilson's fiancée. Wilson, who worked as foreman under his
> grandfather's supervision at the Florence Cotton Mill, was last
> seen in his green Chevrolet truck traveling southbound on Val-
> entine Road. He is said to be wearing a pair of shoes made of
> alligator leather, which belonged to the deceased.

Elma looked for the word "lynch" but didn't find it. A lynching,
she knew, would imply that the man had died at the hands of persons
unknown. Somehow all those persons unknown had managed to pin
it on Freddie Wilson, and though Elma felt no more love for him and
now felt not even pity—he'd had it coming forty ways from Sunday—
what she did feel was bewilderment, fury, and finally relief, that her
father had managed to get off without a scratch, clean as a newborn.
The reporters sat with Juke in the rockers on the porch, on the scattered pine stumps, drinking coffee and eating corn pone with chitlins
and talking till the sun went down. He told stories about growing up
on the farm as a boy with String Wilson, the story about the skunk
they'd caught in a rabbit trap, the story about String carrying a po-

tato in his trouser pocket for a week because Juke told him it would turn into a rock. There were stories of Juke's heroics—the one about saving String when he'd fallen down that well, and saving the drunk who'd wrecked his tractor in the creek (it had crushed the man's legs like twigs—that was why you'd never catch Juke Jesup on a tractor). He'd saved a dog too just a few months back, from the burning shell of a car—it was how his arm came to be burned, he said. The bitch of a hound had run oft. Some kind of grateful! When the next reporter came, he told the stories again. He could tell stories, Juke could. He could talk the hind legs off a donkey. And the reporters could listen. They were paid to listen. If they left with their pockets a little heavier, weighed down with jars of gin, it was just to make sure they listened right. None of the stories made it into the paper, and except for a quote here and there—"I reckon God saw that judgment was made"—Juke stayed out of the papers too. It was a tragedy, the papers said, a shame. But what could be done in a case like this?

Only one paper, the *Macon Testament*, printed an editorial. It was also the only paper that used the word "lynch." It was one of those big-city dailies. On Tuesday morning, after delivering her eggs, Elma was seen reading it at the crossroads store, hiding behind a tower of condensed milk.

> For three years, it seemed Reason had come to Georgia. The Klansman had been evicted from the Governor's mansion, and lynching with him. Then, in January, Irwin County brought Georgia back to that dark era. Now that her record has been broken, why not trample on it? The tragedy in Irwin County will go down in history as truly barbaric, but at least the sheriff had a confession. Here we have nothing, no evidence but a bruised ego and brute justice.

"Miss Elma? You all right, honey?"

Mud Turner peeked around the tower of cans. Elma pressed the paper to her chest. Mud thought she was holding it funny, like her arm was broke.

"Of course. I'll be taking my flour, if you don't mind."

At the checkers table on the porch of the store, Jeb Simmons and his son Jeb Junior sat hunched over the *Testament*. Elma looked like she was in a hurry, but Jeb got up to help lift her wagon down the step. "Don't worry, Miss Elma," he said. "Don't nobody care for no city rag."

"Don't nobody care for no opinionating," said Jeb Junior. They called him Drink. That was what he liked to do.

"That reporter show up round here, we'll send him home directly."

But he'd already shown up. He was the reporter who'd shown up on Sunday. And not just a reporter—Q. L. Boothby, the editor and publisher himself. He was an important man in Macon. Head of the hospital board, the Masons, and a member, it was said, of the Commission on Interracial Cooperation. ("Nigger-lover club," it was said.) He came back to the big house again on Tuesday afternoon, after the editorial was out, and Juke, who'd brought home the paper himself and made Elma read it aloud, was ready, with Jeb and Drink and five or six other men, men who'd been there on Saturday night and men who wished they'd been. Q. L. Boothby didn't make it to the porch. Elma had watched from the window as he backed down the steps, his hands half-raised in surrender, then got in his car and drove back to Macon.

They hadn't bought the *Testament* since Ocilla. If they had a nickel to spend, they spent it on the *Messenger*, whose editor had money in the mill, whose regular order of gin was as big as any in the county. But the end of January, a thousand folks in the next county had mobbed a colored man for raping and killing a teenage white girl. They said he cut out her eye with a knife and left her on the road to die, and when they found him, they tore him limb from limb, joint by joint, pulling out his teeth with pliers, before they strung him from a tree and burned him. Elma's father had sent her to the store for all the papers the next day, and he'd had her read him every word. He couldn't read but a handful of words himself, and never took to his daughter teaching him, or his wife before her. When Elma was done, he said, "To think I was just there on Tuesday. I coulda caught me quite a sight."

It was said that the chief of police kept the man's skull on his desk as an ashtray. One of the little girls from Creek Baptist claimed she had visited his office with her friend, the police chief's granddaughter, and he had let her hold it. She claimed she had a piece of it in her pocket, and all the children gathered round to see it, but it was just a pig knuckle in wax paper, and everyone was disappointed.

———————

It wasn't a nod, Elma told herself. She had not nodded. She had lowered her head, then lifted it to find her father's eye, then lowered it again. Lowered, lifted, lowered. A hesitation of the chin, no more. She had not given her permission. Her permission was not required. What was she to do to stop fifty men from carrying out what they were bent on carrying out?

Freddie would have done it anyway, with or without Juke's help, with or without Elma's blessing—that was the way her daddy put it. Weren't no stopping him, he said again and again, weren't no stopping him, until she came to believe it as he seemed to. "You ain't done no wrong," he said, and that was all—they were not to speak of it. He didn't mean that he, her father, was to blame. He meant to absolve both of them. There was no one to blame, because there had been no wrong. All the blame there was, and there wasn't much, he tagged on Freddie. Elma didn't know whether that had been his aim all along or whether he'd been lucky enough for Freddie to accept the blame before Juke could offer it. She didn't know if, in private, her father saved any blame for himself, if he prayed to God outside of a church pew, if the body that swung in her nightmares swung in his too. She supposed she wouldn't ever know. Genus was buried in the ground and her father was out in the field like it was any day of the week, for though it was July and laying-by time, there was ragweed to cuss at.

Elma moved from room to room, sweeping the floors clean, across the breezeway, her elbows tucked to her sides. If she kept her head down, her chin lowered, if she didn't look out the kitchen window, her eyes would not catch on the gourd tree. The gourd tree would not be there. And if she didn't sing, no one could hear her. No one could say, What are you doing, Elma Jesup, singing like you don't have a care in the world?

———————

In the first days, there was only brief mention of the babies, and usually the press got it wrong. One paper left out Winna; another said they were mulatto twins. It was only after one paper reported that the two babies born to Elma Jesup were of decidedly different complexions that the other papers sent their reporters back, and Juke came in from the fields to invite them inside. Now that their attention was off Genus Jackson, he didn't mind being in the papers. The babies he almost seemed to be proud of. "Ain't no use hiding them," he said to Elma. "Might as well grab us ahold a some fame." Besides, it was good for business. The reporters came thick as field mice, with their folding cameras and notepads, standing shoulder to shoulder on the porch steps, wanting to take a look at the twins. They aimed their cameras over the edge of the cradle. They left with more gin, paying Juke directly now, having gotten a taste for it. This would piss George Wilson off something good, but what did it matter now? Juke had already pissed George Wilson's pants off.

In the weeklies Juke brought home from the crossroads store, Wilson and Winnafred were the same inky gray, bound in blankets, sleeping. But the headlines spelled it out. The one in the Atlanta paper said, GEMINI TWINS BORN TO COTTON CO. WOMAN. Elma read the articles to Juke. After a while she got tired of the papers and made up stories. "There ain't nothing about us in this one. It's just about the price of corn." Then Juke wanted to know more—what was it about the price of corn? "It's fine," Elma said. "It's holding steady."

She swore off the papers, but in a few days she was dashing down to the crossroads store to read them again, searching for some mention of the children. She couldn't tolerate the thought of them being talked about behind her back. It was like hearing her name whispered in church and not being able to tell who'd said it.

First of August, Elma flinched at the word "lynch" in a headline in the *Testament*. She hadn't been expecting it. It was the babies she was looking for. But it wasn't about Genus Jackson. She looked closer. An elderly Negro politician who owned forty acres in Montgomery County, sixty miles from Florence, had been flogged over the head by a mob of masked men. The men had come to his door late at night and roused him from his bed, where he had been asleep with his grandson. They put him, barely conscious, in the back of a truck, drove him to Toombs County, and left him by the side of the road. At dawn a white farmer on his way to Vidalia with a load of tobacco found the Negro in his bloody pajamas, and the Negro offered him seven dollars to be driven home, where he died of a cerebral hemorrhage.

There was outrage in Montgomery County. The Negro was an important man. A delegate to the National Republican Convention. Secretary and treasurer of the Widows and Orphans Department of the Negro Masonic Lodge, with an office and a secretary. Recently he had run for chairman of the Montgomery County Republican Committee, and before he was elected he accused his lily-white opponents of fraud. He implied, some said, that they were poor white trash. "That's all right," one observer reported them saying at the convention. "We'll see you later about that."

It was the second official lynching of the year, the article stated, though a July incident in Cotton County was still under scrutiny.

Elma did not read the article to her father. She didn't even bring home the paper, just read it standing next to the tower of cans, folded it up, and buried it back in its pile. Maybe now, she thought, the reporters would be busy in Montgomery County. She stepped out onto the porch of the store. The Coca-Cola thermometer read 96 degrees, and Elma's collar was damp with sweat, but now her neck went cold and she shivered. She had not seen Genus's body but now in her mind she saw the old man in Montgomery County, on the side of the road in his nightclothes, saw him there on the Twelve-Mile Straight in front of the crossroads store like a dog dead in a ditch.

"Can I help you with that wagon?" asked Drink Simmons, half standing up from his table.

"No, thank you."

"You look right peaked, Miss Elma."

"I'm all right, thank you kindly."

"You hear any word from that fiancé of yours?"

"What are you asking after?"

"I never took Freddie for yellow." Drink shrugged. "I wouldn't up and leave my woman nor my younguns, even if the law was hot on my behind."

Elma bumped her wagon down the steps and into the sun, and now her body flashed hot. She would not think about the man in Montgomery. It was easier to be mad. "Don't you and your daddy have some squirrels to shoot, Drink?"

The people of Cotton County were distracted from Genus Jackson, and it was the twins who seized their attention. Through August, as the corn grew high in the fields and the next truckload of pickers showed up, people came to see the babies. They came from church and town and neighboring farms, bearing booties and blankets, biscuits and pies. Mary Minrath, the home supervisor who last fall had been sent from town to help with the canning, brought the peach cobbler that had taken honorable mention at the Cotton County fair. Bette Hazelton, the bank manager's wife, brought a box of second-hand clothes she'd collected from the congregation at Florence

Baptist. Camilla Rawls, the doctor's wife and the president of the local chapter of the WCTU, brought two golden-edged, pocket-size Bibles. "Every child of God needs his own." Even the chain gang that made its way down the road left a gift stuffed in the mailbox, a bouquet of blue hound's tongue picked from the shoulder of the Straight. They came by cart and by foot and by automobile, Hoover wagons and two-wheeled jigs, feigning errands to the crossroads store, delivering news. Some clucked and cooed; some shook their heads. All of them prayed over the cradle. "Haven't seen you in church, Elma," said Josie Byrd, whose daddy owned the biggest peanut farm in the county. She was leaving for Emory, for nursing school, and she wore a new pair of leather shoes, white with white laces, so clean they hurt Elma's eyes. "They got Mary Collier in your place in the choir, and pretty as she is, she sings like a gopher frog."

Elma said she'd be back in church when she was ready, when the twins were old enough to travel. And the women left with a knowing nod, sometimes a hand on Elma's shoulder. "If I didn't see them with my own eyes," Josie's mother whispered to Josie on their way out the door, "I'd say those babies came from two different wombs."

A week after delivering the cobbler, Mrs. Minrath returned in her starched apron, her leather ledger at her side, saying, "Those tomatoes in your garden aren't going to can themselves."

Elma said she wouldn't be needing any help this year, thank you kindly. "We got our hands full with the babies."

Mrs. Minrath pursed her flat lips. "Then it would seem you could use all the extra hands you could get. Especially in times like these. And without any womankind around."

"I got my Nan. She's a plumb miraculous canner. We been canning since we was tall as the hem on your dress, Mrs. Minrath. Even without a book to write it all down in."

Mrs. Minrath looked around Elma and into the house, where Nan was holding Wilson. She shook her head. "Poor children," she said, and turned and walked down the steps.

People came to help, and Elma sent them away. It was true that she lost some tomatoes—her father let her tend the garden, but alone she couldn't pick them fast enough. She canned what she could, and the peaches and berries too, and pickled the peppers and carrots, sweating over the stove. She ate the cobblers and biscuits and pies, hating every bite, but she was hungry, and so were the babies, and they were delicious, those wicked, wicked pies. She fed the chickens and the guineas and the hogs and the mules, trapping a high-pitched hum in her mouth, and milked the cows, April and June, Anna and Margaret, and separated the cream from their milk, saving the skim for the hogs. "It's all they want us for, ain't it, girls," she said to the cows, tugging the full, furred mounds of their teats. "Milk, milk, and more milk." When she was held up feeding the babies and couldn't get out to the barn until dawn, their udders were engorged as globes, veined with rivers of ducts. "Ain't it the worst, girls," she said. When she was held up with her chores and forgot to feed the babies, her own milk would mess the front of her dress, and then there was no ignoring it. And then she'd pull the shutters and sit back in the rocker and settle a baby into her lap, or two if she could manage, closing her eyes and letting the ache ease, and then there was nothing in the world but the babies, no visitors, no reporters, only their billy goat mews and the buttermilk smell of their warm heads.

One sunny morning at the height of summer, a truck pulled up in the dirt driveway and a woman with knee-high boots climbed out of it. Her short hair was yellow as a cornfield. Elma stood barefoot on the porch, fiddling with the pins that held up the great pile of her hair, as the woman made her way up the driveway and reached to shake her hand. Elma feared she was from the home demonstration club or the WCTU, on a mission to save her vegetables or her soul. The woman said, "I'm here to see the Gemini twins."

Elma let her hand fall, loose as a dishrag. "They're not Gemini," she said. "They're just regular."

She was a dog breeder on her way to Florida, come all the way from Atlanta. Out of the wooden truck bed, where a dozen dogs yapped, she scooped up two Labrador puppies, one the color of butterscotch, the other oily black as a crow. "They're called Castor and Pollux," she said. "Every child needs its own dog."

Her father came in from the field and thanked her and the dogs jumped on him and he laughed. What was there to laugh about? Elma watched their pink tongues lapping at her father's hands. This was their reward for killing Genus. Dogs.

"We can't keep them," Elma said to the woman. "We got enough to look after with the babies."

"Course we can," said her father. "Dogs look after theyselves."

And he made Elma take the woman into her room, where the babies now shared a larger crib that Juke had built. The woman leaned over the sleeping twins but didn't pray. "Would you look at that," she said.

"Please don't touch the babies," said Elma. "They're still fragile. They were born small."

"They look strong," said the woman. "Especially this boy here. That's hybrid vigor."

Elma joined the woman at the crib, pulling the quilt to Wilson's chin.

"Most people don't believe a woman can have two babies from two fathers at the same time. They think it's witchcraft, don't they? Or just tales from Bible times?"

Elma felt a sudden pressure in her chest, like a blush, or a rush of milk.

"With dogs in the wild, it happens all the time. You take any bitch in heat, they's as good a chance as not that every mutt in the litter's gone have a different daddy."

"That so?" said Elma, head cocked. One of her pins sprung out of her hair and she bent to pick it up, then took it between her lips, chewing it over.

"Your babies will be fine," the woman said. "Black or white, they're fixing to be strong."

———————

Of course, Wilson wasn't true black. Nor was he red like Isaac's child Esau, though under his skullcap was a rusty shock of hair, like the bronze wool used to scrub the pans. When he had grown into his skin, he was a warm, loamy brown, the color of the earth tilled for seed—sand and silt and clay mixed together. And when his eyes finally settled, when he could stare back at the faces that loomed over the crib and hold them in focus, they were a pale gray-green. You didn't have to look twice, some said, to see those eyes were Elma's.

Winnafred, though—already she was called Winna Jean, or just Winna—took after her father. When her skin cooled from the pink of infancy, she was white as a gourd, with Freddie's sun-bleached hair, even before she'd seen the sun. It wasn't until years later, when the twins spent their days running between the house and the fields and the barn, that their freckles came out, like stars appearing in the night sky. If you wanted to believe they weren't twins—and at some point, everyone did, even the twins themselves, as often as they wanted to believe that they were—their freckles were there, finally, to connect them, Castor and Pollux joined in their immortal constellation.

When they were still babies, Elma dressed them head to toe, even indoors, even in summer. She wanted to protect them, to hide them, to make them more the same. You couldn't blame her. After all, Juke said to the visitors, she'd been expecting only one. When she was pregnant, singing "All the Pretty Horses" to the baby kicking in her belly, she'd sewn six identical guano sack dresses, stitching them together with hay bale twine. When two babies came instead, she dressed both of them in the sacks. If she could have, she would have stitched the babies together at the waist, like Siamese twins. Sometimes it seemed she wanted to believe Wilson and Winna were one child, or that she needed others to believe it. It didn't matter how the babies came to be. Babies were babies. Even Juke believed that.

"Course I love them both the same," Elma told the women from church, the reporters who tracked white clay across the floor. She followed them with a broom. "All children live in the kingdom of God, don't they?"

And they nodded with certainty, saying "Amen" and "Praise His name."

But they were thinking of all the things she might have done with that baby, all the doorsteps she might have left him on in the middle of the night. The colored school. The colored church. In a basket on the creek. She could see the scheming in their eyes, the stories they were writing in their heads. Just like they wondered what had happened between Elma and Genus Jackson in the cotton house or creek or cornfield, a cornfield she hadn't even been in, but they were following her there.

In some of their eyes, doubt. They had seen their share of mulatto babies. The Jesups were as liable as any country family to have some black blood along their line, black blood that decided to rear up and show itself. (The white Youngs who owned the tobacco plantation and the black Youngs who owned the juke joint? "You think they ain't kin?" a white farmer, drunk enough, might be heard to say to his wife. This was raised as a diversion, because that white farmer might himself have a favorite colored girl in town, or in a shack, and likely as not his wife knew the girl's name.)

It wasn't a miracle, some thought, just a disgrace.

———

But mostly people believed. Folks in Cotton County were believers. They believed in Jesus foremost, and every holy cow and sheep in the barn he was born in. They believed in the Promised Land. It was far away, the Promised Land, on the other side of the world, but they believed that Jesus meant for them to be here, in Georgia, in the land of cotton, their own Promised Land, hard as times were. Jesus and Mary and Joseph were their people, country people suffering under the sun, and the people of Cotton County would be redeemed. They believed in Redemption, that their losses on battlefields, their losses in cotton fields, would be remembered and repaid in the Kingdom of Heaven. They believed in the Commandments. They believed in work, and rising early, and the crops in the field, and the rain that nourished them, never did they believe in the rain more, now that there wasn't enough of it. They believed in progress, in automobiles and airplanes, and a few of them in the tractors that sat like jungle beasts in their barns. They believed in Charles Lindbergh. They believed in Ty Cobb. They did not believe in Herbert Hoover, but they prayed for him. They believed in prayer, and praise, and warm meals, in the kindness of strangers. They believed in their neighbors. They believed in Georgia, its clays and creeks, in the heavenly mists that drifted over the fields in the morning. They believed in ghosts—for what was the Almighty but the Holy Ghost?—and they believed in miracles. They believed in an eye for an eye and a tooth for a tooth. Getting caught not believing was like getting caught with your hand in the collection plate. "Any faithless fool tells you your babies ain't kin," Juke said to Elma, "you tell them the only sin the Lord don't pardon is the sin of nonbelieving."

So they believed that the babies were twins. Because if they didn't believe, then they didn't believe Genus Jackson was one of the daddies. They'd have to believe that the daddy was someone else. They'd have to believe that a mob of white men killed a black man for no reason. And they couldn't believe that.

Except the black folks. They knew what their white neighbors were capable of. They believed in the same things the white folks believed in, except they didn't believe in the white folks. (Some of them didn't believe in Georgia. Some of them believed the only Promised Land lay north.)

Except they didn't believe in outsiders, either. Neither the white folks nor the black folks believed in outsiders. None of the folks, black or white, knew Genus Jackson. If they had, maybe one of them would have been seen crying on a porch, or writing a letter to Walter White, or taking up a collection for a funeral.

So even Ezra and Long John and Al believed the story that was told. They sat on their stools at Young's and talked it over. Ezra said, "Boy done come to the wrong town."

Long John said, "Never did like that hunchback boy."

Al, who was the oldest, who had sons of his own, said, "He all right. He just a poor child of the Lord. Poor child done fell for the wrong white girl."

He'd been lucky while he was alive, Ezra said, he'd been treated too good, put up in that shack without paying a penny. Besides, the boss gave them a pint of liquor every harvest, and his daughter, at Christmas, she made them pies.

FOUR

THERE WERE FOURTEEN BOOKS IN THE BIG HOUSE. THE THREE Bibles, including the babies'. The family Bible, marked with the birthdays and deaths of Jessa as well as Ketty, was kept on the mantel, where it collected the yellow light of the fire, and from which Elma read a passage aloud at the table each night. There was a book of fairy tales by the brothers Grimm. A book of poems by Edgar Allan Poe, a gift from Elma's schoolteacher, Miss Armistead. The *Farmers' Almanac* (each January the old edition went out to the privy). And a children's encyclopedia, in eight illustrated volumes, called *The Book of Knowledge*, which Juke had bought for Elma's birthday from the rolling store when it was a good year for cotton. If Nan hid a volume of the encyclopedia inside her corn-shuck mattress, nobody missed it, least of all Juke.

In a house full of secrets, one of the first was between Nan and Elma. The winter Nan was six and Elma was ten, their throats began to ache in the middle of the night. Juke looked in Nan's mouth and saw her throat was coated with what looked like gray putty. He thought it was a clump of clay she'd eaten. Then he looked in Elma's mouth and saw hers was the same. The next morning he drove them into town, to Dr. Rawls's office, and the doctor said it wasn't dirt but diphtheria. Juke carried Elma into her exam room, then carried them both into the colored room so Elma could talk for Nan. "She's got the chills."

"How do you know?" asked the doctor.

Elma shrugged. "She told me."

They had their own way of talking, even then, their own system of signs. Elma knew how to watch Nan and guess what she meant, like a game of charades. Elma guessed, and Nan nodded. It was that first time when they were quarantined in a shack behind the house that Elma taught her to read. She'd put on a bonnet, because that's what her schoolteacher Miss Armistead wore, and if Elma couldn't be a farmer like her daddy, she wanted to be a schoolteacher. Nan would trace the letters in her tablet with a pencil, repeating each one in her head. No one bothered with them there. Nan's mother, Ketty, who couldn't read herself, passed them their meals through the window, and when spring came and Juke looked again into their mouths and declared them cured, he burned the shack to the ground, the tablet with it, but the letters stayed in Nan's head. They were three months in the shack, and three months Elma was out of school.

So while Elma read Juke the morning news, or a letter from his people in Carolina, Nan played as dumb as he was. She had no tongue to prove herself, and in this her silence kept her safe. She hung the wash. She shook the dirt from the peanuts. She cooked and canned and patched the holes in Juke's overalls where his knees had worn through. She waited for her father to return. She waited and she waited. She looked out at the road and listened for the automobile he would arrive in. In the daylight, it mattered little that she could read and Juke couldn't, but there were certain nights when it helped to know she could open *The Book of Knowledge* and go away for a while, get lost in Antarctica, or in Paris, France, or Baltimore, Maryland, the place her father lived, a place that seemed just as magical and just as far as the pyramids. In this way the words on the page paved a gentle road to sleep. She'd nibble on the white clay she kept on a pantry shelf in an old coffee tin her mother had used for the same purpose. Ketty said it was natural, just as chewing cured tobacco leaves was natural—it was God's own bounty and it made a day go down easier.

It was on those nights, the nights when Juke came for her, that having no tongue was a mixed blessing. If she'd had a tongue, she could have said no. But would a word have stopped him? Was it better to have no tongue if a tongue was no protection?

The first time he took her to the still was the night they buried her mother. It was just for the gin then. Juke said she was ready for a man's drink. The log cabin was off to the west of the house, beyond the corn, just up the bank from the creek and not fifty feet from the road, but hidden from sight by long-skirted pines and thick-waisted oaks and the Spanish moss that looked to Nan like witch's hair. She had heard Elma say before that her daddy was out at the still—some nights he even slept there—but she couldn't imagine what it was for, or what it looked like, only knew that she washed his tumblers and that they weren't for tea. She had seen the cabin only once, when a trail of blackberry bushes brought her there, like bread crumbs to a gingerbread house.

That night, he sat her down on an old stool made from a pine stump. The cabin was dark, lit only with a candle; Elma was in the big house, asleep. The air was musty, close; it smelled of a sweetness she'd never smelled before. He offered her a sip from his mason jar, and the sweetness filled her nose and her mouth, burning all the way up to her eyes, which filled with tears. The gin dribbled down her chin, as sometimes happened. Juke laughed a not unkind laugh. She did too, and the sound was big in her ears.

The second time, he showed her how the still worked, let her touch the cooking pot, the thumper keg, the condenser that was cool to the touch. He let her play on the barrels. She hopped from one to another like a cat. He watched her while he whittled away on a piece of pine. He carved her a little wooden cat. "You just a curious little cat, ain't you?"

The third time, he had her sit on the mattress, this one filled with Spanish moss, which he slept on when he had a big batch going. Under the mattress he kept a twelve-gauge shotgun, which he took out and stroked with a square of wash leather in the light of the candle. "Know who gave me this gun?" he said.

Nan shook her head.

"Your daddy."

She wanted to reach out and touch it, but she didn't. It was an object she'd seen a thousand times, as plain as his tin of tobacco, but now it shone with a new brightness.

"You remember your daddy?"

Again she shook her head. She did remember him, she thought she did. She sometimes dreamt of the tickle of his mustache and the smell of his corncob pipe. But it was easier to say no.

"Damn shame he left," he said, shaking his head. "Ain't no man who can leave a child. I wouldn't never leave you like that." He reached under her and slipped the gun back under the mattress. "Even Elma never been out here," he said. "Even Elma I don't 'low to have no man's drink." And it was true she felt a little special—her momma dead, her daddy gone, and the boss man paying her attention—even as she held her nightdress tight around her hips. The gin pumped warm through her heart.

The fourth time, he told her to lie down, weren't she tired from that gin and the late hour? He told her to close her eyes. He told her to put out her hand. She did as she was told. In her palm he placed what felt like a marble, and when she opened her eyes she saw that it was a pearl. "It belonged to your momma. Must have lost it while she was cleaning the big house." He wanted Nan to have it, for luck. It was smooth and white with a bluish sheen, like the skin that formed at the top of a bucket of milk, a tiny hole pierced through either side. Nan held it in her hand until she was back in her own room, and then she hid it too, in her corn-shuck mattress.

The fifth time, he lay down beside her. He stroked her braids, which had gone wiry. Such pretty hair, he said, but weren't she lonesome, no momma to tend them?

And like that.

When her body had become a woman's, he told her it was word from the Lord that she was ready to know a man, like the Bible called for. But it meant he had to pull away and do his business on her chest or belly or on the wool blanket, which she washed in the laundry come Tuesday. "I'm too old and you too young to raise no youngun," he said, almost merry.

She never fell asleep there in the cabin, always waited for him to get up and go outside to make water, then went ahead of him back to the house, where she could sleep on the other side of the wall from Elma. Later, on her own mattress in the little room off the kitchen, she tried to settle her eyes on a book, the gin cooling in her veins. She supposed she could have run from him. She could smash a jar and cut him with it. She could take his shotgun from under the mattress and shoot him with it. In her room, when he came for her, she could make a ruckus, waking Elma. On nights he was rough and quick, when he had no kind words for her, or no words at all, she wrote a letter to Elma in her head. Telling.

But what could Elma have done, even with a tongue? What power did she have to stop her father?

It would be worse, Nan decided, if Elma knew. Worse than the shame of being under him was the shame of being under him inside Elma's head.

She wouldn't wait for her father to return any longer. She would go to Baltimore and she would find him. She would look up his name in the phone book. Sterling Smith.

———

Some nights, when Juke came to her room, it was to tell her that she was wanted to deliver a baby. Then her heart pounded with relief. Suddenly she was awake. She hurried to dress and take her mother's satchel—her birthing bag, she'd called it—and go outside, where another man's truck or wagon sat in the driveway. Usually it was a wagon, and the driver was colored, and the wagon was headed for the Youngs' farm or the Fourth Ward or Rocky Bottom, the ragged country beyond the Fourth Ward where Negro croppers tried to make the ground yield. Juke watched from the porch as she rode away, and though she had a long, uncertain night ahead of her, for a few hours she could escape.

"You ain't no granny woman," one father told her, sizing her up. "You ain't no more than a granddaughter." Most mothers she didn't meet before the labor, and by the time a father discovered how young she was, it was too late to find someone else. But before long her silence relaxed them, loosened their mouths. Nobody talked as much as a man driving home to his wife in labor in the middle of the night. They talked about cotton and corn, about their families waiting, whether the mother had had an easy pregnancy or a hard one. One man recounted an entire baseball game between the Chattanooga Black Lookouts and the Atlanta Black Crackers, a game narrated to him by his cousin, who had been there.

A mother in labor, though, didn't like to be talked to. There wasn't much Nan needed to say that she couldn't say with her hands. A wave to tell her to push, a different wave to tell her to stop pushing. A hand on the forehead, or a hand in hers, for comfort. Quick, steady hands. "You look just like Ketty," the mother might say, and the words gave Nan courage. Each time the baby came, Nan loved it. She bathed it and bundled it and held it as long as the mother would allow. The next morning, after the sun had risen, after Nan had been made a cup of coffee, after the brothers and sisters had tumbled naked out of their bed to see the baby, after the afterbirth had been planted in the field to ensure a good crop the next year, the father would drive her home.

On the way back, he talked less. His nerves had calmed. He was tired. Maybe he was thinking about next year's crop, whether there would be enough to feed the new child. They were poor folks, every one of them, log walls lined with newspaper and pasteboard boxes, no clean towels but fertilizer sacks. Sometimes they paid Nan in hen eggs or gourds, once with braided brown bread the mother had made herself, in the early waves of labor, once with a handful of caramel milk-roll candies, seeing how young she was. Once she tasted them, Nan might have liked to be paid in caramel milk rolls every time. (Some folks thought she couldn't taste at all, but she could taste fine; she could taste with the stub of her tongue what it took another person a whole tongue to taste.) Ketty'd had a tongue for bartering, but even with a tongue Nan might have only accepted what was offered. What right had she to what little a family had? One mother of six offered Nan the baby itself, and Nan had stood there and rocked that baby, a girl, and imagined taking her home, a baby that looked to her like family, better than any doll baby, and then handed the child back to the mother, hoping she would never know how pitiful her parents' love was.

But there was a kind of peace in those Rocky Bottom cabins, miles from any crossroads store. A body could farm what little land he had a right to, or have as many children as she liked, and be left alone with their seeds and their rags. So many children they were giving them away, so what was one more mouth to feed? It would be easy enough for her to stay. They were her people out in those cabins. She could earn her keep. She'd saved half her earnings from her deliveries, which she squirreled away in the inside pocket of her satchel. If she got two coins, she put one in the satchel and gave Juke the other. If she got four, she gave him two. It wouldn't be long before she had enough to put together and make something with. Before her mother had died, she'd told her, "You stronger than folks think. You got a strong mind and strong hands. You be ready to go out into the world soon enough."

But then there was Elma. She was her people too. If she told

Elma, maybe Elma would come along with her. The idea made Nan dizzy with hope. Leaving would be easier, less lonely, with Elma. It would be safer. Even grown men, whole families, the ones who were streaming north on the trains to Washington, D.C., to Philadelphia and Harlem, had to leave under cover of night. She heard about them on her calls, folks who were pulling up their roots and planting themselves in the snowy cities where you could walk down the sidewalk without having to step off when a white person came along. You had to be careful. If you were a sharecropper, you had to find a way to get out of town before word got out, or the planter would find a way to make you stay. George Wilson might send his grandson out for you, or the sheriff. Even her father had had to ride a freight train, the story went, when he left for the North.

There was one family that lived in a shotgun shack in the Fourth Ward, just over the tracks. The mother was expecting her third child. Ketty had delivered the first two, and Nan expected to be called for the next, but they never called. After enough months had passed, Nan concluded that the mother had lost the baby, but later she learned from the family next door that they had up and left for a place called Scranton, Pennsylvania, where the mother had people, and the neighbors had been as surprised as Nan. The father, a diabetic who had worked in the picker room at the mill, had complained to Freddie Wilson, the foreman, that his feet grew numb when he was on them for too long, and Freddie had told him that he should be grateful for the work and do it without complaint, and that if he didn't want to stand he could kneel on the floor and clean it, every square foot of the mill. So the man had waxed the floors, scrubbing on his hands and knees where the white women stood spinning, and though he kept his eyes on the floor, Freddie would say, laughing at himself, "You looking up that girl's dress?" and whack him with the straw end of his broom. When he was done cleaning the floor, Freddie made him lick it. "Taste clean?" And then, because twelve hours had passed and his next shift was coming on, Freddie sent him back to the picker room.

And not long after, before anyone knew to say good-bye, the man had taken his family out of Florence. He sent a letter to the neighbor saying he was working in a printing factory, where the hours were just as long but where at least he could operate his machine sitting down. The neighbor told Nan that the third child was born in a hospital, and they named him Zane.

She wondered what it would be like, leaving. If Elma went along, they'd be in separate cars, Elma in the white car and Nan in the colored, and then she might be no safer than if she'd escaped herself, the two of them traveling along in their separate compartments, as they were now. But she'd be among her own on the train. She'd be safe there. But they were strangers. How would she get by—how would she communicate with the passengers, with the conductor, without Elma? How would she get what she needed when she got to wherever she was going? She could write what she needed on a piece of paper. When she was safely out of the South, she could do that, couldn't she? The thought made her fingers itch. It was exhilarating and it was terrifying, the thought of making her way in the world without Elma. She would hand over a piece of paper to a stranger, and the stranger would look at her in confusion and disgust. Or the stranger would nod in understanding.

But she was far ahead of herself. She had not even brought herself to write the words to Elma, telling her why she wanted to go. And if she did, maybe Elma wouldn't believe her. Maybe Elma wouldn't come with her after all. Why would she come with her? What made her think Elma would choose her over her own blood?

There was a white man who'd owned the land that neighbored the Youngs' tobacco farm, and he bred mules. When Nan's mother was young, she'd learned a thing or two from him about the ways of animals, the ways horses and donkeys were the same and the ways they were different. Those mules were the reason, Ketty liked to say, she became a midwife. Nan had long known that mules were beloved in the country for their tough hooves, their good health, their endurance, though they could be stubborn; Juke often said Elma was stubborn as a mule. But it wasn't stubbornness, Ketty told Nan: a mule had a sense of self-preservation. She made two proud fists and struck her chest with them. When a horse was startled or scared, she said, it would flee; a donkey, on the other hand, would freeze. Mules were like both of their parents, sometimes running, sometimes staying; that was what made folks think they were stubborn. They're just confused, said Ketty. They couldn't overcome their own nature.

That was Nan. She was like a mule, she thought, fleeing and freezing. Her father had fled the farm; her mother had stayed. And now Nan's head was confused, so much did she want to stay and so much did she want to go.

Not long after Juke started bringing her out to the still, she brought the kitchen scissors out to Elma on the back porch. She ran a hand over her head, scalping herself with her palm.

"You want it gone?" Elma asked. "All of it?"

Nan nodded.

"Oh, honey, I ain't been too good with your plaits, have I?"

And Elma cut it off right there on the porch, Nan sitting on the step below her and closing her eyes to keep from crying. She wanted to cry because of the careful kindness of Elma's hands, and because she remembered sitting between her mother's knees like this, the sun on her eyelids. It was the confused longing she sometimes felt when Juke rubbed the stubble of his cheek on hers—she could almost remember her father's cheek. When Elma was done, she seemed more relieved than Nan. "You look pretty as a statue, honey."

Juke was not angry, as Nan had expected him to be, nor did he ignore her, as she'd hoped. The next time he led her to the cabin, he was as sweet as he'd ever been. He stroked her little breasts and her belly. He kissed the nape of her bare neck. He talked, as he sometimes did, as though she were the only person in the world with ears, about Jessa, about String, about cotton and corn and the fish in the creek. "I ain't ever told no one this one," he said. That night, as she sometimes did, she felt the rush of love in her body, and kept her pleasure a secret from him, and for a while that was enough.

––––––––––

From time to time Nan was asked to perform other acts, ungodly ones, and all she could do was shake her head. She was but a girl, no doctor, no medicine woman, though she knew between the herbs that healed and harmed. "We bring babies into the world," her mother had taught her. "We don't bring them out."

One evening just after nightfall, before Nan had settled into sleep, it was Elma who came for her. Juke must have been brewing at the still. A colored boy was parked in an automobile out front, and a white girl sat in the back. Nan stood under the eye of the moon in the driveway, her bare feet cold on the dirt. "You the midwife?" the boy said. "We come to call on you." When she didn't come closer—how did the two of them end up together in such a fine car?—he said, "You can make a baby go away?" Through the open window of the car, he held a ten-dollar bill. The girl sat with her hands crossed over her belly, staring into her lap. Nan could smell the leather of the seat, the freshly printed paper, and her knees trembled. With ten dollars, she wouldn't need to find another cropper shack to earn her keep on. With ten dollars, she could buy a ticket on a train.

"You hearing me, girl? You as dumb as they say?"

In the road, Jeb Simmons's truck slowed, the headlights sweeping over them like eyes. The boy squinted in the glare, and when the truck had passed, Nan snatched that ten-dollar bill from his hand and marched back into the house. Maybe he thought she was coming back with her bag. But she shrugged at Elma, went into her room, and buttoned the door, heart slamming. She took volume I of *The Book of Knowledge* out from under her mattress and pressed the bill between its pages, then closed it and hid it again. If the boy was fool enough to follow her into a white man's house, she'd ring the dinner bell, and Juke would hear her.

But the boy didn't follow. What could he do? For all he knew, Juke Jesup was in that house. He didn't want trouble. She never saw that boy again.

When she finally heard the car drive away, she took out her satchel and counted the money. With the ten-dollar bill, she had eighteen dollars and fifteen cents. That was enough, she thought, for a train ticket to Baltimore, where her father lived. If she was going to run, this was the time. If she was bold enough to steal ten dollars, she'd be bold enough to board a train. Alone—she didn't need Elma.

First she had to get a ride. The mail truck was known to carry folks into town—Elma did it from time to time when her father needed yeast from the Piggly Wiggly, more than the crossroads store carried—but Mr. Horace, the mailman, would carry no Negro. She could walk, but the walk was long—six miles—and she worried Juke would be after her in his truck, even if she walked along the creek with her feet in the water. It wasn't safe. Even the dogcatcher had been known to round up loose-foot Negroes, to turn them straight over to the jailhouse, or worse.

But there was a mother of four out in Rocky Bottom, just beyond the Fourth Ward. She was due in August. Her husband had borrowed a truck to drive out to the farm and tell Nan to be ready.

She would be ready. After the baby was delivered she would refuse the ride back to the farm. She'd walk the short distance into town, walk to the train station. At the ticket window she would write down the word "Baltimore." She would buy a ticket for the colored car. She moved the ten-dollar bill to the pocket in her satchel, along with a dress, a wax sack of white dirt, three caramel milk rolls she'd saved, a sharpened pencil, her mother's pearl, and volume I of *The Book of Knowledge*, her favorite, which featured a one-paragraph entry on Baltimore, Maryland, and a picture of the city, the buildings stacked like wedding cakes with pastel-postcard frosting. She had a picture in her mind of walking past those buildings with her father. They were holding hands, taking up the whole of the sidewalk, and then there was snow falling very beautifully and she would be wearing mittens and her father would wrap his scarf around her neck.

She would not pack the wooden cat Juke had carved for her. She would not write a letter to Elma, apologizing for taking the book, for leaving her behind. She would not explain why she was leaving. Why explain now? She was leaving so she would not have to explain.

August came and went. The corn hung heavy in the fields. The baby didn't come, and didn't come. And then one morning late in the summer, a new field hand came. Nan stood at the well as she watched Juke open the tar paper shack for him. Inside, the man—or was he a boy?—opened the shutters and hung the rag rug out the window, and with the window framing his face his eyes alighted on hers. It was like spotting a kingbird on a branch outside the kitchen window, that sudden flash of its yellow breast. She knew it would fly off, she knew his eyes would look away, but for a moment the wings beat in her chest. On his head was a woven corn-shuck hat, the silk fibers glowing gold as he leaned his head out into the sun. He lifted the hat, then lifted his hand. She hesitated, then lifted hers in return. And just as she did with a birthing mother, she felt that her hands were all she needed, that they were better than any word.

The baby came, a girl, on a rare rainy night early in September. She took her time but then came quick. In fact, by the time Nan arrived at the house, the nine-year-old daughter and the landlord, who owned the truck, had already delivered her. The mother sat there stunned and smiling, the baby right as rain. It was not what Nan had planned. When the father offered to drive her home, she nodded. She told herself it was because of the trains, which weren't running at that hour of the night. But she asked him to let her off down the road a ways, so the truck wouldn't wake the big house, and instead she went to Genus Jackson's shack.

She had been too young when her father left that shack to know about the proper ways of love, and at times, when Juke talked mean and she felt lonely, she wondered whether her father had loved them at all. Why hadn't he come back like he said he would? She didn't know that Sterling and Ketty had spent years trying to conceive her in the bed Genus Jackson slept on, or that they kept at it in that bed even after she slept in it beside them, no louder than a bee pollinating a flower.

She'd known since she was small how a baby came into the world, knew the bloody blossom between a woman's legs, but it wasn't until she was nine years old that she learned how they were made. Her mother had always told her that the Lord planted babies in their mothers, just like He grew the cotton and the trees. But one morning Ketty woke her early to take her to a call in Rocky Bottom. The house was down a long dirt road no wider than the wagon, and in the field outside an old man leaned on a double-foot plow behind an older swayback mule. They could hear the mother before they were in the house. Ketty liked to keep Nan close, but she must have sensed trouble—she sent her out to the yard to play with some girls her age. They must have been the woman's daughters or nieces. Nan did not like to play with the children at the houses she visited because they didn't understand that she couldn't speak; their faces were ugly with confusion and then ugly with meanness, and always she was subjected to some inferior role in their game: the maid; the monkey in the middle; once, the dog. But these children were friendly and curious, and the littlest one had legs that weren't full grown, they were like the legs of a rag doll, and her sisters or cousins had to carry her around and set her down on a rock or a stump. Her name was Ketty Lee, for Ketty, Nan understood, had delivered her. The fact made Nan proud. She spent the day running the acres with those girls, playing hide and go seek and picking flowers along the road and plaiting them in their hair.

When her mother appeared in the yard with her satchel, she did not speak to Nan, and she did not speak to her on the ride home, and spoke to the man driving them only to say that she was sorry. It wasn't until they were back on the farm that she told Nan both the mother and baby had died. She told Nan this to explain her own silence and to dispense with it. Did Nan know that a mule could be born to a stallion and a jenny? That was what a girl donkey was called, and its baby mule was a hinny. Usually it was the other way around—a jack and a mare, since a little donkey could climb up on a big horse just fine, little men climbed up on big women all the time, because women with wide hips, birthing hips, they could push out a baby with ease, that was what was prized. Ketty kept talking, waving her dishrag; Nan sat at the kitchen table, her head full of questions. Well, at times a big male horse was allowed to climb up behind a little donkey, for that happened as well of course, a woman was wanted no matter her size, big or small, black or white, a man could climb on top of you and have his way, and the stronger the stallion was, the easier way he had. But the jenny? She was smaller than a horse; she did not have an easy way. She kept the baby inside her a month longer than a horse did—a full year—and in that month, the mule grew big. Sometimes, too big to foal.

That was what had happened to the mother in Rocky Bottom. Her hips were too narrow to let the baby's shoulders through. And the baby had died inside her, and then the mother had died, and there was nothing Ketty could do.

"It was a white man's child," she added. "As far as the talk can tell." Ketty was washing the table now, though it wasn't dirty. "Could be the Lord didn't see the child fit for this world."

Nan thought her mother was scrubbing out her helplessness, her guilty feelings. It was the same look she had when she spoke about Jessa. But it was Nan who felt the guilt fall on her like a bucket over the head. All day long she had played with those girls, laughing, teasing, closing her eyes against the sun while they plaited her hair. It was as though her careless happiness were to blame. She remembered little Ketty Lee, and wondered if her legs had fallen limp from her mother's womb. Was it something Ketty had done, something that looked like the devil's work but was really God's will, like cutting out Nan's tongue?

She couldn't ask Ketty the questions she wanted to ask. What was she trying to tell her? Was she warning her about childbirth, or the ways of men, or the ways of white folks? How did a man climb up on a woman? Were Nan's hips, so narrow, so unlike her mother's soft ones, wide enough for a baby? Would she be wanted?

And then Genus came to the farm, and he was the answer to the questions she couldn't ask. Her mother had not explained the feeling that a man climbing upon you induced, did not mention that what she had mistaken for a rush of love with Juke was sometimes accompanied by the feeling in the chest of spotting a kingbird on a branch.

Most nights for two weeks she visited Genus in the tar paper shack, and on those nights, Juke didn't come for her. Some nights, Genus led her down to the creek. Her secret made her bold, kept her out later, longer. Afterward they lay on their backs side by side on the shore, their skin drying in the night air. She had learned not to eat dirt with most folks around but she scooped up a handful of cool white clay and put it in her mouth. Genus laughed and did the same. He hadn't eaten dirt before. He said it tasted like rain and she thought *yes*. He took another handful and smeared it on her cheek. She laughed. He smeared some on her neck and on her belly and he licked it off and she laughed some more.

He talked as much as Juke did, but his words let her breathe; he didn't talk at her but up into the sky, at the stars. He reckoned he was from Georgia, but down about the Florida line. He reckoned he was eighteen, maybe nineteen. His father had died when he was small. His mother sent him and his sisters to live with an aunt and uncle after that, and he never did know his birthday. Never did learn to read or write. He'd gone to work in one neighbor's cotton field, then another neighbor's corn. He'd seen a white man have his way with a molly mule. On a boxcar, he'd seen a black man kill a white man. The

white man had kicked the black man between the legs. Later, while
the white man slept, the black man sliced his throat with the jagged
lid of a tin can, then kicked his body off the train. He'd seen another
man dead in a cornfield, this one black. He'd worked in a canning factory for a time, but standing still was worse than moving on his feet.
He needed the fresh air, the sun on his neck. He had a rotten gut. It
was inclined to kill him someday, he said. Pain like the devil, day and
night, though he'd never seen a doctor. He tapped a spot under his
left nipple. Nan put her hand there, lay her fingers in the grooves between his ribs, and under her thumb she could feel the faint rumble of
his heartbeat. He reached across her and cupped her head behind her
ear, his thumb tracing the hair at her temple, and she remembered the
girls from Rocky Bottom, the joy she had felt with the sun and their
hands in her hair, and again came the stab of shame for her own happiness. "Maybe it ain't my gut," he said. "Maybe I got a rotten heart."
He said Nan was the only thing that made the pain pass for a time.
Before Nan, he'd never been with a woman. "Ain't never told that to
no soul," he said, his hand over hers, hers over his ribs. "Suppose you
fine at keeping secrets."

Would she have told him about Juke if she could? Would she explain why she was expected at the big house, why, when Genus said,
"Less stay out like this all night," she had to slip her hand out from
under his and leave him? Part of her heart wanted him to know, of
course. So he could save her. So he could take her away. But the other
part was glad she didn't have to. She didn't want him to know that she
was spoiled, that Juke had fouled her already. She wanted to believe,
as Genus did, that she belonged to him as much as he did to her.

The next night that Juke came for her, he came early, when Nan
was still in her bed. She followed him out to the still. Afterward, while
he made water in the woods, she took a pint of gin from the shelf above
the mattress, hid it under her nightdress, and waddled back to the big
house with the jar between her thighs. She hid it under the mattress,
beside the book. The following night, she brought it to Genus's cabin.

"You take this from the boss?" he whispered.

She put a finger to his lips.

"You wanting to have us a fine time?" It was dark in the cabin, but she could feel the smile in his voice.

She shook her head. She wouldn't be having any. She was soured on the taste. She tapped the spot under his heart, the rotten part. She held the jar there. He lowered his head and nodded. He understood. It was to help with the pain. He said, "I'm much obliged to you."

On the night the seed was planted, Juke was waiting for her on her mattress in the pantry when she returned from the creek. Her night-dress clung to her wet skin and her hair was pearled with water.

She took a step back into the breezeway. Her first fear was the gin—had he noticed it was missing, one jar among so many jars? Or the book—had he discovered it under the mattress? Then she feared Elma would hear. Or did she want her to hear? She could have walked across the breezeway and slipped into bed beside Elma, and then everything would have been different. He would have left her alone, gone back to his bed. But instead she stepped into her own little room, thinking she could quiet him, thinking she knew how to quiet him. She closed the pantry door softly behind her. His face was dead as a stone, and she knew then that he knew. He was drinking, the tumbler nearly empty.

"Where you been, girl?"

The tongue is the worst curse, her mother had told her. Ketty's grandmother had been beaten by her master for running from his bed, but worse? Worse was the shame of lying. Worse was having to look at his white face and say, "I like it" and "I love you." There was dignity in silence, Ketty said, in keeping your truth inside.

"Cat got your tongue, kitty cat?" He kept his voice low. He sat up in her bed, placed the tumbler on the floor, and wrapped his hand around her thigh. "You been swimming at this hour?"

She mimed washing, rubbing soap through her hair.

"Washing?" He yanked up her nightdress, plunged his face between her legs, and sniffed. "You ain't washed good enough." Then he yanked her down to the bed, rolled her onto her back, and pinned her against the wall. "I seen you knock on that nigger's door," he whispered. His breath was flaming with drink. "You think y'all are here to skinny-dip? That how you repay me for the food on your plate? The roof over your head?"

Nan shook her head.

"You ain't live in that slave shack no more. You ain't no slave. You live in my house now. You know how many folks'd like to sleep in this here big house? That how you repay me, run back to that shack?" He was slurring. "Don't let me see you with him again. You hearing me? I see you within ten feet of that door, I'll kill him dead."

She might have stroked his cheek to calm him, she might have kissed him, but he was holding her down, one arm to the bed, one arm to the wall. She wished her nipples didn't show through her wet nightdress. She wished her rabbit heart weren't beating so quickly. Surely he could feel it in her wrists. You could take away the tongue, she thought, you could put out a person's eyes, but still the pulse betrayed your fear.

Across the breezeway, through one board-and-batten wall and then another—thick walls built by George Wilson and two hired Negroes whose names he did not know and painted some years ago a milky blue, now fading—Elma sat up in her bed. She had been sleeping, or had been trying to. She had been trying to scare away the image of Nan and Genus in the creek, but every time she closed her eyes, it floated into her mind again like a ghost. When she thought she heard a thump against the kitchen wall, she thought it must be Nan returning from the creek, and then when she heard another, she thought it must be Genus in there with her, and though it was beyond her belief—that Nan and Genus would be so bold in her father's house—it was not beyond her imagination. Once the idea was in her head, it wouldn't turn her loose. She sat up in bed, remembering suddenly the night a few weeks back when a man had come to the house looking for Nan to deliver a baby. Elma had looked all around the house and the yard, but she couldn't find her. The man had left in a huff and a panic. And though Nan had been at the still with Juke, it seemed clear to Elma now that she'd been with Genus, and humiliation knocked her flat on her back. She stuffed her pillow over her face, to drown out the noise and to muffle the sound of her own tears.

What was happening in Nan's room was beyond Elma's imagination. She would have sooner imagined that the noises came from the wall itself, the house coming to life, growing a mouth, giving voice to its ghosts. That was the way Nan felt suddenly—that the walls that had protected her had now betrayed her with their thickness, not keeping her safe but trapping her. This was not her home. Home was the tar paper shack Genus Jackson lived in, before he lived there, before he slept in the bed she used to share with her mother. She thought herself back there now, walked herself from the cabin down to the shack. She wished herself all the way back, the taste of tobacco and clay on her mother's lips, the smell of her father's pipe, the warmth of the grits cooking on the woodstove in the morning. She would even wish away Genus, though her heart seized like a fist when she thought of his name—Genus, who was settling into that bed now, oblivious as Elma. She wished he'd never set foot on the farm.

There was no wool blanket. It was back in the cabin. Here in her room, Juke did not pull away. She could feel his seed seeping into her, thick as egg yolk. Through the mattress, she could feel the shape of *The Book of Knowledge* under her back. She kept her eyes on the pantry shelves beyond him, the okra she'd pickled, the sorghum syrup, the cornmeal, the salt.

Afterward, he cried. "Don't do me like that again, honey," he said. "Don't make me do that again." There was no uglier sight in the world, Nan thought, than a naked white man crying.

FIVE

B EFORE SHE GOT IN THE FAMILY WAY, ELMA HAD BEEN SET ON going to the teacher's college in Statesboro. It was where two girls from her class said they were going. Elma had the grades. She just didn't have the money. The fall of her last year in school, she tried to get work at the Piggly Wiggly, at the theater, at the crossroads store. She even put up a notice on the bulletin board at church: ELMA JESUP. MOTHER'S HELPER AND HOUSEGIRL. CLEANING. COOKING. SEWING. Nobody hired her. Every week she checked the board to be sure the note was still there. Then one Sunday, on that same bulletin board, another notice caught her eye: the Florence chapter of the Georgia Woman's Christian Temperance Union was offering a college scholarship to "a young lady of good character."

Elma liked school. She just didn't like the people there. Boys had always liked her because they liked her daddy's liquor. They thought they might come out to the farm and get into his stash and get under her dress. They called her Red. Clever! They said, "You wanna go have a pull from my bottle, Red?" They pawed her braids. "You watch them town boys," her father told her. Freddie was the only one he didn't mind. The girls weren't particular about her because the boys were, and because they thought she was white trash and a drunk, and because already they were following their mothers to the WCTU meetings at the Hotel Chanticleer. In fact Elma had never had a drink—"Ain't for womenfolk," her daddy said—and that was fine by her, she didn't like the way it smelled on a man's breath and made a man loose and rough and mean.

There was no reason, she thought, she shouldn't have that scholarship. She'd get out of Florence and become a schoolteacher, and if it meant joining the WCTU, she'd do it. She told her father the dollar was for her graduation cap and gown, and though he grumbled about it, and had to collect it in coins, he gave it to her. She asked Josie Byrd if she could go with her to a meeting after school, and Josie Byrd said certainly, it would be grand, and loaned her a felt hat that looked like a bathing cap. Only later did Elma discover that for every new member you brought in, your name was entered in a raffle for a year's supply of Octagon toilet soap.

The women at the Hotel Chanticleer all wore rhinestone broaches and white ribbons and strands of evening pearls down to their navels. They poured Elma tea and piled her plate with shortbread cookies and said, "How do you do?" She knew Tabitha Quick and Carlotta Rawls and of course she knew Parthenia Wilson, she had opened her legs to Parthenia Wilson's grandson in the bed of his truck the day before, but by the time she was shaking Mary Minrath's hand, she understood they were pretending they didn't know her, that they were forgetting that she was Juke Jesup's daughter. They were meeting her for the first time. And maybe they were! Maybe she would be reborn, fatherless, in the WCTU! Elma understood this was because they wanted her dollar, and they wanted her to sign, at the end of the meeting, their abstinence pledge. And yet she let them court her. She let them compliment the felt hat that wasn't hers. She told them what soap she washed her hair with and let them stroke it. She answered questions about her favorite subject in school, her favorite church hymn, her favorite meal to make for supper. Is this what they did in women's clubs? Eventually they began to speak in a code. They referred to each other as "Comrade" and "Sister"; they spoke with reverence of their "Foremothers"; they spoke with disappointment of "unfortunate girls." They spoke about Hoover (well, the white-ribboners believed in Hoover) and about "rum and ruin" and "the flag of booze." They spoke with growing concern about how they might bring Christ to the country, to the Negroes and halvers, the heathens and drunkards. Tabitha Quick said Georgia was in such a state of debauchery that if God didn't intervene, "Black heels will be on white necks."

Elma didn't understand. She thought of black necks. But this was before the lynchings had started up again. "White necks?" she whispered to Josie.

Josie tried to shush her. Elma did not seem to be the only woman ruffled by the phrase. Josie whispered back, "They mean the Negroes will take over town. The ones at the saloon."

"Young's, I believe it's called," said Tabitha Quick.

"Not the Robert Youngs," someone clarified.

"They belong in the county camp," said another.

"Let's not pretend it's just the blacks. White heels on white necks too."

"Perhaps one white heel in particular," said Mary Minrath under her breath.

"Perhaps one redneck in particular," said another woman, more loudly.

"Might as well be a black heel," said Mary Minrath.

"Enough," Tabitha Quick said, standing up to pour more tea.

"She could be useful," said Mary Minrath, and only then did Elma understand they were talking about her, and about her father.

Parthenia Wilson was quiet. She fanned herself with her newspaper. It was her silence that infuriated Elma. Elma shat in the same privy Parthenia Wilson had once shat in. She didn't want to be reinvented by her; she wanted, even then, to be recognized.

Someone said, "We don't mean to make you feel unwelcome, honey."

Another said, "We couldn't be more pleased to have you."

Elma put down her tea. She didn't know what to say. Was she to defend her father? What was it they hated about him? Was it just that he was a bootlegger? Or that he was friendly with Negroes?

She thought of the way her father protected the still. She was not to visit it. She did not care to visit it, she had no fascination with it, only a fear of it and a fear that it would be taken away. Her fear was her father's, that the still might be destroyed and him with it. Sometimes when a car came for Nan in the middle of the night and he was one kind of drunk, he'd come running from the cabin with his shotgun, mumbling about "guvment men." For all her shame about her father's work, she knew that, without it, they'd be as poor as any of the croppers on the Straight, as poor even as the Negroes in Rocky Bottom.

She didn't want to betray her father. But she wanted that scholarship.

She looked around the hotel lobby, the circle of women with their tea saucers in their laps, all of them waiting for her to speak. They were not looking at her like she was a young lady of good character. They were looking at her like she was an unfortunate girl. The scholarship, she knew, was not hers. She did not know that it had already been promised to Josie Byrd.

Parthenia Wilson had said nothing, but she was the target Elma settled on. "Takes more than one white neck to bootleg," Elma said. "Takes a rich white neck, from what I hear."

Parthenia Wilson paused her fanning for a moment.

Elma looked at her and said, "Your grandson don't care what color neck I got. He just cares about necking."

Parthenia Wilson opened the newspaper she was holding and appeared to begin to read it. She did not remove the newspaper from in front of her face for the rest of the meeting.

Elma might have been excused if it had not been considered impolite. Besides, they wanted her dollar. She didn't give it to them. She didn't sign the abstinence pledge. They spent the rest of the meeting organizing a meal train for Bette Hazleton, who was suffering from pleurisy.

After the meeting, Josie Byrd's mother carried her back to the farm in their Ford. She saw Mrs. Byrd scanning the farm for the cabin, her eyes moving right past the stand of pines along the road. Juke asked her where she'd been, and she told him. She couldn't lie. She gave him back his coins. "It's low, Daddy," she said. "Folks look on us like we're low." She waited for the whip of his temper, but he was the right kind of drunk—merry—and he said, "That still is the reason you ain't eating hog hearts."

So Elma did not become a schoolteacher. She did not go to the teacher's college in Statesboro because she didn't have the money and because already, sitting in the lobby of the Hotel Chanticleer, she was pregnant. Her father pulled her out of school that winter. Soon her belly would start to grow. Her father kept her home from town, from church, made sure she couldn't be seen from the road. Folks in town went up in arms about a baby born without a ring on the momma's finger. Didn't matter if the ring was made of corn silk, long as it was a ring. It had happened to a girl at the mill last year and the other spinners had made sure George Wilson found out. He sent her back to Marietta with her baby on the train she'd come in on. Elma thought that girl was lucky, to be sent away from all those judging eyes. She had come back six months later with a baby and a husband. No telling if the husband was the father of the baby, but that hardly mattered.

Freddie had said he was saving for a ring, but Freddie had all the money he needed. He stopped coming around the farm so much, and then he stopped coming around at all. Before she stopped going to church, before she was stuck on the farm, folks told Elma he was lay-ing out all night in the mill village, where he was sometimes seen on a porch with this girl or in his truck with that one, having a big time. She wondered if it was what she'd said to Parthenia Wilson in the Hotel Chanticleer, or if Freddie would have dropped her anyway, if his grandmother's disapproval was a handy excuse. She couldn't let it go; she wrote him a letter. *Is it your grandmother who don't want you tied down?* she asked. *And if she don't want you tied down, is it tied down at all, or tied down to me?* She didn't expect a response, was disappointed but not surprised when day after day the postman brought none. He had probably never gotten the letter, she told herself. His grandmother had surely intercepted it.

When her father was yet another kind of drunk—very drunk, tired, weepy—he'd tell Elma her mother would be proud she'd got-ten so far in school, even if she didn't finish. Elma's mother, Jessa, hadn't gotten past the fifth grade before she came to town to work in the mill, and Juke hadn't gone at all, had been sent into the field at six years old with a ham biscuit, a bull-tongue plow, and a john mule named Lefty. After the babies came, he told Elma that her mother would be proud she was such a good momma herself, and though Elma mostly wore a serious face, like a white stone mask, some color rose high in her cheeks then. Jessa had lost her chance to be a mother, and when Juke watched Elma soothe a crying baby on her shoulder, he looked as pleased and loving and haunted as if he were watching his dead wife herself. And though the baby would be calm by then, he would cross the room and take it in his own arms, rocking it, hum-ming a song only it could hear, saying, "Come on and give Grand-daddy some sugar," saying, "Come on and hug my neck." Sometimes he came in from the field and went straight for Wilson's crib, lifting him up to study his face.

At times, Elma missed the notion of a husband. When she was lying awake at night, nursing a baby, she thought it would be nice if there were a grown body sleeping next to her, if she could reach over and touch a man's bare back. But it wasn't Freddie she wanted there. Just because her pride was hurt didn't mean she was sad he was gone. Sometimes it was Genus's long, slim back she imagined, when she couldn't keep the picture from her mind, but then she saw him disappear into the woods in his union suit, the same suit he was hanged in, and then her mind reared up and trotted away like a horse with a snake on its heels.

One morning in that blazing and interminable month of August, when Elma arrived with her wagon at the crossroads store, a man she didn't recognize offered to help her carry the eggs inside. No one else was about—not Jeb Simmons nor his son Drink, no one playing checkers on the porch. Or had she seen the man before? The sun was in her eyes. She could manage fine, thank you, but he wouldn't hear of it. She held the door open for him while he carried in the crate, placing it on the shop counter, behind which Mud Turner eyed her, cigarette hanging from his mouth.

Overhead, a ceiling fan spun. Elma stood with the man just inside the door. "Must be nice to step off the farm," he said to her, and that was when she placed him—the sharp-edged suit, the neat mustache. He took off his hat and introduced himself: Q. L. Boothby, the editor of the *Testament*. He'd driven down from Macon that morning. Wasn't it a fine morning? But already so hot. "A good morning for a Coca-Cola, Miss Jesup. What do you say?"

Behind the counter, Mud raised an eyebrow. The last time Elma had had a soda was with Freddie, at Pearsall's drugstore in Florence. Winter, before she was showing, before he'd stopped calling on her. They'd just seen *Anna Christie* at the theater next door, Elma's first talkie, and her heart was still pounding with the thrill. Ordering her soda, she tried to imitate Greta Garbo's voice—"Gimme a vhiskey, ginger ale on the side. And don't be stingy, baby." Freddie laughed. Excepting the colored one, there were no saloons to order a drink

from in Florence, just the cotton mill, where it was mostly the men
who drank from mason jars on their porches. Elma's father wouldn't
let her set foot in the mill village, but here she was, out on the town
with her fiancé, Freddie Wilson, whose family owned the biggest
business in town, the whole glittering evening, her whole life, before
her, and who cared how Freddie got his money, it was the way her
father got his money too, and it was buying her a movie and a soda.
The bubbles fizzed in her belly. Or was that her baby, kicking already?

Elma tasted that ginger ale now, cool and sweet, the tinkle of
the ice cubes as she stirred them with her straw. She looked at Q. L.
Boothby, his hat still in his hands. He was as finely dressed a man as
she had seen, his black Oxfords shiny as a piano, a blood red handkerchief flaming from his breast pocket.

She said, "Sir, you don't scare off easy, do you?"

He said, "I won't take much of your time."

From Mud he bought two bottles of Coca-Cola and carried them
to the checkers table on the porch. Elma might have learned her les-
son about daydreaming, but for a moment she imagined that they
were on a date. That they were somewhere else and she was someone
else and the man across from her was her fiancé. She thought a fiancé
might be better than a husband. The promise of a mate, without the
burden of one. The beginning without the end.

"How are the babies?" Mr. Boothby asked.

Elma twisted the cap off her Coke and watched its breath escape
from the bottle. She'd had no more sleep than a mule the night before. Winna Jean had been up crying half the night, and she'd only
sleep at Elma's breast, with Elma propped straight up in bed. And
Wilson had a case of the runs so bad that Nan had to cut more diapers out of an old sack apron and double them up, and slather lard
on his poor red behind. It was best that Elma should be so tired, that
she should sleepwalk through those nights. Then there wasn't enough
sleep between them to worry about which baby which of them cared
for, or whether Elma should feel grateful or guilty or bitter that there

were two of them to care for the babies, and two babies instead of one. Elma said, "The babies are fine."

"Appears to me you must be plumb tired of all the attention those babies bring. Sweet as they are."

Elma took a cautious sip of her soda. Yes, it did taste just as sweet as Heaven. He was warming her up, breaking her down, but it did feel good to sit on a porch and talk to a stranger. "I only want to keep them safe. All types of people coming in, it agg'avates em."

Mr. Boothby held up his hands, as if to show they were empty. "I understand, I understand. I've got children of my own."

Here Elma's fantasy paled a little. Now she pictured Mrs. Boothby. Did she have an electric kitchen up in Macon, with a Frigidaire and an electric stove?

"I have no interest in your babies, Miss Jesup, miraculous or not. I'm a newspaperman. We call our publication the *Testament,* and we do pride ourselves on seeking the truth." Mr. Boothby lowered his voice when he said, "It's the Negro Mr. Jackson I have an interest in."

Elma folded her hands in her lap to hide their shaking. Bill Cousins passed by on his way into the store, tipping his hat and saying, "Morning," his eyes taking them in. Elma felt her heart speed up. No one, of course, would believe Mr. Boothby was a friendly acquaintance, let alone a suitor, but if Bill Cousins recognized the man in the suit, he didn't say so. If he did, he might incite a mob against Elma herself. She might be burned at the stake for talking to a big-city reporter, even if they didn't know his politics. There were things no one wanted known by the outside, and no one knew that better than Elma. When the door had closed behind Bill, she said, "Well, I'm sorry to tell you, Mr. Boothby, but the Negro Mr. Jackson died a few weeks back. Figure you would have read about it in that paper of yours."

Mr. Boothby smiled. "You don't say. How did he die?"

"I didn't see it myself."

"How did your father say he died?"

Elma paused. "He was swung up."

"So your father was there."

"Didn't have to be there. There was a picture in your paper with the rope hanging from the gourd tree. It's all accounted for."

"And who is responsible for hanging the man? What do the accounts say?"

"Sir, don't you have a Roosevelt to cover?"

Mr. Boothby cocked his head. "Pardon?"

"Your friend up in Warm Springs. The one you're building the polio hospital with. Sounds awful important. It's about alls your paper is like to talk about."

Mr. Boothby laughed. "Well, you do keep up with the *Testament*, don't you? I'm mighty pleased."

Elma sipped her soda, then guzzled it. She could feel her defense dissolving, and she allowed herself not to care. Talking about it was better than not talking about it—it was the not talking about it, the silence her father had enforced, that was so heavy. "Freddie Wilson swung him up. He even traded shoes with him. But he ain't my fiancé no more. I don't know where he is, and I don't care to know. He ain't worth a milk bucket under a bull."

Mr. Boothby smiled. He withdrew a pipe from a pocket inside his jacket and lit it. He had no notebook, no pen. "That's what the autopsy confirmed. I know the man who performed it. I can attest to its accuracy. It would be one thing if the man were shot dead first, then hanged without protest. What I can't seem to understand, but which everyone else in the state of Georgia seems to understand just fine, is how one man managed to hang another live man all by himself."

Elma was beginning to sweat. Even in the shade of the porch, the morning heat crept into her collar, under the braid pinned to the nape of her neck. Her mind stuck on the phrase from the paper, "Cervical spine." She said, "Freddie, he had a gun. A rifle. Maybe he trained it on him." She shrugged. "Like I say, I didn't see it."

"Appears to me, it's hard to hang a man while holding a rifle to his head. If it were me, I'd put up a fight. Give him a kick with my alligator boots. What's more likely is there were others who helped Freddie. Maybe many others."

If Elma stepped down from the porch and looked over her right shoulder, she could see her father's cotton coming up. No flowers yet—just green. She could stand up and walk home. If she called out, her father might even hear her voice.

"What I'm saying," Mr. Boothby went on, "is that your fiancé may be taking the fall for his associates."

"Associates? All Freddie associated with were drunks."

"He worked for your father, Freddie did."

"He was foreman at the mill. Freddie said farmwork was for coloreds. He was coming up under his grandfather." That was all Freddie talked about, taking over the mill when his grandfather retired. This is all fixing to be ours, he'd say, parked on the hill overlooking the mill village.

"I'm not talking about farmwork," said Mr. Boothby. "Or millwork, for that matter."

Elma blinked out at the road. She wondered if Mr. Boothby had ever had a drink in his life, and if such a man was worthy of pity or admiration. A pickup passed, a green Chevy like Freddie's, and for a moment she held her breath. Then she saw it had Alabama plates. "I don't know about Macon," she said, "but in Cotton County, that's about the only kind of work we do."

"Oh, I know about your industries here. What do you know about George Wilson? He owns the cotton *and* the cotton mill, does he? And the mill isn't all he runs, what I hear. How's he find time for it all, is what I wonder."

"He's got brothers up near Atlanta who help with the business. And Freddie helps him. Helped him."

"With what part?"

"I wouldn't know. I don't spend much time at the mill. The village is full of riffraff."

"Was Freddie part of the riffraff?"

Elma snorted a soda bubble. "Yes, sir."

"How so?"

"He liked to carry on. Tear his truck around the village. Get into fistfights. Once he got shinnied up and shot the headlights out of his own grandfather's Ford, and blamed it on some poor fool. Went and got him fired quick as you can say Wilson. He was the king of riffraff. He liked to call himself King Cotton, fancied himself royalty, fixing to take on the family business. But he couldn't even take on a wife and child."

"Why not?"

"Don't ask me! Ask him! He had nine months to put his pants on, same as any daddy. His family's got enough houses to put us in, that's for sure. All we'd need was one." Six months along, her father had carried her over to the Wilsons' house, where Freddie had been raised up by his grandparents in his father's old bedroom. Elma's father had made her wait on the porch in front of the parlor window, her full figure framed like a picture. She saw Mr. Wilson, then his wife, heard Freddie's voice deep within the house, and then the curtain was drawn and a colored girl brought her a lemonade, sour and full of seeds. After five minutes her father came through the door, jammed his cap on his head, and got in the truck. He didn't say a word. By the time they turned onto the road, Elma knew that Freddie would not be marrying her. Her baby would not have a Christmas stocking on the Wilsons' mantel.

She had given up on a reply from Freddie, but there it was in the mailbox a few days later, her name in his loopy, second-grade cursive: *Dear Elma.* It was both, he admitted: his grandmother didn't want him tied down, and didn't want him tied down to her. *She don't care for country people,* was the way he put it, and she was almost grateful for his gentleness. He apologized not for dropping her but that her father had been sent away from the house. *I did want to marry you,* he wrote. That was all, and at least there was that.

"Least my own father took up for the babies," she told Mr.

Boothby. "Gave them a roof. I'd rather be in his house than any of those linthead shacks at the mill." Of course her father's house too was owned by the Wilsons, the house and the fields and the food they put in their bellies. They owned their shit and the outhouse they shit in. And a Wilson did not marry his property. He would just as soon marry a Negro in a cabin. That afternoon when her father had driven her to their house, the Wilsons didn't yet know Winnafred, didn't yet know that she was said to tumble around with a Negro for the nine dark months inside Elma's belly. But even before she was born, they had disowned her.

Mr. Boothby placed his pipe on the table between them. "I'm mighty sorry for the trouble you've been through."

"I'm not the one in trouble. Now it's Freddie. What's he the king of now?"

"Well, I'd ask him if the law could find him. And his grandfather isn't keen to talk to the papers. Nor none of the folks at the mill."

"Can't blame him entirely. Both his parents died when he was a tot. His daddy was a war hero. Freddie was always toting that shotgun around like a soldier."

"And his mother?"

Elma told about how after his daddy died she went crazy with sadness and was sent to the lunatic asylum in Milledgeville. When she was little and acted up, her father would tell her, "Straighten out, or I'll send you to Milledgeville."

"The sanitarium," Mr. Boothby clarified.

"She died of tuberculosis." Freddie'd been ten years old and hardly knew his mother, had visited her only a handful of times. Elma thought his grandmother had made Freddie frightened of her. Parthenia Wilson had warned String not to marry a girl from the shop floor. It was one thing to play around under their skirts, another to set up house with them. All those hours standing at their machines made their minds weak, she said. She'd not give Freddie the same blessing. It was she who'd sent String's widow away.

Mr. Boothby shook his head. "Pitiful place," he muttered. He looked as though he was going to push further, then stopped. He drained his Coca-Cola and stood. Elma was filled with a funny combination of relief and regret. It was the feeling she had after getting a crying baby to sleep—even though she finally had some peace, she always felt a little lonesome.

"I have just one more question." Mr. Boothby lowered his voice, looking down at Elma through the round lenses of his glasses. "You'll have to excuse my directness. I don't ask out of prurient curiosity, mind you. I ask because I'm after the truth. Miss Jesup, did that Negro do what they say he did?"

An automobile passed. Elma watched the dust rise behind it and then settle, listened to the rumble of the engine disappear. She would not answer. She would not nod.

"If he did, your fiancé might be handed a short sentence. Knowing the way they uphold the law in this state, he might even go free. I just want to see the proper people held accountable."

Mr. Boothby stepped away from the table, and then Elma felt his shadow at her side, and his hand on her shoulder. "God bless you," he said, and then his hand was gone, and then his shadow was gone. Elma sat at the table for a few minutes, then left her half-finished soda and led her wagon home, forgetting to bring a sack of flour in exchange for the eggs.

———

The next day, there was no mention of Genus Jackson or the twins in the *Testament*. But there was mention, in the three weeks that followed, of four more lynchings in Georgia. On September 8, a Negro accused of killing the chief of police was shot in his bullpen at the McIntosh County jail. The prisoner's blood was said to drip through into a white woman's cell below. On September 25 in Thomas County, a Negro accused of strangling a nine-year-old white girl on the roadside was seized by a mob at the county stockade, filled with bullets, and dragged behind a car from Magnolia Park to the court-house. Some said the man had once raped a Negro woman, though his only convicted crime in the county was theft and concealment of stolen goods, for painting a black mule white. Three days later, in the same county, a Negro who had testified in court against two white men accused of raping a Negro woman was killed by four white men who came to his door. The men had been disguised by the women in their family with makeup and dark glasses. And on October 1, up in the Piedmont, another Negro accused of killing another chief of police was taken from his cell at the Bartow County jail, brought to the county fairgrounds, and swung up by the neck from an electric-light pole. The Negro's brother, also held in the jail, hadn't heard the mob come in the middle of the night, and didn't learn of his death until the next morning, when his brother's shoes were brought to his cell. After the last one—six lynchings, not counting Genus—Q. L. Boothby wrote in an editorial that an epidemic had returned. "The devil has settled in Georgia, and if we don't exorcise him, I fear he's here to stay."

All of these things were in the paper, but Elma didn't read them. She was forbidden from going back to the crossroads store. The day after she sat with Q. L. Boothby, when Juke stopped at the store for his chewing tobacco, Mud Turner wasted no time telling him about the Macon reporter. From then on, her father delivered the eggs instead.

She didn't know that, in the years that followed, when folks said, with admiration for a fellow's cleverness, "He could paint a black mule white," they were referring to a Negro dragged through the streets behind an automobile, not three months after Genus Jackson was dragged down the Twelve-Mile Straight.

After she returned from the crossroads store, exhausted, over-heated, Elma found both babies napping. She lay down on her bed in her clothes, didn't even take off her shoes, and with the crook of her arm laid over her eyes, fell into sleep. She dreamt of Freddie's truck, a row of tin cans tied to the back of it after their wedding, the two of them driving down the Twelve-Mile Straight, man and wife, and then tied to the truck was Genus, and the cans and his body were dragged down the road together, tangled, clanging, the sound the sound of her wickedness, for there was Elma in the passenger seat.

She shot up in bed, fist to her heart. The clanging went on. Was she still sleeping? She stood and walked to the window, following the sound, and as she crossed the room she allowed herself to hope that she had dreamt it all, that none of it was real.

No—she was awake. It was the gourds in the wind, rattling like skulls.

SIX

"GEORGIA WAS BORN DRY," THE WHITE-RIBBONERS LIKED TO say. "The pity of it is, she did not stay that way." The colony of England's poor and persecuted, every schoolchild knew well, was the first state to try Prohibition. It lasted only seven years. By the time it came around again, in 1908, most of the counties, including Cotton, had already voted themselves dry, but that fact didn't stop Reverend Quick's wife, the choral director and a prominent member of the Florence chapter of the Woman's Christian Temperance Union, from singing every Sunday, to the tune of "Dixie":

> From Georgia Land so fair and bright
> King Alcohol has taken flight,
> Praise the Lord! Praise the Lord!
> Praise the Lord! Georgia Land!

Juke Jesup had before then become well acquainted with King Alcohol. He was eleven and still called John when he took his first sip of moonshine under the railroad trestle behind the cotton mill, then spit it in the river. "Taste like turpentine," he said, but he went back the next afternoon and took another sip and didn't spit it out. String Wilson's older cousins, who visited each summer from the piney woods of north Georgia, had built a crude still in a shed behind the mill. Down by the railroad, they liked to get String and Juke drunk, then spin them in circles and watch them fall to the ground, laughing. Once String landed in the fire pit and nearly burned his left leg off. Juke had to drag him into the river. Another time, the cousins dared String to cross the mill dam and he slipped and fell twelve feet into the water and nearly smashed his head like a watermelon on the rocks below. Then Juke had to drag him *out* of the river. String was always getting into trouble. It wasn't his fault; he was too good-natured, too game, too skinny—that was why he was called String. He liked to let folks spin him around. He grew up helping his father in the mill, then, like Juke, married a spinner and had himself a baby. When the war started he got it in his mind to go across the waters and fight, and he came back to Georgia in a coffin made of such fine mahogany that Juke couldn't help but run his hands over it. String did love to whittle a piece of wood.

It was the same year the boll weevil came to Cotton County. No one knew where it came from. For all Juke knew it had stowed away in String's coffin and traveled all the way from Europe. Juke remembered the first time he'd seen one, on the pink petal of a cotton flower, common as a cockroach, but with a snout as long as its legs. He'd plucked it off and crushed it between his fingers. That was May. By June, the field was full of them, the grubs eating through the bolls the moment they hatched. In September, String's father, George Wilson, drove his automobile out to the farm. He snapped a boll of cotton and cupped it in his palm, studying the pod of seeds that never grew. "It ain't your fault, honey," George said. "It ain't no one's fault." They stood out there until the sun went down, Juke in his straw hat, George in his white suit and bowler, looking over the ruined field. That year they lost nearly all the crop.

After her son died, Parthenia Wilson never missed a day of

church; her husband never went back. String's widow threw herself off the mill dam and broke her leg and smashed up her face and was sent to the sanitarium, and Freddie, seven years old, moved into the mill house with his grandparents. The old copper still on the river rusted over, until Juke, coming by each evening to sit with George, remembering what String's cousins had taught him, got it running again. In the upstairs office of the cotton mill, George and Juke drank peach brandy, talking about String and about the farm where, as boys, the two had played. Juke said, "You weren't too keen on me painting him with tar," and George laughed and said he didn't remember. "You ain't remember? You said he weren't to play with me no more." George waved his hand. Back then, he said, the world was no bigger than the farm. On a farm, you played with who was there. On the phonograph, George played the same song, dragging the needle back to the beginning as soon as it ended. *They'll never want to see a rake or plow, and who the deuce can parleyvous a cow? How ya gonna keep 'em down on the farm after they've seen Paree?*

George's son was dead; Juke's wife and his father, a sharecropper on the Wilsons' land long before Juke was born, were dead too. Liquor had a way of making tender feelings duller and sharper at the same time. After a long day plowing, a farmer liked to enjoy a whiskey as much as anyone. Those who were vets liked gin. They'd gotten a taste for it in Europe. George and Juke got a taste for it too. George taught Juke to care more about the liquid in his glass than how fast it got him pissed, and Juke could play fancy as George Wilson. He imagined String in a bar in France, where the gin flowed freely, a pretty girl on the bar stool next to him. For the mash he tried barley, then red wheat, then rye, alternating the cover crops winter after winter; he planted a grove of juniper trees. In the west hundred, which had been cotton, he planted peanuts and corn and the sorghum cane that went into the gin. "Diversify, son," said George. "Don't put all your eggs in one basket. That's the key to staying ahead of nature." In with the berries Juke tried everything he could find on the farm—

rabbit tobacco, blackberries, tea leaves, pecan paper shells, then on one inspired summer morning settled on the silky white petals of a cotton flower. He brought a jar from that batch to George and George smacked his lips like an English lord and said, "By God, it tastes clean as a cotton field." The cotton might have closed its fists to Juke but he'd take of it what he could. That was the kind of goddamn ingenuity only a poor man was capable of, but Juke Jesup, goddamn if he would be a poor man one more day.

Sheriff Cleave shut down the still within a few years, claiming it belonged to an unknown group of mill workers; the *Messenger* ran a photograph of him hacking into it with an ax. But it was Parthenia Wilson, not the law, they needed to divert, along with Camilla Rawls, the doctor's wife, and Tabitha Quick, the reverend's wife, and their whole bonneted mob of the WCTU. The operation had outgrown the shed, anyway. In the wooded acres in the southwest corner of the crossroads farm, just up the bank of the creek, Juke Jesup built a log cabin with a new copper still so shiny he could see his face in it, and one night in 1921 the first cases of Cotton Gin, as it came to be known, were driven into the mill yard in Juke's brand-new Model T truck. George Wilson was there to receive the shipment, which was warehoused in an upstairs storage room of the mill, just inside the office. George never called it a partnership, but that's what it was, with agreements like any other. Juke carried out the production. George handled the business. Farmers drove their cotton into the yard and left with their truck beds full of gin, the cases clothed in the mill's cotton seconds. Just keep it out of the hands of the mill folks, George warned. They had to be in the right mind to work.

That first year, while the boll weevil grubs still wormed their way through the fields of Georgia and the price of cotton dropped from forty-two cents to ten, Juke and George made four times as much on King Alcohol as they did on King Cotton. Enough to give Sheriff a case on the first of every month.

When the Wilsons left the farm and moved into town to the mill, Juke's father said they needed some womankind about, so he married a girl he'd met at a camp meeting in Coffee County, a dark-haired, thin-lipped creature closer to Juke's age than his father's who liked to clean Juke's pecker in the washbasin. Tug, tug, tug, the same dazed satisfaction with which she milked a cow, and when to Juke's astonishment he yielded into the water his own milk, "There you go," she'd say, "all clean." Sometimes she seemed almost to laugh over him, a joke between her and herself, and Juke wanted to be in on the joke. "You bigger than your daddy," she said once, "but he ain't no bigger than a boy's," and all at once in his chest came a feeling as unstoppable as the one between his legs—as much pride as hate, hate for her and her ugly thin-lipped mouth, hate for his small-peckered father, hate for himself for the way his body went limp and helpless under her hand.

Each month, on certain afternoons, he was sent down to the creek to fish—"Go catch supper"—while his father and stepmother thrashed about in their bed like a couple of trout in a pail. When the red rags appeared over the ledge of the outhouse, it meant his father would disappear into the woods and shoot squirrels. From this game his stepmother would produce a stony kind of stew, which the family would consume in penitent silence, the stew thinning to a squirrel-colored broth, until the next time Juke was sent to the creek, and then it was fish cakes for supper, battered with hope, crispy. After the meal, she drank primrose tea, and then at last the tea did its work. Juke was to be a brother. For a time there was bacon and cobbler and warm beaten biscuits from their own wheat—it was the year they grew wheat—and fish fry and fish cakes and fish stew, for Juke was sent down to the creek every day, for hours. He began to take his baths there. His stepmother told him he was old enough to wash himself.

He took off his shoes and rolled up his pants legs and waded in and pretended String was still there with him. Their feet knew every stone in the creek. The sun was warm. The fish were small but they were plentiful. They filled the bucket. Juke carried it down the road back to the farm, where one afternoon he returned to a red rag hanging over the outhouse ledge, the bloodiest yet. In church, the neighbors offered a prayer for the Jesup family's loss.

Not long after that, on a Sunday morning, Juke's stepmother packed her things. His father didn't try to stop her—she could take her worthless womb back to Coffee County—but first he sent Juke out to the creek for another hour and took the stepmother, whose name was Jenny, to their narrow bed. Juke could hear her screams from there. If anyone else heard, they pretended they didn't. When Juke came back his father told him to go in the house, it was his turn in the bed with her. Juke was about twelve by then and he reckoned it was. He had not had to tell his father about the washbasin—his father seemed to know that she should be punished, and in this knowledge Juke was assured of the righteous order of things.

So the ghosts Juke lived with were many, and they still inhabited the big house when Elma was born into it and Jessa joined the ghosts. Juke would not remarry. A mother was a mother; she couldn't be swapped out for a suitable substitute. "Go forth and multiply," the Reverend Quick reminded him. "Have you some sons." But childbearing was the bloodiest business Juke had known, bloodier than the slaying of hogs, which didn't profess to be anything but slaying. His father had survived on the farm with one child; so would Juke.

This was a gift, Elma was meant to know, a sacrificial offering dangled by her father so often it became like a dark, shiny fruit. She was inclined to reach for it and snap it off the branch. What was so wicked about a stepmother? A momma to plait her hair like Ketty did Nan's, to let down her hem, scrub behind her ears? In church, she busied herself by fancying all the ladies who might make her daddy a good wife. Each family took up a whole pew, eight sandy heads, ten, a dozen. No one got lonesome in a family like that. Elma and Juke knew what it was to be the only child in a house, to roll over in bed without knocking into someone else. They knew the power of ghosts, and imaginary friends, and real ones. They knew how easy it was to fashion a sibling, even when the sibling slept under another roof, with a family of its own, even if it was a family hired and not born by blood.

Good night, my sister, my brother, they thought, from under the other roof. Tomorrow we will meet at the creek.

SEVEN

MANFORD RAWLS'S OFFICE WAS ON MAIN STREET, NEXT DOOR to Pearsall's Drugs and down the street from his home. It was the only doctor's office in town. There, between the hours of eight and four, he gave shots, set breaks, dispensed medicine, depressed the spotted tongues of children with his wooden stick. He was a stubborn old white man, no traveling country doctor. If you went into labor in the middle of the night, you fetched a midwife. If you caught a fever in the evening, you waited until morning. One night when Nan was nine, returning home from delivering a baby with her mother, a man flagged down the truck they were in, his flannel shirt a bloody belt around his waist. His stomach had been cut with the glass of a broken bottle, and Nan watched as Ketty took out her satchel and sewed up the wound with a needle and thread, the man lying on the green corn husks in the bed of the truck. He was a colored man; the driver was too. The driver, who two hours before had become a father, left the man with a jar of Jesup's Cotton Gin on Dr. Rawls's step, where he slept until the morning, and even then the doctor made him wait until he saw a white woman with a rash on her legs.

But when Dr. Rawls learned about the twins, when word had reached him that their mother had no intention of parading them into town, he made an exception to his hours. On a Friday evening, he drove his beady black Plymouth out to the farm. The puppies heard the engine and went tearing out to see who it was. He was a white-mustached man who'd begun to stoop, the pale, shaven flesh of his neck wrinkled as a rooster's comb. He wore a black suit and a black Homburg hat and carried a black satchel, listing to the left with its weight, his right ear listening toward the sky for some signal.

"Babies need to be seen," said the doctor, coming through the breezeway to the back porch, where he lifted a towel from the rocker that had not been offered him and seated himself in it. Nan and Elma were giving the twins their weekly bath, both babies squeezed into the aluminum tub, their skin soapy blue in the last hour of sunlight. The day was cool and crisp, the first day that felt like fall. Nan had been enjoying the evening, her hands in the warm water, the babies splashing. The doctor looked at them admiringly, as though they were a pair of his own prize pigs.

Juke sat on the top porch step, his shaving bowl between his bare feet on the step below, a tumbler of gin at his hip. His left cheek was smooth, his right still bristly with red and silver and gold. When Dr. Rawls took a seat, Juke shuttled the glass to the third step. He turned and tipped his straw hat, but he didn't take it off, and he didn't stand up. "Doctor."

"Mr. Jesup."

"These younguns got a sickness I need to know about?"

The doctor lifted Wilson out of the water, slipped him straight out of Nan's hands like a fish. Nan and Elma were still crouched behind the tub, and Nan moved to stand up, but Elma yanked her down by the hand that wasn't holding Winna in the bath, then slipped it into hers. The doctor settled Wilson onto the towel on his lap. "I'm just here for some preventive care. Standard practice."

Juke slipped his straight razor into the bowl of water and leveled it against his right cheekbone, scraping it down to the wedge of his jaw. You could hear the blade on his skin, rough as a rake over stony soil. He was not going to offer the doctor coffee. He was not going to tell any stories. "Is it standard practice to call on a patient after supper?"

"In exceptional cases it is."

"Don't make no exception for us, please. These babies are as standard as they come. They got ten fingers and ten toes, same as anybody."

The doctor was combing through Wilson's hair with his fingers, inspecting his scalp, and Nan had to squeeze Elma's hand to keep from leaping up again. "Miss Jesup," the doctor said, not looking up, "you want your children to be healthy, don't you?"

"Course I do." Elma let go of Nan's hand, scooped up Winna Jean, and wrapped her in a towel. "That's why I keep them at home, so they won't catch nothing."

"They's plenty a child can catch on a farm, even out here in the country air." From his satchel he removed his stethoscope and fit the disk to the boy's chest. "You folks don't need me to remind you." He turned his head and, for the first time since he'd arrived, met Nan's eyes. "Tetanus. Smallpox. Diphtheria." She remembered the first time he'd pressed that cold stethoscope to her skin, and the first time he'd pressed his tongue depressor to her bottom lip. When she opened her mouth and he saw there was nothing to depress, he jumped back as if she'd bitten him.

"They're preventable diseases now," the doctor said. "Medicine has come a long way." In the doctor's lap, Wilson stared transfixed at the shiny faces of his glasses. The doctor took a loaded syringe from his bag and sank it into the naked baby's thigh, as casually as he might stick a cooked turkey. Wilson opened his mouth and released a cry.

Nan released a cry too. She shot up from the porch floor and clapped her hand over her mouth. It was the kind of cry she tried to keep inside, a lonesome, ugly cry, like an animal in pain. It had been so long since she'd made the sound that it sounded alien to her own ears. The others looked at her, eyes wide. She didn't care. Without Elma to hold her back, she rushed to Wilson and took him in her arms.

"Doctor!" Elma said, and Nan was grateful for her voice. "What in Heaven!"

Wilson howled. Nan bounced him. Then Winna Jean, in Elma's arms, began to howl too. Then, suddenly at Nan's feet, Castor and Pollux joined them.

Now Juke did stand up. He took the final step up to the porch. He wasn't a tall man, but his legs and scarred arms were ropy, and he had a way of making himself appear bigger, of filling a doorway with the wings of his shoulders. The skin at his open collar, already pink with sweat, went a shade redder, and his jaw, still wet, went stiff.

"Doctor, this mother would kindly like a warning. As a courtesy."

The emptied syringe still dangled between the doctor's fingers, his thumb on the depressor. Juke palmed the razor.

"Of course," said the doctor. He dropped Juke's glance and looked out at the fields, maybe looking at Genus Jackson's shack, maybe looking for the still, maybe for the quarantine shack that had been burned when Nan and Elma were small. The babies had quieted a bit, the puppies with them. They lay down at Nan's feet. The doctor said, "I reckon you grown folks are due for shots as well."

"Ain't no need for shots for no grown folks," said Juke.

"A man's impervious to no illness." The doctor opened his case, displayed more glass vials. "I can do it here. No need to make the trip into town."

"Put them shots away. Ain't no one stuck me yet and I don't intend to change that. You can stick the babies, but then you'll be on your way."

The doctor looked as if he might push further, but he replaced the vials in his bag. "You know something," said the doctor. "All my years in medicine, I've never seen twins with separate paternity. I know some doctors who would be mighty interested in this case. It's a rarity, I'll tell you that. Something to be proud of." He sat with his legs crossed at the knee, the creases of his pants legs sharp.

"Proud?" It looked to Nan like a smile curling the corner of Juke's mouth. "I ain't ashamed of my grandchildren, make no mistake. But I ain't proud for one minute of their 'paternity.' Neither way."

Dr. Rawls gave an ambiguous tilt of his head. He still seemed to be waiting for some sound from above. "The Lord works in mysterious ways."

"I reckon He does," said Juke.

Juke looked on as Dr. Rawls gave Winna her three shots and Wilson the last two, and in the middle of the howling, the baby boy, like a fountain cherub, sent an arc of urine across the doctor's creased pants legs. Elma rushed over with another towel, but the doctor laughed. "Well, aren't you just full of piss and vinegar?" Elma laughed a relieved and joyful laugh. Wilson laughed too, which made Juke laugh in turn. Nan made no sound at all. She stood with her hands behind her back, clasping each of her elbows to give her hands something to hold. What sound was there for the joylessness she felt then? Relief, yes, that the doctor was leaving, that he'd discovered nothing, but disappointment too, that he was leaving, that he'd discovered nothing.

The doctor bounced Wilson on his knee. "That's a good quality, son. You keep pissing and spitting, you hear? You're gone need to in this life." The doctor blotted his pants with his handkerchief, kissed the top of Wilson's head, and handed the baby back to Nan.

"I'll send a bill."

———

After the doctor's black car disappeared down the road, though, after Juke downed the rest of his gin and stuffed his gums with tobacco, he took Wilson from her again. He wrapped him tight in his towel and rocked him back and forth. He wasn't laughing anymore. "Seems I told you not to open that door to nobody," he said to Elma.

"He ain't nobody. He's Dr. Rawls. And he walked straight to the porch himself!"

"He ain't to set foot in this house again, you hearing me? He ain't to set foot on the porch."

"I thought you said we got nothing to hide. He ain't the police. He ain't the papers."

"I ain't ascaired of the police or the papers."

"But you ascaired of an old man?" Elma put a little smile on her face to show she was teasing.

Juke shifted Wilson in his arms and gave her a serious look. "That old man knows people. George Wilson, for one. People in Atlanta. All the way to Washington. He's an old man with a ticket to Heaven—he ain't got nothing to lose. He's been sniffing around here before and I don't need him sniffing around again."

"You don't want him knowing you're a shiner or you don't want him knowing you're daddy to a Negro?"

Juke was looking out to the field. Perhaps he was listening for a passing car, for other listening ears. Nan waited for him to reply. She thought he might strike one of them, or both. Then she saw him remember not to. When he spoke, his voice was low. "Neither one his business, and I reckon they ain't yourn, either."

"One of them is," said Elma. "You made it my business."

"Quiet. We don't talk of it. Even in this house, on this porch, we don't talk of it. You hearing?" He cupped a hand over Wilson's ear. It was true—they did not talk of it, had not talked of it since the day Wilson was born. "And you," he said, turning to Nan, "alls you gotta do is keep quiet, and you ain't even do that?" He spit his chaw over the porch railing, shaking his head, and returned Wilson to her arms. "Put a diaper on this child."

They retired to their side of the house, Nan to hers. There was no window in the pantry where she slept. For that she was glad. She could sit on her pallet and nurse Wilson without any eyes on her but his.

Juke would have liked both babies to stay all night in Elma's room, and for Elma to tend to them when they cried. "You can feed him just as easy," he'd said to Elma when the babies were a few weeks old.

"You worried we gone have midnight visitors, Daddy?" Nan thought Elma suspected what she did—that the only midnight visitor Nan might have was Juke himself, that he wanted to be able to come to her room again, without Elma or the babies getting in the way. He had not come to her room since the babies were born, and she had Elma to thank for that. "I ain't agreed to be no wet nurse," she told him. "He don't like my milk none anyway."

During the day, when folks might be about—the neighbors, the hands, visitors dropping in—they had to be careful. Nan couldn't pay Wilson undue attention. If folks came by, sometimes Juke would make Elma suckle Wilson right there on the porch, just to show, though it was true he didn't take well to her breast. Mostly he turned his head and cried. Folks turned their heads too. So did Nan.

But mostly it was all right. She liked it best when she and Elma cooked together in the kitchen, the babies lying on their bellies on the rag rug at their feet—didn't matter then whose baby was whose. Didn't matter if Elma said "your baby" or "my baby" or "the twins"— they were the babies, and they didn't care what they were called. If Nan had her hands in a pie crust, Elma changed Wilson's diaper. If Elma was out in the garden, and Winna woke from a nap crying, Nan didn't think twice before she put her own nipple in the girl's mouth to calm her. (Well, maybe she thought twice, but rarely three times.) Winna liked Nan's milk as much as her own mother's. It was Wilson who was particular, though when Nan was out on a call all day and night, and he was hungry enough, he relented.

When the babies were just a few weeks old, she had left Wilson with Elma to go on a call in Rocky Bottom. The woman—she was more like a girl, Nan's age, with no children yet—was just seven months along, and Nan knew before the baby was out that it would be born dead. "It ain't been moving," the girl said. "Used to hiccup. Ain't hiccupped in two weeks." Afterward, after she had delivered the baby, the girl had been shocked and silent, and there was little Nan could do except wrap the baby in a blanket. It was a boy no bigger than a swamp rabbit, and covered in a pelt of rabbit fur. But four days later, after the girl's milk had started to come in, her mother and father drove her out to the farm to ask Nan what to do. "She's swolled up awful," the mother said, and the girl, still in the wagon, sat up straight to show her. It was a trip of perhaps nine miles, a long way to come, Nan thought, for such a question. But then the mother looked around her toward the big house. "I hear the girl got twins up in there. She could use the help of a wet nurse, I expect. The boy really colored?" Nan shook her head firmly. "Can't you ask her?" the mother went on. "We wouldn't ask for much." But Nan refused, and Juke did not come out, and Elma did not come out, and she knew that the family would come no closer to the house. And though she had sent away the poor girl with her poor bloated breasts, still she had nightmares of the family returning to take Wilson, not just to nurse him but to keep him, to replace the swamp rabbit baby, who had been buried, the mother told her, in an apple crate. He wouldn't take it, Nan wanted to tell her. He wouldn't drink from you.

Tonight, even Nan's milk didn't calm him. He was fussing, ornery from his shots. Or was he cutting a tooth already? When did they start to come in? She wished she could ask the doctor, for she knew nothing about how babies grew after they came into the world. Everything she knew she had learned with her own eyes, watching Winna and Wilson. They were as unalike as any two babies ever were, and their skin was the least of it. Were they foolish to think that the world would believe they were twins, or was it just that every two babies were as unalike as these, with their own faces, their own fingers and toes, some webbed with dirt, like eraser dust, some instead flecked with the white dust of snake skin?

Without putting down the baby, she stood and stepped over her pallet to the pantry shelves, where she found a jar of sorghum syrup. Still holding him, she unscrewed the cap and dipped in a finger and pressed it against his gums. He closed his mouth and sucked. She knew nothing about babies, but she knew Wilson. She knew he was hers, as much as she was his.

She lay down on the pallet, Wilson pressed against her side, her finger still in his mouth. His eyes were glassy with tears but still now, his nostrils caked with dried mucus, like flakes of pastry crust. He smelled of pastry crust, of honey wax and vinegar. She put her own nose inside the tiny bud of his ear, where he had a heartbeat, steady and distant. He was her companion now. He had replaced Juke in her bed. For this she loved him, despite herself. She hadn't asked for it, she hadn't expected it, but it wasn't to be denied, the surge of milk so strong she felt the blood in her veins run faster. Here it came, swift and certain, like the full bucket at the well after you gave it a few strong tugs. If that wasn't love, what was it?

His eyelids were fluttering closed, fighting sleep, like a trapped moth's wings. She lifted her gown and dabbed another bit of syrup on her nipple. Slowly, she slipped her finger out of the baby's warm mouth and slipped her nipple in. He took to it blindly, his eyelids resting now. And then the love filled her chest and she was helpless against it. A sleeping child was easier to love than a waking one, she'd learned. Or maybe it was that, with his green eyes closed, it was easier to pretend he belonged to Genus.

Would she have loved the baby more if Genus were his father? Or was this the only way, that God took something for every gift He granted? He had taken her mother home but had made Nan a mother. He'd taken Genus, but He'd freed her from Juke. Would she go back, and agree to spend her life under Juke, if it meant Genus would still walk the earth?

Yes, she told herself, yes. She'd spend a thousand lifetimes on her back. She'd walk herself backward out of his shack, out of his life, to see him again framed in the window in his corn-shuck hat, shaking the rug, the moment before his eyes discovered hers. She would watch him from a distance. That would be enough.

EIGHT

THE TWINS WERE BOTH BORN IN THE BIG HOUSE, EACH CHILD IN its own time. Before they were twins, though, before they called them the twins—to others, as well as to themselves— they were two babies growing on separate vines. As spring came to Georgia, Elma thought of the baby that way, marveled at the tomato plants (planted on Good Friday, the luckiest day to start a garden), the green fruits first as small and hard as acorns, then growing heavier, hanging lower; she weighed them with one palm and held the other to her belly, which was growing too, as firm and round as fruit. After she left school, she dressed in Juke's overalls and walked the garden—it was as far afield as he would allow her—pulling june bugs from the leaves and waiting for Freddie to come to his senses. No one knew she was carrying, or at least no one said they knew. Her daddy told folks she was needed on the farm and no one blinked an eye. Freddie would pull up any day now in his lizard green truck. He wouldn't make a big show about it. They'd sit on the porch and drink sweet tea, and the ring would be in his pocket.

She was five months along when she discovered her belly wasn't the only one growing. Nan and Elma were working hip to hip in the kitchen. Nan was frying eggs. Elma was soaking black-eyed peas. Nan lifted her apron to wipe her brow, and below it was a small mound, unmistakable. Nan dropped the apron, and still, there it was. Nan was so skinny, it was hard to see how Elma hadn't noticed it before.

But Elma's mind did something then. It hopped over Nan's belly and trotted off. Already it was becoming good and fast at trotting, her mind. It ignored the racing of her heart. She drained the beans, then realized the beans needed more soaking, and then she stumbled out to the well to fetch more water, walking as she did with her arms straight at her sides. Genus was out by the shed, chopping wood for the cookstove, the slow, steady sound of his ax chipping too close to her ears, and Elma's heart sped up again and her hands shook and she spilled half the bucket down her legs, but still she kept her mind far away, at the edge of the fields.

Juke, he'd noticed first. Out at the still one night, he'd passed his hand over Nan's belly and felt the mound—round where before it had been so flat it was nearly concave. He pulled away from her, sat up on the mattress. He asked her if she was with child.

Nan looked to the wall. Sometimes it was awful convenient, her having no tongue.

"You can't answer, but you can nod. You good at that." He put his finger under her chin and turned her face to his. "Answer me. Alls you gotta do is nod or shake your head."

He waited for her to respond, thinking already of what to do. He knew people. He knew everyone. But Nan was the only one in the county who handled woman's matters. What was she to do, take care of it herself? Word was Dr. Rawls took care of that kind of thing, if the pay was high enough. But he wouldn't lower himself to ask the doctor for help, even if he told him it was a field hand's child.

He felt her body relax. She nodded. But there was something in her nod—a different kind of fear—and now it was Juke's body that tensed.

"It's mine, ain't it?"

Did he want it to be his?

"Answer me, girl."

It would be better, of course, if it wasn't his, if the baby was colored. That it would have a proper mother and father. He was nearly forty years old and he had never to his knowledge given any woman but Jessa a child.

She raised her shoulders and looked to the wall again. Juke dropped his hand. He could see it was true, that she didn't know. How could she know? And how could he have been prepared for the rage and disappointment, that the child might be another man's?

He did what his body knew how to do. He finished having his way with her, thinking, This will be the last time. He had only let go inside her once. Maybe that had been enough. But now he did it again, laying claim to what was his, because what harm could it do?

When he was done, he lay back and reached for his chaw and, naked, crossed his legs at the ankles. He told Nan about the colored woman whose tit he'd suckled on as an infant, having no mother himself. "Maybe that's how come I got a taste for darkies," he said. (It was a joke known across the county. "Ain't Jesup's fault he a nigger lover," white folks might be heard to say. "He been drinking nigger juice since he was a boy.")

By the time Elma's mind came around, calmed down, it was evening. She took another look at Nan at the supper table, her belly sitting in her lap, the same size as Elma's. What a fool she had been, daydreaming about Genus, following him at night, when here he had been making love to Nan. She had tried for months to unremember that vision of them in the creek, but here was the proof. And then she did something else that surprised her. She said, right there, laying the gravy on her daddy's potatoes, "Looks like I ain't the only one expecting." She said it cheerfully, teasingly, as though she was gossiping about someone else at church. If she said it with a smile in her voice, then she wouldn't feel the snap of her heart like a twig, for in her mind, Nan was carrying Genus's child and now they would both be on the farm for good, together, a family, and Elma would be both a spinster and a whore.

Juke nodded over his potatoes. "I reckon you're right."

"Nan? Is it true?"

Nan looked from Elma to Juke, then nodded at the table.

"I seen my mistake now," said Juke. "You shoulda been sent to church. Your momma and daddy would be right disappointed."

"Ain't your fault, Daddy. Her momma didn't send her to church, either."

"She ain't hired to go to church," Juke said. Then to Nan, "You ain't hired to go to church. You ain't hired to get into trouble neither."

"Daddy, don't say 'hired.'" Elma sighed a laugh. "Look at me. I been to church, and I'm in the same shoes, ain't I?"

"You in those shoes 'cause Freddie Wilson's all hat and no cattle. Tell me why I shouldn't run him out of town tomorrow."

"'Cause you still holding out he'll marry me, Daddy." And that was what he wanted—for his grandchild to be a Wilson. She didn't add that part.

"It's the only right thing," he said.

"You saying Nan and Genus oughta get married?" Elma stuffed her mouth with potatoes. Why had she gone and said that?

Juke looked sideways at Nan. She had not touched her food. "I got one who can't talk, one who can't stop talking." It was not the first time he'd said it. "You don't need to make up for her tongue." He chewed for a while, thinking, muttering. "Hell of a time . . . two more mouths to feed." The cuckoo clock above the mantel ticked.

Juke nodded his head toward Genus's shack. "Is he the man?"

Another moment, and then another nod. She could make her face look like a child's when she wanted to.

"Tell me why I shouldn't run him off this farm." His voice was lower now, as though Genus might hear him.

"Daddy—"

"Quit mouthing! How do I know that nigger ain't had his way with you too?"

"Daddy!"

Juke shoveled in a forkful of ham. With his mouth full, he said, "Reverend Quick will marry them. He's married niggers before. Reckon it's only right. Niggers belong with niggers." He pushed his plate away and leaned back in his chair. After supper, Elma knew, he would pour himself a tall drink and take it out to the back porch. Elma and Nan would be left to clear the table, and at least then there would be the comfort of silence, no sounds but the familiar ones of china and silver.

But now Nan still sat with her head hanging. Juke said, "Reckon you going back to that shack. Reckon you shouldn't never have left it."

NINE

T
HE COUPLE ARRIVED IN SEPTEMBER IN A BEAT-UP MODEL T WITH
a license plate from New York, the colossal silver lily of a
phonograph player blooming from the back window. The
puppies barked alongside it as it made its way up the dusty driveway.
For a few clenched heartbeats, as they stepped out of the car, Elma
was sure they were there to see the twins. The story had reached
across the telegraph lines all the way to New York City, and here they
were to take their picture, to record them on their gramophone. She
had the bone-tensing fear that they might take the babies too. When
they asked for Juke, said they'd heard in Florence that he might be
looking for hired help on the Wilson farm, Elma felt her heart relax,
and then cool into a flat, dull stone. Her pride was hurt, just a little.
Their names were Sara and Jim.

They sat on the back porch, admiring the babies on Elma's lap,
while they waited for Juke to come in from the field. Nan poured
them iced tea, and the man said, "You folks do like it sweet, don't
you?" Elma's heart stuttered when the woman asked if Wilson was
Nan's, but she kept her voice steady. "No, ma'am," she said. "They're
both mine."

Juke took them in on the spot, even though they were outsiders to Florence, even though he had enough willing hands in town. "Can't pay you a penny," he said, "but I can give you three meals and a roof." He took them in, Elma suspected, because they were young and white and new to town—they'd come all the way from New York, almost as far as Canada, where no one had ever heard of the Gemini twins or Genus Jackson. "New Yawk!" Juke said, putting on his best radio voice. "Y'all talk just as straight as a skyscraper, ain't you?"

"Not the city," Jim corrected him. "We're from Buffalo."

Juke shrugged. "At's a city, ain't it? What you kids doing down this way? Don't you know everyone here's running north?"

They'd been up and down the coast between Buffalo and Georgia and beyond—all the way down to Indian River, Florida, where they'd worked in the citrus groves that summer. They still had a crate of grapefruit in the backseat of their car, along with a basket of wool from a Vermont sheep farm and bolts of fabric from a garment factory in New York City. Because her father asked her to, Elma helped them carry their things to the tar paper shack behind the big house. Genus had left nearly nothing behind, and what he did have Juke had ordered that they burn. The shack had been swept clean. Now boxes and suitcases filled the room, overflowing with books and trinkets and clothing, a banjo, a guitar, the phonograph, fabric in orange and purple and periwinkle blue, a bolt of lemon yellow spilling from the bed to the floor. The couple moved busily about, saying how comfortable the cot was and what a pretty view, as though they were moving into a fancy new hotel. Elma watched from the doorway, arms folded.

"You must have loved growing up here," Sara said to Elma. She dug into the peel of a grapefruit and scalped it with her fingernails. She had fast, small hands, calloused and strong, her bare arms golden brown from the sun. Her face was square, with broad cheekbones and coffee bean eyes, and she wore her black hair in a braid down the length of her back. She handed Elma a wedge of the fruit. She had no idea who'd lived in this shack, did she? Elma didn't know whether to be disgusted or relieved.

Elma pressed it tentatively to her lips, tasting the bitter and the sweet. She nodded at Sara's question—was it a question?—filling her mouth with a brave bite now so she wouldn't have to speak.

"Isn't it a marvel?" Sara said. "Here it's peaches, right? You grow any Georgia peaches on this farm?"

Elma shook her head. "Just cotton, mostly. Some peanuts and corn."

"Jim, we got to get our hands on some Georgia peaches."

"If you say so," Jim said, putting on a twang. He held out a palm and Sara deposited a piece of grapefruit in it. He lifted his fedora in thanks, and under it Elma saw that his head was nearly bald. "You're a Georgia peach now, ain't you?"

"You better watch out," Sara said. "Before you know it I'll be cooking you grits."

Jim popped the fruit in his mouth, picked up the banjo, and with one foot propped up on the bed, began to pluck out a love song about a Georgia peach who cooked him grits. He made up the words as he played, rhyming "grits" with "shits." His voice filled the room, blew out the open windows. Out in the yard, Castor and Pollux began to howl, and he sang louder, so loud that Elma felt his voice thrumming through her bare feet, the twang that sounded as though he had a mouth full of scrap metal. It was Sara he was singing about, but it was Elma's voice, wasn't it, that he was making fun of. "She can't cook worth a fart, but she's stolen my heart, my sweet Georgia peach!"

Sara rolled her eyes, hiding her smile. She'd heard songs like it before. "Baby, that was delightful. You're a regular Irving Berlin."

"Who's Irving Berlin?" Elma asked. Her mouth still burned with the grapefruit, with the acid shame of never having eaten grapefruit before. She wanted more, but she didn't want to ask.

"Elma," Sara said, taking both her shoulders in her hands, looking her deep in the eyes, "we're going to teach you a thing or two."

"Or three or four," sang Jim on his banjo. "Or maybe more."

When the doctor's bill came, it came on a Sunday morning, when Dr. Rawls knew Juke would be in church. A colored boy on a borrowed bicycle pedaled barefoot all the way from Florence. He made sure Elma was the one to open it before she scurried back into the kitchen. Inside the envelope, tucked behind the bill, was a letter typed on onionskin paper. Nan stood with Wilson on her hip, watching her read it. It took a moment for Elma to see that it wasn't Manford Rawls's name on the letterhead but Dr. Oliver Rawls, Emory University, Atlanta, Georgia.

"Atlanta," Elma whispered, as though it were the name of a holy city. She thought of Josie Byrd's spotless white shoes, the knee-high boots of the yellow-haired dog breeder.

Oliver Rawls was the youngest son of Manford Rawls. Elma remembered him vaguely. He was ahead of her in school, far enough that he was graduating from high school when she'd been learning arithmetic. Mostly she remembered his limp, first on crutches, then on a cane. A head of dark curls, and round eyeglasses like his father's. Now he was a doctor like his father, a hematologist. He studied blood. He had heard about the twins from his father—"an exceptional case indeed." Would Mrs. Jesup—he said *Mrs.*—consider bringing the children to his laboratory in Atlanta for a few tests? Nothing invasive—just some blood work. "Our blood reveals more about ourselves than you can imagine."

Elma was leaning against the stove. When she'd finished reading the letter aloud, she dropped it to her side. "Blood work," she spat. She felt sick. Then she raised the letter and read it once more, to herself. "No one's gone stick those babies again," she said, "not if I have any say." But she kept her eyes on the page. "Some big-city scientist thinks he's putting his hands on my babies?" She looked up, remembering Nan, remembering her father wasn't in the room. "*Our* babies," she said quietly.

Then her eyes found the note at the bottom of the page. "PS," she read aloud. "I understand travel may be difficult. My father is willing to carry you to Atlanta, and I am willing to compensate you for your trouble."

Elma lowered the letter again, this time creasing it a little in her fist. "Some big-city scientist thinks he can buy me like a hog?" She produced a laugh. "I'm fixing to burn this with the rest of the trash," she said, but she put the letter in the pocket of her apron and kept it there, and spent the rest of the day singing a tune inside her closed mouth.

———

Sara and Jim were good hands. Juke taught them how to take the peanuts out of the ground, to thresh and stack them, to bale the hay. He taught them how to top and strip and cut the sorghum, and Nan and Elma helped to mill and cook and bottle it. When the cotton wanted picking, Sara and Jim made a game of it, racing to see how fast they could fill their bags, the way Elma and Nan had done when they were small. Their hats bobbed along the west field, Jim's voice filling the air with songs of rabbit-tail cotton and candy-cloud cotton, cotton soft as a baby's cheek. The other pickers stayed along the road, taking their midday meal under the lacy shade of the cottonwood tree, while Sara and Jim ate at the big house. They'd come back for harvest because they needed the work, Ezra and Long John and Al, and because Juke had been good to them. (Al's wife had begged him not to return to the farm, and Al had said, "He all right. He won't do me no harm," and his wife said, "Just don't be coming back to town dragged by no truck," and kept all three sons at home and said if they even looked at a white girl she'd kill them herself.) They kept their eyes on the ground, away from Elma, away from Juke, away from the gourd tree, and they didn't come near the house. At the cotton house, when it was time to weigh in at the end of the day, they didn't meet the young couple's eyes, but Jim tipped his hat as though he didn't notice, and whistled, impressed, at the biggest pull. Usually it was Long John, but on a day when Long John didn't come, it was Jim himself who picked two hundred and eighty pounds, more even than Juke, who was not shown up but proud. "They teach you to pick cotton in New Yawk, Jimbo?"

For supper there were boiled peanuts and greens and salt pork and beaten biscuits soaked in syrup, and Jim and Sara remarked over every bite, falling over themselves, and even Nan couldn't hide how pleased she was. After the meal, the men would throw horseshoes in the scrubgrass yard while the women washed the dishes. Then Sara would bounce a baby on her knee while Jim played his banjo or guitar on the front porch, "Travelin' Blues" and "Buffalo Blues" and "Boll Weevil," and they'd all listen, shelling field peas while the sun went down. After a while, the music eased even Elma. The voice Jim used was his own. He sang and the dogs howled after him. When they howled too long, Juke threw the pea jackets at them, and they ate them up. One evening a chain gang limped up the Straight, their sweat-soaked handkerchiefs hanging like bright tails from their back pockets, and as they leveled the ditches Jim played them "Birmingham Jail," and they sang along, and then, wanting to give them something brighter, he played "Ain't Misbehavin'," and they sang and danced too, even the shotgun guard Lloyd Crow, who was known to enjoy a pint of gin with Sheriff Cleave now and then, clapping his hands along to the music before moving the men on. Jim and Sara talked of their travels—speakeasies and soup kitchens, revivals and picture shows, the camps along the flooded Mississippi. Many nights they'd slept in their car at the edge of shantytowns, giving shelter to those who needed it. At marked houses, they begged for food; at farms they worked for milk and eggs; they stayed put until they had enough to buy or trade for gasoline; then they kept going. For a while Jim had run rum in Philadelphia, but he got into some trouble and they went south. They'd been traveling for three years. Now they were twenty-three, and Sara wanted a baby.

"I can't stand it one more minute," she said, taking Winna Jean into her lap. "I've got to have one."

"Another mouth to feed," Jim said. "No, thank you."

Sara blew a raspberry on Winna's cheek. "Babies eat nothing but momma's milk. Look at this momma! She's got two and they're still fat as can be."

"They don't drink milk forever, darling."

"Well, by the time they're through, times will be better."

Juke laughed from his rocking chair, sending shreds of tobacco flying from his mouth. "Maybe in New York they will. In Georgia, times is always lean."

"We never have missed a meal," said Elma, not looking up from the peas.

Juke said, "They're a blessing, no matter how lean the times."

––––––––––

Harvest went on. In the evening, there was celebration, but in the daylight hours, the fields had a way of keeping your mind on the ground. The seeds grew, no matter what was happening in the big house. They managed to keep the weevil away, but that year there were army worms. If you sat dead quiet on the porch, you could hear the shush of their chewing through the fields. Juke used all of Elma's good flour to make an arsenic paste, and early one morning while the dew was still on the cotton he and Jim crept into the field and lay the poison down. Then when you sat on the porch the only sounds were the cricket frogs and your own lonesome breath.

For a time it seemed that a new season had come. The floorboards were cool in the morning. The gnats were gone. In the yard, the guineas squawked; the one Elma had named Herbert did his rain dance. All year long they'd prayed for rain along with him, but at picking time, they prayed it stayed away, at least until they'd plucked all the cotton from the fields. The second week of October, though, brought a steady storm, not strong enough to lay the cotton flat, but long enough to keep them indoors for three days. When the rain stopped, they'd have to rush to empty the west field of cotton, if it wasn't ruined already. For now, there was nothing to do but stay indoors. While Winna and Wilson took their morning nap and Nan started on the churning, Elma packed a basket with hoecakes and dashed through the rain to Sara and Jim's shack. Juke and Jim were out at the still, and Sara was sewing something she held behind her back while she opened the door.

"I brought dinner," said Elma, shaking the rain out of her hair.

"Aren't you sweet," Sara said. She held up her sewing: a doll. "You caught me. It's for Winna Jean."

Elma took it from her. "Ain't *you* sweet!" She couldn't help it. It was no guano sack rag baby. It was made with what looked like flax cloth, and it was wearing a yellow rose-print dress with a flax cloth apron and black felt Mary Jane shoes.

"It's not finished," Sara said, taking it back. "She's got to have button eyes."

"She's pretty as a picture," Elma said.

"Well, I'll tell you the secret. It's the cotton she's stuffed with. Finest cotton in all of Georgia, from what I hear."

"Oh, yes! I bet it is."

"Your daddy won't mind I took some?"

Elma waved her hand. "Daddy's got so much cotton he won't miss a doll's worth."

"But it's not his, exactly, is it?" Sara placed the doll against her pillow and sat down beside it on the cot, and Elma put the basket on the table.

"Might as well be. It's George Wilson's field, but he ain't set foot in it but once a season."

Sara nodded knowingly. "He doesn't want to get dung on his trousers."

"Fine by me. Better than coming over every day to complain about this or that. The Cousins, down the road? They don't have barely a minute of peace. They all live in shacks, a whole mess of kin on that farm. The planter, he's brother to one of the wives, he's always out on the porch of his house pointing his finger, saying do this or do that, and in what order. He once made little Lucy Cousins take out all the stitches in his socks and put them back again. Least Mr. Wilson stays out of the way."

She didn't say that he'd stayed away for some time, that he and her daddy had fallen out. When the weevil came and so much cotton was lost, when he seemed to be one of only a few landowners with any money left, George Wilson had bought up farm after farm. Before long, he didn't have time for the crossroads. When there was business to be done, Juke had gone into town, to visit with him at the mill. And then the babies were born, and Genus was killed, and as far as Elma could tell, her father stopped going to the mill at all. She had seen nothing of the Wilsons.

"You like that," said Sara. "For people to stay out of your way."

"Not you!"

"Well, maybe that's because I haven't asked you about the twins yet."

Elma sat down in one of the wooden chairs. Then, remembering for the first time where she was, she stood up again. She could still smell the smoky char of the fire that had nearly burned the shack down. "What about them?"

"How they look so different. I mean—"

"I know they look different," Elma said sharply. She busied her hands in the basket. Then, more gently, feeling her tongue go loose, she said, "I didn't ask for two babies." She had thought that sentence hour after hour, it had lived silent in her head, and there it was now, out on the table. She laid the hoecakes side by side. They were heavy as rocks, made with the low-grade flour left in the back of the pantry, and Elma wished she'd made something else instead. "They have two different daddies, is how come. They're twins, grown up inside me at the same time, but they ain't all the way kin."

"That's something," Sara said, wide-eyed.

"Alls I'll say," Elma said, but she'd already said more than she ever had, even more than she'd said to the newspaperman—when had she ever had a real friend to talk to, who could talk back!—"Alls I'll say is one of the daddies is Freddie Wilson. The landlord's his granddaddy. More like a daddy."

"The one that owns the farm?"

"He ain't no more than a dog. Freddie, that is. Granddaddy too, I reckon. Folks look down they noses at the baby for his skin, well! The Wilsons ain't no better! They don't even take up for they own."

"You sure these Wilsons don't have mulatto blood, and that's how come Wilson's dark? It's the uppity white folks, the ones with the slaves in the family—"

"Oh, no!" Elma shook her head. "Not the Wilsons. They're pure as cotton. No. No. They're two daddies. That's alls I'll say. Nature has its own ideas, I reckon."

"I reckon it does," Sara said, trying on the word.

"You think a mare ever thought she could mate with a donkey?"

Sara considered it. "I reckon she mates with whoever she pleases."

"Well, the first mare that gave birth to a mule ought to have been as surprised as me. But you think she'd have loved him any more if he'd been a horse?"

"I reckon not."

"They're both gone now, the daddies. One is dead and one might as well be." Elma fingered the envelope in the pocket of her apron. "That's alls I'm like to say about that."

Sara crossed the room and touched her hand to Elma's shoulder. "Thank you for the lunch." She took a hoecake from the table. They both took bites. The rain tapped against the tar paper roof.

"You ain't spent much time near livestock," Elma asked her, "have you?"

"Can't say I have."

"A mare don't mate with whoever she pleases. She mates with whatever ass is penned in with her."

Sara laughed. Before she could stop herself, Elma asked, "How do you keep from getting caught?"

"Do what?"

"From getting pregnant."

Sara didn't flinch. "You ain't spent much time near Catholics, have you?"

"Can't say I have."

"You know your time of the month, don't you?"

"I don't bleed anymore, not while my milk is in."

"Well, you count it. Just before or just after your time is the safest. It's the time in the middle you worry about."

Elma nodded, though she didn't quite understand.

"Good thing about my time of the month is that it's my time, not Jim's. He might be the one getting caught, come Christmas."

Now Elma laughed. She smoothed her apron. "A letter came from Atlanta." She slipped it out of her pocket. "Some doctor at Emory University wants to study on the babies."

"Study on them? What for?" Sara reached for the letter and lowered herself into a chair.

"He wants to see how come twins can have two daddies, I guess. I ain't gone let him, though."

"Why not?" Sara didn't look up from the letter.

Elma sat on her hands. Could doctors really tell if two babies were twins? Could they even tell if they were brother and sister? She said, "I don't want my babies poked and prodded. I don't want them in a medical journal. They ain't specimens!"

"But he says he'll pay. Times are hard!"

"How do I know he'll pay? How do I know I won't get there and they'll take the babies away?"

Sara snorted. "Elma, Emory University is a respectable institution. They're not going to take your babies. Tell them your terms."

Elma shivered at the word. Her "terms." Yes, she had set terms before—she had set terms with her father. That was the word for it, wasn't it?

"Tell them what you demand in order to cooperate with their study. Atlanta's all the go! Have you ever been?"

Elma shook her head.

"Well, it's bigger than a bread basket, let me tell you. The men aren't bad to look at, either. Oh, you're going to love it! You can take our electric!"

"I don't know how to drive. Well, I know a little."

"I'll teach you!"

"Sara, I can't. I'm much obliged, but I can't leave. Daddy would never let me, for one."

"He sure keeps you down on the farm, doesn't he?"

Elma took another bite. For a moment a dry cake of panic lodged in her throat. What did Sara know about her father? About Nan? Was Elma the last person to know what was happening in her own house?

"I don't mean nothing by it," Sara said.

Elma could see that she didn't. She swallowed. The rain was lightening up on the roof. She had a flash of herself, like a remembered dream, flying through Atlanta on a streetcar, holding her hat tight to her head. If her father could leave the farm, if her father could go to the city and be someone else, why couldn't she? She had told him her terms before. She would set her own terms now.

She said, "How'd you get your hands on that electric, anyway?"

Sara smiled around a mouthful. "You can get your hands on just about anything if you're clever enough."

"You stole it?"

"It's on loan from my uncle up in Buffalo. He used to like to kiss me with his tongue. I figure he had it coming. First he lost the car, then he lost everything else in the crash."

Now the hoecake sat like a stone in Elma's stomach. To Nan, her father used to call himself that, an uncle, just like she'd called Nan's father Uncle Sterling. "Come on and hug Uncle Juke's neck. Come on and give Uncle Juke some sugar." Then he stopped. Was that when it had started up, with Nan?

Her mind fell upon something. She closed her eyes and followed the branches of the tree. If her daddy was Wilson's daddy, then Wilson was not Winna's brother but her uncle. The only person he was brother to was Elma.

So if the doctors discovered the babies were kin, well, that was because they were.

Sara was still talking about the car. "Wasn't all I took. All that good cloth doesn't come cheap."

Elma sat up. "You stole that too?"

"Do you know how much the dress factory pays? I prefer to call it 'souvenir harvesting.'"

"Harvesting!" Elma swatted Sara's arm. "Well, lucky for us, we got nothing for you to harvest. Nothing but a handful of cotton."

"Just watch out. I might take me a souvenir baby."

Elma laughed. Her ears listened for the babies, but all she heard was rain. She knew she should go to them, but she felt frozen in place. Nan was there. Her father wasn't. Let Nan listen for them. That was what Nan wanted, wasn't it? Same as Elma. To be mothers to their children. To share them, even! But to be mothers with their whole selves, not to be split into fractions. She allowed herself to imagine it: Nan and Elma living in the big house with Wilson and Winna. Her father gone from the farm. Not gone from the world, like Genus. Just disappeared, like Freddie. Gone! Sara would be there too. In the shack, making dolls for the babies. After doing the doctor's study in Atlanta, maybe they'd have a little money to live on.

Then, still laughing, she felt the air go out of her lungs. She looked sideways at Sara, thinking how strange it was that you never really knew anyone, that no matter how much your heart warmed to a stranger, she'd always be a stranger to you. She caught her breath. She was dizzy with fear and envy, certain of some unavoidable loss. It wasn't just her children she feared losing. Harvest was nearly over. Sara and Jim never stayed anywhere long. Soon they'd be gone, their automobile with them.

After their meal, when the rain had quieted to a lazy drizzle, Sara and Elma raised the windows and hung their heads outside. The guineas had come out again, honking nervously through the yard, through the coal black ash of the old shack they liked to nest in. High above the sorghum, a purple martin emerged from a gourd. "That's a funny scarecrow," Sara said, pointing. "Instead of scaring the birds away, it gives them shelter."

"We like those birds," said Elma. "They catch the skeeters."

"I'll tell you something, Elma. They do no such thing."

Elma studied the gourd tree. Someone—her father?—had removed the length of rope, or it had been blown down in the storm. Looking at it with Sara beside her, it was almost just a gourd tree. "Maybe it's an old wives' tale."

"You Southerners have peculiar ways of keeping some in and others out."

A lock of Elma's hair had fallen. She took a pin from her bun and then stabbed it back. "Do we now."

"It would be one thing," said Sara, "if it worked."

TEN

NINE TIMES OUT OF TEN IT WAS WOMEN WHO GOT HIM INTO trouble. He had red blood coursing through him like any man. But the day Juke met the girl who would be his wife, it was String he had his mind set on seeing. He'd been sent by his daddy to the feed and seed in town, and he took their john mule, Lefty. They had a barn full of mules then, mostly spritely young mollys who could plow in their sleep, but Lefty was the only john, and Juke's favorite. He was near big as a horse and spotted black on white clear through his mane. He'd been George Wilson's favorite too. It had been George who'd finally taught him to turn right.

It was 1901, just after the Wilsons had built the mill and moved from the farm into town. George Wilson and his brothers had inherited a hill of money from an uncle in the railroad business. In a few years George had grown bored of planting, of buying up land all over Cotton County. He got it into his head to buy rights to the Creek River at the edge of town, where the river and the Straight and the new railroad converged. He borrowed more money from his brothers in north Georgia, one in the turpentine business, another in sawmills. He found builders and then mill hands in the same way, by riding his horse from farm to farm. He needed Juke and Juke's father at the crossroads farm, but he pulled whole families from cropper cabins five counties around. On the train from Marietta, George's brother sent cars full of farmers' daughters in search of work. He sent the sheriff around to the Fourth Quarter to find loose-foot Negroes. The sheriff offered them the chain gang or the picker room. They chose the picker room. All of Florence was mighty proud of that mill.

Juke wanted to see it himself. So, after fetching the three sacks of corn seed, he tied the mule and its cart to a gum tree by the road and walked down to the river to wait for String to walk home from school. It was springtime, the wiregrass along the river wild with cornflower. Juke kicked off his shoes to chase tadpoles. When String came along the railroad and saw him, he let out a yelp of joy. "What in Hades you doing out here?"

The Wilsons' new house was the biggest house Juke had ever gotten close to, with a porch that wrapped around three sides. From the front porch you could see the cotton mill straight down the hill, three stories of bricks and as long as a freight train. The Creek River rushed rapid out of the woods there, feeding into the new dam that formed a pond at the head of the mill. To the east you could see the three-acre garden Parthenia Wilson had planted for the mill families, and Lefty, still tied to the tree by the Straight. To the west you could see the mill village, where the mill families lived, just a dozen clapboard bungalows then and more rising before Juke's eyes, houses no bigger than the shacks on the farm, the spaces between them no bigger than each house. And the Wilsons owned all of it. At ten years old, John Jesup—he was not yet called Juke—had traveled no farther than Macon, hopping the freight train with String and his cousins, and that city, with its smokestacks and street trolleys and brick-paved block after block, had left him feeling nauseous with longing and homesickness and the penny candy String's cousins had stolen from the sweets shop, though they had plenty of pennies in their pockets. There was so much to see he'd had to close his eyes.

That was how Juke felt on the porch of String Wilson's new house. He wanted, and he didn't want to want.

String seemed to know not to invite Juke inside. He left his school satchel on the porch and snuck Juke into the mill through the picker room in the basement, where colored men were opening bales, standing up to their knees in clouds of cotton. They paid the boys no mind.

"Looks like they in Heaven," Juke said to String as they passed through.

String laughed. "This here Heaven is the onliest place you'll find darkies in the mill. We won't hire them for nothing more." Up a narrow staircase, they came to the shop floor, the biggest room Juke had ever been in. A wall of windows, tall as silos, stretched from his elbow all the way up to the ceiling, and down the room, laid out like pews, was row after row of spinning machines, a girl standing at each one. "Look like church," said Juke.

String laughed again. "If there was only girls."

"That's the church for me," said Juke. "Bout as hot as church too." He took off his cap and fanned himself with it.

"We hire girls for spinners, mostly. Ain't nothing to it." String kept his voice low, and over the sound of the machines, Juke hardly heard him. "Most of the work boys do in the spinning room is sweeping."

"You sound like you the boss already, tombout all this hiring you doing."

"My daddy's learning me on the floor." String fetched a couple of push brooms hanging from the wall and handed one to Juke. "You know how to sweep?"

"I live on your daddy's farm, don't I?"

"Just push it around while we walk about, and Mr. Richard won't give us no trouble."

Juke put his cap back on his head and did so, following String down the line of machines. The women were studying so hard on their work that they barely raised their heads at the boys. They were too young to be called women, too tall to be called girls. The spinners all wore their hair in the same high, heavy pile, like a round loaf of bread on top of each of their heads, and their hair was dusted with the flour that was cotton lint, cotton everywhere, down their dresses, in the air, catching in Juke's broom, so much cotton that he felt he might sneeze, and then he did.

As he passed a girl at her machine, she looked up at him. This one was a girl, no bigger than Juke. She wore her yellow hair like a girl's, in a braid down her back, with a red satin bow hanging limp at the end of it. She wore a calico dress to her chin and a dirty apron and no shoes on her dirty feet. "God bless you," she said to Juke, and then returned her eyes to her work.

"Thank you kindly," said Juke, leaning on his broom. Like him, the girl had freckles, and he went near cross-eyed staring at them. "Ain't you hot in here," he asked, "standing at that machine all day?"

"Reckon we all hot," said the girl, not looking up.

"Y'all oughta open the window and let in some air."

"Daddy won't let them," String cut in. "When the breeze comes in it musses up the threads."

"That so?" said Juke. He took his cap off again and wiped his brow with it. Already he was damp with sweat. "How old are you?" he asked, yelling over the whirr of her machine.

The girl said she was twelve, and though Juke was ten he said he was too. He hadn't thought to ask the girl her name, but as they pushed their brooms into the weaving room, String told Juke it was Jessa. She'd come to the mill on the train from up near Atlanta, and she had no family but the one she boarded with in the mill village. "And she ain't no twelve years old," String said, "no more than we are. Twelve's the youngest we're supposed to hire."

He left only with her name. Jessa, Jessa, Jessa. The sun was setting over the mill village when Juke emerged from the mill. The mill hands, finishing the second shift, were making their way to their porches.

Juke didn't yet know if he loved the mill or hated it. His stomach was empty and he hoped String would ask him to stay for supper but he didn't. Juke's eyes adjusted to the dusk, the open air. He'd forgotten the mule, he'd forgotten its name, he'd nearly forgotten his own legs and how to use them. He was both relieved and panicked to see him there—Lefty—like a baby shocked to tears when its mother returns to a room. "Good boy, Lefty. There you are. Did you think I left you, Lefty boy?" There was Lefty, there was the cart, but inside it were only two bags of corn—one, two—and Juke had bought three. That much he knew.

His daddy whipped him good, of course. It was darker than pitch when Juke and Lefty finally returned to the farm, and his daddy came out of the house and hauled Juke down from the mule. Juke tried to explain, but his daddy ripped a branch from the chinaberry tree and right there under it by the light of his lantern switched his behind. Juke's father was angry about the stolen seed, but he was angrier that Juke had gone to the mill. "That ain't the place for you," he said, panting, after Juke was good and whipped. "Ain't this house enough?" He couldn't feel his behind but he could feel the wet warmth on his legs and hoped he hadn't messed himself. He was relieved to see it was blood.

Come August, Juke took Lefty to the mill once more. His sore behind had healed; enough time had passed that he was willing to risk another one. This time he didn't see String, who was out riding freight cars with his cousins. But he took what he'd come for, a cart full of corn, sickled down from the garden in broad daylight, not near as much corn grown from a sack of seed, but it would have to do. Juke Jesup had a long memory, long as the shadows laid across the Twelve-Mile Straight on the ride home. He closed his eyes, feeling the sun press against his lids, remembering the tremor of the train as it made its way from Macon to Florence, the stolen butterscotch on his tongue, the taste of the city's sickly sweetness.

It was two summers later, just after his stepmother left the farm, when he saw the girl again. She was standing at the same machine, a few inches taller, her braid a few inches longer, and Juke watched her unnoticed. At the other end of the room String and his cousins were horsing around with the other spinners, hiding under their machines and tugging their aprons from below to scare them, pretending they were getting caught in the machines. Then one of the girls, distracted, really did get her apron caught. The machine tore it clean off and ate it up. The supervisor tossed the rest of the boys out and Juke dropped to the floor where he stood and hid behind her machine. She was concentrating so hard she didn't see him as he made himself flat and rolled under it. That machine was hot as a woodstove, and under it was a film of cotton lint no broom could reach. He was afraid he might sneeze again. Juke's shoulder nudged an empty bobbin and set it scattering across the floor, but she didn't notice. From under the spinning machine, lying on his belly, he looked at her bare feet, the delicate map of bones and veins, the cotton lint caught between the webs of her toes. If he looked close, and he did, he could see that her legs swayed slightly as she worked, the muscles in her pale calves tensing. If he had a few more inches, he could have looked up under the hem of her skirt. But it didn't matter. It was her feet he loved. Two years of saying her name under his breath, and now he was close enough to touch her. His ears full of whirring and his nostrils full of cotton, his pecker went hard as a broomstick against the wood floor. His hand drifted up, but instead of taking hold of the edge of her apron, it closed around her ankle.

Quick as a chicken, she leapt back and yelped, knocking his arm against the hot metal frame of the machine. Then it was Juke who was yelping.

"I'm sorry," he said, crawling out and getting to his feet. "I didn't mean to spook you."

"What in Heaven you doing down there?"

He held his wrist to his chest. He'd burned it something awful. "You got the prettiest feet in Cotton County."

She looked hard at him, her eyebrows knit, and then unknit, then knit again. The girl at the next machine leaned around it to get a look at them, but no one else came by.

"Reckon you're fourteen now," he said, smiling like an idiot.

"Reckon you are too." The hair around her face was damp with sweat, her dress so wet it stuck to her arms.

"Still is hot as Hades, ain't it?"

"Go on and follow them boys out."

"My name's John Jesup. My daddy runs George Wilson's farm. We work like mules, but at least we got air to breathe."

"Go on now, John Jesup," she said. "You gone get me in hot water."

"Your name's Jessa. You don't got to tell me. I'll be going, now, Miss Jessa, like you say."

Before he did, he fetched the runaway bobbin from the floor, lifted the closest window, and propped the bobbin under the sash. From the narrow space under it came a breath of country air. "You can blame it on John Jesup," he said, and Jessa smiled lengthwise at him, not meeting his eyes as she went on spinning. "I aim to be in hot water anyway."

That was the second time he met the girl who would be his wife. That time he left with a scar on his wrist the size and shape of a pea pod. He told his daddy he'd burned it in a campfire he'd built with String, but for the next twenty-eight years, until that scar was lost inside another web of burns, he'd tell the truth to any stranger who asked. "She done branded me like a bull, right then and there."

His weakness was for women, and the only thing that made it worse was liquor. Best place to get both was Young's, the colored juke joint in town.

He led String there for the first time when they were fifteen, crossing the railroad tracks into the Fourth Ward through the dark. When he'd heard the field hands talking about it, he'd imagined something grand, but it was just a shack slapped together with corrugated tin, flimsy as a soup can under the full moon. It leaned like a drunk on the Easter Hotel next door, a two-story brick building with boards over the windows, though they didn't close out all the light inside. It was said to be run by an old colored woman named Easter Moore, who had five daughters she rented out to men in the five rooms. Out back, on the clothesline between two gum trees, several pairs of ladies' stockings tiptoed in the breeze. Juke could hear the piano and smell the barbecue from the tracks. "We ain't allowed in there," String whispered. "They'll skin us alive."

"We allowed anywhere we please." Juke leapt over the tracks. He was near grown, his father's boots pinching his feet. "It's them ain't allowed places."

Inside, the men did not skin the boys alive. They glanced uneasily at one another, then relaxed, then smiled. The man at the upright piano did not slow his playing. Juke held out his palm and String dropped his dime into it and Juke slapped it on the counter.

"You looking for barbecue?" said the man behind it.

"We like two corn liquors, please."

The man laughed, his white teeth the brightest thing in the dark room. "You would, would you?" His eyes waited for a nod from someone over Juke's shoulder. "All right. Just a taste." From under the counter he took a jug of piss-colored liquid and began filling two glasses. "This your first drink, son?"

The power of the coin and the power of the liquor made Juke feel drunk already. "Naw. But this here's my first time in a juke joint."

Again the man laughed. "That right?"

Juke laughed back, so they'd be laughing together, and after he'd downed his glass and most of his friend's he wandered outside and nearly took his head off on the clothesline, then fell down and rolled onto his back and laughed some more, the stars pulsing gently above him.

He couldn't get back fast enough. Every night he could take Lefty and steal away into town, he'd beg String for a nickel or a dime. When String stopped lending him money, he collected scrap metal and threw papers and stood at the crossroads with his wagon, selling squash and corn and cabbages. His daddy was proud, took him for an entrepreneur, didn't know half the money was going to the Fourth Ward. "Gotta get me back to that juke. That liquor like to light my skin on fire."

"Juke, juke, juke," String said. "That about alls you can say."

He didn't remember who made the name stick—String or the bartender. Before long only their daddies still called him John. Juke's daddy didn't worry much where the name came from. It was a nickname like any other, a Jack or a Jake, a Butch or a Buddy or a String. The women on his lap, the daughters from the Easter Hotel, whispered it in his ear, "Juke, Juke, Juke," women with names like Epiphany and Sabbath, who wore stockings that felt like liquid under his hands. Juke could feel their skin and the burn of the liquor, the same golden honey glow, the whole way back to the farm. Lefty slowed the last few miles, and Juke's daddy would worry about him in the morning, wondering why was he so plumb tired, good for nothing son of a bitch, couldn't hardly take two steps without falling over. Juke was better than the mule at hiding the night on him, chewing on a handful of the pennyroyal that grew wild along the road. He didn't return to his bed, just brought Lefty straight to the barn and began the morning milking, resting his forehead on the cow's warm side, dawn brightening the corners of his moonshine-sweet sleep. In his dreams, Jessa was the one on his lap, the barefoot girl from the mill, her long legs pale as milk straight from the cow's tit.

One black winter night, drunk and wanting, he left String on his porch and staggered into the hushed mill village. It was so cold Juke couldn't feel the ears under his own cap. In the house he thought was Jessa's, he thought he saw a candle burning in the window. He'd seen her a few times in the years since he'd burned his wrist, but not enough. He scrambled down into the blackberry bush outside the window, pressed his fingers to the smooth glass. He felt his body go all cold, then all hot. He played his fingertips on the pane, tapping out the blues in his head.

"John?"

It was a man's voice, gruff and full of concern. Juke squinted at the lantern bobbing toward him.

"What in Hades you doing out here, son?"

George Wilson, bareheaded, wrapped in a coat, stepped down the hill with the light.

Juke saw now that he was only a few yards from the Wilsons' house, that the house he'd chosen was not a house at all but the Wilsons' own shed. Through the window, he could make out the dark shapes of shovels and hoes, shiny as arrows.

The liquor lapped inside Juke's skull. He tried to think of which lie to tell, and figuring it would hide the rest, settled on a truth. "I'm looking for a girl."

Mr. Wilson chuckled. "Don't keep no girls in the shed, honey. No girl who'd like to court in the middle of the night."

Juke's legs felt weak. His body had gone cold again, bone cold. "I didn't mean no harm," he said. He fell to his knees and let his sick out, out into the frost-studded dirt, in the cone of light from George Wilson's lantern.

"Oh, for pity's sake," said Mr. Wilson, taking a step back.

It had been five years since String, without a word, had asked Juke to wait on the porch, assuming as Juke did that that was the way his father would want it. What was Juke to make of it now, the way Mr. Wilson invited him in without a second thought, opening the door and stepping through it himself first, leaving Juke to follow and pull it closed? In the Wilsons' sitting room, Mr. Wilson gave Juke a tumbler of hot tea and a cotton blanket that smelled like a woman. Not like

Epiphany and Sabbath, who smelled of sweat and salt and hair oil. It smelled like lavender soap. It smelled, Juke imagined, like a mother. He sat back against the cool, duck-feather pillows of George Wilson's sofa, String asleep somewhere above him, willing himself not to cry. "You boys got enough sense to at least cavort a little quieter," Mr. Wilson said. "Your daddy's like to have your hide, should he find you been laying out at all hours of the night, smelling like a juke joint."

"Well, that's my name, ain't it? Juke. You can be calling me that now, sir."

Juke spent the night there on the sofa, and at dawn Mr. Wilson sent him to fetch Lefty in the woods. George intended to hitch his carriage to the mule and his mare and drive Juke back to the farm. He'd tell Juke's father just enough, that his son had been sick, that he thought it best to let him rest there for the night. That would call for enough whippings, George thought.

But when Juke found Lefty, he was lying on his side on a bed of pine needles, as though he'd just settled down for a rest himself. "Get on up, Lefty," Juke said. When the animal didn't rouse, Juke thought he'd been got by a coyote, or a boar. But it was his big mule lips, blue and barely trembling, that gave him away. Over Lefty went the cotton blanket. Perhaps the sun would warm him. But after George and Juke had reached the farm, then returned to the woods with Juke's father, Lefty was like a block of ice, his brittle legs useless. "He's worn out and half froze both," said George. Juke's father hitched a rope around his middle and together the three of them tried to raise him up. Lefty shifted and slid across the ground. He was an old boy, George reminded them. He didn't have but a handful of years left. George had known that spotted mule as a boy himself, traveled with him up and down the Twelve-Mile Straight a thousand times, worked him across every godforsaken acre of that farm. They had to tie two of their handkerchiefs together, Juke's father's dull one and George Wilson's bright one, to make a blindfold. George tied it over the animal's eyes. Then Juke's father handed Juke the twenty-two. "You do it."

"Ernest," said Mr. Wilson. "He's just a boy."

"Go on," his father said.

"Ernest, you make that boy shoot that mule, I'll have you out that big house by tomorrow."

"Thas all right," Juke said, taking the gun. "I can do it."

"Ain't a boy's job," Mr. Wilson said. "That's my mule and I don't want it taken out the world by no child."

So Juke's father took the gun. Solemnly he aimed it between Lefty's glassy eyes and pulled the trigger. The next week, Mr. Wilson would send the mule breeder out to the farm with a young molly named Mamie.

Juke and his father were made to dig a hole for him. The clay was so solid that Mr. Wilson sent his yard boy with another shovel, and then String snuck out to help, and Juke and his father accepted it. They were ashamed but also desperate, which made them more ashamed. By the time they were done, it was coming on night, their fingers frozen to their shovels. They buried the mule there in the pines by the railroad tracks, on the land owned by George Wilson.

———

There was love between the two men still. They had loved String first. Then, because he was kin to String, they had loved Freddie.

When Juke had driven his daughter out to the mill, good and pregnant, he had sat there again in George Wilson's sitting room, drinking lemonade a servant girl had poured him. Elma waited on the porch. "I can't no more control my kin than you can control yours," George told him. When Juke replied that if Freddie didn't step up, he would step down, George just laughed. "Honey," he said. "You think I couldn't put any man in the county in that house?" He patted Juke on the back as he walked him out.

George had called his bluff. Nothing had changed. Juke had continued his deliveries to the mill, though he didn't see him again until the middle of that night in July, when George was awakened by the sound of drunken gunfire. From his porch, in his nightclothes, he could see his grandson's truck under the moon, parked in the middle of the village. At first he'd thought it was a deer or boar he'd shot and dragged behind him. Then he saw Freddie cut the body from the truck, and then Freddie looked up at George on the porch and saluted him. It was a habit the two shared, their way of saluting String, but what would String think, George wondered, about this? George did not return the gesture, but he didn't run out to stop him, either. Freddie got into his truck and drove off, and then a dead man was lying in the road.

If what Sheriff had told Juke was true—that George Wilson wouldn't stand for his grandson's name to be dragged through the dirt—then Juke would face him. He wouldn't hide. Guilty men hid. Guilty men ran. Freddie had run faster than Juke could've bet on. Juke hadn't even had to oil him up. He hadn't had to draw the picture for him—how unkindly the law would look on him, how many years on the chain gang he had coming if he stayed. He didn't even have to say, "Let me clean this up, son. I'll take whatever's coming." He didn't have the chance to tell him because he was gone.

So Juke didn't wait for George to send the lynch mob back for him. After Sheriff left and after church, he drove into town, following the tracks that Freddie's tires had made in the mud, between them the shallow rut the body had left in the road. He found him in his office at the mill.

"For pity's sake, son," George said to him, and let him in.

It wasn't what Juke had expected. George didn't look outraged; he merely looked tired. It was because he hadn't been there, Juke realized. He hadn't seen it with his own eyes. Old man thought his boy was coming back, but there was no coming back from what they'd done. Both of them. Freddie and Juke. They'd done it together.

Juke settled into the calfskin chair. He began to pour himself a drink. Then George took the glass.

"And all that?" He nodded to the scar tissue that crossed Juke's arms. "You burn the darky up too?"

"Saved a dog," Juke said. "Some months back."

"Only dog you saved was yourself."

Juke unrolled his sleeves. Most delivery days George carried a pistol in his pocket. Juke wondered where it might be today, under his pillow or in the drawer of his desk. "Eye for an eye. Ain't the good book say? That man harmed my blood."

"An eye for an eye? Then you'd reason I should take an eye too? Shall I kill you now, now that you've harmed my blood?"

"Freddie harmed himself. It weren't my truck the man was dragged behind. That's what I aim to tell you. I didn't want it this way, George. Weren't no stopping him."

George stood over Juke, holding his glass, and Juke, feeling he should raise his eyes up to George's level, stood too. When he was upright he realized he was standing because he was leaving. George had only let him into the office to dismiss him from it.

"Why'd you keep him on?" George asked.

"Who? Freddie?"

"The Negro. After you knew what he was up to with your daughter. What your daughter was up to with him. Hard to keep that girl out of trouble, I reckon, but folks say—"

"Ain't nothing to keep her out of except a certain Chevy truck."

"I gave you too much authority. That was my mistake. I gave you a false impression. I let you hire and fire any man in the county, and look how you squander my goodwill. That boy's playing around with your daughter, you don't do nothing but give him a kick in the ass?"

"I got too much forgiveness in my heart, I reckon."

"No. You got a heart full of hate. You wanted to keep him there, where you could see him. You'd rather have a man in that shack you were born in who's lower than the low-down white trash you are. You wanted someone to beat on. You wanted to feel the size of your own pecker."

Juke said nothing.

"I know you, son. I know you because I lived in that house too. And because all day long I play you like you played that poor nigger."

"Alls I aim to say—"

"I know. An eye for an eye." George shook his head. "I can take an eye," he said, "whenever I please. I can take both your eyes, the farm and the still both." He drank the gin in Juke's glass. "But why blind myself?"

ELEVEN

NAN WAITED FOR JUKE TO CALL ON REVEREND QUICK ABOUT the wedding. Her belly grew to the size of a ten-cent watermelon. The child inside her thumped and thrashed. She counted the seconds between its kicks. She read *The Book of Knowledge*. Chicago, Constantinople, Crete. She read that a daughter ripe in her mother's womb contained all the eggs that would make her own babies. She imagined herself cocooned like a spider in Ketty's womb, and Ketty in her mother's, and Ketty's mother in her mother's, the slave who kissed her master with her cursed and cancerous tongue. Nan prayed the child inside her was not growing eggs of its own. She thought of the baby girl so worthless she was offered as payment for her delivery, and she prayed it was a boy. Let it be a boy. And let it belong to Genus.

"You be ready to go out into the world soon enough," her mother had told her before she died. Was she ready? She did not consider herself young. She was fourteen. With Ketty she'd visited mothers that young, or nearly, mothers who'd been married off to neighbors, cousins, railroad men boarding on their way through town. When she was small, playing house in the quarantine shack, Elma was the mother, Nan the child. Now Nan would play mother. She would marry Genus, live in the tar paper shack as her mother and father had. They would raise a family. "Reckon it's only right," Juke had said, and Nan had sat at the table looking into her lap and felt her face flame with hope. She would leave the big house and return to the first bed she'd slept in, to the room that smelled of sweet tar and hominy grits and nearly burned milk. It was a better future than she'd been set on.

In the early weeks, she'd waked every morning to a curdled stomach. She let it out in the privy, in the weeds, once in the bucket she was filling with April's milk. "You got the flu, honey?" Elma said to her that time, and sent her back to bed. When her bleeding didn't come, and didn't come, when she knew that a baby was growing inside her, she did what her mother had taught her never to do. She brewed a tea. Black cohosh, chamomile, pennyroyal. For three days she drank it in the morning, at midday, in the evening. It tasted like death, like dirt—not the creamy richness of white clay, but the deep-earth dirt of a grave, and that was what she was doing, she thought, she was making her womb a grave. On the third day, drawing water, a pain reared up in her gut so fast she fell to her knees at the well. The yard flashed yellow, then red. She felt the hard dirt under her knees. She felt a wetness on her face and put her hand to her lip. Blood. She was bleeding from her nose. And the sight of her own blood reminded her that she was alive.

She remembered her mother praising the mule, thumping her chest: *self-preservation*.

She wiped her nose with her apron and tossed it in the privy, covered it with lime. She splashed the tea into the weeds. Her body would offer up no more blood.

She had done as Juke had said—she had stayed away from Genus. He didn't dare come to the house. She could see him trying to catch her eye in the yard, and she walked around his eyes, away from them. It was better that she was with child, she decided. Now he would stay away from her. If the child was Juke's, at least Genus would be safe. That was called a sacrifice.

But then Juke had said he'd call on Reverend Quick, and then Nan carried the load of her belly with her back straight, her face up. What had been a curse was now a gift. She prayed to God for forgiveness, for the tea. She waited. Juke kept both the girls in the big house, hiding their bellies, doing their yard chores himself. At dinner, Elma asked what was taking so long, and Juke said the reverend didn't take to marrying off a girl so young without shaking her father's hand first. "And I say, What in Hades do you reckon I am?" Elma asked why Juke hadn't told the Reverend Nan was older than fourteen, and Juke said if he was going to tell a lie in front of the Lord he'd better save it for the gates of Heaven. Juke said when he found the time—did they reckon he had all the time in the world, running a still and farming two hundred acres and now hanging the wash like a woman?—he'd go to the Fourth Ward and find him a jackleg preacher.

Juke did not behave as though he was preparing to marry Nan away. Or maybe it was his way of preparing. He took her to the still nearly every night, saying, "I reckon this be the last time, before you going off to be a child bride." The crab apples of her breasts had grown soft and full, and Juke liked to latch onto them like an infant. She closed her eyes and bit down on her jaw. "You gone be a fine momma," he said. "Yours gone be the sweetest milk," and she hated the pride that reared up inside her hate, "sweeter than any cow's in the county. Sweeter than any gin. I'd like to say I'm through with you but I'm like to be drunk on your milk, Nan."

On the nights she was brave and Juke was drunk, drunk enough not to notice, she took a pint of gin from the shelf before leaving the still. She walked it to Genus's shack, put her arm inside the open window, and left it on the table below. It was an offering until they could be together, until she could stand before him in the daylight, her figure full.

The third night of this, she was six months with child. When she put her arm in the window, Genus grabbed hold of her wrist. She flailed, trying to get loose, but his grip tightened and she held still. "Why you never come see me no more? Huh? Why you leave a man lonesome?" There was no glass in the window, nothing but a wooden shutter raised by a rope like a puppet's mouth, and she feared it might close on her head. The night was black but if she looked into the window she might see him, so she closed her eyes and listened. "You think liquor's enough for me? It ain't." Any moment now Juke would be coming down the path. She tried to break loose. Felt she might choke on the stub of her tongue. "I ain't harm you," he said, feeling her fear. "I ain't never harm you. I ain't did nothing for you to do me this way."

Nan did something then that she hadn't done before. She hadn't done it with Juke, hadn't done it at all since she was a child. Genus still gripping her wrist, she cried. At first she had to call it up, the only noise she could think to make, the only way to get him to turn her loose, so she might run free back to the big house before Juke came upon them. But once the sound was free of her chest, the tears followed, hot and fast. "Nan!" Genus said, as though to quiet her. Then, more gently, loosening his grip but taking her wrist in both hands now, sliding one hand up her arm to the shoulder, as though trying to pull her through the window, "Nan. You ain't got to cry. You ain't got to be lonesome. You tell me. You squeeze my hand if you mean to say yes. He harming you? The boss man? He the one keeping you away?"

She cried. Her shoulders shook. It was terrible, the sound she made, the sound of her own strangled voice, and her hate stood up and turned on Genus. Juke had no intention of allowing them to marry—what a fool she'd been to believe his word!—but what kind of man would want to marry her? A girl with no tongue, a girl who made a sound like that? Was he as bad as Juke, loving only her silence after all, her weakness? What good would it do to tell him? What could he do to protect her? Quick as a whip, she slipped her arm from his hands and ran back to the big house.

The next night, Juke didn't come for her. But the night after that she smelled his breath on her face before she opened her eyes—the salt pork and greens she'd made him for dinner, the sharp sting of gin. She rose and followed. The moon was full. Her belly was big now, so in the cabin he turned her over and hauled her up onto her hands and knees. She thought of the story Genus had told her about the white man he'd seen having his way with a poor dumb mule in a barn, and all the love she'd felt from Juke, for Juke, rose up and disappeared, insubstantial as fog. She was no more than a molly mule in a barn, except he treated Mamie only with kindness, calling her "Old girl" and stroking her ears until she brayed with joy. At least when she was on all fours he couldn't see her cry, which Nan now found she could do without making a sound at all.

Afterward she stood at the edge of the field where the woods thinned into stony wiregrass, watching the moonlight pick out the distant roofs of the big house, the barn, the privy, the shack. A sandspur caught her under the arch of her left foot, and she stood on the right to pluck it off, balancing the weight of her belly, shifting the pint of gin under her left arm. She thought she could hear Juke making water in the woods, but her ears were playing tricks on her—he was too far behind. He would stay back at the cabin, have one last drink, pack his jaw full of tobacco. She had time. She could make it to the shack, leave the gin on the table. She could almost make out the window. Was it open? It was the same window she had first seen Genus through, the day he shook out the rug. She remembered the way he raised his hand in greeting, and she felt that hand snaking up her arm again, felt the tenderness return to her chest. Surely he had enough gin to last him a week, a month. She had told herself that the liquor was her way of making amends, of offering the only peace she could give him, but now she needed his hand on her wrist. If he asked her to, she would squeeze his hand. She would stand under the light of the full moon and let him see the round bulb of her belly. And if he loved her he would take her away. There was time, wasn't there, to take her satchel, still packed, the bills still folded in waiting. She would leave with the nightgown on her back, no underclothes to speak of. They needed time only to put shoes on their feet. By foot, they would travel the Twelve-Mile Straight as far as it took them. It all had been there in her mind, squirreled away, and now she turned it loose and it came unfurling like a spool of thread. Before dawn, they'd be close enough to town to meet the train while it was slow. He'd hoist her up into a boxcar. What did they need a ticket for? What did they care for a marriage certificate?

She aimed for the shack. Yes, the window was open. It was April. Spring. Her nose filled with the humid night, thimbleweed and arrowhead and aster. She ran, the pint bouncing under her arm. She picked up a sandspur, another, didn't stop to pull them from her feet. Her feet were thick as hides! The night breeze rustled the sorghum, knocked the gourds. Ahead, between the shack and the big house, the clothes on the clothesline lifted in the wind, a family of paper cutouts. Before she could make it to the shack, from behind a white sheet hanging on the line, a shadow stepped out into her path.

She skidded in her tracks. Nearly dropped the gin. Genus took her by the wrist and yanked her behind the sheet with him. "What you doing out here? This time of night? Where he taking you, Nan?"

She put her finger to his lips. He was tall, taller even than she remembered, and she held on to the high mound of his shoulder and placed her cheek on the smooth part of his chest, where the buttons of his shirt were open. He still held her wrist and she could feel her own pulse, wild under his grip. He didn't seem like he was set on it, he looked like the idea came into his head right there, but when she raised her face his mouth was on hers and he was lifting her up by the waist to bring her close. His tongue filled the empty cave of her mouth. The breeze came again and for a moment the cool sheet wrapped around them, and they made a sound like laughter.

Then Genus lowered her to the ground. She could feel him step back. Take her in. His hand traveled down her nightdress to her belly, and just like that the baby gave a swift mule kick to her ribs. Genus jumped back.

"Nan," he said.

Nan nodded. What else could she do? How could she tell him all she needed to say?

"Nan," he said again, letting his hands drift back to her belly. She covered his hands with her free one. She wanted to take his hand and run, back to his shack for what things he could carry, back to her room for her satchel, but it was too soon, or too late—Juke was behind them, coming back from the cabin, he'd be upon them before they knew it, and then there he was, regular as rain, the distant thud of his boots on the clay path, the lantern through the sheet first as small as a firefly, then growing with every step.

She put her hand to Genus's mouth again, sealing his lips between her fingers. She froze against him. Why had he gone and waited for her like a fool? There was nothing to do now but make themselves trees. She made her eyes focus on the flimsy shield of the sheet, inches from her nose. She could smell the lye soap in its fibers. The clothes should not have been left on the line overnight, but Juke was slow with their chores, sloppy. She could see where he had tucked the corners of a sheet over the line instead of letting them hang. The rusty clothespins would stain.

Just before the lantern was upon them—was it aiming for the big house? or for them?—she remembered the pint. If he didn't kill her for standing out here with Genus, he'd kill her for stealing his gin. It wasn't far to the shotgun he kept at the still, nor to the twenty-two he kept in the big house. She slipped the jar under her nightdress, lodging it high between her legs. And just then the breeze returned and blew back her gown and blew back the sheet, so that it clung around their bodies like they were a couple of corpses, and if Juke hadn't seen them before he saw them now. She wanted to rip the sheet off the line and roll down the hill in it with Genus, roll right into the creek.

Juke ripped the sheet down for them. "Looky," he said. He was drunk, his breath poisoning the night. "You get lost on your way home? Can't find no bread crumbs?"

"Yes, sir, I reckon we both did," Genus said, and she loved and hated him for his quick, lying mouth. "Nature called out to me and I heard footsteps on the path. I was just visiting on the sound."

"The privy sets behind you, boy."

"At times nature calls me to the woods, sir."

In the light of the lantern, Nan could see a smile on Juke's lips. He worked the tobacco along his gums. Where she had expected to see anger, even fear—surely he wouldn't want to be discovered following Nan back to the house—she now saw a playful pride. He was drunker than she'd accounted for. "At times nature calls our Nan to the woods." He still held the sheet and as he put his arm around Nan's shoulders, it billowed behind her like a veil. "Sometimes to this shack, that cabin. Lord knows where else! Nature calls out like a bitch in heat! Look what she got to show for it!" Now he reached his arm around her and grabbed her belly and she stumbled forward, and the jar began to slip and she squeezed her thighs tighter.

"Look, boy," Juke said. Nan realized her eyes were closed. Slowly, she opened them. Juke held the lantern to her belly. "You see now? Say so. You lose your tongue, too?"

Genus glanced up. "No sir," he said quietly.

"Ain't no telling whose child that is. It's the Lord's child. The Lord will tell His story by and by."

Her eyes were open and she could see Genus's close and for all her will she couldn't look away.

"We'll wait and hear the story. I'll 'low you stay on this farm and wait with us. If that baby's all darky, I'll marry her off to you myself." He still had his arm draped around her, heavy as a log. "If it's a mulatto child, now that's a different story the Lord will tell. If that's the story, you can take your leave. I'm nigger lover enough to raise up a mulatto, but not enough to let it get raised up a bastard by a nigger field hand. The Lord help me if He ain't made me a nigger-loving man!" He tossed the sheet over his own head. "You lucky you landed on this farm and not in town, boy. Them Klansmen's mighty powerful nigger haters thataway!" He howled like a ghost, swaying back and forth. "Powerful liquor haters too. They like to tar and feather me worse than no nigger. Boo!" He jumped at Genus, knocking Nan's arm, and again the jar slipped, this time almost to her knees. She clenched her legs tighter yet. Juke laughed, still swaying, his sheeted face turned up to the sky now. "Oh, the Lord has made me to love a nigger too much."

Genus was bent over, his hands on his knees. Was he having another pain? Was he going to be sick? Or was he going to lunge forward, take Juke down? With the sheet over his head he was as easy a target as he'd ever be. Could you suffocate a man with a bedsheet? Could you crack his skull with a mason jar?

"Ain't right," Genus said.

Juke was still laughing, swaying. He didn't hear.

"Ain't right," Genus said more loudly, standing up straight.

Juke stopped laughing. He whipped the sheet off his head, tossed it to the ground.

"You supposed to be like kin to her. Ain't right to do your kin that way."

"What you know bout who she kin to?"

"Clear as the morning she ain't got no mother nor daddy. You the only care she got."

"And I done cared for her! The Lord knows it. I always done a good part by her. When others would a turned a pickaninny out in the cold I kept her head dry and her belly full and the Lord help me if I done cared for her too much." The sound came into Juke's voice, the sound that meant he would start to cry, and then he did. He held the lantern high and cried under it, chewing his tobacco like a punishment, tipping his face up to it as though to a liquor glass, which perhaps in his drunkenness he thought it was, then cried some more, in disappointment. "I care for her like my own. Nan"—he turned to find her now—"I done cared for you like my own blood." Nan stood under the clothesline, squeezing her legs closed, her feet still pricked with sandspurs. She prayed to the Lord that he would stop crying, that he would go back to yelling, for if she only hated him it would be easier to run, or to kill him, or both. And this too: she did not want Genus to see that he cared for her. She did not want him to see that she had once cared for him.

"We're fixing to take leave come morning," Genus said. "We'll be out your way. I'll be the one keep her head dry now."

Lord help her if her heart didn't swell up and her baby's too, hearing those words.

"I'll kill you first." Juke spat his tobacco at Genus's feet. "You hearing?"

"It's what she wants. You care for her, you let her go."

"How in Hades you know what she wants? She tell you with her tongue?"

"You the one who done it, ain't you?" There was disgust in Genus's eyes. "You the one cut it out."

Juke stepped closer to Genus and put his finger in his face. "Her own mother done it! When she was just a babe!" He turned back to Nan, knocking her jaw with the lantern as he spun. "And I done spooned milk into your bloody mouth!"

The jar slipped and fell. There was no time to stop it. She had time only to pray that it wouldn't shatter. It did. It split against the ground like a melon, spraying shards against her legs. It sprayed Juke too. He jumped back. So did Genus. When Juke was done flinching, he looked her up and down, his face bewildered. "Girl, look like your water done broke." He crouched down to the ground, picked up one of the larger shards, crescent shaped. Her legs burned. Now she prayed that he would go back to laughing, or even crying, that his anger would stay away.

"It's mine," Genus said. "It's for me. I got pains in my—"

"You the one been skimming my jars?" He stood up, stepped closer to Nan. "Here I thought my counting was oft."

"I got pains inside. I'm the one took it."

"It was you, uh?" He turned back to Genus.

"Yes sir. Forgive me, sir."

"You taking what's mine?"

"Yes sir."

"Ain't enough you stealing her sweet parts, now you smuggling my gin up in there?" He swung the lantern, with purpose this time, struck Genus under the chin and knocked him on his back. Quick as a fox Juke scrambled on top of him. The light had rolled away now but in the dimmer dark Nan could see Juke holding the shard to Genus's throat.

"Tell me why I oughtn't slice your neck."

Had Nan simply forgotten Elma, or had she lacked the faith to pray she might come for her? All those years she hadn't saved her, and here she was at last, racing down the porch steps, screen door slamming behind her. "What in Heaven!"

But before she was upon them, the sheet, tangled tight as a wick around the lantern, burst into flame. The fire made a sound like the wind, and then the wind found the fire and the fire found the toe of a pair of Elma's stockings on the line, then a dress of Nan's, then a string of Juke's shirts. Juke leapt up and stomped on the sheet with his boot. He was the only one wearing shoes. Elma ran to fetch a bucket of water, cursing the well for its slowness. What could Nan and Genus do? She helped him to his feet. They watched the clothes light up the night.

They might have run then. Later, Nan would think, Lord, why didn't we run? Let Juke chase after them in the truck, let him send a mob after them and string them both up. At least they'd have that night, running free on the road like the spooked horses they were, the fields burning behind them.

They didn't run. Instead they chose the way of the donkey, the possum: call it self-preservation, cowardice. They stayed, played dead, played nice; who were they to overcome their nature? They found another pair of buckets and fetched water from the creek. They could hear Juke's screams as they climbed back up to the yard. By the time they returned the fire was all but out and Juke was rolling on the ground. He'd cut the clothesline from the big house with the shard of glass, but not before the fire had caught the sleeve of his shirt.

Nan did not have to think. She ran to Juke and emptied the bucket over him.

He lay at her feet, the wet, smoking hulk of him.

Genus stood beside her, his bucket full.

In the light of morning, in the yard that smelled like the smokehouse, they could see where the fire had blackened one wall of the shack. They could see where it had left Juke's right arm in bloody scales. He walked to Jeb Simmons's farm and Jeb drove him two towns over to find a doctor who wasn't Dr. Rawls. "Y'all three best be here when I get back or I'll put Sheriff on your tails faster than you can say daddy." By afternoon he was bandaged up and home again, settled on the porch with a tumbler of gin. He told Elma and Nan to stay indoors. Through the kitchen window Nan could see that Jeb had his son with him, and in the back of his truck was a stack of pine logs. She thought they were there to patch the shack.

But with Genus's help, and with Juke looking on, they built a new one. It sat where the quarantine shack had been, at the edge of the yard, not far from the gourd tree. Twelve by twelve, no windows, and a door that locked from the outside. And into that shack went Nan and Elma, who were sick with diphtheria again, or so Juke told anyone who would listen. And there they would stay for the next three months, out of sight, until the babies came.

TWELVE

W HEN THE NOVEMBER RAINS PASSED, THEY SAVED THE COT-
ton, Juke and Jim and Sara, Ezra and Long John and Al,
what there was to be saved. Elma would have liked to be
out there picking with a baby on her back, but Juke refused, asking
the McArdle boys for help instead. In return he helped them slaughter and smoke their hogs, which they wanted done by Thanksgiving,
and the moon was waning so they better get to it, then traded a case
of Cotton Gin for fatback and lard. The ears and tongue and feet
went to Ezra and Long John and Al. Last Thanksgiving, Elma remembered, they'd slaughtered their own hogs, and Genus had taken
a heart, cooking it over the fire in the yard and eating it alone in his
shack. "Everything but the squeal," Ketty had liked to say. It was she
who'd said it wasn't time to kill a hog until it was cold enough to see
your breath. This year, that meant they would wait.

Juke went into town to have the rest of the cotton ginned and
made ready to go to the Cotton Exchange in Savannah. Eleven good
bales, all told, piled as high as the house in the bed of the Ford and
in Jeb Simmons's Chevy, the last bale in Jim's convertible. Most years
Juke sold George Wilson's cotton right back to him. Last year, when

he'd used the Cotton Exchange, he put the cotton on the train. This year Juke didn't have occasion to ask George his opinion. He hadn't laid eyes on the mill since July, had Jim drive his shipments to the mill. What in the hell was the use in driving all the way to Savannah, George would say, as he'd said last year, when his cotton ended up back at his mill? The use was that Juke would get to unload two trucks of hooch—if you didn't look close, you couldn't see the cases hiding under the bales—and spend his harvest money on city liquor and city women, and damn if an old man with a grudge was going to keep him from his trip. Times were hard. Juke had to diversify, to stay ahead of nature. Couldn't put gin on a train, now could you?

While Juke was at the cotton gin, Elma baked a pecan pie and walked it to the Cousins' farm, Winna Jean on her hip, the puppies trotting along beside her. While the women fawned over the baby and the boys fawned over the pie, she asked Lucy Cousins to carry a letter to town on her bicycle, slipping her the envelope and the rag doll Sara had sewn for Winna, and Lucy's eyes went wide and she nodded.

That night, while she cleared the dishes, Elma told her father the twins needed baptizing. Nan was putting the babies to bed, and Juke was at the woodstove, starting the first fire of the year.

"Good girl," he said, giving the logs a poke. "I reckon it's about time."

"On Sunday. Before you leave for Savannah."

"What's the hurry? You done waited four months already."

Already the fire was filling the room, warming her cheeks. In a few days she would put the babies in an automobile and travel with them to Atlanta, where men in white coats would poke and prod them, where they would reveal or not reveal what she wanted to keep hidden. For an escape from the farm, for a few dollars of her own, she was already risking too much. She did not dare travel that distance without the Lord's blessing.

"I don't want to wait no longer," she said. "The babies are ready and so is God."

"All right, then. I'll talk to the reverend tomorrow."

"And I want it done in the creek. Not in the church, with the whole congregation looking on. Those are my terms."

Juke raised an eyebrow, then lowered it. "You getting comfortable with setting terms." He spit into the fire. "That's all right."

She'd wanted the seclusion of the farm, her woods, her creek. Never mind that the creek had been spoiled twice, first by what Genus and Nan had done there, then by what the men had done, dragging Genus from the water. It would be hers again. It would be the twins'. That was where God would find them.

Besides, she wanted Nan there, and Nan wasn't allowed at Creek Baptist.

But now, through her woods, to her creek, their cars and wagons and horses parked along the Twelve-Mile Straight all the way to the Creek Baptist Missionary Church on the other side of String Wilson, came a stream of people—neighbors, strangers, the entire congregation, who would not be kept away. In two days word had spread from Reverend Odus Quick to Reverend Quick's wife, who taught Sunday School at Creek Baptist, to Florence Baptist and First Methodist and Grace Primitive Baptist, to the members of the Florence WCTU, to their husbands and sisters and cousins, to their kin in Ben Hill County, their kin in Albany, to the editor of the *Messenger* and the *Valdosta Daily Times*, who ran notices in the Saturday papers. Word spread through the home demonstration club, through the Masons, through the mill, over the party line, over the counters at the crossroads store and Pearsall's and the Piggly Wiggly, in the chairs of the barbers and beauty shops, through neighbors trading eggs for milk, through the Jew who sold brushes door to door, in kitchens, on porches, in the fields: the Jesup twins will be saved on Sunday. Only as Elma watched them all trample over the pine needle path in their Sunday shoes did she wish for the protection of the church, a building with walls, which could hold only so many people.

But here they were, gathering along the narrow bank—some had come early, claiming the best vantage points; a few families were picnicking in the grass, catching the patches of morning sun through the trees, as though it were a Fourth of July camp meeting and not the Sunday before Thanksgiving. Just over Elma's shoulder were Nan and Sara and Jim, and down the bank a ways were Al and Al's wife, Cecilia, and their three sons, the only black folks who dared show, their fishing poles over their shoulders, as though to say they'd just happened down to the creek, though they were miles from home. There were the Henrys and the Nevilles and the McArdles, Jeb and Drink Simmons, sharecroppers and shopkeepers, the vets who begged for change outside the feed and seed in town. There was Sheriff Cleave and his wife, and Dr. Rawls and his wife, and Elma's schoolteacher Miss Armistead, and Josie Byrd, home from Atlanta for the holiday, her white nursing shoes traded for a dainty-heeled pair of black Mary Janes. There was Mary Collier, showing off a round belly and a new husband, a ruby the size of a june bug on her finger. And there were reporters, a team of them, the black eyes of their cameras already blinking at her. The only other time there had been so many people at this stretch of the creek was the night of the hunt for Genus Jackson.

Elma turned her back to them. That was what she would do— she would face the creek, and the reverend with his Bible, the blood-colored ribbons that had marked his pages for as long as Elma could remember, and then she could pretend they weren't there. It was just Elma and the babies, Winna sleeping in her arms, Wilson babbling in her father's, both babies bundled in the long-sleeved gowns sewn by Bette Hazelton, the bank manager's wife. The bank had gone under and taken with it most of the money in town, including Dr. Rawls's retirement savings. Elma had learned this from her father. "That's why I keep my money buried in the Lord's earth. Best bank they is."

Talk was that the Hazeltons were set to move to her sister's in Augusta by the new year, but the windows of the First Bank of Florence still featured the silk roses Bette Hazelton had arranged there, proud as bridal bouquets. And there she sat in Elma's front room yesterday (nowhere to sit but on a straight chair), unwrapping the gowns for the twins. The finest white cotton, with matching bonnets and a dozen tiny pearl buttons sewn down each front and lined underneath with terry cloth—"To keep them warm," said Mrs. Hazelton, lifting the hems to show her. Elma's sympathy for the woman hardened into a brick of envy and shame. Bette Hazelton had no money in the bank but she had yards and yards of fine fabric and a Singer sewing machine and jars of shimmering buttons, more precious than jewels and coins. Elma had planned on dressing the twins in their regular old sack dresses, had planned on it even after Mrs. Hazelton left the gowns, thinking the Lord didn't give a hoot for pearl buttons, hearing the edge of pity in her voice, of judgment—who dared baptize their children in a creek in November?—but this morning, admiring the gowns in the tissue-lined box, she decided to hear the blessing in her voice instead.

She could hear Mrs. Hazelton's voice now, if she listened closely. She could hear all their voices whispering along her neck, the cold grazing her collar. Under her denim chore coat Elma too was wearing a white dress, the cornflowers not entirely faded, and Sara had braided her hair and pinned it in a neat coil at her nape. But she could have been wearing a guano sack herself and no one would have noticed—it was the babies they wanted to see. She pressed Wilson's cold cheek to her own, tucked the quilt—her mother's quilt—over the baby's shoulder. The sun hung above them, cold and runny as pudding. The reverend chatted in a low voice with one parishioner, then another. What was he waiting for? To her left, her father rocked Winna, murmuring nonsense in her ear, swinging now and then to face the crowd, to nod hello and raise a hand to a new arrival, like a groom giddy with nerves. At his bedside, he kept a framed photograph taken at his wedding, Jessa wearing a hat stacked high and wide with ribbons, like a wedding cake; Juke, clean-shaven, smiling an open-mouthed smile. Elma inhaled a sharp lungful of cold air. He was her groom now, she thought, and she his young bride. And what did that make Nan? Nan, who wouldn't get her wedding, either? Was she one of the brides too? These were the babies they would all raise together, and though he didn't know it, the reverend was there to bless not just their babies but their unholy union.

In Juke's arms, Winna was bleating, the sound she made when she was tired. She called Winna her little goat, Wilson her little sheep. She didn't love Wilson any less, did she? Well, it wasn't a matter of amount. Her love for him, it was just differently shaped. Her love for Winna was primal, an extension of herself, like loving the blood that ran through her own body. She did not choose to love Winna, but she chose to love Wilson. Not because he had Negro blood—she loved Nan, didn't she?—but because he had her father's. Because the love he was born into was an ugly one. She was his sister, after all— she loved him with the love of an older sister. She loved him as she loved the runt of the barn cat's litter. Milky-eyed and scrawny, the kitten had died after three days, even while Elma had spooned him the cows' milk. She loved Wilson like that, a love that was akin to pity, because the world did not presume to love him. And though she would have loved him no matter what, now her love was a perfor- mance. She kissed his doughy cheek.

Ketty used to tell her to stand up straight. "What you doing with your head hanging to the floor? Let the world see your face. Let God see His work." Now Elma straightened, shifted Wilson to her other shoulder. She found Nan's eye, but Nan wouldn't let her hold it. Ketty was dead but her voice was the one in Elma's ears. How odd, Elma thought, that Nan was the one here with her, and yet her voice was as unknown to Elma as Jessa's. What would it sound like, Nan's voice? What would she say on this day, the day her son would be baptized with someone else's name? Wilson John Jesup. Juke had managed to set his name in there as well as George's. George might have forsaken Juke's kin but his name would be there on the reverend's tongue. And Nan, her arms empty, what could she do but stand there and listen?

"Dearly beloved," the reverend began, and the crowd quieted. Elma lowered her head again. She would make herself a statue, a sculpture of a praying woman. "We gather today to welcome into our fellowship and into the Lord's eternal and holy Church Winnafred and Wilson." The reverend's lisp, which Elma had imitated along with every other child after her Sunday school class, eased her a little. His wife, Tabitha Carlson Quick, was his first cousin, and word was that years ago they'd had a son born with his intestines on the outside instead of in, and he didn't live but three days, like the barn cat's runt. Elma kept her eyes on the catfish whiskers that grew here and there from the great rashy gullet of the reverend's neck. "Baptism is an outward and visible sign of the divine grace of our Lord and Savior Jesus Christ. Our Lord said, 'Let the children come to me, do not hinder them; for to such belongs the Kingdom of God.'"

Elma let the words warm the back of her eyelids. She realized she was closing her eyes. She was no longer just a statue but a real praying woman. "Praying's just bending God's ear," Ketty liked to say. She was bending God's ear. She was asking for His grace.

"These are dark times," said the reverend. "Suffering times. Sickness! Slaughter! Hunger! The Lord's messenger warned Job, 'The fire of God is fallen from Heaven'! But the Lord is testing us, as He tested Job. Let us not, my friends, fail His test! Let us not charge God foolishly. Let us not grow weary, grow weak. Let us not lay our hands on one another. And let the devil not tempt you with the abomination of alcohol! For then will we turn our eyes from God. Then will we fail His test. My friends, let us wash away the devil's poison."

Elma had eaten nothing for breakfast. Her stomach felt sick. She stole a glance at her father, whose eyes were closed. Behind him, Nan and Sara and Jim had their eyes closed too. Jim opened his and looked at Juke, then closed them again. Elma prayed quickly, repeating the words in her head: *O Lord, O Lord, O Lord.*

"Tis the season of Thanksgiving," the reverend continued. "Today we offer our thanks to the Lord for the miracle of His children. We offer our thanks for Wilson and Winnafred, chosen by the Lord to live among us in harmony and peace. In baptizing them we ask the Lord to wash away the sins of their fathers. O Lord, shower these children with your steadfast love, accept them into your Kingdom, for in you they are saved."

From the crowd on the bank came an infant's cry. Loud, hungry. Would Elma's milk trickle for another baby's cry? It wasn't particular for Wilson. She pressed him closer to her chest. She had hate in her heart for that ignorant baby on the bank, and now she prayed for that hate to be washed away with the rest of her sins. She prayed for that baby, and for Reverend Quick's baby, for his soul. She prayed that Wilson and Winna might cry on a riverbank and no one would pay them any special mind. She prayed that they would be saved, but from prejudice, from prying, which was its own damnation. She prayed that they might lead a life of glorious obscurity, of loneliness even, that they might run the acres of the farm, as she had, unwatched by anyone but God in the sky.

The reverend put his hand on Elma's shoulder. It was time to bring the babies into the creek. She turned and followed him to the edge of the water. Her feet knew the path, but they were heavy in her shoes. She would do what needed to be done.

"Dunk them devil babies!"

Her eyes shot into the crowd. She almost laughed. At the elbow of the mother with the crying baby, another child, a girl of no more than ten, stood clapping her hands. A gasp went up here, a chuckle there. "Dunk em!" a young man echoed.

"You shut your foul mouth!"

It was Sara, swinging around to face the crowd. Jim stepped toward Elma and put a hand on her elbow.

"Hush," said the mother of the girl, drawing her roughly by the shoulder. "Only one of them baby's from a devil seed."

"Enough!" the reverend said, just as Juke cried, "This child's done no harm! He's done no harm!"

Another man said, "Only Satan can plant two separate seeds in a woman's womb. She must be saved too! Ain't much count to save just the babies."

"Bless the Jezebel's womb!" called a woman.

Elma stared through the crowd. "Don't listen to them," Sara whispered to her fiercely. "Don't listen to that white trash." But Elma was listening. She was thinking, Bless it! Amen! O Lord, bless it! She welcomed their words. She hoped they would throw stones. She hoped they would burn her at the stake. Not because she had been fouled by a Negro, but because she had nodded. She had nodded, and given her permission, and then they had taken a man's life. "Just look at me," Sara was whispering, but Elma was looking at Nan now, Nan who stood with head bowed, her eyes closed—how wonderful prayer was! letting a body hide her eyes from the world—but she wished Nan would open them just for a moment. Nan had not been in the room the night the men had hauled Genus into the big house, wet from the creek. She had been hiding across the breezeway in the pantry. She had not seen Elma perform her affirmation. For all Nan knew, Elma had denied it, had defended Genus to his death. And she wanted to tell her now: that it was her fault. That she might be punished for a lifetime, she might be ostracized, she might sacrifice her own reputation to keep Nan safe, but that still the punishment wouldn't be enough.

And was this even what Nan had wanted? She had not asked Elma to save her. Perhaps she had been wrong to think so. Perhaps for Nan there might be no fate worse than this, watching someone else give her baby to God.

Nan did not open her eyes. Elma looked past her, into the crowd. She fixed her eyes on the one other still face she could find. It was a familiar face. It stared back at her from under the rim of a broad felt hat, eyes filled with a frigid and ancient disapproval, of Elma or the crowd she did not know. It was Parthenia Wilson, Winnafred's great-grandmother. She appeared to be alone.

"Enough!" said the reverend, putting a hand on Juke's arm. "Sinners, let us throw no more stones! To you I say, come receive the sacrament yourself, sinner! God will turn away no sinner who asks to be saved. We are all sinners, this mother the least of us. If she's borne the devil's child, it's God's will that we cleanse the sins from all our backs. Remember that we must love even the Whore of Babylon, Mother of Harlots and Abominations of the Earth, for she too is holy. She is all of us. *And he saith unto me, The waters which thou sawest, where the whore sitteth, are peoples, and multitudes, and nations, and tongues.*"

She stood. She bore it. It was true, some of it. She had not borne the devil's child—it was Nan who'd done that—but she was pretending to; she was colluding with the devil. Why didn't she stand and point a finger at her father? Why wasn't he the one they were throwing stones at? It was beyond her courage. She was not brave after all. She could not bear it after all. So Elma's mind went away as the people of Cotton County drifted down to the water like thirsty cattle and waited for their turn to be saved, the cameras clicking after them. Elma's mind went away and dreamt, and maybe that was God, after all, saving her.

In the days that followed, a vicious influenza appeared, with a fever and a cough and a mucus, green as the creek, spit into hand-kerchiefs and tin cans and chamber pots from Macon to Valdosta. Dr. Rawls, who had chosen not to take the sacrament that day, had a line outside his office all the way down to the First Bank of Florence. "What did you reckon would happen," he asked, "walking into a creek on winter's eve?" He prescribed cold and grippe tablets and sent his patients home to bed. Some tried nose drops; some tried tea; some tried whiskey. Some tried lady's slipper and granny graybeard and bloodroot. But it hung on, this sickness, for some until Christmas, for some into the new year. It was said that it was the worst flu in those

parts since the end of the Great War. It was said to kill a grandmother
in Ocilla, an infant in Fitzgerald, and a whole family of five in Jeff
Davis County. It was said to reach the dogs and the cattle and the
chickens, to infect their eggs, which people fried for breakfast, making themselves sick all over again.

It had started, folks believed, that morning at Creek Creek. They
said the devil's seed had tainted that water. Some women vowed not
to wash their clothes in the creek. Some men vowed not to take its
fish. They hadn't been saved that day but infected, and now the sick
was everywhere, in the water, in the air, like the weevils in the fields.

Well, that was what came from bothering a poor girl's burden,
said some, those who weren't at the creek. First raped by a Negro. Bad
enough she had to raise the child up. Couldn't the girl find some salvation?

Folks got sick. There was no more to it, Elma knew. She did not
believe that anything extraordinary had happened that day, other
than her own humiliation.

But that was later, after her mind had returned to her. After the
baptism, back on the farm, Elma saw her dress and her denim coat
dripping from the line, her wet shoes drying on the porch steps, and
that was how she knew, without needing to see the picture in the next
day's *Messenger*, that she had been lowered into the water with the
rest of them. The dogs were sleeping on the porch. The babies were
wrapped in blankets. For a moment she thought it was Ketty's lap
they were in, but it was Nan's. Nan looked as old and tired as Ketty.
Elma too was wrapped in a blanket. She was a mother, Nan was. Four
years younger and Nan was as much a mother as Elma, and look—
now she was mothering Elma too.

Juke did not seem to be about.

"It's over?" Elma said. She sat up straight in her rocker, feeling her
mind warm again.

Nan nodded. She passed Winna Jean to Elma and Elma put her
to her breast.

They had done what they needed to do. Now, if something should happen to the babies, God would protect them. Elma caught Nan's eye, and this time Nan let her hold it.

"You ready?" Elma asked. She was asking the babies and asking Nan.

Nan kissed Wilson's head. She nodded.

Elma looked to the sky, the weak sun. What she wondered was would her shoes be dry by the morning, when she would wear them to Atlanta, taking the children with her.

THIRTEEN

THE PLACE HE WAS BORN WAS CALLED OVID, THOUGH HE DIDN'T know it. It wasn't a town, just cornfields and a creek and a collection of cabins. He was born in 1912. His father's name was Treman. His mother's name was Martha. She was half Apalachee Indian. The cabin he lived in with his mother and four sisters was in Florida, but the fields they worked were in Georgia. The privy was in Georgia. The creek began in Georgia. He would die in Georgia.

One of his sisters was his twin. Lacy. She wasn't right. From the time she was an infant she cried day and night. She never could form words, just that screech, like a chicken hawk circling. His older sisters helped feed and bathe and dress her. She drooled so much that their mother knotted a diaper around her neck, the same diapers she was wearing at five or six years old when their father died. He had a rotten gut. It was rotten from moonshine or else the moonshine eased the pain. After he died their mother got a taste for it too. There were weeks, after the corn was gone, that they lived on blackberries and grasshoppers, he and his sisters catching them in jars. When his mother decided she couldn't care for them all anymore, he was relieved. He had long, wandering legs already. She might have sent Lacy to a lunatic asylum, but instead she kept her and sent the others away. They were ready for work.

After he was gone, first at his auntie and uncle's, then at their neighbors', then at another neighbor's down the road a piece, it was Lacy he was homesick for. His older sisters used to sit in a circle on the porch, singing and plaiting each other's hair, an unbreakable chain. They had voices like angels. They smelled like the sun. The Lord had scattered the three of them in kitchens and cornfields, one all the way to the coast, like a bird flew seeds from place to place. But it was Lacy's scream he heard when the rooster woke him each morning, Lacy's dead limbs that weighed down his mind when his cotton bag dragged behind him, heavy as a grown woman. She was the one their mother had chosen, but he was the one who was free. What he knew was that the cord that bound him to their mother had been coiled around her neck. It did not yet seem cruel then that their mother had told this to him, a little child. Some nights he dreamt it was his neck the cord choked, and he woke gasping.

On the day they buried their father, their mother distracted by grief, Lacy wandered off and ate through a whole ear of corn, husk and cob and all. Genus was the one who found her under the porch in a pool of her own sick. He was proud of himself, but his mother, standing above him, kicked him in the mouth. "You supposed to keep her in your care!"

He hadn't understood that Lacy was his responsibility. No one had told him. But he was her twin—he should have known. He heaved her up and hauled her down to the creek and washed her, picking the kernels out of her hair, saying, "You be all right, Lacy, you be all right." He washed the blood from his mouth. She was not all right. She groaned. She didn't squawk. It was the only time she was quiet. Lord forgive him if he enjoyed that quiet while it lasted. He could look on his sister lying with her feet in the creek and see her beauty. He'd only seen her quiet like that when she slept. They had grown up inside their mother together but he did not feel yoked to her until that day, and not long after he was sent away.

The thing about being yoked to a body was the cord was always clawing at your neck. But if you had no one to call kin, as Genus didn't after he left his auntie's house, it was just you and your own two feet. He took to telling folks it was a mule who'd kicked him in the mouth, and soon enough he almost believed it himself.

His feet carried him from town to town and farm to farm. He slept in barns and boxcars, in a barn he shared with a gray molly mule named Baby, and on the most peaceful night of his life, in a canoe he found on the edge of a lake. It was riddled with bullet holes, but it floated fine. He didn't know that the lake had no name. Drifting alone under the stars that night, he might have had no name himself.

He'd had enough Bible learning from his auntie to know how to talk to God. She sang gospel songs and tribal songs both. He hummed them as he walked the roads. He spent a goodly amount of time thinking on how to fill his belly. He still had a taste for grasshoppers. By then—ten, twelve, fourteen—his belly was paining him awful. It wasn't his stomach but his liver, or so a white man told him when he pointed to where it hurt. Was he a drunk? the white man wanted to know. Whatever it was, it felt like he was being eaten from the inside. It felt like his insides were disappearing themselves. Maybe he had what his father had. Maybe he had bad blood. After a day's work, when he could find a quiet barn or field, he liked to tug on his manhood. It helped to keep his mind off his gut. He didn't think on womenfolk when he did it. He spent most days not laying eyes on any womenfolk at all.

When he came upon the crossroads farm, he hadn't said his own name in many days. He saw the cotton in the field that wanted picking, the stand of pines beyond it in the fog, and he straightened his bent body upright and his heart stood up in his chest. It stood up again when he saw the girl at the well, her arms as thin as cane reeds, and all day as he watched her in the cotton from under the brim of his hat, when she brought him dinner under the cottonwood tree, and again when she came to his door in the rain and peeled off her wet dress. He said his name. She could not say hers, but he heard her voice loud as a bell, and then he learned what manhood was for.

She had brown eyes, Nan did, but if you looked close they were ringed with ocean blue. "That's ink from God's own pen," he told her. It was what his auntie had liked to say about the Bible. He had stood on a beach and seen the ocean once, so much of God's glory his eyes stung with salt.

He didn't think of the pain in his gut then and he didn't think of Lacy. It was later, watching the girl as she picked—her name was Nan, the boss's daughter told him—that Lacy came to his mind. Maybe it was because they had the same affliction, that neither one of them could talk words. They were the true twins in that way. But where Lacy screamed, Nan was silent. Nan looked to have all her mind and then some. What was the opposite of a twin? They were like two sides of the same penny. It seemed to Genus now that Nan might scream if she could. Maybe she once had, and that's how she'd lost her tongue. The carrying on Lacy did seemed like the way black folks felt most of the time. She protested. Growing up was learning not to protest. "Do what the boss man say," his auntie told him when she sent him down the road. "Your reward will come in Heaven."

He watched the black bird of Nan's hat skimming across the field. He had to bend over and catch his breath, from the heat and the burning in his gut and the sight of his sister standing silent under the sun, if she'd grown up into a woman. Was she a woman now? Or still a crying child?

He shouldn't have left her with their mother. He should have stayed.

"You be all right, Lacy," he'd said, his mouth full of blood. "You be all right."

———————

He made friendly as he could with the men in the field, if only to ask them questions. What had happened to Nan's family? What had happened to her tongue? The men raised their eyebrows and shook their heads. Daddy gone, momma dead, they said. Her momma was a medicine woman. She'd delivered all three of Al's sons. Ezra, the little man with the mustache, said, "She make a witch's brew of the girl's tongue. Try to make herself a cure for her sickness, try to outsmart God." He shook his head again. Genus eyed him. He didn't believe it. Why would a mother cut out her child's tongue?

"Now she live in the big house," Long John said.

"Yes, sir, ain't no mistake," said Ezra. They inched down the row, keeping their eyes on their hands, out of hearing of the girls, who edged along the row closest to the house.

"My woman sure enough would like to sleep on a pillow that soft," said Al.

"God put her there," Ezra said. "Ain't no mistake. Her momma take away her talking, the Lord gone make sure she got a soft place to rest."

"She got a soft place to rest, all right."

"See all this cotton?" Long John asked Genus. "This ain't the whole of it. Boss ain't just no cropper. He running a blind tiger."

Genus didn't know what a blind tiger was, so he kept quiet.

"He make hooch, son. White mule. Call it 'Cotton Gin,' think he clever. All the white boys in town be guzzling it like it the blood of Jesus."

"But he be at Young's ever Tuesdy. Tell you what. Drinking God's own corn liquor."

"He ain't just there for the corn liquor, brother."

"You ain't none how, brother."

The men laughed. "You see them girls at Easter's," Long John said to Genus, "you won't be asking after no skinny-ass, dirt-eating cotton picker."

Miss Elma, the boss's daughter, was the one who would know Nan. Problem was the two girls went about their picking elbow to elbow. He had to get Elma alone. He loosened the hinge on the gate to the chicken yard so he might help her with it again, but she didn't take to the trap.

Then one evening after picking he looked down the ladder of the hayloft and there she was, standing beside the hay bale he'd thrown down, and under it, a crushed slice of blackberry pie.

She asked about his tooth, his back. She had her eyes on him and now he saw her too. The first time he'd seen her she was in overalls, like a boy, but now she was wearing a dress that clung tight. When he asked about Nan, she kept her answers small. Then he took his questions for a walk.

"Miss Elma, where Mrs. Jesup at? With the Lord, like Nan's momma?"

She fidgeted with the pins in her hair, and he could see that her fingertips, blistered as his own from picking, were stained with blackberry juice. "When I was born. Never did know her. Her name was Jessa. Jessa Lee McBride, before she married my daddy. Daddy says she was born to be a bride, right through her name."

"I'm powerful sorry. My daddy gone be with the Lord hisself."

"The Lord, He takes care of them," she said.

"How long ago was that? When you was born?"

"How long? Seventeen years."

"And how long since Nan was born?"

She cocked her head, not trying to remember but deciding whether to tell. "Fourteen. Just a youngun," she said. And then her face went still as stone.

She was a sight, Miss Elma was. Smelled like sweat and flour and the soap he used to wash in the creek. Eyes like the green stones at the bottom of that creek. It was the longest he'd been this close to a white woman.

It was his weakness, that smell, the taste of the blackberries on that fork. He should have taken it as a warning. He should have run from that barn before she said a single word. But he had stood there and talked an hour away with her, forgetting she was a white girl, forgetting she had a daddy. And then her daddy appeared and took the hoe from the wall and then he remembered.

Not long after that, Nan stopped coming to the shack. When he saw her in the yard, in the field, she kept her eyes ahead of her. She stayed fixed to Miss Elma like there was a string between them. He wouldn't dare come within twenty feet of Miss Elma anyhow, not with her father about, but it seemed both of their hearts had hardened against him. Then he found the first pint of gin on the table below his window. His heart stood up in his chest and then fell like a boot.

One morning when the boss went to pick up the hands in town, Genus found Miss Elma alone in the field and risked a question. "Nan looking all right to you?"

"She looks all right to me," she said.

"She ain't taken ill?" He tried to hide his teeth behind his lip when he spoke.

"Right as the rain." Her face was still stony, but he could see that she was looking hard at him, at the bruise that had made corn mush of his jaw. "Say something."

"Miss?"

"There. Your tooth. The shark tooth. What happened to it? Is it gone?"

Genus covered his mouth with his hand.

"My daddy did that, didn't he?"

Genus did not nod. "You ain't did nothing. That tooth been wanting to come out."

She rolled the left sleeve of her dress up to her shoulder, tucked it under her cotton bag. He tried to look at her eyes and not the glistening hairs growing in the hollow under her arm, red as the hair on her head.

"Well," she said, not looking at him now but out at the field, "I'm sorry just the same."

Lord help him, he let her into his mind. All those nights without Nan, he couldn't help it. That night, when he lay down for a tug, his mind raised Miss Elma's dress up to her waist as she stood at the gate to the chicken yard. Then there was Nan at the gate, asking to come in. Well, come on in, girl. Only womenfolk in his sight on that farm, Lord forgive him, he had a hand on both their behinds.

He came to regret it, once he learned the devilment that went on in that house. He came to feel sorry toward those girls like they were his own sisters.

Uncle Mastiff, the uncle his mother sent him and his sisters to, he wasn't a good man. A drinker, a gambler. Three little girls in that cropper cabin with him. All of them slept on the rug. Genus would watch as his uncle came from his room in the night and put his hands under their nightdresses. Ellen, Agatha, Doreen. He remembered their names from the same deep, dreamlike place he remembered the names in the Bible. They were girls as yoked to their fate as Bathsheba or Hagar. They were as quiet as Lacy was loud. They pretended to sleep. Genus pretended to sleep. What else might he do? He was six, seven years old. Before they moved down the road to find work, he found a pint of paint thinner and poured some into his uncle's flask. He didn't know what it would do. Let God decide.

All that behind him, he should have known what Nan was doing in that big house. He should have suspected the boss. The boss had been kind, too kind. Genus had been blinded by that shack. Call it a shack—it was a house. With a bed and a stove and a window that closed against the cold. How many winter nights had he slept in barns, waking up with frost on his boots, praying he wouldn't end up on the chain gang? He'd not been restless to leave that bed, especially when Nan was in it. He'd looked at the tar paper roof above him each night and said to himself, Boy, you have found you some luck.

Lord forgive him. Now it was spring. The girls had spent most of the winter indoors. Genus reckoned that's what women did, but he'd been hiding them, the boss man, while their bellies grew. Now the men were planting for the season to come, and he would not be there come harvest. He was ready to leave. He would take Nan with him. He'd live under God's stars the rest of his days if he had to. He would not lie back and pretend to sleep.

The morning after the fire, after the night Juke had come across them under the clothesline, he found his chance. After the boss hobbled off to the Simmons farm to catch a ride into town, Genus tossed everything he owned in his cotton bag, put on his corn-shuck hat, and crossed the yard. Shards of glass still pebbled the ground. The burnt clothesline lay in the dirt, the laundry scattered around it fried as breakfast. He'd never been inside the big house. He didn't knock, just came in the right door from the breezeway. Nan and Elma were sitting at the table. Nan's foot was in Elma's lap and Elma was cleaning the cuts on Nan's legs with a cotton ball. The sight of her there in the daylight, the sun glaring off the canisters of flour and sugar in the kitchen behind her, her hands on her round belly—Genus went to her, let his bag fall to the floor, and dropped his head into her lap. He felt her fingers on the back of his neck.

"You all right?" He grazed her legs with his hand. "You cut up good?"

"Be careful!" Elma said. "You'll make it worse."

He stood, picked up his bag. "Come on, Nan. We aiming to take our leave."

Elma stood too. "What's this talk of leaving?"

"Leaving. Fetch your things," he said to Nan.

"She ain't fetching nothing. She ain't no dog."

"You talk for her, miss?"

"I do, in fact! Been talking for her long before you came round."

Genus shrugged his bag onto his shoulder. "Maybe you ain't been choosing the right words."

"Go on then. But you ain't taking Nan."

Her belly was as big as Nan's, her pale breasts swelling out of the top of her dress. He pictured her again with her skirt up around her waist and went sick with shame. She was not worth a tug. Cold as all the white women he'd known.

"Sure as the devil I am."

"I won't abide no more of this talk."

"I won't abide no more of this business!"

"What business?"

Genus threw up his hands. Did she not know? "The business of your daddy carrying on with Nan."

Elma looked at Nan. Nan looked down at her lap. The sun was coming strong in the kitchen window and Genus had to shield his eyes with his hand.

"He told me hisself last night, standing right there under the line." He pointed to the yard. "He as like as me to be daddy to that baby."

"No," Elma said, shaking her head. "I won't allow that talk."

"It's the Lord's truth, Miss Elma." He could see now that she hadn't known, and he made his voice soft. "I'm sorry to bring it on you."

"What's this talk?" she asked Nan. "Nan, what are these lies he's telling me?"

Nan wouldn't look either of them in the eye. She was holding her elbows across her belly, rocking back and forth like there was already a baby in her arms.

"He's my daddy." Elma pointed to Nan but wouldn't look at her again. "He's like a daddy to her too! Just like her momma was momma to me."

"Who's to know but the Lord that he ain't had his way with her momma?" He was asking out of kindness, out of concern. "Who's to know he ain't had his way with you?"

Elma shoved him. Sent him and his cotton bag sprawling backward against the table. "You quit that nigger talk!"

Nan leapt up and righted him. He bent over, Nan's arm around his back.

"Go, nigger! Go! You hearing?" Elma pointed out to the road. "We done fine on this farm without you. But Nan's staying here."

Nan stamped her foot. They both looked at her. She put a hand on Elma's upper arm and squeezed it twice. Was she comforting her or protesting? Or giving her warning? Genus felt the sweat coming down his temples. Whatever Nan was saying, he could see that Elma understood. He had a vision of making a family with Nan. It was a vision he'd conjured before, he realized; it didn't take long to come together now. They'd ride the freights north. He'd find work and an apartment and Nan would buy their groceries in a market and cook their meals on an electric stove. The baby would be born and they'd raise it in peace. When the baby cried, Nan would need no words to comfort it. A mother had a way. Before long Nan and the baby would have their own language too. But what about Genus? Would they always be strangers to each other? Or would she be the only stranger? His own secrets would spill like too much rainwater on the dirt. Whatever secrets Nan had kept from Elma—they were both squeezing each other's arms now—Elma knew more about Nan than Genus ever could.

"You don't want to go," Elma said to Nan, quietly, like she was trying to calm a nervous mule. "This is your home, Nan. You were born in that shack. You ran in them fields. You raised up here. Your baby wants to be raised up here too."

Nan tapped Elma's shoulder and looked down at her belly.

"Where you gone live, the pair of you? Where you gone find a house as fine as that? You gone live on the bread line? You gone ride train cars? That's a fine life for a youngun."

Genus put his arm around Nan's shoulder. What did it matter what their life looked like? What did it matter that he knew little of

Nan's past? They'd leave it behind. They'd be new as the babe Nan was carrying.

"These ain't slave times," Genus said to Elma. "You can't hold a body captive no longer."

"I know that," Elma said, insulted. "But my daddy don't. You take off with Nan, you reckon he won't be on your tail hotter than a slave master?"

Genus felt the sharp edge of the shard pressing into his neck, the one Juke had held to him the night before. He squeezed Nan's shoulder. His uncle Mastiff? The paint thinner hadn't killed him. What had killed him was a hunting knife. After his auntie and uncle's house, after the first neighbors', word reached Genus in the cornfield down the road that Mastiff had stolen a white man's horse and sold it to pay off a debt. He'd been missing for perhaps three weeks when Genus came upon a body in the corn. Hard to tell at first who it was, but there were his uncle's scaly green boots, heavy as hooves, the ones he said were made from a gator he'd killed himself. Genus knelt close. The corn stalks shushed. The skeeters buzzed about his uncle's bloody shirt. The knife still stood alert in his chest, stiff as an ax in a stump. Should he tell the overseer? Would the overseer think Genus had killed him? *Had* he killed him? He hadn't even thought to wish him dead, and yet here before him was his wish fulfilled. Genus was perhaps ten years old. He had no use yet for a pair of boots of that size, but one day he would. He had no shoes of his own, and he had aims on walking. He took them off his uncle's feet and left his body in the field and left the farm, carrying those boots in his cotton bag until they fit his feet without falling off, and then he reckoned he was grown.

Genus had felt no sorrow for him. God had decided in the end, and Genus had no quarrel with God. Now he felt no sorrow, but a dread catching flame in his gut. Out the kitchen window, beyond the gourd tree, the fledgling cane stalks caught the burning light.

He was not a killing man. He had sisters. They had taught him to sew.

"Y'all ought to know," Genus said to the girls, "if I end up dead, it's by that man's hand. And if he ends up dead, it's by mine." He would take what came to him, he decided. He was tired. He wouldn't fight, but he wouldn't call him sir. He would hold what he could of his manhood.

"Stop that talk," Elma said.

"It ain't what I'm aiming on. The Lord won't like it. But that's why I'm staying. That's why we staying, Nan. We got a baby coming. We don't need no white man hot on us." He nodded at Nan. Her eyes were shining with tears. He wished to God he knew what they were for. "We wait it out. Yeah? We see whose face this baby got. Lord hear me, I'll be here no matter which way. Yeah? But the Lord hear my prayer this baby won't have no devil face." He looked to Elma, who looked to the window. "And then the devil won't have no more use for us, and we can get on out from around here. Yeah?" He nodded to Nan. He had put on the voice he'd used with his sister. *Less put on your dress like a good girl, Lacy, yeah?* But Nan was nodding back. Was he saying what she couldn't say? Was this what she wanted? "And I keep you safe here. Lord knows I keep you safe. We put it in God's hands. Less pray on it," he said. He took Nan's hands in his and she bowed her head to his chest.

Then she stepped away from him. She turned one of his hands loose and held it out to Elma. Elma's face was flushed and tired, her hair coming loose at her neck. She put her hand in Nan's. She didn't look at Genus, but she offered him her other hand. He remembered her fingertips stained with blackberry juice from the pie she had brought him, and he let his hand enfold hers. The girls bowed their heads. They were women now, Genus reckoned. Maybe this was the day they were grown, like the day his feet fit his uncle's boots. He knew the women bowed their heads because he was watching them, even as he prayed. And holding their hands, he could see them. It must have been God's light that filled him. He could see Elma's hard, bitter heart, calloused as the claw of her hand. He could see she was yoked to Nan like a sister. He could see her fear and her hate and her love. And he could see Nan, the two rivers cutting her cheeks, and he could see now that they were tears of relief. The boss was gone, and they stood alone in the big house. What she wanted was peace, and for the moment, she had it.

———————

So they would wait. He was gifted at waiting. He waited for rain. He waited for the baby. The pain under his ribs flashed like lightning.

When the shack had gone up—what could he do but help to raise it?—he reckoned he was building her prison. She was trapped. The Lord forgive him: they should have run while they had the chance. Out his window, he could see it not a stone's throw across the yard. The lumber smelled fresh as the forest. He watched the boss deliver their meals and take away their piss pots and he studied on the ways he might kill him if it came to that. He kept a sharpened shard of glass in the chest pocket of his overalls. He sipped the Cotton Gin he'd squirreled away under one of the floorboards. He slept in his shoes.

But in time, he came to think of Nan's shack as a safe house, or at least a holding cell. If Nan was in prison, Elma was her guard. Genus could not be with her there, but neither could the boss. Genus had promised to keep her safe, and by building the shack he had done it.

"That a quarantine cabin?" he heard a neighbor ask on the porch.

The boss said his daughter had gone and caught diphtheria again. Couldn't be too safe, he said. The neighbor said she'd offer a prayer in church.

He'd said nothing about Nan. He'd left Nan out of the shack and out of the story. Not one neighbor, Genus realized, would ask after Nan. No white folks would know she was gone. From time to time a colored wagon came up the drive, looking for Nan to deliver a child, and Juke turned them away, saying she'd taken ill. And what could the driver do but turn and leave? Genus felt that cane stalk shush in his chest, like the devil's breath in his lungs.

He took another sip from the pint Nan had left him. It might have been brewed by the devil's hand, but it felt like the Lord's kindness. It eased his limbs. It quieted his gut. He tried to remember the light that had filled him, holding the women's hands as he prayed. He'd felt the Lord was speaking to him, not in words but in light, the way Nan spoke to him.

He didn't have much time, he reckoned. If a white man didn't kill him, his guts would eat him from the inside out. Wouldn't be much longer till he couldn't do farm work anymore.

He looked out the window. It was springtime, and evening, and the Lord was dropping the yard into shade. The brick well where he'd first seen Nan stood quiet, the silver bucket filled with the last of the sun. Above the big house, a flock of martins fell upon the tin roof like a net.

FOURTEEN

F OR YOUR OWN GOOD," HER FATHER TOLD HER, AND SHE HEARD
the sound of the lock.

And then, for a while, the world was the size of the shack,
no bigger than the first one they'd been in, when they'd truly had
diphtheria. There was Nan's corn-shuck pallet, which they shared on
the floor, which was full of splinters. There was the little table her
father had built and on top of it they kept the candle, the cup, and
the blue water pitcher with the chipped spout. Under it they kept
the chamber pot. Before long Elma's eyes hurt from looking at the
same things—the pallet, the candle, the pitcher, the pot—and she
closed them. When she closed them, she found that she could hear
everything on the farm. She heard the cars on the road, and the
McArdles' wagon, which had one mule, and the Carlisles' wagon,
which had two. She heard the road scraper pass. She heard her father
swear at the barn cat when she killed a loose chick. She heard a bird
build a nest in the eave of the shack. She imagined the nest was made
of twigs and Spanish moss and corn husks, much like their own mattress. She'd seen blue jays build such nests before, but the sound the
bird made, like the squeak of a mouse, told her it was a martin.

"Nan, honey. It won't be so bad. It'll be like when we were small."

Before long it almost was. There was solitude. There was safety. There were hours and hours to lie on their backs—when had they last spent a whole day lying on their backs?—feeling their babies kick. There were three meals a day, delivered by Juke and prepared by Glory, the colored grandmother he'd hired five days a week to do the women's work, telling her what he told everyone else, that the girls were suffering from the strangling disease. Every piece of her food was browned to a crisp, fried beyond recognition—was this a ham hock or a horseshoe?—but it was food that Nan and Elma didn't have to cook. Sweet Jesus, to be served food! After a week, Juke in his guilty feelings allowed them the Bible, then in another week the newspaper and some needles and thread for sewing, then a tablet and pen, which Elma said she wanted to draw pictures with, having no window. She could see an ease come over Nan's face when the pen was in her hand. They played tic-tac-toe, dreamt up names for their babies. Nan wrote down "Ketty" and "Sterling." Elma wanted Jessa for a girl. If it was a boy, he would be George Frederick Wilson IV. Elma practiced writing "Mrs. George Frederick Wilson." Juke said as soon as Freddie came to marry her, he'd turn her loose, and though Freddie was a coward and a brute and most of the time she didn't love him, that was what she set her mind on. Freddie would come to his senses. Reverend Quick would marry them in a quiet ceremony at the creek—her belly was too big for any church. She would be free from the shack and Freddie's grandfather would build them a house a hundred times the size of this one. She sketched her wedding dress and a nursery, a baby carriage as pretty as a bonnet, which she could push around for the world to see.

He was protecting them, her father had explained. The neighbors, the field hands, the passing cars on the Twelve-Mile—what would they think if they saw the girls' growing bellies, and the girls living still in Juke's house, no rings on their fingers? No one knew Elma was

pregnant except the Wilsons, and they weren't admitting it to themselves, or anyone else.

So what despair there was, what restlessness and vengeful rage,
in time it all settled like dirt shook from a rug, because a body, Elma
learned, could adapt to anything on earth. Even what despair that
thought brought she had no choice but to accept. She had no choice
but to accept the bowl of blackberries her father brought, though they
both refused to eat them. They reminded Nan of the path to the still.
They reminded Elma of the pie she'd baked for Genus the night she'd
come upon him with Nan at the creek. The next morning she'd fed it
to Mamie, and for days Mamie's snout had been blue-black. Genus
asked Elma, "What she get into?" and Elma said, "I baked her a blackberry pie."

Now she heard Genus and Mamie plowing the west field, his
voice deep, her bray high. "Come on, girl, just a little more, good girl,
come on." She watched Nan on the mattress, eyes closed, stroking her
belly. She watched her listen. She watched her pray.

In the quiet hours of night, hours when Nan slept beside her perhaps
more soundly than she ever had, Elma's mind would drift to what
Genus had told her the day after the fire. She had managed to scare
the words off. Why should she believe Genus Jackson? He'd had an ax
to grind against her father ever since that day in the barn, when her
father had gone in after him with a hoe. Maybe Genus was as slippery
as Freddie, trying to slide out of marrying Nan. Or maybe he just had
his mind set on upsetting Elma. That Nan's baby might be her father's, that her father and Nan . . . it was as preposterous as accepting
that her father was her mother, or that Nan was a rabbit, or that there
was no God in the sky.

Yet there was Nan, sleeping beside her, and there was her belly,
undeniable.

One night in the shack, Genus's words crept back to her like a hungry dog. Her mind leaned back to all the noisesome nights in the house, and all the nights Nan's bed had been empty, even before Genus came around, and then it was Elma who was crying, careful not to wake Nan.

She had heard the rumors about her father and colored women. He wasn't the only white man in town said to frequent Easter Moore's. He wasn't even the only white man in town said to have a colored concubine. But Nan was a child. Nan was family.

If it was true, it was unforgivable. Was she supposed to forgive such a thing? Wasn't that what the Bible taught? She sat up and lit the candle. Nan didn't stir. In the Bible she found the passage she'd marked: "For if you forgive men when they sin against you, your heavenly Father will also forgive you. But if you do not forgive men their sins, your Father will not forgive your sins."

She was a sinner, like her father. She'd had lust for a colored boy in her heart. Envy of a colored girl. Would God find it worse that they were colored? Her father would say so. But she had always envied Nan! Now, another kind, the sick sort of envy that was more like betrayal. She looked at sleeping Nan, whose affections her father had sought in secret. Oh, she hated her for it! She hated her for making her hate her father. And she hated herself for hating both of them. She hated Nan's baby, whoever the father was. She hated Freddie. She hated Genus, who had chosen Nan instead of her. She hated the sweet stench of the blackberries, which in the hot shack were turning more every minute, graying with mold. She hated, God forgive her, her own baby. She loved her too. Please, God, she prayed, let it be a girl. Let it not grow up to be a man. She could not think of a man alive she didn't hate. She had hate in her heart, and she could hardly stand the feeling of hating so much. To smother it, she lay down on the pallet and pressed her belly up to Nan's back and wrapped an arm around Nan's neck. Nan flinched. She scrambled toward the wall. Elma felt the fear in her, the way her bones seized up before she was even fully awake. That fear was her answer. She did not need to ask. But she asked anyway.

"Nan," she whispered. "I'm sorry I woke you."

The candle threw Nan's shadow up against the wall. Her chin was tucked to her chest, the wings of her arms tucked to her sides.

"Is it true? What Genus said about Daddy?"

It was late, or early. The nesting martin had begun to chirp in the eaves. Suddenly Elma was sorry she'd asked. She did not want to hear the answer. She could close her eyes, refuse to see it.

But her eyes were open when Nan, looking over her shoulder, nodded. Her shadow, flickering on the wall, nodded with her.

"I'm sorry," Elma said, her voice still small. "I'm sorry I woke you. Go back to sleep."

After a moment Nan turned back to the wall. In a moment her body relaxed on the mattress.

Elma sat with her head between her knees. She closed her eyes. She would look at nothing, think of nothing. But the smell of her own body, under her arms and between her legs, sickened her. She smelled like a man. She smelled like an animal. She felt the sick gathering in her, like an egg in her throat. All at once she couldn't help it—she let it go. There was no place to do it but on the floor between her feet.

"I'm sorry," she said, gasping. Nan was awake, a hand on Elma's back. "I'm sorry."

The next morning when her father brought them breakfast Elma threw the bowl of blackberries over his head and into the yard behind him. "Make me sick," was all she said to him.

He brought her a bucket of kerosene and water and made her clean it up, and the summer came on deep and the box swelled with the hot stink of her sick, and even after her father took pity on them and drilled them some holes for air—high up, too high to see through—the shack reeked to high Heaven for the rest of their days there.

———————

One morning, they woke to the sound of chirping. In her half sleep, Elma thought it was crickets, or mice. Nan woke too, sitting up.

Through the drilled holes, pins of light shone through. They both looked to the eaves. "Babies," Elma said. She couldn't help smiling. Above their heads, as they'd slept, the martin's eggs had hatched, and now she was a mother.

It was Elma's eighteenth birthday.

She kept the days marked in the front of the Bible, on the page before the family tree, but the giant eggs of their bellies were a calendar of their own, measuring each day. Nan pressed her hands to Elma's belly like a man marking the height of a horse. Every finger width their bellies grew in circumference was another week, and though Nan had littler bones than Elma, and narrower hips, their bellies measured the same—thirty-two fingers, then thirty-three, then thirty-four. There were forty weeks in all and not many left. She wrote it all down for Elma. Then they tore the page from the tablet and lit a match and burned it.

Thirty-five centimeters. Thirty-six. Elma heard Genus humming at the well. (Nan closed her eyes.) She heard the McArdles' rooster. She heard her father going to the barn to milk the cows, then, later, her father taking them out to pasture. She heard April's call in the west field, thin and worried, and then June's reply, low and comforting, in the north.

Oh, to be out to pasture! Tethered to a tree or a fence post, but with enough rope to wander in the sun.

But later her father would bring the cows back to the barn and lock them in their pen.

"For your own good," he had told her when he'd locked the girls in the shack. Now it occurred to her that he might have been talking, in a different way, to Nan. Was it for Nan's own good that she was locked up? Was it himself he was shielding her from?

It was true: he had not touched her here. And the thought filled Elma with a warm hope: that her father might want to protect Nan as much as he wanted to trap her. That he might love her as much as he hurt her. And that what he knew he needed was a wall between them.

Before long the shack would come down. But Elma, she would be the wall.

That night, after blowing out the candle, Elma pressed her belly up to Nan's back and wrapped her arm across her neck. Nan reached for her wrist. "When we get out a here," Elma said, "he won't be bothering you no more. I'm a take up for you now. I don't know how I'm gone to do it, but I'm gone to."

FIFTEEN

B LESSED DAY FOR A DRIVE," SAID DR. RAWLS FROM THE DRIVER'S seat. "My momma liked to say a Georgia fog was just Heaven coming down to earth for a visit."

Out the window, the mist hung low and silver as the Spanish moss, the oak branches meeting above the road in a lace of praying fingers. Elma rode in the front and Nan in the back, a baby on each lap. It was among the conditions Elma had spelled out. Nan was not to be left on the farm. She was needed to help care for the children. The men's trucks had left before dawn for Savannah, and the doctor's black Plymouth had arrived not long after, when Sara was still wrapping the warm biscuits in the basket. Elma offered one to the doctor now, and he took it, saying he was much obliged.

"I remember when you girls were small," he said. He drove with his shoulders hunched, his nose nearly touching the steering wheel, his hat nearly touching the windshield. When he braked the car, he did so uneasily, with a long hand lever shooting up from the floor. "Y'all should a been in a hospital, in proper quarantine. But it wasn't so common back then. Y'all two was peas in a pod. Put two bodies in a cabin together all the summer months, any body like to catch it."

He took a bite of the biscuit and swallowed. "It's a right ugly illness. Course it ain't common at all to go and catch it not once but twice. When I heard your daddy built you another shack, I had to scratch my head."

The car came out of the canopy of trees. The road opened into farmland, gently rolling, the morning sun burning faintly at the horizon. "A right ugly illness," Elma agreed.

Through the cold breath of the fog, at the side of a crossroads, a white man stood beside a truck full of winter squash, orange, yellow, green. Before long Cordele passed by the window, and then Nan was the farthest north she'd ever been. She warmed Wilson's tiny hands in her own. She told herself she was just on a trip like any other, imagined Dr. Rawls was driving her to some Negro cabin to deliver a baby and not to a laboratory where white doctors would stick Wilson with more needles.

"Doctor," Elma asked, leaning forward, "what all are you fixing to do to the twins?"

"Why, we'll just take some blood is all." He had to raise his voice to be heard over the sound of the engine.

"I don't want em bothered any, you understand."

"No, ma'am. Won't hurt no more than getting their shots."

"We need the money, is the only reason, like anyone else."

Nan liked to believe this was true, that this was what had driven Elma to accept the doctors' invitation, despite the risk. How could anyone refuse? It was money that Elma would be able to keep herself, without her father's knowing. They could save it for the babies. Whatever happened, the babies would come first, the babies would be safe. "Besides," Elma had argued—she could feel the fear in Nan's silence—"they can't find out nothing about their daddies in a hospital. The babies is kin, after all! Don't worry, Nan," she said. "I won't let no one find out."

"Of course," said the doctor now. "We find it to be a fascinating case, is all. From a medical perspective. My son and I, that is."

"Is he a baby doctor, then? Your son?"

The doctor chuckled. "No, he aren't no baby doctor. He's like to have a fainty spell if he saw a woman give full birth." He cleared his throat. "He's trained as a physician. But now he studies blood. Sickle cell disease, to be particular. Leave the sick bodies for an old man like me. He might at least study on the poliovirus, if he's going to look in his microscope all day. Oliver had polio as a child. He's still stiff with it. He might be able to do some good, studying on the poliovirus. But he just looks in his microscope all day, looking at platelets and cells."

"Sickle cells?" Elma said.

"Yes, ma'am. Common among Negroes." He described how sometimes their red blood cells were shaped just like a sickle wheat was cut with, holding up an ancient, hooked finger. "Ain't much to be done about it, but he's going to see what he wants to see in that microscope."

"Don't know what a doctor studying on sickle cells wants with my babies. Wilson don't have no sickle cells."

The doctor lifted his left ear to the roof of the car. "It's just some blood work is all. We like to make sure the babies are healthy and growing strong."

"Wilson don't have no sickle cells, does he?"

"We don't know until we test him, honey. Could be he carries the trait. Wouldn't know just by looking at him."

"What's it do? What kind of sickness do them cells cause?"

"Ah, honey. Don't get yourself worked up yet. It's a rare disease."

"You said it was common among Negroes, Doctor."

"More common than in other folks is all."

It was cold in the car, even in their coats, and Nan held Wilson close to keep warm. He lay bundled and sleeping in her arms, his eyelids reflecting the gray outside the window. The windshield wipers beat back the fog. "Genus Jackson," the doctor said, trying out the name. "Genus Jackson, when we did the autopsy, we discovered he had no spleen."

Nan sat frozen. She clung to Wilson as she'd clung to Genus that night behind the hanging sheet, making herself a tree, but she could feel the wheel of her heart turning, the blood spinning through it.

"A spleen's the organ filters the blood." The doctor tapped his left jacket pocket. "This man's spleen, his own blood, had sucked it dry. I never saw a thing like it."

"He had the sickle cell disease?" Elma asked.

"That's right. All the signs of it, and worse." Nan saw Genus bent over in the field. She saw his hand over his ribs, the same place the doctor had touched. "Seems the man weren't long for this world anyhow."

"You want to know if Genus, that man, passed it on to Wilson."

"It's a hereditary trait, yes ma'am. There's a chance."

If she'd had a voice she might have asked them to turn the car around. She wanted to be back at the shack, the place where Genus had been, to see it with these new eyes. She wanted to tell him what she now knew.

But what did it matter? Nothing was changed. Genus was dead. Wilson did not have the disease because he was not Genus's child. The doctors' tests couldn't reveal that, could they?

Nan watched Elma cover half her face with her hand and look out the window. "That's all right," she said. "We'll just see, won't we. Ain't no use worrying now, like you say."

"That's right," said the doctor, his voice brightening. "No use worrying. God will tell us the story in His time."

Wilson was heavy as a block of ice. She shifted him to keep her arms from falling asleep, fingered her mother's pearl in her dress pocket. For their trip to the city, Elma had lent Nan her chore coat. Nan was wearing her own best blue dress, but it had grown so small she couldn't close the top button. Sara had loaned Elma a belted wool coat and a proper dress, lemon yellow with a white bib collar, and a pair of cream-colored leather pumps that Elma said pinched her toes. Elma and Sara had talked on and on about Atlanta, how the lampposts would be hung with wreaths, about the trolley cars on Peachtree

Street, how there might even be snow. Elma had said she wanted to eat a sandwich at a lunch counter—pulled pork, or maybe corned beef, with a Coca-Cola, or maybe a ginger ale—and watch the people go by the window, and Nan, sweeping in the corner of the kitchen, marveled at how Elma had gone back to being a schoolgirl on picture day, unchanged by motherhood and what had happened to Genus. And now, looking out the window at the world going by, the world that too was unchanged—a boy pedaling a bicycle with a basket of newspapers, a bright yellow school bus at a stoplight—Nan saw that the things she'd thought made them more the same than anyone else were but provisional, and that Elma had more in common with a rich white girl from Buffalo than she had with Nan, who had lived in her house with all those ugly secrets in her mouth.

And why were they keeping the secret still? Wasn't killing a man a sin worse than what Juke had done to Nan? Why was that the secret worth keeping? In the beginning, it was Nan who Elma had claimed to protect, but now it seemed, as the car sped farther and farther from the farm, that it was Juke they were protecting. And Nan closed her eyes at the thought that in protecting her father, Elma was protecting herself. For what would she do without her father?

"Well, what I said before, about taking precautions. I suppose it's possible to be too safe. I once saw a Negro child operated on. No more than ten years old, and her spleen swollen to the size of a yam. They took it out, hoping her body would go on without it, but she died not long after. Her body couldn't go on without that spleen. They shouldn't have sliced that poor child open. It puts me in mind of your mother, Nan." In the rearview mirror, the doctor caught her eye and wouldn't turn it loose. "Now, she was a good Negro woman. The best granny midwife in Cotton County. But she did you more harm than good, cutting out your tongue the way she did."

"She meant to save her, Doctor," Elma said, looking over her shoulder at Nan. "That sickness, it's in her family's blood, just like the sickle cells, passing down and down the line."

"I know she meant a kindness," said Dr. Rawls. "But I remember before she went out to the crossroads, when she worked in the tobacco barn out the other side of town, like her mother before her. She weren't the only one of them workers with sickness in their mouths. But by the time she came to see me it had gone too far. What could I tell her but to stop chewing them leaves? By then it was too late."

Wilson began to stir awake in Nan's lap, a gas churning in his belly. There were too many words for her to take. Sickle cells? Tobacco leaves? She looked to Elma for some sign, some recognition that the doctor was mistaken about this too. She wanted to seal off her ears with wax. She wanted to be back in that shack, the grits and the coffee on the stove. All this big world outside the window, this long road out in front of them, and still it was that shack her mind was after.

"Me, I won't even circumcise an infant anymore. A bloody mess, and to save em from what? It's not our place to go slicing children with our scalpels, guessing God's wishes." He shook his head. He was wrong, the doctor. It wasn't the leaves that had made her mother sick. Her mother was smart as a conjure woman—she knew the way a sickness worked. "But I suppose it's like the Jews and their practices. It's not for me to judge." He finished the biscuit, chewing it dryly. "Yes, your mother was a good woman, Nan. I once saw her coax a baby out by shooting pepper up its momma's nose with a soda straw. She did sneeze that baby right out! I reckon you learned a good deal from her."

Elma said, "Yes, sir, sure enough she did."

"It don't mean nothing to me, you going round delivering younguns. I got more than I can handle, Lord knows. I can use all the hands I can get, specially with the Negroes. Use your hands, girl. You may not have a tongue, but you have good hands. You hear?" He sat up tall, putting his face close to the rearview. To Elma he said, "Ask her to show that she hears."

Still Nan delivered babies, but now her colored patients had dropped off and were replaced by white ones. Now that Castor and Pollux were there, it was the dogs that called her out of bed, barking at a car or a wagon in the driveway, not a visitor inquiring after the babies but a father set to have a baby of his own. Before the twins were born, no white folks but the most desperate would allow a girl of fourteen to bring their child into the world on her own, let alone a dumb Negro, Nan heard it said, unless they'd called on her mother before. Now they came from as far as Jeff Davis County.

Some of the white fathers talked about Genus Jackson, in voices they might use to talk about a car wreck or the Crash or the other unavoidable and tragic affairs of the world. "Appears to me they wouldn't have been no mob if it hadn't been for no hooch. But then, they probably wouldn't be so many younguns in the world neither." Some of them were more direct. They said, before they even reversed out of the driveway, "That the gourd tree they hung the darky boy from?" and pointed and whistled.

The colored fathers, the ones who still came, did not talk about Genus. After Genus was killed, most of the colored fathers did not want to come near the farm, so their sons and daughters were instead delivered by their sisters and mothers and the fathers themselves. (Nan had heard that one father, whose son Nan had delivered, had severed his newborn daughter's cord with a rusty piece of hog wire and she had developed an infection and died. She'd heard that another had left his pregnant wife to go north. A cousin was left to help her deliver the child. Some said he was going to send for the family once he'd found work in New York, and some said he had a white woman up there, and some said no, he had a white woman here in Florence, and the reason he'd left was because her husband had found out and he didn't want to end up like Genus Jackson.)

The white mothers looked at the babies Nan handed them with curiosity. Maybe it was just the way a new mother looks at her new baby, but Nan thought they were looking for some sign. "Hello, darling," one mother said to her child. "Now you can say the same hands that brought the Gemini twins into the world brought you into the world as well." In an Indian cabin in Meredith, a pair of twins came out fast as Winnafred and Wilson were said to have come, two black-haired boys identical down to the swollen peaches between their legs. The mother and the father looked at their sons with some relief and some disappointment, as though all at once they'd been spared a curse and deprived of a miracle.

If her mother could see her now, delivering white women's babies, driving in the backseat of a white man's car, would she say she'd done good, that she must do what she had to do, that dollars were dollars, white or black? Or would she tell her to bundle up her baby and jump with him from that car and get as far as she could get?

In the front seat, Elma looked back at Nan and nodded. Nan slipped her hand out from under Wilson and rubbed his belly. His eyes were open now. Her breasts were getting full. She made Elma wait for it, but she returned the nod.

"She hears," Elma said.

The doctor settled low into his seat again. "All right, then. Good girl." He began to hum a quick little tune. "I sure could use as many hands as I can get. I aren't going to live forever, and now the bank's lost all my savings, I'll be working till the day I die. Don't have no use for a hematologist in Florence, but a baby doctor, that we could use. Or a family doctor, for that matter. No use telling that to Oliver, though. He got no patience for talk of coming home. Six children, all married off with they own families, all but the youngest. That's my Oliver. Who's to take my practice now? Who's to take my patients, on a Monday like today? If he were home, Oliver could."

"We're much obliged to you, Doctor," Elma said, "for carrying us."

"Oh, it's no trouble. Gives me a chance to lay eyes on my son. Though we're fixing to be late, with this fog." The road ahead, still veiled with mist, glowed white in the headlights. The doctor craned his neck up at the sky through the windshield, and the babies, both awake now, as though sensing something there, looked with him. "My momma liked to say a fog in the morning means sunny skies in the afternoon. A day that begins in a cloud all around, where you can't see your own hand in front of you, that's the day that ends up so clear you can see the Lord's face in it."

Near Macon, Dr. Rawls pulled into a filling station. The slick-haired attendant, a white boy, put his hands on his hips as he leaned down to the driver's window, his jacket tight across his muscled arms, and glanced past the doctor into the passenger seat. From under the cuff at his left wrist, Nan could see the inky scales of a sailor's tattoo, and Nan could see Elma see it too. Elma sat back, lifting Winna off her lap and placing her on the seat, and patted the twist at the back of her neck. Sara had fixed her hair with a dozen pins last night, and Elma had slept sitting up. Foolishness, Nan's mother would say. Mothers always had a thing to say, even the doctor's mother. Now Nan wanted to seal her ears against her mother's voice. Because it was foolishness, Elma and her hairpins, but Nan might have wanted her hair put up if she could. And maybe it was foolishness to drive head-first into a hospital of white doctors, but what choice had her mother left her with, chewing enough tobacco to kill herself dead? How was she to know her mother wasn't the biggest fool of them all?

She remembered the leaves her mother chewed, the same color as her hands, the way she'd crumble off a piece and keep it concealed against the roof of her mouth, like a secret. Even after she came to the crossroads, she chewed them. Juke grew no tobacco, but she got it when she delivered babies back on the tobacco farm, kept it hidden from him. Sometimes she was even paid in tobacco. Folks knew what she liked.

It was a cold blanket that was falling over Nan, the empty, upside-down feeling of knowing more than the person who'd brought her into the world. There was anger under that blanket, anger at the doctor for knowing so much, anger at her mother for knowing less—Nan stretched the crippled stub of her tongue, searching for purchase—but there was pity too, and she settled there, for it was the easiest to sit with. All this world passing by her window, and her mother had seen none of it!

After the car pulled back out onto the road, Elma asked the doctor if she might let down the window for a minute, and into the car rushed the cold burn of gasoline and manure and the emptied fields. Nan's lungs choked with it. Her eyes watered. She held Wilson in her left arm and pressed her right hand over her ribs, just under her heart, like she might plug up a leak.

———

That part of Emory University was not in Atlanta proper. It was in the pines outside the city, a fortress of vast stone buildings with tile roofs the color of the clay in that part of Georgia. The fog had burned off but it had left the sky dull over the empty campus, like a yellowed bedsheet hanging on a line. No students roamed the paths with their books tucked under their arms, no co-eds in fur coats and white nursing shoes. "Must be on holiday already," said Dr. Rawls. "Here she is. Anatomy Building." He parked the car and cut the engine, and the silence roared in Nan's ears.

She peered up at the building. Anatomy. She did not like the sound of the word. It was a stout, colorless castle. It looked like a prison. She thought of Freddie Wilson's mother in the sanitarium.

Dr. Rawls raised his wristwatch to his eyeglasses. "Late," he said. "It's near one o'clock." The old man had been driving nearly six hours, stopping only for gas, eating nothing but biscuits. Both babies had slept much of the trip, lulled by the road moving under them, and now they were hungry too.

The doctor nodded at Elma. "You ready, ma'am?"

Elma said she needed to powder her nose, if he didn't mind.

"Of course, of course." He stepped out of the car. While he made his way to the passenger side and opened her door, Nan tapped Elma's shoulder and held Wilson against her breast.

"And the babies need to be fed," Elma added, stepping out.

"Of course," said the doctor. "Let's go see Oliver first. Then we'll let you settle yourselves."

Inside the doors, Dr. Rawls spoke to a woman behind a desk, who led them down a flight of stairs. The basement corridor was lit by electric lights, one after another, the bulbs hanging in wire cages above them. From behind the closed doors along it came a dizzying, chemical stench, like bleach and pickles. Nan did not like that smell. Her skin went stiff with gooseflesh. The all-overs, her mother had called it. "Formaldehyde," Dr. Rawls apologized, drawing his handkerchief to his nose. At the end of the hall, the woman used one of the keys hanging from a chain around her neck to unlock a heavy wooden door. Inside wasn't a laboratory but a long, dark office lined with metal desks, mint green. At the end of the room, under a small, high window, sat three wooden armchairs. The dull sun came in through it, lighting the green linoleum floor like a river. All the desks were empty but one, every inch of it stacked with papers, a dim lamp, a microscope, and a typewriter, whose keys a young man sat tapping. When they came in he stood and, with the aid of a wooden cane, walked rigidly across the floor to them.

"Hello, son!" said Dr. Rawls, dropping his satchel and taking him in both arms. When the doctor removed his hat, the men were the same size, small and lean, each of their round eyeglasses reflecting the other's. The doctor stood in his black overcoat, the son in shirtsleeves with an ink stain blooming over his heart. "You've grown three new whiskers since I seen you last," said the father, giving the son's shoulder a pat, but the son was smooth-faced, his dark curls cut close to the scalp, only showing themselves at the top.

"And you've grown some wrinkles, Doc."

Dr. Rawls laughed.

"I grew some wrinkles of my own," the son went on, "just waiting on you to arrive."

"They was a mighty heavy fog. I says, 'We're going to be late,' and sure enough we are." Dr. Rawls released his son and stood aside. "I brought along some folks from Florence. This here's Mrs. Elma Jesup."

Nan saw Elma flinch at the "Mrs." It was meant as a courtesy—Dr. Rawls would not introduce a mother with a "Miss." But who had she married—her father? Herself?

"Mrs. Jesup, this is my boy Oliver. Dr. Oliver Rawls."

Dr. Oliver directed a nod toward Elma. He looked unsteady on his feet, like the air had gone out of him. "Ma'am."

"She's mother to these two bouncing babes."

Elma swung Winna around to face him. Her blanket was slipping off her shoulders, and she'd begun to cry. "This is Winnafred Jean. And this is Wilson John." She put a hand on Wilson in Nan's arms.

"And this here's Miss Nan," said Dr. Rawls.

"She's our chore girl on the farm," said Elma. "And a big help with the babies."

"I reckon she is," said Dr. Oliver. "Pleased to meet you both."

"She don't speak," said Elma. "But she can hear just fine."

"She's coming up to be a good little midwife. Delivered the twins herself."

"You don't say. Must have been quite a miracle to take sight of."

"I don't think of the babies as no different from any others," said Elma over Winna's crying.

"Of course," said the doctors at the same time.

"We're just interested in the science," said Dr. Oliver. "It's a rare chance for a doctor to study a case of separate paternity. We call it 'heteropaternal superfecundization.'" He smiled. "Had to dust off an old textbook to remember that one. Of course, it's clearer to the eye when the babies are of different races."

Elma nodded, her eyebrows knit, shushing in Winna's ear. "These babies ain't gone sit still till they've been fed. Is there a washroom, please?"

"Yes, ma'am. There's a ladies' room down the hall on the left. Don't have a colored one, I'm afraid. Suppose we'd have to go over to the service building."

Elma looked at Nan. Nan was relieved to see she didn't want to leave the babies with the doctors, not alone, but her bladder was as full as her breasts. "She don't need one right yet."

"A washroom is no place to nurse a child," said Dr. Rawls. "You can sit right here in one of these chairs. We're physicians. Aren't nothing we've not seen before."

Again Elma looked at Nan, telling her to sit tight, she'd have her turn soon. "Yes, sir. I'll use that washroom first."

"I'll take the baby," said Dr. Rawls, taking off his hat and coat. His son hung them by the door. Elma handed Winna to Dr. Rawls. "Hello, old girl," he said to Winna after her mother had left the room. "Are you full of piss and vinegar too?"

By then Wilson was crying also, tugging at the buttons on Nan's coat. She worked free of the coat and Dr. Oliver took it from her, hanging it on the hook next to the doctor's. He told her to sit down and make herself comfortable. She did. Even without the coat, though, it was warm inside, the building pumped through with a hot breath of air.

"Take the envelope from my coat pocket there, son."

Dr. Oliver did, then turned the envelope over and opened it enough to brush a stack of bills with his finger. He whistled. "I don't understand why they put on Andrew Jackson. What was wrong with Grover Cleveland?"

"He was another Hoover, that's what. Couldn't manage a dimestore, let alone a depression."

"Bet you're glad to see a Southern boy on a bill for once."

"I'm glad to see twenty dollars in one place these days, son. Don't think I didn't take one for my own pocket. Gasoline ain't cheap."

Dr. Oliver shook his head, then tucked the envelope into his shirt pocket. "This girl, she's on one of Wilson's farms?"

Dr. Rawls nodded, bouncing Winna on his hip. "Her daddy Juke Jesup works a couple hundred acres out by the crossroads. Cotton, mostly. But they've diversified." He raised his heavy white eyebrows. Winna was whimpering after her mother, Wilson carrying on in

Nan's lap. From the far end of the room, Nan couldn't hear much over the sound of the furnace and the sound of the babies' crying, but she could hear enough. "They've got a little of everything going, and then some more. They keep the sheriff nice and warm."

"You didn't tell me she was so pretty," said the son, finding a corner of the desk to lean on. He had to use the cane to pivot, as though his feet were stuck to the floor.

Dr. Rawls chuckled. "I don't think she knows it herself."

"Red hair and all those freckles. She could play a farm girl in the movies."

"I'm afraid that red hair got her into the trouble she's in now. It's no wonder Wilson's grandson took a shine to her."

"And the Negro who was killed?" He looked around his father at Nan, wondering if he should go on.

"She can't speak nor write," said Dr. Rawls, lowering his voice, and his son matched his tone.

"She can hear, as the girl said."

"*If* that Negro is the father. That is the question."

Dr. Oliver settled his cane across his lap. "We'll see what his blood tells us. I can't guarantee it'll give us an answer. Not without samples from all the parties." He said something else Nan couldn't hear over Wilson fussing in her ear. The baby was fiddling with the top button of her dress now, the one that wouldn't close.

"Well, Wilson's boy is on the run from the law. I couldn't likely chase him down and ask to stick him with a needle, could I? I tried that with Jesup and the brute wouldn't let me near him. He nearly cut me with his razor first. And Wilson too, after I came up empty-handed. We got to come home with some kind of answer or that man is like to be very disappointed."

"And what's it matter to you? You in with Wilson too, Daddy? You been putting on a hood and running round with them fools?"

Dr. Rawls scoffed. "Son, I'm too old to be in with anything, except in bed with your mother by nine. Klan's running out of steam, anyhow. It's them Black Shirts taken over their call. I take no um-brage with the Negroes."

"But you see no need for medicine that might help them."

The doctor waved a furious hand. "I'm just helping bring the truth to light!"

"Ah, the truth. What's the truth about you scraping all his women clean?"

The doctor winced. "Please don't be crude."

"It's a crude procedure."

"It's simple and it's safe and I'm not the only doctor to do it! God knows in times like these we don't need any more bastard lintheads running barefoot in the mill village. More village idiots to grow up and join the Black Shirts—surely you can find good in that? I do what I must do to keep in that man's good graces. And if I'm letting him pad my pockets, it's because I hope to leave you and your brothers and sisters more than a mustard sandwich and an IOU."

"All right, Daddy. Easy now. You get worked up, we're going to have to call a doctor." Dr. Oliver shook his cane at him gently.

"I'm not certain we'll find one here. They got an awful lot of mi-croscopes and fancy equipment, but aren't a man around who can count a pulse."

"All right, now. If our fancy equipment is no use to you, go on and solve your little country mystery by counting a pulse. See how far you get."

Dr. Rawls grumbled something too low for Nan to hear. "Where is that girl? Poor child probably hasn't pissed in a proper toilet in her life. Suppose she can't find the flusher." He paced in front of the empty desks. Then, in a thunderous whisper, leaning Winna away on his hip, as though to keep her from overhearing, he said, "That man Jesup's been in the bed of every colored gal in the Fourth Quarter!"

"So's George Wilson himself, if talk is true."

Dr. Rawls waved his hand. "He keeps clean. White women. Mill girls."

"Mill girls," Dr. Oliver repeated.

"I'd bet my last dollar, if I had one, that there child belongs to one of Jesup's colored gals. It all stinks to high Heaven!"

The doorknob rattled, and there was a knock. Dr. Oliver opened it to let in Elma, who had her wool coat over her arm. She stood in the middle of the room. She patted the back of her hair. "Ma'am," he said. He went to the desk and removed the envelope and handed it to her. "This is for your trouble. We here at Emory are mighty grateful."

Elma accepted the envelope. She held it between her fingers for a moment, then tucked it unopened into the pocket of the coat on her arm. "Thank you kindly, sir." She gave Dr. Oliver a nod. Then to Winna, she said, "All right, honey. Come here and stop that fussing. Dr. Rawls gone leave you in Atlanta if you fuss that way." She took her from the doctor's arms and sat in the chair to Nan's right. "You hungry too, honey?" she asked Wilson, who still clawed at Nan. "All right now, let me get your sister on first." She laid the coat over Winna and pulled it up to her chin, and in a moment the baby's cries quieted. Elma did not have to tell Nan that she planned to nurse both babies there, to make a show of it. She just had to raise the tent of the coat and Nan knew to slide Wilson under it, but after a few moments, he still wouldn't settle. Nan tried to catch Elma's eye, to ask her what to do. She was confused, her mind filled with all the doctors had said.

Dr. Rawls, he had his eyes fixed on the window above Elma's head. "When you're done here," he said, waving toward the coat, "we'll just put the babies on your knee, just like on your porch at home. We'll shine a light in they eyes."

Elma nodded. Wilson fussed and kicked, and Nan reached under the coat to try to help him latch.

"We'll just take a look-see right here," said Dr. Rawls, mostly to himself now. He lowered himself into his son's desk chair. "An old man needs a rest," he said. "Still feel like the road's moving under me." A moment after sitting down, his eyes fell closed and his breath deepened. Then Wilson cried out again and the old man startled awake.

"I'm sorry for the hollering," Elma said, struggling. "I been in the car so many hours I'm right full of milk. Wilson's so hungry he don't know how to get on."

Nan studied on a square of tile in the floor, trying to clear her mind. It was a swirl of greens. Mint green, forest green, sea green. So what if she'd never seen the sea? A body could imagine near anything.

She could feel the milk then, though she pretended she couldn't. Like when she used to hear Juke's footsteps coming for her room at night and she'd tell herself no, it was just a mouse, it was the house settling, it was just someone walking through her dreams.

If no one asks you for the truth, her mother told her, then it's not your turn to tell it. Nan did not, could not tell anyone that her given name was Nancy, that the family name that came from the masters of her father's people—Smith—was lost when her mother died, that no one asked her for it, that if someone had, she might have answered, "Jesup," for that was the only family she knew. She told no one that it was her tongue that killed the cotton in 1916, the year she was born. It was her tongue that called the boll weevil to Georgia. Ketty had buried it in George Wilson's field, with the sorghum seeds that had been brought to the South by African slaves. She had hoped, she said, for a good year on the farm; that was what was expected of you. Instead the cotton closed its fist that year and refused to grow. Ketty laughed. She hadn't known that was what she'd been wishing for all along, not a bounty but God's curse on the field. Nan had given her voice for the white man's misery. To hear her, Ketty said, you wouldn't know hers was the most powerful tongue in all of Georgia.

Or was that story more foolishness from her fool mother's tongue?

If Elma had noticed what was happening in Dr. Oliver's office, she might have sacrificed her coat so Nan might cover herself instead. If Nan's mind had been quicker, she might have stood and crossed the room to fetch her own coat hanging by the door. She might have gone in search of the washroom. But her mind wasn't in the room. It had gone to the sea. It ignored the needling in her chest. The wet was the waves; the warmth was the sun. She left them all behind—Elma, the doctors, Wilson's crying, her mother's voice too. She was holding Genus's hand on St. Simon's Island, a place he had told her about once, where the beach was white as a field of cotton.

Maybe Dr. Oliver had his eyes on Nan so they'd have a place to land, to keep them off Elma. He leaned against the desk across from them, his cane resting at his hip. His arms were crossed in front of his chest. White men had looked at Nan before, but even Juke's eyes stopped at her skin. Dr. Oliver looked inside her, like she was under one of his microscopes. His glasses caught the light from the window. He was staring straight at Nan's heart. Nan looked down too. Sure enough, her insides had spilled out. The front of her blue dress was dark with milk. Her dress was like two colors of the ocean, the shallow part, and then the deep.

"Daddy," said Dr. Oliver, and he nudged Dr. Rawls with his cane.

Dr. Rawls sat up, awake, and looked where his son was pointing. It took him a moment to see. He said, "For the good Lord's sake."

Elma's eyes followed the doctors'. Her face was resigned. Her face was peaceful. Maybe, Nan thought, Elma would not have covered her if she could. Maybe this was what they both had counted on, hoped for; maybe they had wanted to let go of their secret all along.

What could she do? She unbuttoned her dress. She took Wilson from Elma's lap and fit his mouth to her breast. He quit crying. Inside and then all around her, a fear grew as big as the room. But alongside it, sure and quiet, a new relief flowed like a river. In front of the white men's eyes, Nan fed her son, and she was happy.

SIXTEEN

I T WAS WINNAFRED WHO WAS BORN FIRST.

By the thirty-seventh week, they'd shed their dresses in the shack. Wrapped their heads in their aprons. They stunk worse than the hogs, who at least were granted the dignity of a mud bath. Once a week Elma's father left them a washtub and they squatted beside it, rubbing the soap under their arms, between their legs. Elma tried washing her hair in it but as soon as it was dry it was wet with sweat again, and as the sweat dried it went stiff as straw. Nan's hair grew out. In the light of the candle, Elma tried to plait it. She sang "I'll Fly Away." She read the Bible aloud. "'A woman when she is in travail hath sorrow, because her hour is come: but as soon as she is delivered of the child, she remembereth no more the anguish, for joy that a man is born into the world.'" She said, "What do you suppose 'travail' is?" The onionskin pages of the King James were soaked through with the sweat of Elma's breasts, those mounds so monstrous they seemed to belong to someone else. The book lay open upon them. She slept. She woke. Already her breasts wept milk. Their bodies were as ripe and round as summer squash.

The last days of June, Elma's plug of blood fell in the piss pot.

She thought of her mother. She was scared. But Nan nodded knowingly and patted her arm. Nan wrote on the tablet—she liked writing her messages, now that she could—*Wont be long now*. She seemed, Elma thought, almost cheerful. She'd never seen her so determined, so calm.

Elma's father had never let her go with Ketty and Nan on their deliveries. "Leave em to their colored work," he said. "Ain't nothing for your eyes."

But once, when Elma was twelve, a father who'd come to the crossroads farm to fetch Ketty had his wife with him in his wagon. Ketty'd taken one look at her and seen there was no time to go back to their house, so she took the woman to her own shack. She barked at Nan to put a clean sheet on their bed, and Nan barely had it on when the baby slipped out of its mother and into Ketty's hands, quick as a calf. Elma looked on from the doorway. She'd thought of childbirth as a long and painful process that ended as often as not with a live baby and a dead mother. But this mother had not died. She'd sat up in bed, unbuttoned her dress with one hand, and put the baby to her breast with the other, its umbilical cord still attached. It was the woman's ninth child.

Now Elma tried to summon that woman's face, her sense of purpose and calm, the same casual expression she might wear while shelling beans. She breathed. They waited through another day and night. They did not hear Genus's voice, but they heard his footsteps across the yard. By the middle of the second day, the pain came all around Elma, like a belt. "In my back," she told Nan, and Nan nodded and rubbed her there with her tough, narrow hands. In a while Nan rang the bell, and Elma's father came.

"Got to wait," he said, standing at the open door. Elma looked past him. There were no men about. She told him she couldn't wait. He said he'd be back when the sun went down, and closed the door.

The pain came in waves, came and went. She would have the baby here, on this filthy mattress, if she had to. She tried to breathe. She tried to keep that mother's face in her mind, but it drifted. All she could see was her own mother's face, bloodless.

A mother is the only one who can tell the story of her baby's birth, and her mother was not there to tell it. Nor was Ketty, the only witness. Elma had always imagined that day as a single bloody picture. Jessa on the blood-soaked bed, and Ketty holding Elma. Or had Ketty passed the baby to Jessa? Had Jessa held her before she died? Did she go fast, fast as the pains that were coming on now? How was Elma to know that the next one wouldn't be fit to kill her?

She shifted onto her knees. She was naked as a cow, her red braid a sweaty tail. She didn't care who heard or saw her now. She made a sound like April made before a storm.

Why hadn't she asked Ketty while she could? She had known, somehow, not to. Her father's sadness and Ketty's sadness were one, cold and quiet as a bucket.

It had happened to her father's mother too. Both of them had killed their mothers coming out. The Lord saw it happen all the time.

Nan was breathing out of her nose, snorting like a horse. Elma couldn't follow. She could barely breathe at all. What good could Nan do? Even Ketty couldn't save her mother. She was in the Lord's hands now. And if the Lord took her, he would take her from this filthy shack.

Then, footsteps. Elma thought they were Genus's at first. The door opened and her father stood there in the afternoon. "All right." He looked away from his daughter's nakedness. "Quick, while nobody's about." There was discomfort on his face, and panic, and also relief—his daughter was alive; the baby hadn't come. Of course. He too was afraid.

Once Nan had helped her get her dress back on and helped her into the house—Juke put her in his bed this time, which was bigger than hers—the pain came furious. It was not the mattress her mother had bled on. That one Ketty had dragged into the yard and burned, not wanting Juke to see it. This one—it was clean; her father had slept on it alone, doing his business with women, with Nan, in other beds, hadn't he? Hadn't he that decency? She felt she might retch like she had in the shack and then a pain came like a lash and she did retch, soiling the bed. She had not been warned about that part, but Nan covered it with a towel and rubbed her back, her hands telling her it was normal, honey, it was fine.

She rolled over and got on all fours again. It was her back, the baby's head pressed on her tailbone. It was stuck there, she thought. Elma crawled down to the floor. Nan let her. The floorboards were flat and cool and worn smooth. Nan brought a piss pot. Elma retched into it. She retched into it again. When the hollering reached a certain pitch, Juke appeared with a pint of gin and made her get back on the bed, she weren't having no baby on the floor. She had never had a drink before. Her father had always been careful to keep it from her. But in between pains she took it gratefully. The burn in her throat made her holler, but it distracted her from the burn in her back. "Atta girl," her father said, patting her hair. "Atta calm you right down. You're a strong girl, honey." Then another pain came and he left the bottle and went back to pacing in the breezeway.

The liquor didn't numb the pain in her back. What it numbed was her head. Her head was outside now, cooling in the air. She could breathe. She could see that it was coming on evening. The day went on with no care for what happened in the house. That did calm her. The guineas still squawked in the shade. The flowers still grew. Elma breathed. Her father was right. He was strong and so was she and so was Nan. Nan readied her instruments. She knelt between Elma and under the tent of her dress checked her again. (Three months naked in the shack, and now she was wearing a dress!) She was teaching her, Elma realized. Soon Elma would have to do the same for Nan.

Nan might have been in the early stages of labor herself, her baby dropping down into place, her narrow hips making room. She had never given birth before—how was she to know that the pain in her back wasn't from lying for months on the pallet on the floor, or from kneeling before Elma for the four hours she pushed? Four hours she pushed, holding one of Nan's hands or both, gripping so tight that Nan couldn't grip them back. She'd seen mothers push that long before, and longer. Helping a mother push was easy for her, easy as baking a loaf of bread, and when the baby came out right, she felt the same satisfaction of seeing the loaf of bread come out right, golden and round, with no knots or bruises. Dozens of round, golden heads she'd guided out of the warm ovens of their mothers, hundreds of hours she'd spent holding the hands of those mothers as they pushed, so how was she to guess, when three days later she was the one on her back in the bed (not Juke's bed, no—there the baby might have refused to come out at all—but her own bed, the dead silent mattress with its hidden book) that she wouldn't know the first thing about how to push a baby out?

Elma, she had pushed and pushed with all her might, every muscle marshaled for that purpose, the muscles in her neck even pushing, her eyeballs mad with burst blood vessels when she was through. When the baby girl came out sunny-side up, her face lifted up to Heaven, it was no wonder her mother had been in such pain. "It's a girl!" or "It's a boy!"—that was what Ketty had always said first thing, but Nan had no choice but to hold the baby up for the mother to see for herself. Elma tore a bad tear, but she was so glad it was over, she was so glad to hear her baby girl's cry—a girl!—that she didn't even feel Nan sewing her up. "Am I bleeding?" she asked, and though there was always blood, Nan shook her head. It was the same kindness Ketty had made Jessa, saying, "You good, honey, you doing real good," kneading her belly like she might pump a heart to start it beating again, then stitching as fast as she could, then kneading again, then stitching, even as the blood made gloves of her hands. The life went out of Jessa while her baby girl lay dazed and docile at her breast, both their bodies slick with blood and chalk. Ketty had let the baby lie there as long as she liked, smelling the smells of her mother's neck, taking what warmth was left of her body.

Now Elma lay with her daughter at her breast as Nan sewed. Dozens of women she'd sewn up, careful as she'd darn a pair of baby's socks, but three days later when it was Nan on her back in her bed, clenching her mother's pearl in her fist, she was as fretful as a newborn herself, her knees shuddering so bad they knocked against each other. She pressed them together, trying to keep her bladder shut, but she felt the wet leak out on the mattress. Elma cleaned it up as Nan had cleaned Elma's sick, with a warm towel and a calm voice. She did her best to soothe her, showing her how to breathe, as though Nan hadn't been the one to teach her. Elma didn't know a thing, she didn't know about the woman in Rocky Bottom who had died along with her baby, she didn't know that birth, if you did it wrong, killed you both. She was still shuddering, it was the room, too small to breathe in, the chipping blue paint, the room where Juke had pinned her against the wall and left his seed inside, and Juke now pacing out in the breezeway again, this time rocking an infant in his arms. Already he loved his granddaughter, and Nan couldn't take any more love from him. She couldn't bear to birth a baby he might love. She didn't know it was the same with her grandmother, and her great-grandmother too, and the woman in Rocky Bottom who had died with a white man's baby inside her, that they all had thrashed in their birthing beds, fighting their babies back. How could they force a child out the same dark door it had come through?

The tongue is the worst curse, Ketty had told her. There was dignity in keeping your truth inside. But the truth was fixing to come out, it was fixing to burst like that jar of gin that dropped from between her legs. She wanted to reach down and sew herself shut. If her mother had wanted to save her, she might have sewn shut the lips between her legs instead of cutting out her tongue. She might have sewn shut every womb in Cotton County, saving them all some trouble. If Nan had any love for the infant girl crying on the breezeway, she might do her the kindness now, clean as a doctor skinned a baby boy's pecker.

The girl came first, the boy three days later. They were not born with their cords braided like streamers on a maypole, but the boy was born with his own cord noosed around his neck. Nan had to sit up and squat on the bed, to feel the weight of the earth under her feet, before she could find the muscle to push him out. "That's it," Elma said, her eyes locked on Nan's, their arms locked too. Her face was lit up with excitement—she was doing it, Nan was pushing—and Nan hated Elma for being through with this and loved her too for that look that tricked her, that told her she might soon be through with this too.

And then it seemed she was. When she felt the baby's head emerge, she rolled back and reached down and cupped it in her hands, and when she felt the cord, her mind sprang back to life, and quick as she'd loose an errant stitch, she reached down and lifted it with the hook of her finger. She didn't have time to think about whether it might be kinder to let the baby die before it was all the way born. Half born, its head out and no other part—still the child could be anyone, anyone's—again she felt the mason jar of gin she'd hidden between her legs that night. It was what it felt like to hide her love for Genus, to try to keep it in. Genus was out in the field now, or out in his shack, oblivious as far as Nan knew to what was happening in the house. Cord loosened, Nan lifted the baby by its shoulders as it slipped out onto the bed. He was blue for a minute, and as Nan beat on his back she beat back her fear, and when he cried and pinked up, and opened the eyes in the wrinkled golden raisin of his face, he looked, she thought, like an old white man. Already she could see that it was Juke's. A boy, but Juke's. She'd gotten half her wish. That was about as good as the Lord gave.

In the truck, out on the Twelve-Mile Straight—when he was a boy they called it Twelve-Mile Line, or Twelve-Mile Pass, though it passed through to nothing—Juke drove to town. When he was a boy there

Nan scuttled over to the baby and scooped her up. With a baby in each arm she sat with Elma, who lay perfectly still on her side, her left arm spread crooked across the floor.

"You the momma now," Juke said, taking out his tobacco tin. He opened it and stuffed the tobacco against his teeth, back where the molar hung black and loose. "You think we can stay in this here house? Folks find out I'm daddy to that child? You think I can sell another pint? You think Nan can deliver one more nigger baby? We fixing to be on the bread line quicker than a fart." The baby, the girl, was crying, and the baby boy now cried too. "You the momma now, honey. Get on up. You all right. You a strong girl. You got to get on up and be a momma, you hearing? Nan, get her up."

Elma sat up on her own, clawing at the floor on her way up. She said to Juke, "You ain't never laid a hand on me."

"I still ain't. I kicked a chair over's all. Ain't a man allowed some anger?"

"You ain't never done me no harm. But you been bringing harm to Nan."

Nan still crouched behind Elma, cradling the babies to her chest. Juke kept his eyes from her.

"I'll do it," Elma said. "I'll be momma to him. But you ain't to lay a hand on Nan."

Juke stopped his chewing. "I ain't never hit her neither."

"You done worse! You ain't to even look at her. You ain't to touch her. If I see you near her room, I'll run straight to George Wilson and tell him you the daddy. I'll tell the sheriff. Anyone who'll listen. Then you'll be on the bread line if you ain't on the chain gang. You hearing?"

If Juke had been looking at Nan, he would see that her eyes were bright with fear and hope. She too was waiting for his reply. But he was looking at Elma. Elma may have been made in his own image, she may not have known a cent about her momma, but she was her momma through and through. She could spit the same fire. And all he could do was stand back in admiration.

He was done with Nan, anyway. Really done this time. So be it.

"All right, then," he said. He turned to the door, trading his field hat for his town one. "I got business in town. I'm coming back with the daddy to both those babies, now. You get it remembered."

It was near on noon when Juke arrived at the mill. He circled the village in the truck, hanging his head out the window, asking after Freddie. He found him on a porch of one of the shacks, a cigarette in one hand and a jar of gin in the other and a fat brunette on his lap. The girl was ten kinds of ugly, but she had a rump that was wide and soft. Juke was smiling when he pulled up to the shack and lowered the window and said, "Freddie boy, you a man all right. You a daddy twice over."

Why did he come? Juke didn't know. Maybe he was drunk enough to be curious. Maybe he was after trouble already. They wouldn't get full drunk until that night, after they returned once more to the mill and filled the beds of their trucks with men, men just off the second shift who didn't mind making use of the Cotton Gin Juke had brought for them, Juke pumping them with gin like he might load a shotgun. His shotgun was in his lap. Maybe that was why Freddie got in the truck. They were drinking now as Juke drove, sharing the pint Freddie had brought with him. He was hearing his daughter say "Momma" and the crack of her elbow on the floor and he drank and drank some more. Freddie asked what were their names, and Juke told him they hadn't settled on ones yet. It wouldn't be until later that Juke named them both, after he'd given up hope of taking Wilson as their last name and made it the boy's Christian name instead. "They your kin all right. No doubt."

But Freddie did doubt it, standing over the cradle, another cigarette burning in his hand. The babies were sleeping now. Freddie didn't say hello to Elma when he came in the door. He said, "He don't look like no Indian. He look like a nigger bastard."

"You reckon?" Juke said, looking again at the baby's hair, his mouth. His fool eyes were playing tricks on him. He blinked and the baby looked white, white enough. Blinked again, and he saw black. Black enough. Juke was drunk enough to do what he thought he would do. It too had been sleeping in his mouth, black and rotten. He was remembering how light Nan's skin was when she was born, how it darkened as she grew like a loaf of bread tanned in the oven. Before long the boy would grow dark too. He would be black enough. Too black.

It was not Genus Jackson's child, he knew this for sure, or sure enough to bet the farm on it, if it were his to bet. He dipped a finger across his gums and lifted out the tobacco. "Which one of em," Freddie was saying, pulling back the curtain. "Which one of em I got to kill."

Perhaps he was expecting to see more than one, but he wasn't schooled in farm ways. It was laying-by time, and there was but one man in the field, a distant black shape in the green cotton.

And Juke said his name, as though giving it to a newborn child. He named him.

———

Genus Jackson's mother, Martha Jackson, wanted to call him Gene, but his father, Treman, thought a man ought to have a full name. What was the whole name for Gene? she wondered. She'd had a Great-Uncle Gene. He had a full white beard and he'd brought clementines at Christmas. She had always been fond of him. His full name had been Eugene, but she didn't know it.

Genus, said Treman. And that was that. They never did call him anything else.

They did not dare give their children middle names. They were not so wasteful with their hopes.

(Genus's three older sisters, however—who would marry and move north and settle together in a row of shotgun houses on the edge of a frigid city of concrete and brick—would have ten children between them, and each one had a middle name, some of them two.

Although none of the sisters would read the newspapers of Georgia, and none of them would discover what had happened to their brother, they gave their children the middle names Genus and Lacy, for the little twins lost to the wilds of the South.)

Genus Jackson did not dare approach the house the first time he saw the Ford skim across the road toward town. Not in the daylight. He could hear the cries—he was sure now that they were two different cries—when he came to the cottonwood tree for the midday meal. Glory, the maid, had been gone for four days, taking her frying pan with her. His stomach had emptied itself of the last of her lard, but now it was too empty. He had lived for four days on biscuits from Al's wife, hard as gourds. What his stomach wanted most was a bowl of field peas, buttered and salted the way Nan made them, not cooked beyond complexion, the way his aunt had done it and his mother before her, but still firm enough to hold their color, the smart pink irises of their eyes. When Miss Elma emerged from the house that noon, making her way down the back porch steps and across the dirt yard to the cottonwood tree, his heart didn't know whether to rejoice or lay down and die. In one hand, she carried the basket of sandwiches for the others. In the other, a bowl of peas. This she handed to Genus, but she barely raised her arm, as though the bowl was too heavy to lift. She looked at his face once, then hid her eyes under her hat. Her belly was flat under her apron. He had not laid his eyes on her nor on Nan in three months.

"Miss Elma, Nan's all right? Is both babies born?"

Elma nodded. Genus did not know that Nan could read or form letters. He didn't know that she'd written on the back of a bill from the crossroads store, before she burned it in the cookstove, the thing that Elma would say, which was, "Come to the back porch soon as you can. If he's still gone when dark comes on."

But the truck came back that afternoon and the boss climbed out with another white man. Genus kept his head down over the weeds he was chopping. The glass shard was in his boot, sharp against his ankle. Then, quick as they arrived, they left again. Genus stood in the field, watching the truck disappear for the second time that day. He heard the bump of the tires over the intersection. Then it was gone.

He does not wait for dark. He goes to the shack and washes his hands and face and neck in the basin on the shelf with what water is left. Then he takes off his shirt and washes under his arms and changes into the other one and then puts his corn-shuck hat back on his head.

When he comes out, Nan is waiting for him on the back porch of the big house. A bundle of a baby is tucked under her arm. Maybe it's the way she stands above him, but she looks taller, and her hair is longer, round and full as a head of cotton. Her belly too is flat. Her eyes are wet. She is shaking her head as he comes up the steps. It takes him an hour, a whole day, to get to the top. She doesn't need words to say what he understands. He finds that he has no words either. She shifts the baby so he can see.

The baby is small as a squirrel, with a little squirrel's face and, when Genus lifts the edge of his diaper, a squirrel's nut between its legs. He has not seen such a small baby before. She starts to offer the baby to Genus to hold but he is afraid to. So instead he settles into one of the rocking chairs on the porch and settles Nan into his lap. He holds her and she holds the baby and they rock.

He can't say whose face the baby has. Who can be sure but the Lord? It's the Lord's face. It's a squirrel's face. It is not the white devil face he has feared. His sisters had a single doll baby between them, a white doll baby their mother found and brought home. Their father called it the devil baby. He saw what he saw and the boss will see what he will see. What Genus sees now is that it doesn't matter. Now that the baby is drawing breath in the world, now that a white man has claimed it for his own, there isn't any changing his mind, and there isn't any way he'll see fit to keep Genus on, not with Genus knowing all he does, which isn't everything, not nearly, but it's enough.

He is tired. He will sleep tonight and wake up in the early hours of Sunday and take his last bath in the creek. He will wash this place off of him. He will walk down the road he walked in on. He has been here nearly as long as he's been anywhere else.

But for now he will sit in the shade of the porch. For now it is his porch, his house, his farm he is watching from his chair. The cotton is green, tall as the knees of the cows, who are out to pasture. Two are in the grass between the dirt yard and the garden, the long ropes around their necks yoked to the gourd tree. The other two are in the north field. His belly is full of peas from that field and butter churned from the milk of those cows. His lap is warm with his woman. His son— for now, it is his son—is sleeping.

II

SEVENTEEN

T HE WAGON CAME SLOW. TWO HORSES, ONE BLACK, ONE WHITE, led it down the dirt road. It was December, early enough in the morning so that the blades of grass were still webbed with frost. The eyes of the men in the fields lifted from the ground to watch the wagon make its steady course away from town. Women on porches held their hands over their brows, shielding their eyes from the feeble winter sun. What sort of a wagon was it, and where was it headed? It was as tall as a train car and half as long, each side enclosed with bars, and inside, if the women squinted, they could see the men in their striped uniforms, lying in their bunks stacked two deep and three high, some supine, some leaning on an elbow and looking out, and then they could catch their eyes, dull and dark, staring back. They were the men who had been seen along the Twelve-Mile Straight before, leveling the ditches, dragging their feet in their chains, but never in a wagon headed west, to the place where the dirt road ended, where the Creek River drip-dropped into a trickle. Driving the wagon was Lloyd Crow, a shotgun across his lap, and as he passed each house he nodded his greeting. Another shotgun guard, Hank Talvey, hung off the back. Two bloodhounds trailed behind. By the time the wagon reached the farm farthest down the Straight, then kept on, the two croppers in the field were scratching their heads.

"What in Hades they after?" one asked the other.

The other man lifted his hat at Lloyd Crow and watched the wagon disappear over the little hill. He said, "I heard it, but I didn't believe it. I do believe they gone pave the Straight."

Inside the cage were a dozen men, the four white across the top and the eight Negroes in the bunks below. The youngest was a boy of fourteen, who'd stolen a crate of milk from the porch of a white woman in the Third Ward. The oldest was old as the pines. He claimed to be a Civil War vet, forced to fight for the Confederates; they said he was sentenced to ninety-nine years and a dark day. That was why his uniform was the color of a paper bag, while everyone else was in stripes. He liked to be called General, though the warden re-fused. Every prisoner was to be called by his last name. Problem was, now there were two Smiths on the crew—a white boy, in the camp but two weeks, and a Negro, next oldest to the General, in the camp two years. The older Smith was forty years old if he was a day, silver in the stubble of his cheeks, but still round with muscle, shoulders near as wide as a shovel laid across them. The man had been called Smith until the white boy had turned up, and then the warden said the white boy would be called by his last name, the colored man by his first. The colored man was proud to be known by his Christian name, but thought any man should be given the same respect as oth-ers. So last week at breakfast, when the warden called him, he made the mistake of saying, "Call me Smith." He'd thought, too late, to add, "Sir." The white Smith had shrugged his shoulders, mouth full of breakfast, and the warden had taken the colored one for a stretch on the Georgia rack. The rest of the crew could hear the rope's tighten-ing and the man's hollering over their grits and coffee. It was not his first time on the rack nor in the sweatbox—he had a mouth on him he couldn't keep closed—but it was the first time he passed out, chin hanging to his chest. When he came to an hour later, after the ropes around his handcuffs were loosened, he'd messed himself, and was made to clean his pants in the creek. A week later, his shoulders still ached where the arms had nearly been pulled from their roots.

Now they were set for a new camp. That's what they'd been told. The older Smith tried to keep his eyes on the coming work. They were to leave behind the warden and his rack and his sweatbox, even the cursed cage where they slept. They'd been chosen, the twelve of them, to build a settlement at the abandoned end of the Twelve-Mile Pass, to help the men from Macon who'd won the road contract. Soon the contractors would bring their trucks and their scrapers and pavers, and the chain gang would bring the sweat. "Good-bye, boys," the warden had said. "Remember: bad boys make good roads." They would raise the tents they would eat in and sleep under, as well as a kitchen tent and a blacksmith shop and latrines, made from the land's own pines. As the wagon bumped over the road, he tried to think of it as noble work that was waiting for them, as though they were pioneers cutting through the wilderness. Better than digging ditches. He hoped he wouldn't have to dig latrines. That was cotton-picking awful work. And he had picked some cotton in his day. He had picked cotton, and dug latrines, and logged pines, and chipped turpentine. He had not made it to the steel mill up north. He had not even made it out of Georgia.

Always there was something keeping him back. Seasonal work, picking cotton or peanuts or peaches, another opportunity he couldn't pass up, another chance to fill his pockets with enough to get where he needed to go. The freights were full of folks heading north, but also full of reasons to stay a little longer, a little longer—folks who knew a fellow who knew another who was looking for workers. Their brains were rotted by liquor, but they were full of ideas. He was different. His mind was clean of poison. Back then, he'd had only one idea, which was to put miles of road between him and the woman who had broken him. Whether he did that in a steel mill or a turpentine camp didn't matter much to him.

Only thing was that once you were in the camp, there wasn't any getting out. Same as sharecropping, worse. Turpentining, you were in over your ears. The overseer paid you up front, then owned your ears and your eyes and the feet you stood on till you earned them back. They were no better off than slaves buying their freedom. Those who fled the camp fled to Florida. It was harder to get dragged back over the state line. He thought about following them.

Then he'd gotten word from a neighbor back home. His woman had passed. He had not seen her in more than ten years. And now their daughter was without a mother. When he fled, he fled home.

He was not ten miles from Florence when two deputies on horses had rounded up a whole train car of hoboes and filled the jailhouse with them. He was tired by then of running, and glad for a dry roof, a bed that stood still. That was more than two years ago. He had been released after a year, only to be picked up again, a day later, for vagrancy. Then back to the county camp he went. He had to give back the eight-dollar set of clothes he'd been given on his release. Back to the camp, back to the mosquitoes and the shackle sores and the stink of shit in the pan under the cage, worse than any smell on the farm. After he was back the second time, there was always something kept him there. A loose tongue. A fight with a fellow convict. "Impudence" was the word in the warden's log-book. He couldn't read but the warden told him so. Sometimes the warden took him for a stretch. Sometimes he just stretched out his sentence. Three months became six. Six months became a year.

Now it was the end of 1930, and he had dug every ditch in Cotton County. Hard times had gotten harder. The road gang was filled with men who had stolen bread and coats and tomatoes off the vine, some asking to be caught. He too found himself resigned to it. He had lost sight of the farm. He could no longer call it clear into his mind. He could not remember what his woman's cooking tasted like, no more than he could remember his mother's. In the camp at least there were three meals, salt pork and corn pone and enough sorghum syrup to make you sick.

His stomach was full of that syrup now, too sweet. When the road ended, the horses found some shade to settle under and the shade made the cold colder and the cold made him sleepy. The supply truck hadn't yet arrived. "Y'all just sit tight," said Lloyd Crow, stepping down from the wagon. "Don't you go anywheres." There was nothing to do yet without the supplies—the tents and stakes and hammers, the saws to fell the trees—so they waited in their bunks. They'd been given no coats, only wore their union suits under their clothes, and striped knit caps already dusty from the road. They lay and listened to the creek and the birds. He heard a robin call, and through the bars saw its orange breast among the trees. He did not like to look at the trees, though. He had seen enough pines for a lifetime. He closed his eyes. With nothing to distract him, he thought he could hear the fish swimming in the creek. Had it been summer, he'd have liked to take a swim in that creek himself. He daydreamt awhile about summer, and then maybe he really was dreaming—he was dropping into sleep. Already he could hear the General, in the bunk below, begin to snore. When was the last time he'd been idle enough to fall asleep before the day began? When was the last time he'd been out in the country at this hour without a shovel or pickax in his hand?

At the turpentine camp, it was a hack he carried, chipping away the face of pine after pine, the gum filling box after box. The work was no harder on his hands than farm work, but it was harder on the mind, his eyes hanging the same distance from the same bark hour after hour. Maybe he wasn't made for mill work after all. On the farm, at least, there had been more kinds of work than he could keep up with—wood to chop, mules to feed, rattlesnakes to scare from under the peanut stack. There was a gopher tortoise liked to hide under there too. It was coming back into his mind now. Elma had fancied the tortoise her pet. He'd found the animal dead on its back under the drying peanuts. A rattler had got her, or else she'd fallen over from old age. He'd buried her in the woods down by the creek, where Elma couldn't see.

He was old as that old gopher now. Would the girls recognize him, if they got close? He'd recognized them, even from a distance. Wasn't it them? With his eyes closed, he saw their two figures, women now, standing on the porch set back from the road, shielding their eyes from the sun as they'd watched the wagon pass. In their arms, they each held a baby. At their feet, two dogs barked at the hounds.

Nancy. She had been little more than a baby herself when last he'd seen her. Now she looked like her mother. Slimmer, slim as a telephone pole. But that was Ketty's high round forehead and square shoulders and proud mouth, and that was the way Ketty stood, still and stiff as a tintype. Again he felt the wagon pass by, the wheels turning, the porch growing more and more distant, and though the farm was but a few miles down the road, he felt it was years and years behind him, that he would never get back to it, that he would never see the woman on the porch again, and he had to remind himself that it was his daughter, not his wife, and that he'd been the one to leave them.

He chased them from his mind. Opened his eyes. Better to see the cursed pines.

"Looky." The prisoner in the bunk above was hanging his head upside-down. It was the new white boy named Smith. Their ankles were shackled as well as their wrists, but the white men's were loose enough to stretch. Something was wrong with the boy's right eye. It was closed, or nearly closed. His other eye was a baleful shade of blue. In his hands he held a length of string.

First thought the older Smith had was to get the string around the boy's neck. Instead he asked, keeping his voice low, "Where you find that?" It wasn't cheap twine but good cotton string, the ends of which the boy now knotted together to form a loop as wide as his chest.

"Out in the yard before we set oft. Central camp's not far from the mill. Figure I got me some cotton mill string."

"Mighty nice string," he allowed. The two guards were in the sandy clearing a good twenty yards from the cage, pacing out the campsite. "What you set on doing with it?"

He thought the boy might have something clever in mind. One-eyed boy, you had to wonder what kind of trouble he found. Choke the guard with it, or pick the lock of his shackles. Could you pick a lock with string? When the boy said, "You ever play cat's cradle?" he had to keep down a laugh. The boy's hands darted twice through the loop, forming a crisscross. When he was a boy himself it had brought to mind the legs of an ironing board. The sight of the shape now filled his lungs. He had taught Elma to play the game, their hands swooping in and out of each other's like birds.

He couldn't help himself. He found his fingers remembered what to do, pinching the string, ducking under, coming up for air. It was hard enough to do with his hands cuffed, harder still with fingers stiff from the cold. The white boy's wrists hung heavy. Their fingers did a clumsy dance. But the white boy laughed an approving laugh. "Thas right," he muttered. "Now you on the trolley!"

It was foolish, playing with the boy hanging down from his bunk like that. Crow spotted them from a good distance. He climbed the steps to the cage and unlocked the hatch.

"What you boys busy with?" He came up the aisle. "Hand it over, Sterling."

Sterling did.

"You boys doing child's play? Y'all need some men's work?"

When the trucks arrived just before noon, Mr. Crow handed him and the white boy a pair of shovels and walked them out to the woods with a ball and chain. "Privy, boys. Two-seater. Then y'all Smiths can do your child's play together in the shitter. Blacksmith and white-smith." Crow laughed. "How you like that?"

Crow wasn't half the devil the warden was. He was dark as a

crow, with oily black hair he slicked back under his hat and an oily black mustache. He liked to say he was half Cherokee, half Mexican, and half American. He liked to tease the men, called them women's names, Sissy and Mother and Sally. He joined them for hymns and prayers on the Sundays the preacher visited the county camp. Sterling had been on his crew once before, on this road, just after Elma's babies were born—the Gemini twins, folks called them—and Crow had let him pick a handful of blue hound's tongue from the ditch they were digging and leave it in the mailbox. Sterling had not laid eyes on the girls then, and he wondered if they'd ever reached Elma. He wondered if the Buffalo nickels he'd sent to that box had ever reached Nancy. He'd stolen them from a white boy, the son of the overseer at the turpentine farm, shook them right out of the pockets of his dungarees drying on the line. Figured his debt to Georgia was steep enough anyhow, too steep to pay off.

———————

"Sterling Smith," said the one-eyed white boy. "You got people in these parts?"

They were meant to dig a hole six feet deep and three across, big as a grave, and they weren't but six inches in. The clay was cold, packed solid. Digging it was like digging concrete. To the boy's left, Sterling said, "Ain't got no more people."

"They dead?"

"All about."

The boy asked Sterling how he ended up on the chain gang. Sterling started to tell him, thinking out a way to answer without answering. The first time, on the train, there was nothing to be done. But the second time, a year ago—he'd been let off the gang with his eight-dollar clothes, and he'd walked to Young's, where he stood under the leaky tin awning, rain coming down around him, no money in his pocket to go inside—would he have gone inside, if he'd had the money?—smoking his last earthly cigarette. Standing there.

Free. Why stand there frozen, getting rained on? Why didn't he walk straight to the farm, to his daughter? He remembered the stroke of her little fingers in his mustache. Her little heart pumping like a bull-frog in her chest as she slept against his. And yet all night he'd talked himself into and out of it, running through the scenarios. It was too late, he told himself. Ketty was already gone. Nancy was already grown. What if Nancy was gone too, and it was just Juke left there? What if he'd have to leave again, tail between his legs? He'd finally fallen asleep in the ditch along the railroad tracks, under a blanket of a rusty piece of sheet metal, and at dawn he'd woken, relieved, to the approaching clip of the peace officer's horse.

"What about me?" the white boy cut in.

"What about you?"

"You want to know bout how come I end up here?"

He had worked beside white men who liked to talk. Another white man might guess they'd had no tongues to speak of, but put them next to a Negro, their tongues went loose, like their aim was to fill you up with words.

"Reckon I got time to listen."

"Held up the cotton bank in Meredith." They'd had a good rhythm worked out, swinging their shovels so they wouldn't knock each other over, but now the boy stopped swinging and rested his chin on the handle of his shovel, waiting for Sterling's response.

"Boy, you got to warn a fellow."

"Watch your mouth. Ain't no boy."

"What you hold up the bank with? A slingshot?"

"Rifle. Savage 99. Woulda used it too, if it ain't get choked up."

"You make out with any money?"

"Oh, yeah. Whole hill a money." The boy started digging again. Sterling followed. "Guard shot at my truck, but I made out anyhow. That's how come my eye got shot."

"Your eye got shot out?"

"Oh, yeah. Clean out."

"Huh. What'd you do with the money?"

"Buried it."

"Where?"

"Fool, think I'm a tell you that?"

Sterling dug. Where the shovel touched his hands, his skin burned with cold. He'd have traded his breakfast for a pair of gloves.

"But what if I told you I ain't need to hold up no bank?"

"What you rob it for, then?"

"For fun, nigger. Christ almighty, ain't niggers ever have no fun?"

Sterling's hands tensed around the shovel.

"Well, I reckon I was feeling risky. Ain't you ever feel like finding trouble? Just to see how hot it is?"

"I ain't got to look for no trouble. It find me itself."

"Ain't the worst I done," said the boy. "Nor the most fun."

From the woods twenty yards off, Lloyd Crow eyed them sideways. Sterling kept his own eyes on the dirt. He would lower himself into the ground, inch by inch. If he ignored the boy, maybe he would stop talking.

"You know the Wilson farm? The original Wilson farm, back at the crossroads?"

Now Sterling lifted his eyes. Could he see it on him? Did the white boy know him?

"We done passed it this morning. The one with the gourd tree you can see from the road?"

"I reckon," Sterling said, his voice hoarse.

"That's the place where them Gemini twins were born. You know the Gemini twins?"

Sterling shook his head, though he did.

"Lordy, lordy. The Gemini twins. They was born to the white whore lives there. Darky baby and a white one. Reckon we seen em when we drove past."

"Thas some mouth you got on you, son. Talking bout a lady that way."

"If she was a lady I'd say so."

"I heard . . . well . . ." Sterling had heard about the mob killing but had not known it had taken place on the farm. He'd thought the man had been killed in the mill village. "I heard there was—"

"Heard she was nigger-raped?" The white boy was smiling. "You right about that. Heard that cropper Juke Jesup dragged the nigger all over the county. You know who Juke Jesup is, don't you?"

Sterling said nothing.

"Oh, he's just about the lowliest nigger lover in Cotton County. Runs a blind tiger. Ain't you heard of Cotton Gin? That's Juke Jesup's Cotton Gin. Lowliest nigger lover. Nigger killer too. Raised up a nigger girl on his farm like his own. You reckon they all living fine now? On that farm? Going on like the Lord don't have a care for it, them niggers and crackers living unnatural under the same roof?"

Sterling tried to keep quiet, but his tongue got loose. He said, "I heard of that kind before. 'Nigger lover.' Spect I ain't never met one. Spect this fellow ain't gone be the first neither."

The boy laughed. "You fixing on making his acquaintance?"

"Don't suspect I'll have the chance. Not unless he ends up on this here road gang. Sound like that's where he belong."

"Spect it is, spect it is." The boy's shovel slipped, and he swore. He started to sing a little song. It was a song they sang on the road, one he must have picked up in his two weeks digging ditches. When Sterling didn't join him, he said, "I ain't sore at you. For losing my cotton string. I got more where that come from. I got enough cotton to last me my lifetime. Fact, my daddy was called String."

String. Sterling did know that name. Rich white boy. His landlord's son.

The boy stopped digging again, and now Sterling followed his shovel over to the ground, landing on his knees, his weight thrown off.

"You got to give a warning, son. You want Crow to find us on the ground?" He rose to his feet. "You reckon that's a way to find some fun?"

"What if I told you my people own most a this county? All the cotton? This dirt we digging?"

The boy shook a shovelful over Sterling's shoes. It caught in his shackle. Sterling kicked it back best he could in his chains. They were good shoes, given to him by the county on his last release. Those they had let him keep.

"Don't do that again, son. I like to knock you over with this here shovel."

The boy laughed. "That right? You aim to end up on the rack again?"

"It'd be worth it, just to knock that smile off your face."

"You ain't know who you talking to, nigger."

"I don't have a care for who your people is. In here you digging a privy."

"What if I told you my name weren't no John Smith?"

Sterling tried the name in his mouth. "John Smith. I heard that name somewheres."

The white boy laughed. "My the only man in this camp ever get any schooling?"

"That the name you give the warden?" Sterling said. "You mean your name ain't even Smith?"

The white boy did a little dance, holding the shovel in the dirt for balance, the chains around his ankles jumping, nearly pulling down Sterling with the weight. For the first time Sterling caught clear sight of the boy's boots. They were covered in dirt, but they were fine. Looked like they were made of crocodile hide.

"How bout George Frederick Wilson the Third?" said the boy. "You heard that name somewheres?"

———

Sterling Smith had dug the ditch down the Twelve-Mile Straight and he had dug the ditch down the road he had grown up on. It was String Wilson Road now, but it had no name but a number when he lived there with his mother and father and two brothers in a shack owned by George Wilson. They worked sixty good acres of peanuts and cotton and corn. They had a dog named Spot and a horse named Gilda Gray. They had piney woods to hunt in. They had a log cabin church an hour's walk up the road. His parents were churchgoing people, and Sterling was the one who gave them grief. When he came home drunk, or with a black eye, or talked back, or was too rough with a brother, or too lazy in the field, his parents didn't raise a hand to him. Instead they both dropped to their knees—never one, always both, as though they had four legs and one heart for the Lord—and prayed. When he was small, they made him drop to his knees too. And he would. He would pray. When he grew older, and wandered farther and farther from the farm, to town, to the juke joint, he stopped dropping to his knees. He closed his eyes and sat down to a sandwich his mother had made, or he walked back out the door he'd come through. He was daring one of them to raise a hand. Sometimes he thought by the looks they exchanged that they were daring each other, that neither one of them wanted to be the first. His brothers got bolder, daring each other to be as daring as Sterling, practicing their black eyes on each other. One night the two brothers, rough-housing, knocked the kerosene lamp into the fireplace and burned the house down, his mother and father and the two brothers in it. At eighteen, Sterling was the oldest. He'd been getting shinnied up at Young's, and by the time he'd returned to the farm, he was drunk enough to wonder where the house had been put. He didn't have another drink after that.

George Wilson had built a new shack for a new cropper family, and found work for Sterling at the crossroads farm down the road. "Old man's got him but one son. They can use all the help they can get." The old man was hard and sad and left him alone, had no harsh nor kind words for him. The son was the same age as String and the same age as Sterling. He was the white boy who liked to dance with the best girls at Young's, went by the name of Juke. Sterling had seen him there across the room. When he had enough liquor in him, he'd cast a look of disapproval or maybe even of disgust across the women's glistening, sweet-smelling heads, but Juke had not returned the look, had not even caught it, had buried his face in a girl's neck. After he stopped going to Young's and started at the farm, Sterling tried to give the white boy the same look across the yard they now shared, but still the white boy didn't return it, didn't even catch it. He gave Sterling the instructions his father had given him, gave him a pat on his back, said, "Lord keep the sun low and the sweat cool," and set off into the north field, Sterling into the west.

For a year Sterling had the shack to himself. He woke early every Sunday to walk the three miles up the road to the log cabin church, where he dropped to his knees and prayed. It was there he met a girl in a blue dress. He asked her if could he see her home safe, and she said yes. She was the kind of girl, he thought, his parents would want for him, a girl who would take care of him now that there was no one else. She had never set foot in Young's joint; she delivered babies on the Young tobacco farm. She was an orphan herself, her father long gone, her mother dead, and together they were no longer alone. They were married in that church, about the same time Juke Jesup married his bride in theirs. For a wedding gift George Wilson gave the men a pair of sweetheart hogs. Sterling's was called Bob and Juke's was called Honey. Bob they slaughtered that winter, and in the spring Honey had a litter and Jessa and Juke readied themselves to have a baby too.

Ketty had a wide waist and a full chest and long, strong legs: she wasn't plump so much as sturdy. Sterling thought a man should have a woman the wind couldn't blow over. Her body softened when she carried Nancy, and stayed soft afterward. "You my buttermilk biscuit," Sterling would say, both hands on her broad backside, inhaling the sweet almond oil in her hair. Some mornings he smoothed a little of the oil in his mustache, just so he could keep her smell under his nose all day. When he was walking rows in the field, he'd spot her churning on the porch, or carrying a basket of tomatoes from the garden, her hips flared out on either side of her apron, and the sight of her would keep him plowing ahead, one foot in front of the other, the thought of her weight on top of him, pressing him to the mattress. At the end of the day there was supper and there was his pipe and there was Ketty.

He could feel her weight still. When he tried to now, lying awake in the new camp, he could conjure every button on her blue dress.

The tents had gone up quickly. His ankles were still chained and under the thin cotton blanket he could find little warmth. In the distance, the coyotes howled at the boars and the hounds howled at both of them. The fire Lloyd Crow stoked outside the tent was no more than the cruel promise of heat, and so he slept in his cap and his boots as the other men did, and that was the worst insult, not the fact that he had no gloves or coat but the fact that he couldn't take off his shoes after a long day of work. When he was a boy, he and his brothers had gone barefoot most years. His mother had wrapped newspaper around their feet in the winter, but he didn't remember his feet getting cold; he remembered the hot water bottle she slipped under the blanket, his feet and his brothers' feet punting it around in the night. And he remembered summer, chasing his brothers barefoot in the yard, the wiregrass smooth, the white clay sun warmed, his feet tough as hides.

Now at least in the camp there was God's breath blowing through the night, the same air his daughter now breathed not six miles down the Straight. Was she awake now? Where did she sleep? He wondered if the white boy was right, if she had been raised in the house by Juke. Of all the scenarios he had conceived after he'd learned of Ketty's death—that she would be sent back to the tobacco plantation, that she might find work as a house girl in town—he had not bet on Nancy continuing on at the farm, and he was reminded of all the years he had missed, the life, the whole life, that she must have formed in his absence. He wondered if his child remembered him, and if she didn't remember him, if she'd been told of him, and if she'd been told of him, what she'd been told. What would he say for himself if he could, knowing she might be able to say nothing in return?

He wondered too, and realized he'd been wondering it for some time, since he'd seen her there on the porch wearing Ketty's face, whether the baby on her hip was her own, and he turned his mind from the thought and from the one that followed.

Ketty had not wanted a child. She had not expected to live long, the women in her family all dead by forty. Her own mother had been born on the same day as a mule on the tobacco farm, and they'd been given the same name, Ruby. The mule had outlived the woman. Why bring a child into a world like that? Where a woman couldn't hope to live as long as the mule in the barn?

Sterling believed the Lord didn't intend to keep two married folks without a child. He did all he could to give her a baby, but she had her woman's ways. She knew the times she was ripe, and those were the times she was good at keeping away from him. Some nights she slept on the floor or the porch just to keep her distance. She said it was because it was hot, or cold, or because she was expecting to be called to a delivery and didn't want to wake him. But Sterling worried her love for him was waning. The blood began to warm in his heart, down his arms, between his legs. At night he let his seed go in the sheet, but it didn't ease the burning in his veins.

Then old man Jesup went to walk with the Lord and Jessa followed right behind him. He was a mean old man and Sterling had not mourned him. But Ketty had loved Jessa. They'd come to the farm around the same time, two girls who'd emerged dazed from childhood to find themselves wives on the fog-draped, dead-end road with its strange scattering of shacks, the nighttime buzz of cricket frogs that was either miraculous or murderous, depending on the minute. They seemed to prefer the company of the other—in the kitchen in the big house, brushing the other's hair on the porch—to the company of their husbands, who smelled like mules, who after a long day planting or picking spoke mostly through grunts, who grunted at the dinner table as they did in their beds, grunting grunting over them. Sterling could only guess what the women talked about. He was sure they laughed at them behind their backs. Maybe they aped them. One night while Sterling was grunting over Ketty she had to keep herself from giggling, and when Sterling had asked her what she was laughing at she said, "Nothing," like she was trying not to remember. He hadn't been able to carry on, had pulled on his pants and taken his corncob pipe out to the porch and cursed her.

He grieved for Bob, who'd been turned to pork before Honey even went to litter. And Honey went on happily lolling in the mud. Bob was needed no more.

When Jessa died, Ketty went quiet. She went into the big house to take care of Jessa's baby. She stayed there for months, until the baby was big enough to sleep well enough through the night without a bottle. Elma reminded Sterling of a baby fox, with a tuft of fox-colored fur on her head and cunning fox eyes and a cry like a fox's, high and full of panic. He didn't cotton to that baby.

"Look too much like her daddy," he told Ketty. Juke Jesup had lost his wife but he had a child of his own and now he had Ketty too, Ketty carrying buckets of warm milk to the house, Ketty washing diapers in the creek.

Ketty said Jessa would want her to be a mother to the baby. "If I had milk in my breasts, I'd feed her myself," she said.

And Sterling had said, "Got to have a baby to have milk. And got to sleep in my bed to have a baby."

After that, she slept in the big house for a week. Said Elma had the croup, though all Sterling could hear was that fox cry in the middle of the night. He couldn't sleep. His mind got to where he thought maybe it was a real fox, getting into the chickens. He rose from his bed and took his shotgun and shot out into the dark, meaning to scare the fox away, but he shot a chicken instead, and it was so full of buck all they could eat from it was a wing. It was a mother, its nest full of eggs gone cold. Juke fed the eggs to Honey and her pigs. He took Sterling's shotgun and Sterling said, "Take it. Took everything else."

It had been his father's gun. A Winchester twelve gauge, one of the few things to survive the house fire. Sterling and his brothers had shot squirrels with it and possums.

For a while Sterling was bad off, so down he thought he might die. It was the cows' milk, he thought; it had gone blinky. For a week he stopped drinking the milk, stopped eating at all; he couldn't stand to be holed up in the privy with Juke Jesup, who was sick too. They sat side by side, letting the sickness pass through them, mumbling to themselves, blaming Ketty. "She left that milk out too long in the barn," they said. "Her head's empty," they said.

When finally the Lord saw to it to plant a seed in Ketty's belly, Sterling's sickness eased. He was so relieved to be alive that for a while he was happy. He thought she might be his alone again. Stop messing with the white folks in the big house. Elma was a girl of four by then, no need for bottles or diapers, though she followed Ketty like a puppy, running along behind her in the yard. Ketty would send her out to the men with the water jug. Slowly Sterling did cotton to her, took to bouncing her on his knee, singing this is the way the ladies ride, holding on to the collar of her dress while she giggled. She called him Uncle Sterling.

That was when Ketty started eating dirt. At first it was just a little here and there, which she'd snatch up when she went down to the creek and nibble from her palm like a handful of nuts. She said it was a thing pregnant women were known to do. Her mother had done it and her mother before her. It helped with the nausea and it helped with the cravings. But then it seemed the dirt became a craving of its own. She still chewed tobacco leaves when she could, but since she'd left the tobacco farm, it wasn't so easy to get her hands on. The dirt was everywhere, and it was free. She would come back from the creek with an old coffee tin filled to the brim with white clay. "That ain't natural," Sterling had worried, and Ketty said, "What's more natural than God's own earth?" She hid the tin under a loose floorboard. Sterling could hear the board squeak in the night, and then her munching like a mouse beside him.

When the baby was ready to be born, Ketty delivered it herself, like a momma mule dropping a foal in the barn. The baby was tongue-tied. "Ain't latching right," Ketty said. When Nancy was but three days old, Ketty went to her satchel and took out her scalpel and ran it over the flame on the stove. Sterling snatched the baby from the bed, thinking Ketty meant to harm her. It was the first time he'd seen such a look in her eye. "I'm just fixing to loosen it," she said, and with the same quiet resolve with which she'd carried Elma to the barn to suckle from the cow's teat—"She got to eat, don't she?"—she slipped the scalpel under the baby's tongue and gave it a nick. "Just a nick," Ketty said, "for your own good," and the baby howled and her mouth dribbled blood but she clamped it down on Ketty's breast and she stopped howling and she ate.

It scared him, was the truth. Ketty's way. She knew more about the ways of the body than he could ever hope to know.

That was what put the thought in her mind, he reckoned. What if she just loosened it a bit more? And a bit more? She knew how to wield a scalpel, how to carve up women when they needed it. "She don't need that tongue," she'd said. "What good's it gone do her?" The baby wouldn't wean, nursed around the clock, and Ketty wasn't like other mothers, she had work to do, she had calls to go on, she couldn't have the child stuck to her all the livelong day. "She gone suck me dry. I got nothing else for her." Sterling had said hush, don't talk crazy. He told her all the dirt she ate was making her mind feeble. But their daughter had just turned a year old when Sterling came upon them in the sorghum cane, Ketty kneeling under the gourd tree, knocking the earth with a shovel. It was spring. The baby was hanging on her back in its sling, her eyes swollen with tears, a poultice tied behind her head and across her mouth like a gag. Around the bloody rag her cries were like little goat mews, the kind of cries a baby makes when it's cried out. "That's geranium oil it's soaked in," Ketty said, as though that explained it. "It's done. I done buried it. She'll be all right now. I gave her something to dull her head. She'll be better off without it."

Sterling had wrenched the shovel from her hands. He might have struck her with it if the baby hadn't been on her back. He wrenched the baby from her sling and lifted the rag from her mouth and cursed her mother. He went to the icebox on the porch and chipped off a diamond of ice and fed it to her, but with no tongue, the baby couldn't get her mouth around it. It dripped down her chin. Ketty stayed out in the field until dark.

"Crazy woman," said Juke, looking on. "Y'all both lost your sense. Y'all both belong in Milledgeville."

Sterling didn't know where to put his rage. He was embarrassed. The white man was standing over him, and Sterling held his mutilated child. When Ketty came back to the shack, the baby finally asleep in her cradle, he beat her to the floor. He'd never done such a thing before. She looked ready for it, unsurprised. He closed his eyes and saw his parents dropping to their knees, his unsurprised parents, dropping down to the floor with Ketty.

Next day Juke saw the mark on her jaw and said, "Fool, you ain't need to raise a hand to no nigger gal. Don't you know?" He laughed and shook his head. "They already come into the world bruise colored."

EIGHTEEN

THE FIRST LETTER FROM OLIVER RAWLS ARRIVED ON THE FIRST of December, delivered not by the boy on his bicycle but by Mr. Horace, the postman, in his mail truck. It was not sent through Dr. Manford Rawls, and it did not contain Dr. Manford Rawls's name; it did not contain Juke's name or Nan's name, and other than "Dear Miss Jesup"—now she was *Miss*—it did not contain Elma's name. If you'd gotten your hands on the letter first and steamed it open, if you had the means to read it, you would not know that Dr. Rawls had carried Elma and Nan to Atlanta just before Thanksgiving; he had not. Nan had not nursed Wilson in front of the doctors' eyes, and Elma had not spilled the truth, like Nan's milk, that he was the child of Nan and of her father, that was why no one must know, because what would become of them? She had not cried. She had not pleaded for their confidence. The doctors had not repaired to the hall, had not from the other side of the door argued in hushed voices, the father objecting, the son reasoning, had not returned to the room, the father gruff, the son wearing the kind of bright smile parents wear for their children in difficult circumstances. Dr. Rawls had not gone in search of a sandwich and a whiskey, his first drink in a dozen years, leaving them all to eat from their lunch basket in the basement, and had not said, upon dropping them back at the farm that evening, long past dark, "I'm too old a man to keep women's secrets," as though Elma and Nan were but schoolgirls spreading gossip in church.

What Oliver Rawls's letter contained was the kind of chatter a cousin might put in a letter to another cousin. News from the city, his work, the weather, his father's health, which had suddenly declined. He wrote about his own brothers and sisters, who had children of their own, and he wrote about those children, his nieces and nephews. Elma nearly fell asleep reading their names, Elizabeth Jane and Jane Elizabeth and baby Camilla Josephine Jane, but she wrote back to say how darling they must be, and he how doting. The letters came one after the other, so fast she could barely reply to one before another arrived, but she did, regular as thunder following lightning, because she felt she owed it to him. In keeping him talking, she felt, she might keep him quiet. His letters were long, five and six and seven pages, all typed on the same onionskin paper, and the ink sometimes rubbed off on Elma's fingers and wouldn't wash. She told her father it was from the newspaper, and hid the letters inside her pillowcase. All morning she waited for the mail truck, her ears standing up straight when she heard any sound from the road. Often it was just the school bus, or the road scraper, or traffic to the crossroads store. One morning it was a wagon from the county camp carrying prisoners out to the pines. With the cold weather, the visits to the twins had quieted, and Elma welcomed the peace, but she did not welcome Oliver's letters. They were a new hazard to head off, another secret she had not asked to keep. She wrapped herself in her mother's shawl, ready, and when the mail truck came she walked fast, but not so fast as to catch her father's attention, down the driveway and over the plank bridge to the mailbox, and when she retrieved one letter from Oliver, she slipped her letter to him into the box.

One morning she was doing this with Winna Jean bundled on her hip just as a car came up the road. Elma slipped the letter into her apron pocket. It was a great, pearl-colored Buick with ivory-colored tires, the spare tire hiked up over the left wheel well like an extra eyeball. It was a fine car, finer than any Elma had seen on the dirt Straight, but she wasn't particular about the way those tires stared at her. The car slowed when it approached the mailbox, and Elma could see that it was a colored boy driving it. Through the window behind him, she saw a woman sitting in the backseat, face hanging close to the window, eyeglasses like two silver dollars and pearls tight enough to choke her. Her hat was blood colored, with a brim a bit wider than the fitted hats younger women wore, topped on one side with ivy leaves and small, tightfisted, blood-colored roses and holly berries frosted with what looked like sugar or snow. The woman's eyes took stock of Elma, then the baby in her arms. Elma's eyes saw all of this like a camera, though it wasn't until the woman had turned her head sharply from the window and the car had resumed its regular speed west down the road that the picture developed and she realized who the woman had been.

To Winna, she said, "That there was your great-granny."

Elma was cold in the wake of the car, as though it had left behind a tailwind. She held Winna closer.

"Can't say what business carried her out here."

Elma remembered something Ketty had said once about a lady they'd passed in town. Elma had understood it was not a compliment. She said it now to Winna. "That was a hat fine enough to build a nest in."

———————

But in fact Parthenia Wilson did have business west of town, west of the crossroads, as far west as one could travel on the Twelve-Mile Straight. She asked the driver, whose name was Frank, to park at the edge of the road behind a stand of pines, where the Buick would be out of the men's sight but they would be in hers, and sent him to fetch Mr. Crow. While she waited she watched the men work their shovels and saws, clearing the land. Were it warmer, she thought, they might take off their shirts and the sun would shine on their broad backs as on the backs of the fishes in the creek. She had known this creek and the fishes in it once. She had washed the laundry in it. She had bathed her young body in it. The men were as young as she had been when she had bathed in the creek.

Mr. Crow came and she lowered her window and said the work was coming along fine, wasn't it? (For though it was the state paving the road, her husband had matched Georgia's contribution dollar for dollar, and had driven the Buick up to Macon himself, the trunk full of Cotton Gin, for the lucky men who had won the road contract, though he told her he was going to play golf.)

Most certainly it was, Mr. Crow said.

What they needed in that clearing was a garden, she said. Just an acre. Corn, tomatoes, peppers, some wildflowers. Even a prisoner deserved God's bounty.

She looked beyond and around him as she spoke, looking at the backs of each of the men, looking at their faces.

A memory rose up in the woods then. It was something she hadn't thought of in years: little John Jesup with his father's sickle, cutting down the corn in her garden. She had watched from the window. She had let him go, thinking he needed it, thinking everyone deserved God's bounty. Now she saw that was how it had started: he had taken and taken from their family, and he had gone and taken her grandson too.

Mr. Crow would take it under advisement. Mrs. Wilson would report to her husband that it was all coming along fine. Her colored girl, whose name was Mag, had baked four blackberry pies for the men, for even a prisoner deserved God's bounty. The driver unloaded the tray from the car. Mrs. Wilson reminded Mr. Crow that they were God's children, all of them. They were mothers' children too. They had mothers and grandmothers, every one of them.

"How many are there, Mr. Crow?"

"Ma'am?" He stood with the tray of pies, which weighed some.

"How many prisoners?"

"A dozen," he said. "They'll be plenty to go round."

"I count ten," she said.

Mr. Crow looked over his shoulder. "They's two digging latrines in the woods," he said.

"You make sure they each get some of that pie, then," she said, adjusting her hat.

Parthenia Wilson had not walked into the creek on the day the twins were baptized, and she did not catch the influenza that took up residence in the lungs of half the population of Florence. Manford Rawls too had chosen to stay on the shore, but he returned from Atlanta to find a line of patients out his office door and down Main Street. He treated them for two days straight, and on the third day, which was Thanksgiving, he woke with a fever, and after breakfast he returned to bed. He did not tell his wife that he believed it to be the whiskey that still sat with him funny, nor the weight of the girls' secret. He said instead what he did not believe, which was that his patients had succeeded at last in giving him the flu. He was not accustomed to being sick, or being cared for. He was not accustomed to lore, the tale his patients told him about the sickness brewing in that creek. But by the second day in bed, it was clear that the flu was what it was, and by the third day, his wife, Camilla, was in bed with him. With a shaky hand, Dr. Rawls wrote a letter to his youngest son, asking him to return home to take care of his patients. It was the least he could do, having not even returned home for Thanksgiving. Dr. Rawls did not say what else was in his mind, which was that, whichever way you looked at it, whether you believed the story or not, those girls, those twins, that family, Juke Jesup, they had brought the illness on him.

Oliver told this to Elma in his letters, told her of the request his father had made. He asked Elma her opinion. Should he come to Florence, the prodigal son returning to his father to beg for acceptance? Or should he stay in Atlanta, where he had important work to do, work his father didn't understand?

Where she wanted him was Atlanta, she thought, far away from home, where her secret was safe. But maybe her secret would be safer here in Florence, far away from any laboratory, where Oliver could keep an eye on Dr. Rawls. She remembered the gentle voice he had used to appease his father, the voice a man might use to calm a spooked horse. If he came back to Florence, she thought, she might see him again. She might like to see him. She gathered all the letters from her pillowcase and looked them over. Was he hiding something from her, or just from her father? She could see he was still being cautious that, should Juke get ahold of the letters, he'd see nothing but a city boy courting a country girl. And then it occurred to Elma that the letters might be just that. That he was asking her what their life together might look like.

She stood up from the bed of wrinkled letters. That a scientist at Emory, the son of the beloved local doctor, might fancy her—the idea struck in Elma a dread and distrust. It had been beyond her reckoning to consider such a man a suitor. She had been so relieved, so grateful for his confidence, that she had carried on their correspondence with all the trust their secret called for. She'd been blind. She saw now that he must be after her for all the reasons he'd kept out of the letters, for business, for research, for the complicated kind of gain that was familiar to men in suits in cities, to men like Manford Rawls and Q. L. Boothby and George Wilson, but not to her.

She sat up and took the ledger in her lap and wrote back to him, *You can write free and honest to me. My father can neither read nor write. You can call him the fool he is and you can call me white trash if you please. Write me please what is in your heart for I won't be taken for the fool you believe me to be.* She spit on the seal of the envelope and the next morning she mailed it.

"We won't be taken for no fools," she said to Nan. In answer, Nan handed Wilson to her. She was carrying Ketty's satchel and gathering her coat around her shoulders. She had been working more often since Dr. Rawls had taken ill. Two nights before she had delivered two babies within four hours, and they were both named Young, a colored one and a white.

The next morning, the men took the twenty-two out to kill the pigs. Elma paid little attention to the pigs; she did not love them; she did not name them; they were like fat, dirty-faced neighbor children she tripped over in the yard as she threw them the scraps. She didn't like to love a creature she loved to eat so much.

So when Juke and Jim went out to do the butchering, Elma and Nan and Sara stayed in, sitting down in the front room to work on an old quilt. Ketty had started it with the two girls years before, piecing together bits of tablecloth and feed sacks and the dresses they'd outgrown, but she had little patience for sewing. She'd used her needle to sew up women's wounds, to keep them alive, and, when necessary, to sew up the holes that ate through the family's clothes. What little time she had on the farm, when she wasn't paying visits, she did not care to devote to sewing squares into quilts. But Elma's hands were restless, empty of letters, and Sara had bolts of fabric that she said wanted quilting. Elma said, "I do feel like putting my fingers on something pretty." She thought she might tell Sara about her correspondence with the doctor, ask for her advice, though she couldn't think how to tell it without telling all of it.

She took the half-finished quilt from the cotton basket under her bed and shook the dust from it over the porch railing. Then the three of them gathered in kitchen chairs around the woodstove and laid the quilt over their knees. Nan had the idea to put the twins in the emptied basket, and found that they could both fit in it propped up on a bed of cotton batting. They liked to sit in it under the canopy of the quilt, where the warmth of the woodstove was trapped, and when the women fluttered the quilt like a flag over their heads, the babies saw the firelight flashing through the tissues of colored squares and laughed, and the women laughed. They studied the old squares and Elma said, "Remember this one, Nan? I think it's from an old apron of your momma's." And, "This one's from the hem of that little ging-ham dress we wore. I wish we had that dress to put on Winna."

Sara said, "How about if I told you this could be a baby blanket."

"Good Heaven!" Elma fumbled her needle. "Are you fixing to have a baby?"

Sara laughed. "I told you I might have a surprise come Christmas. I think I must have been pregnant already when I told you that."

"Oh, Sara, that's grand!" Elma put a hand on Sara's hands and a hand on Nan's. "Nan! You hear that?"

Nan had heard and was smiling her congratulations.

"You hear that, you two?" Elma peeked under the quilt at the twins. "You're gone have you a playmate. Come summer, I reckon?"

"July, I'd say. If I'm counting right."

"Nan can tell you. Once you start to show, Nan can measure you with her tape." Nan nodded agreeably. "She can do all your care and deliver the baby too. She's the best midwife you could ask for."

Sara went back to sewing her square. It was lemon yellow and crawling with green leaves, and against the faded, flax-colored square beside it, it was bright as summer.

"You'll be here," Elma said, "won't you? In the summer?"

Sara didn't look up. "I can't say for certain."

"Does Jim want to stay?"

Sara sighed dismissively. "If Jim had his say, he'd live in that shack forever."

"He wants y'all to raise the baby here on the farm?"

"He doesn't know about no baby."

"Sara! Ain't you gone tell him?"

"I plan on it. Wanted to tell you girls first. That's not all I want to tell you." She rushed on, lowering her voice. "I don't want to be the one to tell you, but I don't want to be the one not to tell you."

Nan was sewing with her corner of the quilt held close to her face and now she lifted her eyes to Sara.

"You girls got to know I never meant to keep nothing from you. I didn't know at first why we came to the farm. You got to know I thought we ended up here same as any place."

Elma gripped her needle. "Jim's in with my daddy, ain't he. He's been running for him all along."

Sara shook her head sadly. "No. No, he ain't in with your daddy. Your daddy thinks he is. But it's George Wilson he's in with. He's in deep."

Elma listened, the quilt moving under them like a patch of ocean, while Sara told her what she'd come to the big house to tell her, bearing bolts of fabric, as though it were a regular sunny morning: that Mr. Wilson had put Jim and Sara on the farm, that he put them there to keep an eye on Juke, and to learn about the still, and to take over the business after Mr. Wilson took Juke off the farm. "He said any fool can plant cotton. It's the gin he cares about. He needs someone to run the still."

Elma's sewing sat in her lap. She felt as though it were her head the quilt was falling over. The room felt close and dark and full of wood smoke. She saw Nan sewing with her eyes wide. She thought Nan too was trying to imagine the farm without Juke on it. Just the three women and three babies, and Jim to do the man's things. "But where's he gone put him? My daddy?"

Sara shrugged apologetically. "It's not just your daddy he's running off."

She looked from Elma to Nan and back.

Elma tore the needle and thread from her square and stuffed them into her apron pocket and stood up. From under the quilt, she slid the basket and lifted Winna out of it. "He's gone just run us all off, then, is he? I suppose you and Jim are set to move on into this house and replace us. You even got you a replacement baby on the way, with no darky blood!"

"Elma. You got to know I had no sights on this. I don't even want to stay. Jim says there was a man killed just before we came, and Juke was the one who did it, and George Wilson wants us to help prove it. I don't want no part in that."

"You don't know nothing about that! Not one thing! It was George Wilson's dog of a grandson who did it, just as bad as my daddy, and it's George Wilson's filthy tit you'll be living on! Have at it! You want to live under George Wilson's thumb? Have at it all you want."

"How am I to know who did it? You folks don't talk about nothing! Mr. Wilson wants us to spy on you, but you're closed up as a bunch of clams! I thought my folks in Buffalo was bad. You folks might as well all be mute."

"We got nothing to say to you," Elma said. She was transferring Winna from hip to hip. The baby's cheeks were hot from the fire and Elma herself felt feverish, the sweat cooling on her upper lip. She felt above all foolish, that she had allowed herself to be suckered by George Wilson, that in her apron pocket was a letter from Oliver Rawls and she had expected to show it to Sara and she had expected Sara to fawn over it as she had the first time, to say, "You're gonna marry a doctor, Elma! That's grand!"

Nan had stood up. She was holding Wilson on her hip as Elma held Winna, standing across from Sara as if to say that their sewing circle was over.

"Mr. Wilson said there's something unnatural going on in this house. I don't know what it is, but I'd say he's right."

"Gone be your house soon enough," Elma said, walking Sara to the door and opening it for her. "You're welcome to it. We'll leave it real clean for you."

Elma listened for Sara's steps across the hard winter earth between their houses, and the sound of the shack door. Behind her Nan was holding her needle between her lips and Wilson was playing with the thread hanging from it.

"Don't worry, honey," Elma said, turning to Nan. "We gone find another place. I got somewhere in mind."

––––––––––

The letters now were short, but they came with greater frequency, on some days more than one, as though he had dashed one off on the typewriter and then, after pacing around his room, thought of another sentence to say. What was in his heart, he wrote, was that he loved her, Elma Jesup, and that he cared not a wink that she was the daughter of a moonshiner and a monster and yes, a fool, that his father's opinion of her father was of no consequence to him, for his father was a fool of his own kind.

I haven't finished but eleven grades, she wrote. I am both a spinster and a whore.

What was in his heart was that he cared not a wink for what the hicks of Florence thought of her. He knew her for what she was, which was a woman of honor and sacrifice. He too wished to be a man of honor and sacrifice, and if she had him, he would mean to be. He knew those children to be what they were, which was not twins and not even siblings, and not two regular country bastards, but, taken together, something the opposite of bastards, something holy.

Did she know of the premature babies at Coney Island? People came from all over the world to see them. He had seen them himself, he wrote, on a trip to New York City as a boy. Tiny, tiny babies no bigger than a man's hand, weighing but two or three pounds. Used to be such small babies would live but a few hours, but now they were kept alive by a doctor ahead of his time, who could practice the miracle of medicine only by making the babies a sideshow. Today, incubators were coming into use in the hospitals in Atlanta, and did she know why? Because of that doctor. As a boy, Oliver had peered into one of those incubators and experienced such awe, such love and fear (for that was what awe was), that he had decided then and there that he would be a doctor, that he would devote his life's work to the creatures that folks might find unworthy of living, but which man, working with God (for that was what science was), had chosen to save.

Where would we live, Elma wanted to know. She imagined a house in Atlanta with scalloped roof shingles shaped like tulip petals. She didn't know where she got such a picture, but it was fixed in her mind.

As a young man, he wrote, he had believed the science he practiced superior in morality to the morality of his father's, for it was a science whose purpose above all else was to serve Negroes, to save the lives of Negroes, to know their blood.

The house would have an electric kitchen, she imagined, and two floors, and many rooms, a long hall with door after door, and they would fill the rooms with their children, hearty, legitimate, clean-faced children with auburn curls.

When he'd seen Nan spilling her milk, he wrote, when he'd seen her courage and the lie that the babies were meant to uphold with their lives, Oliver had understood clearly—though it seemed to Elma that he was figuring it out as he wrote—that the best way to serve Negroes was to work as his father did, as a family doctor, but a good one, one devoted with his whole being, not to serve Negroes by studying their blood between slides of glass but to touch their blood, their milk, the fluids that made them human animals the same as he, with his hands. His father at least had known that much.

Was his hair blackish brown? Or brownish black? She tried to put together the features of his face. She made his eyes narrow, the mouth playful.

Therefore, he wrote, it was his intention to return to Florence and assume his father's practice. They would live in his parents' house on Main Street, for they wouldn't be long in it. After Christmas Manford and Camilla Rawls would move to their daughter's house in Savannah, where Dr. Rawls had a colleague who specialized in influenza.

Still clutching the letter, Elma crossed her room and opened the curtains, as though she might be able to see the doctor's house from where she stood, past the place where the Twelve-Mile Straight became Main Street. It was the same road of a different name, but it might as well have been across the ocean. As a child, she had passed the doctor's house many times, white brick with pine green shutters, and two great ferns on the porch the size of peacocks.

For several days Elma moved about the big house thinking, *Soon I will not look out this window, soon I will not walk on this squeaky plank of floor,* seeing everything around her as if for the last time. She did this with Oliver's letter in her apron pocket, because if it was there, if she could feel its crinkle and weight when she leaned against the stove or knelt to milk the cows, she had a plan. She had Dr. Rawls's house and she had Oliver. She said his name aloud, feeling it in her mouth. *Oliver.* Was that the name she wanted to call to dinner for the rest of her life? To call out in their bed?

Perhaps there was still something else to be done. She imagined herself going to town, taking her daddy's truck, or catching a ride with Mr. Horace, the postman, and knocking again on the Wilsons' door in the mill village. She would demand to speak to Mr. Wilson. She would demand to know if it was true—if he intended to evict her family from the farm. She would say, "How does it feel, putting your own blood on the street?" She wanted to hear it from him straight. Or perhaps Mrs. Wilson would be the one to come to the door, and Elma would hold her eye, longer than she had held it at the baptism, or as she'd passed the house in her pearl-colored Buick. She could see something in that old woman's eyes, some weakness or window, the sense that she was unsettled, vulnerable, that she was looking for something. Perhaps she was simply looking for Freddie. Perhaps that was why she'd been driving down the Straight; perhaps she had her driver drive that Buick all over the county, looking. A woman who

could love a man like Freddie, a man who now seemed to Elma in-
capable of loving a dog or a baby or anyone but himself—surely she
could find some love for his innocent child. Elma would bring Winna
Jean, of course, who had her daddy's blue eyes, clear as if she'd stolen
them, and Mrs. Wilson would see the baby and turn her head, because seeing those blue eyes for too long would be too painful, and
she would retreat into the house and say to her husband, "George,
have some pity."

But she remembered the last time she'd stood on that porch,
pregnant and waiting for what felt like hours for her father to emerge
from the house, and she remembered what pity felt like.

She and her father had been on the same side of things then.
She felt a sick stab remembering it, the blind love she'd had for him,
solid and square, even in his angry impotence. He'd risked his own
pride going into that house, and now she saw it wasn't only pride
he'd lost—he'd lost the farm too. It had started that day, hadn't
it, before the babies were born and Genus was killed and Freddie
disappeared—it was the day her father had had the nerve to ask for
George Wilson's benevolence, to presume that George Wilson might
consider his grandchild and his daughter and himself a kind of kin.
That was the day George Wilson had decided to excise them, to carve
them off his land like a cancer. He might have done it already, if he'd
had another man ready to run the still.

It was her fault. If she hadn't gotten into that truck with Freddie
Wilson, if she hadn't been fool enough to say, "Only if you'll marry me."

After Sara had come to warn her, the day they'd taken out the
quilt, Elma had waited for her father to come in, ready to tell him,
ready to make a plan. She made a pie, because she was sorry for him
already, and because her hands wouldn't stop shaking, but her mind
went off and she burned it. She sat the burnt pie on the windowsill—it
was a pecan pie—and through the window she watched her father
and Jim come out of the smokehouse, talking in their low, friendly
way as they raised water from the well to wash the blood from their

hands and arms and faces. She did not want to tell him then, not with the traitor Jim there. She'd had quite enough scenes in that yard. She'd wait until supper. First there was meat to cook right away, a ham and a shoulder and some sowbelly, and then her father invited Jim and Sara to celebrate the first fresh pork of the year. She gave Sara the smallest serving of pork and the largest of the burnt pie and did not speak to her and did not look her in the eye, only said to Jim, "I hear congratulations are in order." She looked only at her own slice of pie as she listened to Sara, recovering, tell Jim the news, and then Jim yelped and stood up so fast his chair fell over behind him.

After supper Elma pled a headache and, after putting the babies to bed, went to bed herself, while Nan tended to the dishes and Juke and Sara and Jim put on their hats and coats and went out to the porch to pour some gin, because it was time to celebrate. Elma lay on her side in her bed (she did have a headache, she realized) and listened to the carefree notes of Jim's banjo as he played along to the songs on the gramophone. When the notes went high, the dogs barked, and there was laughter.

She would tell her father tomorrow, she thought.

It was the kind of merrymaking, she decided, that could only be followed by plentiful lovemaking. The music played on but already Elma was seeing Sara and Jim stumbling back to the shack, could already hear the squeal of their mattress. He adored her too much to be anything but glad. He would lift her dress. He would stroke her belly, tenderly, and then hungrily, her breasts. What would it be like to be adored like that?

Slowly, as though to ensure she might not notice herself what she was doing, she turned onto her back. She drew the flat, dull pillow from under her head and pressed it to her own belly. She squeezed her knees around it. She squeezed her eyes closed.

In her mind she drew Oliver's face above hers. His eyes were closed and his mouth was open. But he wouldn't stay put for long. Sara and Jim kept floating back into view. She pressed the pillow closer, against her pelvic bone, crossed her ankles around it. And then just when she had Oliver within her reach, just as she moved toward the shudder she'd brought on with the bar of cornmeal soap, there was Genus again, standing naked in the creek, and she sat up and flung the pillow to the floor.

———————

That Tuesday morning she was down at the creek washing laundry when she heard the mail truck. It was early. She leapt up so fast she pulled a muscle in her right calf, and if she hadn't had to hobble she might have made it to the mailbox first. As it happened, her father got there just before she did, and he had an envelope from Oliver Rawls in his hand as she limped over the plank bridge.

"Look like this one's for you," he said. He didn't hand it to her. "Who's it from?"

Elma thought of what lies she might tell. It was from a cousin from Carolina, or from Josie Byrd in nursing school. Instead she settled on a half truth, because she felt it was time to be brave, and because she had another truth to tell him, ready to distract him with. It was time to tell him that too. She said it was from a doctor in Atlanta who'd gone to school ahead of her. She said they'd been writing letters. She said he was thinking of coming to Florence to practice medicine. She did not yet dare say the last name of the doctor, who shared the name of another doctor, who distrusted Juke as much as Juke distrusted him and who was married to the WCTU.

"He sweet on you? That what you telling me?"

Elma said she supposed he was. She had expected him to tear the letter to pieces, but he did not raise his voice. He simply made the noises of possessiveness and doubt a father made at the news of a daughter's courtship. He asked her more questions, but did not ask if she was sweet on the doctor. What would she have answered if he had? Then, grumbling, he relented, granting a blessing Elma had not dared ask for. She stood with her weight on her left leg, her right calf throbbing. She had expected her father to shout. She'd expected him to keep her a barefoot old maid on the farm. But now she understood that he was, above all, proud. She recalled the ease with which he'd accepted the news of her pregnancy. *Long as he'll marry you.* That a doctor should want to marry her was not a surprise to him; it was the divine order of things; it was the easeful life to which he believed his family was entitled, and justice for the loss of her first blue-blood fiancé, who had spurned her. She saw now that she was as much her father's pawn to move about as he was George Wilson's. He did not know, Elma realized, his own poverty, his own wretchedness.

Satisfied, he turned back to the field. She did not tell him what Sara had told her. She was thrown off balance, her right leg buckling beneath her. Let him stand or fall on his own two feet. She would look after herself.

She had fallen for grander ideas before. She had sat with her head on Freddie Wilson's shoulder overlooking the mill village while he said, "This here's all fixing to be ours." Look what trouble that had gotten her. But she didn't see how this proposal, so small in comparison, could trouble her any more.

She moved toward the house, up the porch steps. That Oliver accepted her not in spite of the fact of her poverty, her wretchedness, but because of it—it astonished her. It occurred to her to be insulted, that she might be the object of his obscene fascination, like another race or species, like a two-pound baby.

But she remembered Ketty sitting on this porch, saying, *We are all children of God.* Oliver was a child of God, so was she. And she was poor and wretched, and Oliver loved her that way as God did, as her father didn't, and who was she to want a man who might love her for something other than her true nature?

She went into the kitchen and found the scissors, the ones she'd used to cut Nan's hair. Because it was something she'd read in a book, she tied a lock of her own hair in a ribbon and cut it with the scissors and put it in an envelope. In the accompanying letter, she wrote, *My Nan would come with us, of course, and both the children.*

That Christmas Eve, there was Dr. Rawls's beady black car in the driveway and a knock on the door. Winna Jean was at church with Juke, playing Baby Jesus in the Christmas pageant. Later the story of that night, the one that was told by the town, would center on the pageant, where Winna Jean, who'd been requested special by Reverend Quick, hollered all night, until Pauline Gentry, who played Mary, checked her diaper and announced to the congregation that Baby Jesus had wet Himself. Elma, who'd had enough of the congregation at the baptism, had chosen to stay home with Nan and Wilson. Nan was nursing him off the kitchen, and at first, Elma hissed at her to quit it, there was someone at the door. Then, seeing through the window that it was Oliver Rawls, she laughed with relief. This was the feeling she fell in love with: the exhilaration of being herself, of throwing open the door to their house and letting their secrets out into the night air. What did it matter what he saw?

On the porch he held a baby loblolly tree against his side in a clay pot and two striped stockings, lumpy with toys. He could barely keep hold of the gifts, and she saw that he meant them to hide his cane. He was wearing a gray serge suit and a black coat, and Elma wondered if he hadn't borrowed both from his father. She had the feeling that it had been a very long time since she'd seen him and that she'd seen him just a moment ago. Her fingers were still smudged with the words of his last letter. She'd hoped he was handsome, and that she hadn't only remembered him that way. He was handsome but he was short.

She let him stand there a minute. That he'd assumed the babies needed stockings, and that she'd not thought to make them herself—she might have sewn them instead of wasting time on that quilt—filled her with a quick and dirty shame. She thought to be ashamed too of the unpainted house and the threadbare rug under her feet, of the forks and spoons and knives setting in a tin can on the bare table behind her, rather than laying like sleeping ladies in a drawer. She remembered his father coming to give the babies their shots, how panicked she'd been, how desperate to put a cloth on the table. Then she remembered that Oliver knew what she was and that was why she wanted him, and that she'd intended to offer nothing else. She'd hoped he'd be coming, and she'd worn her daddy's overalls so he could see just how deep in the country she lived.

She took the tree and the stockings from him. "Is that you, Oliver," she said, "or is it Santa Claus?"

She was being silly as a tramp. It was because she was nervous. Why was she so nervous? Here he was standing in front of her. He opened his mouth, then closed it. He took off his hat. All those pages, and now he was struck dumb.

"Look a-here, we don't have much time," she said. She couldn't seem to stop her mouth; she was showing him the tramp she was. "My daddy'll be back in an hour."

Nan caught her look and took the twins to visit with Sara and Jim in the shack. Elma didn't bother making him a pot of coffee, didn't even let him into the front room. She turned him around and led him across the breezeway to her room and took the tree and the stockings and put them on the nightstand. The tree looked so pretty she wanted to string it right then with popcorn and ribbons. Her mother's quilt was on the bed. It was the bed where she had longed to reach out and touch a man's back, the bed where she had clasped her pillow between her legs, and her cheeks flushed with shame and the memory of her wanting. She wished now she had worn a dress and not the overalls, that she hadn't mistaken poverty for homeliness, but it was too late.

"You here to talk to me about cells?" she said to Oliver Rawls.

He shook his head. She took his hat and tossed it on the bed.

"You study on blood all day," she said. "I reckon you got some red blood yourself." She knew the red blood of men, knew it coursed through them whether they lived in a big city or small, whether they were in a hotel room or a truck bed, doctors or preachers or mill men, and she was telling him that she knew, that that was what he'd come for, and that her blood ran red too. Gently she helped him out of his coat. She had the feeling she was undressing a scarecrow.

"I want to marry you," he said. "I came to ask your father's blessing."

"My daddy ain't here, and even if he was, it ain't his blessing to give."

"Your blessing, then."

"You want my blessing?"

"I want to marry you. I want to ask you."

"You want to."

"I do. I am."

"Is that you asking?" She took off his glasses and lay them on the nightstand beside the tree.

"It is." From his breast pocket he removed a little silk coin purse, and from the coin purse he removed a thin gold ring set with a jade stone. He did not tell her that he had taken it from his mother's dressing table, that she was too sick to miss it.

He came close and, when she didn't object, slipped the ring on her ring finger. Without his glasses he looked like a young boy dressed up for church. "Is that you saying yes?" he said.

His dark hair fell over his forehead and his ears were red from the cold. She didn't like that he was shorter than she was, so she lowered herself to the bed. That was how she said yes. She unfastened each strap of her overalls and let the bib fall. Then she unbuttoned the top of her shirt, one, two, three, and her white breasts spilled out. They did not spill milk but stayed full and firm as he stood his cane against the bed and, as though they might do its work of supporting his unsteady weight, lowered his hands to take them. His hands were sticky with the sap from the tree. Later they would laugh at this, but now they were serious.

Genus was standing in the creek, and now Nan joined him—the dark shapes of their shoulders on the water, the sound their voices made together. Elma closed her eyes against them.

Oliver was leaning into her, losing balance. She felt his hands fall from her breasts to either side of her on the bed, where he braced himself. She helped him lower himself to the bed. He sat beside her, breathing heavily. From the pocket over his heart he removed his handkerchief and blotted his forehead with it.

"I'm afraid we don't have enough time," he said.

She tried to laugh. "We don't need much."

"We do. I do."

He caught his cane before it slid from the bed to the floor. It was the kind with a handle that looked like the business end of a golf putter, and resting between his knees now it looked like his manhood risen. She had not heard of men whose manhood couldn't rise, and so she assumed only that he was a gentleman. She sat there beside him, unwanted, with her shirt unbuttoned, her eyes closed again and her cheeks burning, until she thought to button it again. Then he put his hands on hers to stop her. He opened a fourth button and opened her shirt wider, as though drawing open two curtains to have a look at the day. With some trouble, he reached for the glasses on the nightstand. "To see you with," he said. He was blind as a mole rat without them.

NINETEEN

T HE PEOPLE OF COTTON COUNTY WATCHED THE PEARL-COLORED
Buick moving up and down the Twelve-Mile Straight, remark-
ing that it was pretty as a lady's mirror, pretty as a necklace.
They had seen the wagon of prisoners who had been delivered out
to the pines, but knew only that George Wilson was building something out there, that he had tamed every acre in the county and that,
aside from Rocky Bottom, the godforsaken pines were the last acres
left. Talk was that electricity would follow, that telephone poles would
connect Florence to whatever was out there. Some folks felt it was obscene. They didn't want the country littered with telephone poles. The
country should remain God's. They had a postman and newspaper
boys and in his auto and on their bikes they could get news out to the
country just as fast as it wanted to go. These were mostly the men.
The women were mostly of the opinion that electricity meant Frigi-
daires full of food, that telephones meant ringing up their mothers
and daughters in houses far away. The colored women in the Fourth
Ward had more mothers and daughters in houses far away, and more
sons too, in Washington and Baltimore and Harlem. Imagine a telephone line that went as far as that! They were of the opinion that

telephone lines were a fine thing. The white women in the country were of the opinion that if colored women in the Fourth Ward should be able to ring up their mothers and daughters and sons, the white women in the country should too. The people of Cotton County, men and women, white and black, agreed that it was coming and there was nothing to be done, no letters to be written, for George Wilson's will was as high and impregnable as God's. They waited for the men to come down the road as they waited for Jesus to return, with their eyes on the fields but their ears open. They listened.

What a paved road would mean to Nan was an easier time on the way to deliveries. More than once on a dirt road a wagon wheel had gotten stuck in a pothole, or a wagon had lost its wheel altogether, or a horse had lost its shoe. Even in an automobile the drive was smoother on a paved road, and Nan could rest her head against the window in the back while a father talked at her from the driver's seat. She didn't sleep, but let her mind drift out over the road, freer than it could on the farm, over the pages of *The Book of Knowledge*, to Birmingham, Boston, Baltimore, where her father's faceless figure hovered above the city. Often, when she had deliveries in town or on the other side of it, the car or cart drove down the Straight and passed the doctor's house. She knew it was coming when the dirt road went paved and the country was behind her. The brick houses huddled together under the warmth of the streetlamps and the trees stood straight in the yards. The doctor's house was built of white brick, and in the light of the streetlamp she saw the dark porch and drawn drapes and neat chimney breathing smoke into the night. Both doctors were there in that house, she imagined, dreaming peaceful white men's dreams.

In her own dreams her mind would drift to that afternoon she had sat in front of the doctors in the hard-bottomed chair and bared her breast to them. In the dreams she was entirely naked. In one dream, she had pissed herself, as though she had mistaken the hard-bottomed chair for a chamber pot. She woke to find it was Wilson, sleeping against her, who had pissed himself, soaking her dress. Then she woke again and came to realize she'd dreamt that too. Wilson was not in her bed but across the house in Elma's, or in his crib, dreaming his own dreams.

It was the shame and relief of having pissed herself, the wet, irreversible fact of it—that was how it had felt, to nurse Wilson in front of those men. She had crossed a threshold. It was the closest she had come to telling. Let it all be known, she'd thought.

And then they had shut her up again, like you'd clap shut the mouth of a flue. Elma had shut her up, begging as she had for the men not to tell. The men had carried out no tests, because they'd seen with their eyes what they needed to see. And in protecting Elma they were protecting Juke and protecting themselves.

Then, before she knew it, Elma was planning a wedding. She said to Nan, "I got us a plan. We're fixing to move into town, you and me and the twins," plain as she might say, "We're fixing to bake a cake." It was impossible for Nan to believe, so she didn't believe it. Elma showed her the ring, but she didn't wear it. She hid it in among the sugar, in the sugar bowl on the windowsill no one used; they used the sugar from the glass canister instead. She said she didn't want her daddy to know, not yet. She said, "Don't worry, Nan. I got it all in my mind." She made it sound as though she was doing Nan a favor. As though the only reason she was marrying a doctor was to get them far from Juke, as though marrying a doctor was a sacrifice.

Elma didn't act like she was making a sacrifice. In among Oliver's letters, mailed now from just down the road, he sent the McCall's wedding dress pattern she asked for, and she took a lace curtain from her bedroom and the silk from the twins' baptism gowns, for they would not be needed again, and some fabric Sara had left in the big house that Elma said she would not miss. With these she began to fashion her own wedding dress. She would have liked to be married in her mother's dress, she said, but she'd been buried in it. She

sewed when Juke was deep in the field, or at the still, or asleep, working by candlelight and humming as she did so, for she liked to have
her hands on pretty things. She talked to Nan and the twins about
the doctor's house, painted a picture of it for them, the wainscoting
and wallpaper and water that flowed from faucets when you turned
them. And with each detail of the house and each detail of the dress
it was easier and easier for Nan to picture, and harder for her not to
picture. She closed her eyes and ears against it, but at night when she
slept she dreamt of the rooms of the house, the ceilings as tall as a
cathedral's, and Wilson in it, running barefoot, the soles of his feet
clean as the day he was born. It was a sweeter dream than the one
where she nursed Wilson in the hard-bottomed chair. So she began to
allow herself to believe it. She allowed herself that happiness. And she
allowed Elma her happiness, her humming, her planning, because if
they were going to live in the doctor's house, if it was to happen, if it
was their chance, then it would be Elma putting those miles between
Nan's bed and Juke's after all.

As for Juke, he stayed out of her way. He didn't touch her. Instead
he had his hands on Wilson. He ate supper with the baby on his lap,
letting him lick the gravy from his spoon. After supper, while Nan
cleared the dishes, he rocked him in the crook of one arm, singing
him "Bedtime's Come for Little Boys."

> Come here! You most tired to def, po little lamb.
> Played yoself clean out of bref, po little lamb.
> See dem hands now—such a sight!
> Would you ever believe dey's white?
> Stand still till I wash 'em right, po little lamb.

He said it was a lullaby the colored nurse sang to him when he
was a boy, but Nan had never heard it before, and what she wanted
most was to never hear it again.

———

On the last night of 1930, under a sky dizzy with stars, the pearl-colored Buick pulled into the driveway of the crossroads farm. Now that winter had set in and the dogs didn't care to sleep under the porch, Nan had taken to closing them in with her in the pantry at night, so that when a driver approached and the dogs sat up and readied to bark, she could quiet them with a bit of pork rind. With Wilson on the other side of the house, they kept a kind of company for her. Also she'd taken to sleeping in her day clothes, stockings and all. It was warmer, and made her feel safer, that she might just leap out of bed and into her shoes. That was what she did now. She had her mother's satchel and was out the door, which she knew how to close without making a sound, before anyone else in the house had waked.

She was not expecting the Buick and did not recognize it as belonging to the Wilsons. For the first several minutes in the backseat, she wondered if the driver was the father, and wondered where a colored boy had gotten such a fine car. Too late, she remembered another colored boy driving another car, the one with the white girl in the back. When they were out of the driveway and well down the road, he said, "You the midwife? I thought you'd be full grown."

Nan nodded at the rearview mirror.

"It must be you, then. They tell me you don't talk. But you can hear all right?"

Nan nodded, more slowly this time, wondering who "they" was.

"I's sure glad you got in the car with no fuss. I ain't want to lose no job. It was my cousin Tate you took that ten dollar from." He gave her a hard look in the mirror. "He lose his job over that. Scared he might lose more. You think Mr. Wilson need ten dollar? It was my cousin Tate who lose out. He ain't driving no more fancy cars for the Wilsons. He run off to Pennsylvania, working in a sawmill now. He make more money in the mill than driving a fancy car, tell the truth."

Nan put her hand on the door handle. It was a different car from the one that had come before. It had to be. She would have recognized it. But it had been a long time ago—a year and a half at least, before Wilson, before Genus.

"I just hope Mr. Wilson want to give you one more chance. Reckon he got to. Unless he want to deliver the baby hisself, you the onliest hope he has. He got a problem at the mill. Name of Betsy. She a spinner girl at the mill. She kin to the new foreman they got up in Freddie Wilson's place. She in the family way, as they say. He say to tell no one her name but it just come out my mouth. You can hear all right, though?"

He waited for Nan to nod again. The car was moving fast. Even if the car stopped, what good would it do to jump out?

"You ain't seem like no thief. You seem all right. Tate got a brother name Quack, he a deaf-mute. Deaf and dumb, but my momma say don't call him dumb. He can't hear nothing. Born that way. His momma drank a fine amount and my momma say that what done it. He ain't right. But Quack work in that sawmill with Tate, where the saws be making all kind of noise, so my momma say it don't matter none him being deaf. She say he lucky he ain't in no institution. He would sorta make a noise like a baby duck when he was tiny, fore he got sense enough to keep quiet. Thas how come we call him Quack. His real name's Frank, same as me, after our granddaddy."

In the dark car Nan could see the profile of Frank's face, his close-shorn hair and the petal of his right ear and the faintest shadow of a beard on his face, as it was late at night or early in the morning and he had not yet had the chance to shave. He wore wire-framed eye-glasses, and from where she sat she could see the world through a slice of them.

"You ain't even know the night I had. I ain't even had a wink of sleep. I already been all over town. I been to Dr. Rawls's house. You know Dr. Rawls? He the one Mr. Wilson usually call on. But he got the influenza and he can't even get out of bed. His son Dr. Oliver answer the door. He say to call on you. Thas how I come to carry you back to the mill village. I got me my own quarters there. Use to be Tate's. Now they me and my sister Mag's. We got our own shack with a cookstove. She the house girl. Mrs. Wilson treat us pretty good. But Mr. Wilson knock on my door all hour of the night, I tell you what."

He had an easy way of piloting the car, slowing as they approached town, breaking for a dog in the road, as naturally as he'd walk on his own legs.

"I seen some things there, I tell you what." She could tell he was working toward something. "I seen my boss man and your boss man having a fine time at the mill. They be all kinds of girls, spinners I reckon, going in and out of that mill all night. They ain't working the graveyard shift neither. And they be all kinds of liquor coming in and out too. I tell you. Course I ain't seen your boss man there for a time." They were coming to the village now, and the car's tires creaked over the gravel. Nan could see the Wilsons' house at the top of the hill, a candle lighting a wreath in each window.

"That fella got strung up on your farm? I seen him in the road right here." He pointed. "That fella any kin to you?"

He and his sister Mag had heard the gunshots, and seen the body from their window, and they'd locked the door and turned out their lantern and hid under the table until daylight.

————

There was gunfire again as Frank pulled into the mill village. The mill folks were sitting on their front porches, in their truck beds, setting off firecrackers in the street, shooting rifles into the sky. "They just celebrating," Frank said, to himself as much as to Nan, as he eased the Buick around them and into the yard around the back of the mill. "Least they busy enough to pay us no mind." It was the yard where farmers delivered cotton and Juke and now Jim delivered their gin. Carrying her bag close, Nan followed Frank's fast legs through the back door and up a narrow staircase. Frank used a key to open the interior door. The room inside appeared to be a kind of office, with a long mahogany desk and a red print rug on the floor and red-painted walls and a cowhide sofa, where a white girl lay on her side. She was a big girl, boxy, and you had to look close to see she had a belly on her. There was a single lamp in the room, and it was throwing an amber light on the Bible another girl, perched in a leather chair, was reading aloud. When Frank and Nan came through the door, she marked her place and closed the book and stood.

"This my sister Mag," said Frank. "This here Miss Nan. She the midwife. Now, she can't talk back to you none. She like Quack, 'cept she can hear fine. But she gone take good care of you and your baby, Miss Betsy."

Nan hoped Frank would stay, but he nodded his good night. She could see that the top buttons of his shirt were open and under it he was wearing his union suit. He would catch a few hours' sleep after all. She'd been uneasy in the car, but now his voice had become familiar. He left her with the girls, who were strangers.

Miss Betsy was far along, six centimeters and counting. Mag didn't like to talk as much as her brother, or else she was bitter toward Nan, or else she was distracted by Betsy. She went back to reading her Bible passages, pausing when Betsy hollered to say, "Miss Betsy, you got to quiet down," and asking Nan didn't she have something to give her to make her quiet. "I seen Dr. Rawls do it before. He deliver the baby of a lady I used to work for. He just knock the momma clear out and use his forceps to pull the baby out while the momma off in dreamland." She threw her arms out and rocked her head back, imitating a sleeping woman. "Momma wake up and there be the baby, sucking on her tit. He like the sandman, Dr. Rawls," she said. "Don't you have nothing?"

Nan shook her head. She thought if she could knock out a woman she'd knock herself out every night of her life.

Mag gave her a long, cold look, starting at her knees and ending at her face. Then she threw up her arms again, dismissing her.

"You ain't look like no devil." She laughed to herself, and Nan was so relieved to hear the laughter that she joined her. "My cousin Tate got what was coming to him! He think he mighty, driving that car around, playing off like it his, playing fancy for the girls. I would have liked to see the look on his face when you took that money from his hand. Boy had it coming!"

Betsy labored on her side for a good while, the street below swelling with sound now—a new year had come. Guns fired. Glass broke. Someone played a fiddle. Nan had seen plenty of women in labor before, but she had not seen an office so fine, so she let her eyes cast about it. Had she not been so fearful of meeting Mr. Wilson, she might have taken pleasure in it. There were paintings on the walls of ships on the ocean, and a phonograph table, and a bookcase with more books than Nan had ever seen, with leather spines and gold edges. The desk was bigger than her own bed, and seeing it she remembered what was said about the chief of police in Ocilla, that he'd kept a Negro's skull on his desk as an ashtray. But George Wilson's desk had a regular pewter ashtray, a half-smoked cigar resting in it, and a silver ice bucket, and a crystal liquor bottle as big as a milk jug. There was a framed photograph of Parthenia Wilson, another of a young man in an army uniform, and another of Freddie Wilson, as a boy, on a horse.

"Ain't it all fine?" Mag said. She joined Nan at the desk, where Betsy couldn't hear them. "I bet the White House ain't got a room finer than this." Mag lifted the lid on the ice bucket, just to show that she could, Nan thought. "Liquor money," she whispered. "Fella runs gin." Nan raised her eyebrows, feigning surprise, and Mag, encouraged, went on. "You ain't know that? Why, I could tell you some things." She liked to talk as much as her brother after all. "You and me's about the only girls been in this here fine room who ain't been on that there couch." She nodded to the sofa where Betsy was lying with her eyes closed. "Baby went into her on that couch, baby gone come out there too."

Nan raised her eyebrows, but now her surprise wasn't feigned.

Mag gave a wicked chuckle. "Don't think he don't have him a taste for colored girls. Only reason he picks on the white ones is all the spinner girls is white. Only way I got out from under him was tell him I got syphilis. I ain't got no syphilis, but I got a brain." She tapped her temple. "Them poor spinners ain't got no brains. They come on up-stairs and Mr. Wilson pour em drinks in this fine room, and fore long they on they backs on that couch. He old too! His pecker probably look like an old dried root. Them girls don't usually get far along fore he sends em to Dr. Rawls, though. They go in his office with child and they come out, no child." Mag wiped her palms against each other. "I reckon Miss Betsy must a hid her belly good, to get this far. Maybe she got some brains after all. Old man think he the smart one, though, think no one see. But Mrs. Wilson, she no fool. She know how he carry on. I ain't got any qualms to tell you this, 'cause what you hear you can't say back to no one, can you? You remind me of my cousin Quack. He just as gentle a soul as can be. Ain't got a ounce of brains, though."

Betsy was a quiet birther. Mag had to shush her only a hand-ful of times. Nan could tell she was afraid, afraid of pushing out the baby but more afraid of being heard, though the fireworks and fes-tive voices still carried on outside the window. Nan's mother had told her of women who had gotten all the way to birth without knowing they were pregnant. She wondered if the same was true for Betsy, if she hadn't been clever but just blind, if she was not just in pain but in shock. Nan wanted to tell her that she did not need to be afraid. That she didn't need a father to raise the baby, only needed to be free of him, that the easiest part was yet to come. The baby crowned for a long time, a half hour or more, the bowl of its head firm against Nan's hands. Frank came to check on them, the sound of the street follow-ing him upstairs, and Mag sent him away. Finally Nan had to take the scalpel and make a cut, as her mother had taught her. She did not like to do so and would have done it with her eyes closed if she could.

She wondered if Dr. Rawls felt the same way when he did what Mr. Wilson asked him to do. Were his hands steady? Was it the same to him as delivering a child? She wondered if her mother had known, if Mr. Wilson had ever asked her to do the same.

Soon after the cut, the baby's head came forth with the undammed river of Betsy's fluid. One of its hands was pressed to its face, so that the mother had been pushing out the head and the arm at the same time. The baby was a girl, and a loud one. Mag helped to clean and wrap and quiet her while Nan sewed. "She look just like you," Mag said to Betsy again and again, as though to make it true. While Nan sewed, Frank came again, and then left once more. When he returned, Nan was readying her satchel to leave and Mr. Wilson was with him.

In his white suit and white hat, he filled the doorway. She had not seen him on the farm since she was a little girl, and though she was close to grown now, he looked bigger to her, not smaller. To calm her fear she looked at his white shoes. She wondered if Mr. Wilson, like her, slept in his clothes.

"Evening," he said. "Or should I say morning? I ain't seen you since you were just a pickaninny." He lowered his shoulders to peer down at Nan, looking for something in her face. He was looking at her so intently that it took her a moment to remember to look away. "I knew your mother, girl, from the time she was your size. It's a shame she's gone, and I'm sorry."

George Wilson began to cough a wet, swampy cough. He removed a handkerchief, spit a wad of brown phlegm into it, and returned the bundle to his pocket. Then he raised himself up and looked over her shoulder at the girl propped up on the sofa holding the crying bundle that was his daughter. He took a few steps to her and bent over, studying the baby's face the way he had studied Nan's. He looked from the baby to Betsy, then Nan, to the baby again. "You come back with a husband," he said to the girl. "Buy you one if you need to. Come on back when the baby's grown and I'll put you and your man to work.

I'll keep you in a house. But you got to bring the baby back with you, to live in the village."

Satisfied, he took several bills from his billfold and handed them to Frank, saying, "There's a Ponce de Leon coming through the station at four thirty. We'll beat the sun yet." Nan had not seen such a large collection of bills since Dr. Oliver's office. That money had also been George Wilson's, and it was now hung in a dress pocket in Elma's closet, waiting, she said, to pay for her wedding.

He patted his breast pockets as though looking for more. Apologetically he said to Nan, "Miss Betsy clean me out, child. But being as you run off with one a my sawbucks a while back, I reckon we square." He was smirking. "I ain't have a quarrel with you, child. I reckon you a clever gal." His voice was kind now, his eyes still searching. "But Jesup I have a quarrel with, and I ain't intend to send no more money to his household. You get back home now and keep safe. I hope your eyes are sharper than your tongue."

The four of them rode in the Buick together, Frank driving, Nan and Betsy and the baby riding in the back. The mill village had quieted now, the lights going off in the houses along the hill. Betsy was wearing a clean dress, and Nan knew she was in pain, though she looked as numb as a corpse. She didn't say anything as Nan helped the baby to latch onto her breast. Then finally the baby was quiet. Even Frank was quiet. Nan remembered it was the first day of the new year. Likely the baby was the first baby born in Cotton County in 1931. But there would be no picture in the newspaper, no free gift set from Pearsall's Drugs. Betsy had a suitcase already packed, and Nan wondered in what room she would next open it, saying to her baby, before it was a full day old, This is where we'll make a life. Nan thought the open suitcase would make a fine bed for a baby, if the baby lived to wherever they were going.

It was the same town she had traveled through on many nights, the shops and houses dark and shuttered under the moon. Save for a drunk or two, it was quieter here than in the country, where the click of the cricket frogs drowned the night. But Florence, she now saw, was no safer than the farm. She had survived the trip to town, but seen its quiet malice, invisible, like a virus, and all the more frightful because, with its paved streets and electric lights, it looked civilized. Come morning, it dressed up in a white suit and went to church. That was what Juke aspired to be, she thought, George Wilson in a white suit with a girl on his cowhide sofa. But George Wilson had evicted him from that office and soon he'd evict him from the farm, and now in some nether organ, Nan felt pity for him, because to George Wilson Juke wasn't more than that girl on the sofa, whose vanishing at least he had furnished.

At the station, Nan waited in the backseat and watched as Frank bought the girl's ticket, then handed her the rest of the money and helped her and the baby onto the train. She wondered if Frank had stripped one of the ten-dollar bills from the bundle. She might have done the same herself. She remembered the ten-dollar bill she'd gotten from Tate and the white girl, and wondered if she too had been sent away on a train, or if she had been sent to Dr. Rawls, and then back to work at the mill the next day. Why had Mr. Wilson sent her to Nan at all? Was it better to be sent to Dr. Rawls, she wondered, or to be sent away on the train? Was it better to be forced to make your baby disappear, or to be forced to disappear with your baby?

If either one of them had had a momma nearby, or a shack to call their own, they might have sneaked Betsy and the baby away. They might have fed her, clothed her, put her under someone's care. Nan knew Betsy had as good a chance of dying as the baby. They might have taken her to Dr. Rawls, or his son, but they didn't.

They watched the train pull away. Frank returned to the car. Nan remembered her own plan to buy a train ticket at that window, to disappear, before Wilson, before Genus. It seemed a long time ago. She had been thirteen. Soon she would be fifteen.

But she had another plan now. On the way home, Frank drove past the doctor's house, the chimney breathing its smoke, and Nan thought that whatever dark malice now lived inside its doors, she had no choice but to believe it her refuge. Soon Dr. Oliver would marry Elma and he'd be the only man in her house. She would serve him. She would wake early to make his breakfast. She would wash his underclothes. She'd sweep that white man's floor every day of her life if it meant that she'd never cook Juke another meal, she'd never hear that lullaby, she'd never give him another penny. Instead she'd use her own money to buy Wilson storybooks and toy cars and school clothes, and good shoes with laces, and for herself, only sometimes, caramel milk rolls. And inside the house, at least, where they would be safe, she and Wilson could live as mother and son.

Was she a fool to believe a white man might bring her salvation? But who else might bring it, on this earth?

TWENTY

"YOU CAN THANK ME FOR THAT PIE," THE WHITE SMITH SAID TO the black one. He squinted at Sterling with his single, sky blue eye. "My grammy sent it for me special."

The latrine had been finished and they were putting it to use, as Crow had suggested. Around their ankles were their striped pants and their chain, the ball hanging out the privy door like a watchdog. Sterling thought it must have been a white man invented the two-seater so he could have another man to talk to, even when he cleared his bowels.

"I left her a message, like smoke signals, like the Indians done. Like the Hardy Boys. You know who the Hardy Boys is, don't you? Can't you read?"

Sterling shook his head, and Freddie shook his. "They's adventure boys. They do secret codes and such. Anyway I left my grammy a secret code. Know what I done?"

Sterling was paging through an issue of *Progessive Farmer*, which he indeed could not read but it was something for the men to put their eyes on before using it to wipe their behinds.

"She used to sing me a hymn when I was a boy." Now Freddie

raised his voice up big and sang, "'Crown Him with many crowns! The lamb upon His throne!'"

They both took stock of where they were sitting and Sterling shook his head and laughed despite himself and Freddie laughed so hard he had to spit. "We's just lambs on our thrones, ain't we? Boy howdy!" He spit again in the dirt they'd just dug. "You know that one, Blacksmith? 'Crown Him with many crowns'?"

Sterling shook his head.

"My grammy, she used to sing it to me while she made me a crown out of flowers. They was them little yellow flowers like daisies, but with black eyes? They grown all up on the hill of the mill village."

"Black-eyed Susan," Sterling couldn't help but say, and by the time he said it he was sorry he had, because Ketty had grown them.

"That's them. She used to make me a whole bunch of crowns from black-eyed Susans. And she would put the crowns on my head and sing 'Crown Him with many crowns' and call me her lamb. Boy howdy, every boy should have him a grammy like that. You remember last week when we was back in the mill village, cutting back that ditch weed?"

Sterling nodded. It seemed like a long time ago and far off.

"They was all them black-eyed Susans on the hill, and I made up three little crowns, tiny as like to fit on a kitty cat, and I put em in the mailbox."

"What mailbox?" Sterling said.

"My grammy's mailbox. We wasn't but right acrost the street from her house."

"Thas her house on the hill there?"

"Thas my house. Ain't I told you it was?"

Sterling put down the magazine. His stomach hurt all of a sudden.

"I knew she'd know it was me. I seen her on the porch watching all of us, but she didn't see me back. Boy, I'm just about as clever as Joe Hardy." He laughed again. He had a laugh that made Sterling want to claw out the boy's remaining eye.

"Thas your house, and you playing games, son? Why you ain't call out for her right there?" It pained him to think the boy was playing games in front of his own house. And yet wasn't that what he was doing himself? He had been playing games a year ago when he had stood there frozen in the rain, refusing to go home. He had been playing games for thirteen years before that, finding reasons to stay in Georgia.

"I'm a wanted man. Wanted for far worse than that fool warden got me for."

Sterling wondered what the fool warden might do if he put the white boy's head in the privy.

"Did you do it? What you're wanted for?"

"Hell no," the boy said. "I ain't no killer. I ain't even kill a nigger."

"It's you that's wanted for killing that man?"

"Thas right."

"Why you wanted for it?"

"'Cause Jesup done laid it on me! My only crime was knocking up the wrong whore." Freddie pointed an arm out the privy window. "Just over yonder. I used to have her park my truck under them trees, and we'd go to town." He whistled. "We give them birds a mighty show!"

"You telling me you one of the daddies?"

Freddie nodded hungrily. "Guess which one's mine. The darky or the white?" He gestured out the window again. "I like to think it was me who laid my seed in her first. Had I known a darky had got to her, I would a driven out a here like a bat out a hell."

"You knew her," Sterling said. "Elma Jesup."

"Hell yes I knew her. In the Bible way! You sounding like you know her too."

"Naw," Sterling said.

"You sure, Blacksmith?"

"Naw. I don't know no white girls."

"Thas good, Blacksmith. They trouble."

"I don't know no one."

Sterling looked out at the pines. He believed the boy because he needed to. The boy had had no part in killing that man. Juke Jesup had done it. Yes, of course he had. He felt his ancient hate rise up out of bed.

"'Crown Him with many crowns!'" the boy sang. He said, "I'm fixing to show my grammy my face when I'm good and ready." His body let out a sound like hell raining down, and then he laughed again. "Lordy, lordy, them blackberries done run like jam clean through me."

———

Ketty would grow black-eyed Susans to make a poultice for the foot when somebody stepped on a spur or a rock or a spider. She made a poultice out of them when she'd cut out the baby's tongue, packing them into the baby's gums like her own cured tobacco leaves, then wrapping the rag across her mouth and around her head. It amazed Sterling what a body could get used to. You could get used to having no tongue, and you could get used to your baby having no tongue. Seemed it might grow back like a lizard's tail.

It didn't grow back. It was bloody and then it was black and then it was pink again. It was just the stem of it left, like a weed whose root you couldn't pull all the way out of the ground.

Not long after that, Ketty woke up one black midnight to go on a call. When Nancy was young and still nursing, Ketty would take her with her, strapped to her body. She'd deliver one baby with another suckling on her tit. More than once, when a mother had trouble with her milk, Ketty would offer the newborn her own breast. But now Nancy was weaned and Ketty left her behind, in bed with Sterling, and she was crying a terrible tongueless cry and barking a terrible spiteful cough. She was sick with something like the croup. He hoped it was the croup. Sounded like her lungs were coughing up their wrath. He got up and walked her down the length of the shack, and then he got to remembering something Ketty had done with Elma, which was to wrap her up in a blanket and bring her on the porch, and let the cold night air settle into her lungs.

It was March and a fine night for such a remedy. As there was no rocking chair on the porch of the shack, which wasn't a raised porch but just a few planks flat on the ground, and since Sterling was falling asleep on his feet, he lit a lantern and went to the porch of the big house and settled in a chair. He had a full mustache then and the baby liked to pet it. He thought how strange it was that the women had gone from the farm, that they were two men, he and Juke, with little daughters in their care. Nancy's lungs filled with the dewy air and cleared and as he rocked her she settled into something like sleep in his lap. He was feeling pleased with himself. He put his nose and mouth to the back of her little neck, no bigger than a corncob, and breathed her in. The cricket frogs chirped.

The door to the breezeway, the one off the bedrooms, swung open. There stood Elma, five years old, in bare feet and nightdress, her hair a red cloud above her. "Where's my daddy at?" she said.

Now the cold night air burned in Sterling's own lungs. He tried to think. He could not remember a wagon coming for Ketty. He could not remember the sound of its wheels. Perhaps he had slept through it. It was such a common sound, as common as the baby's cries, the guineas' fussing in the yard. But the cold feeling stayed with him, a ghost in his chest.

"He ain't inside?" Sterling said. He didn't whisper, because he wanted to hear his own voice in the night, so he might not be so scared.

Elma shook her head. She did not look scared. If he could have, he would have asked the girl to hold his hand, but he was as afraid for her as he was for himself, of what he might discover. He said, "Go back to bed. I'll find your daddy. He's probably checking on the hogs," because it was the first thing came into his mind. In fact, he did go first to the barn, and looked in on the cows, but the cows were asleep, as were the guineas and chickens and the hogs under the house. The people were the only folks up. There was no truck on the farm yet, and the only way Jesup would make it to town was in the wagon or on a mule, and both mules were there in the barn, asleep as well.

Sterling walked with his lantern in one hand and the baby in the other, holding her close to his chest. He might have put her down on the bed now, but he felt safer with her there over his heart, felt that she was some kind of protection. He looked in the privy and the cotton house and the sugarhouse and the shed. He looked back in the big house, thinking maybe Elma had been wrong, that she'd missed her daddy in his own bed. He'd never been in the man's room before, rarely went any farther than his porch. What he found was a room so empty it left him breathless, not just empty of the man himself but of everything else, save for a bed and a dresser and on top of it his wedding picture in a frame and a tobacco tin and a hat. He tried to remember if the man had another hat he wore but couldn't. He couldn't say why it disappointed him that Jesup's room was as empty as his own shack. He supposed he'd expected that, even if his own room wasn't full of fine things, a big house belonging to a white man would be, even if it was a man he hated.

Sterling told Elma he'd stay there on the porch and wait for her daddy, that she could go back to sleep. He had no shotgun, Jesup having taken it from him, so he sat in the rocker with the baby. It was coming on dawn, the martins waking in the cane field, when headlights came up the Straight, slowed at the driveway, and turned up it. Sterling moved with the baby to the front porch and watched in the near dark as Jesup stepped out of the passenger door and Ketty stepped out of the back. The car was still running, the headlights laying across the porch steps and Sterling's legs as he came down them. By the bottom step, he could see that it was George Wilson sitting in the driver's seat, and he was waving him over. Sterling went to the car window as Jesup and Ketty passed through the headlights to the porch, where they stood in their coats as one broad-winged creature, silent and dark.

"Evening, Sterling," George Wilson said.

Sterling said good evening.

"Or shall I say good morning?" George Wilson smiled. "I was returning Mr. Jesup home when we found your old lady up the road a piece. Says she was walking home after a granny call. Says the Negro wagon busted up. Says the wagon lost not one wheel but two. Says the wheels just rolled right off into the ditch and disappeared. What do you make of that, Sterling?"

Sterling said, "I'm much obliged to you for returning her, sir."

"Lucky we come across her," he said. "There's boars, Sterling. One of my men on a farm up the road killed one last week."

Sterling said again he was much obliged.

"They'll attack at the knees, Sterling. Bring down a full-grown man just as easy as a woman." George Wilson looked at the baby in Sterling's arms. She was awake again and fussing, and Sterling was rocking her, and now she was barking her wrathful cough. "A woman is safest on the farm, don't you agree, Sterling? Where she can tend a crying child?"

Sterling agreed that yes, she was.

"I need a man to be well-rested to do a day's work on the farm."

"Yes sir," said Sterling.

George Wilson tipped his hat and readied himself to reverse the car.

"Mr. Wilson," Sterling started.

"What is it?"

"He took my shotgun, sir. Mr. Juke. I can't keep away no boars if I ain't got a gun. A man needs a gun, sir."

Mr. Wilson looked to the porch, where Ketty and Juke Jesup still stood, an undivided mass. Sterling wished to God he could see their faces.

"I'll speak to him, Sterling."

"Thank you kindly, sir. Sir?"

"What is it, Sterling?"

"Mr. Juke was with you all evening?"

George Wilson looked thoughtful for a moment. Then he smiled. "We had friendly business at the mill," he said. "You get some sleep, Sterling. Settle your mind."

Then he reversed the car and the headlights slipped down the driveway and out of sight.

———

Sterling's mind would not settle. Ketty had gone cold and quiet as a stone, as though it were her own tongue she'd cut out. He'd ask her about the cows, or tell her about the fields, or praise a meal, and she would turn away from him, let him see the broad blank face of her back. She turned her back also to the baby, let her crawl all over the farm while she went about her chores. Once she lost sight of her. Ketty and Sterling searched the two hundred acres, and Juke joined in, cursing them both, and Sterling was sure she'd crawled down into the creek and drowned. It was Elma who found her down in the woods, where she'd gotten into some blackberry bushes. Her face and hands were stained blue-black. Ketty had scooped her up and pounded her diapered behind, then kissed her stained face. Sterling felt satisfied: now his wife would be more vigilant. But the next day the baby was crawling over the acres again. She crawled over to him in the yard, where he was trimming the hooves of one of the mules. Her knees were worn white, and covered in ant bites.

If Ketty was going to turn her back to them both, and sleep on the floor, if she was going to stay out all night delivering babies while she left her own at home with him, and if he said Good morning or Goddamn and her answer was the same, if still she showed her back to him, he might as well tell her his mind.

"You got plenty of time for other folks' younguns," he said. "You gone all day, all night, I'm plowing a field with a baby on my back.

Mule's leading me and I'm leading her. Ain't nothing but a swayback mule to you. Ain't I nothing but a mule?"

Ketty answered that it was God's say how long it took a baby to come into the world.

"How my to feed her?" Her answer—the fact that she'd answered him, spoke words to him—animated him more. "While I'm plowing a field? Know how long it takes to feed a baby grits with a spoon? How my to do it? We got two men on this farm and it ain't nearly enough as it is. I ain't got time to feed no baby with no spoon." He realized he was holding the baby, and he handed her to Ketty. "You make me a mule of a man, Ketty. Folks look on me like a mule. I won't have it." He told her he had cousins in Baltimore who had a bunk for him at the steel mill. He had no cousins, though he had heard from a field hand who did that the mills up north needed workers. There was a war on. Every day, men were leaving Georgia. Why not him? He told Ketty, "You keep doing me like that, I like to up and leave."

Ketty's answer was to bundle up the baby, next time she made a call, and take her with her. Never again did she leave the baby behind in Sterling's care.

That did not bring him peace. Now his bed was empty of the baby too. He did not like spooning her corn grits but he liked having her there in the bed beside him, petting his mustache, her little chest rising and falling, her mouth dribbling drool as she fell asleep.

Sterling's shotgun was not returned to him. He plowed the west field and Jesup plowed the north. Their mules seemed to know not to look each other in the eye.

———————

She'd gone mad, he concluded. She had cut out their daughter's tongue not to save her life, as she claimed, but to keep her silent. All that clay had poisoned her mind.

Later, when he learned it was cancer that killed her—it was an old friend of his mother's who sent him a letter in the turpentine camp, a letter he'd had to ask another man to read him—he thought maybe she'd meant well after all. He wondered how early it had got hold of her. Maybe it wasn't the toxic Georgia clay that had made her crazy but the cancer gnawing holes through her tongue even in those years, or through her mind. When he thought of it this way—it was the sickness in her, it wasn't her fault—his own heart softened against her memory. He lay in the camp now, so close to the farm he could smell the manure and name the mule who made it, and wondered not for the first time if she was buried there, on the farm where they had had their honeymoon and where she had hardened her heart against him. Had Jesup buried her himself? Or was she laid into the ground by her own people?

But she'd had wildness in her even before she came to the farm, he had to remember. She had come to him like a jenny in heat, no stranger to the ways of men. He was no fool. When he'd courted her as a young man, they'd once hung their arms over the fence that divided the Youngs' farm from that of a white man, a mule breeder, and they petted the horses and donkeys and fed them apples and carrots. Sterling looked at the animals with envy—he'd worked in George Wilson's field all day and was hungry himself for apples and carrots. But Ketty looked on them with a kind of benign and earthly accord, her hands stroking their black lips and pink gums, their pink tongues. And the white man, the man who all day long paired animals to his liking, in ten-gallon hat and dungarees and a gold belt buckle, from over the fence he treated the animals with the same sensual calm, putting his fingers in their mouths, putting his mouth even on theirs, and beside Sterling's timid indifference Ketty and the white man were like mother and father to the animals they loved and knew so well, like lovers, and Sterling startled and fled from the thought that that was what they were.

He liked to think that he had tamed her. When they married and moved to the crossroads, she didn't pay visits to the tobacco farm, didn't even suggest them, though her people, or at least her friends, folks she called Auntie This and Uncle That, still lived there, still had a log rolling each spring and a corn shucking each fall, still carved chairs, raised babies, smoked tobacco into the night. It was as though it was a life she was resigned to leave behind. She had chosen to make a new life with Sterling. They never spoke of the mule breeder. Sterling had managed to put him out of his mind, until the night she returned home with Juke Jesup in George Wilson's car, and they stood together on the porch in the shadow of dawn, in the same complicit silence.

That was March. The baby's cough calmed. She had a birthday. Ketty took the baby with her when she went off the farm and even as she went about it, carrying her on her back in the flour-sack sling as though to show Sterling just what she was capable of. The baby came to walking late, so much time did she spend in that sling, but then she did walk and she learned to cling to her mother's knee.

One morning as the summer waned, Sterling woke to find them gone. It was late, the sun was up, the animals moaned hungrily from the barn. Fear rose in his throat: that they had gone for good. That Ketty had turned her back to him a final time, taken the baby and gone back to the Youngs' farm, never to return.

But then he saw that their things were there in the shack with him still: a basket of sack diapers, the baby's silver spoon, the bottle of almond oil Ketty wore in her hair. He scrambled down to the floor and lifted the loose floorboard by the stove: there was her coffee tin of white clay. She would not leave for good, not without taking those things with her. She had strung up an old sheet for privacy, so she could wash in the zinc tub and change clothes without his eyes on her, and now he stood and moved the sheet aside and saw that the few dresses that she owned still hung from the wooden rod in the corner. At their feet, hiding under their skirts, was her satchel. Her birthing bag, she called it. In it she kept all the instruments she used, God knew what they were for, to help a baby into the world.

Now his relief came back up his throat, burning with acid. He thought he might be sick. Because if she didn't have her birthing bag with her, if she wasn't delivering a baby, where was she?

She was not on the farm. No one was. The wagon was gone and so was Clarence. He spoke to the animals who were left just to hear his voice, trying to keep the worry out of it, as though it were they who needed reassurance. "Look like the world done emptied out, Mamie girl." He tried to put his mouth to hers, as he had seen the mule breeder do years ago. She snuffed at him, shook her mane.

They had all left. Jesup had taken all the womenfolk from the farm. Sterling's darkest fantasies had not accounted for such a possibility. He had imagined him taking Ketty. They would go drinking and dancing at the juke, where Jesup had years ago derived his name, stealing from Sterling his people's very pleasure, the only fun God allowed them in this town, on this earth. Now he had stolen his woman too, and they might have a regular room next door for all Sterling knew, perhaps he paid Easter Moore for a room without requiring the use of one of her daughters, for he had found the woman he wanted, he had brought her with him. He imagined them in a room in the Easter Hotel, the windows boarded, keeping out the eyes of the world, and under the lurid electric bulb—for Jesup would want the light on, he would want to see the woman beneath him—they would have each other. In his mind they had each other in the ways of blacks and whites, mules and hogs, on the bed, on the filthy floor, in the back of George Wilson's car—what was George Wilson doing, driving them home?—in fields and in pine woods, in the toilet at the juke, where as a young man Sterling had read on the walls all the ways of women and men, all the ways Jesup and his woman would betray him, because they wanted their own pleasure and above all they wanted his pain. He had found his way from the barn to the shack now, he found that he was naked and kneeling on the bed and that his face was wet with tears. His hand reached for the almond hair oil on the table beside the bed, and it was slick and smelled of Ketty and helped him to do what he found his hand wanted to do. He was alone, she had left him, even the animals didn't love him.

Every Saturday night, after she washed her hair in the zinc tub and before she wrapped it in a rag, she massaged the oil into her scalp. She had let him do it himself once or twice, massage her head in his hands, his nose on the nape of her neck, the sharp smell of almonds.

In all those visions he had not imagined that they might love each other, Juke and Ketty. That they might take their daughters and leave the farm. That they might take his family, and make their own.

He was a fool. He stood and dressed. His hands were still slick from the oil, from his own wretched fluids; he wiped them on his pants. He seized the birthing bag from the floor. Why had he not thought to look in it? The zipper was old and stuck but he got it open and sunk in his hands and extracted from the bag's evil teeth a scarf, silk, long, endless, blue, and another, red, and last a string of pearls, long, endless, his eyes kept seeing them and seeing them as his hand drew them out, pearls as big as marbles, the loop big enough to lasso a bull with. Where had she gotten them. How long had she hidden them. Ketty did not have fine things.

He stormed out of the shack, across the yard, up the back steps of the big house. All of their things were there too: the Bible, the dishes. Where were they. How far had they gone. Why had they left behind the coffee tin of clay, why had they left him behind. He tried Jesup's bedroom door and found it was locked. It had a lock. Hadn't Sterling just been there? Hadn't he just checked the knob? Or was he sleeping again, fool with his eyes closed, he'd let them leave right under his nose. With his shoulder he threw himself at the door, again and again, it was a bead-board door, made of long flimsy planks, he could shoulder it open if he tried. Then he realized it opened out and not in, and then he pulled the knob toward him with all his force and pulled the knob straight off the door. He landed on his back. In one hand he held the knob and in the other, he realized, the pearls, which he had wound around his wrist like a tourniquet. He stood up, dropped the knob, fingered the hole where the knob had been, forced the lock open. He had in his mind that he might find another scarf, some gift he intended for her, a trinket that would connect him to the ones he had already found.

But the room was as empty as it had been the first time he'd stepped into it. The calm of the empty room settled over him. The day had moved on and a sunbeam came in the window and gold flecks of dust fell across it. On the dresser was the wedding picture, the tobacco tin, the hat. It was the straw hat he wore in the field. Sterling remembered now that he had another one, a plaid cap he wore to town. He felt the sense return to him. You are confused, he told himself. The day was moving on. There were animals to feed. Had he fed the animals? Had he fed himself? "Eat something," he said aloud. He realized he was saying it to Jessa, that he was looking at her in the gold frame. In the frame she and her groom wore carefree smiles. She was looking back at Sterling with urgent eyes that betrayed her smile, they were warning him, they were keeping him there.

He turned and saw the dust drifting over the bed. It was as though Jessa's eyes, her hand, had turned his head. He had not considered the bed. The man's bed. A white man did not bring a colored woman into his bed.

He stepped forward. The bed was made neatly. It had a look about it like it had not been slept in for some time. At its head was a single pillow, flat as the blanket, in a white pillowcase. Look here, check here. The pillow was stained slightly with the yellow wax of Juke Jesup's ear. A hair lay in the middle of it. Sterling pinched the hair between his fingers and held it up to the light. Rust red. He dropped it to the floor. Then he bent down as though to kiss a child good night and inhaled the scent of the pillow. The smell was so familiar, as familiar nearly as the smell of his own nostrils, the taste of his own mouth, that it took him a dizzy moment to place it. Almond oil.

Right under his nose.

What Sterling felt as he moved from the room, as he went out into the yard, was a righteous satisfaction. That he had been right, that his suspicions were confirmed, that he had married a woman who made love to a white man under his nose. It was a terrible and harmonious feeling, a feeling that he had been brought back to his senses, that his senses were whole again. Out of his eyes he saw the farm and it was more vivid, truer; he saw that the animals had known, that Mamie had not been rebuffing him, that she too had been giving him a gentle warning, that she pitied him.

When the wagon came up the Straight—so she hadn't left him, so in that way he'd been wrong—Sterling was waiting on the front porch. It was a colored man driving, not Juke, a man who seemed to Sterling familiar from church or town, but no matter. The baby was on Ketty's knee. Sterling raised a hand to the man as his mule turned into the drive. Around his wrist and across his palm he still gripped the strand of pearls. He waited until the wagon had turned around and made its slow way back up the road to town, and then he took the baby from its mother and put it in the rocker on the porch. He led Ketty into Jesup's room and pushed her onto the bed and lashed her with the pearls, on her face until she covered it, then across her forearms and knees as she drew them up, then her hips as she turned, then her back. He lifted her skirt and yanked down her drawers and lashed her bare behind. He could hear his voice hollering. He was saying, "You make a mule out of me." He said, "Right under my nose." The pearls were a poor whip, he couldn't grasp them firmly or dig them deep, and finally the string broke and the pearls flew, scattering across the bed and the wood floor.

In his mind too, a line snapped. He looked around. Through the window the sun had changed. The room was soft now with shadows. He did not know what day it was, what time it was.

Outside, the sun was low and the day was mild and Jesup was standing in the drive. The baby was in his arms. Behind them, behind the mule, little Elma sat in the wagon.

"What's that ruckus?"

"Ain't nothing," said Sterling, coming down the porch steps.

"What you doing in my house?"

"That there's George Wilson's house. And inside it I been show-ing my woman how it's gone be and it ain't none of your concern."

"You laying your hands on that old girl? Boy, didn't I tell you how to treat a woman?"

"I'll take my child now."

"Devil you will."

"Right under my nose. Y'all been making a mule out of me. I won't be no mule no more, no sir. I'll take my child."

"You ain't in your head, Sterling. You talking like a fool. You been getting in my hooch?"

"I'm in my head for once. I ain't no mule no more. I see it clear. I smell it." Sterling inhaled deeply. "I done smelled her in your bed."

"You been in my room, boy? You been in my bed?"

"You ain't denying it, then."

"You can do what you please with your own woman. That's within your right. But you ain't dare set foot in that house."

"I seen the things you gave her. I seen em with my own eyes. She ain't even visiting on babies, I bet, most times."

"What all things?"

"The necklace! The scarfs! All the fine things! Where else she get em?"

Jesup came closer and put the baby down on the bottom porch step beside Ketty's handbag. She had dropped it there when Sterling had hauled her inside. It was leather, mahogany colored, with a brass clasp. "Fool," Jesup said. "I ain't give her nothing. Don't you know I ain't got nothing to give? They's from Mr. Wilson, these things. He done give em to her. Half the croppers in the county be wearing his old lady's castoffs. Old man do a nice thing like that, and you take it out on your woman? You a bigger fool than I thought."

Sterling was shaking his head. "Ain't nothing to do with Mr. Wilson," he said. "I done smell something foul on this here farm. She ain't even visiting on a baby today. I smell it."

Calmly Jesup opened the bag. Sterling expected it to be full of more fine things, but Jesup unwrapped from the sackcloth inside a scissors, a thermometer, a forceps.

The screen door slammed and Ketty came out to the porch. She came weakly down the steps, holding the railing, and picked up Nancy from the bottom step. She passed by Sterling as though she didn't see him. Without speaking, she turned and carried the baby to the shack. Both men watched her back as she went. They heard the door slam.

Jesup helped Elma down from the wagon. He said, "Go play in the house."

She did. Jesup said to Sterling, "George Wilson told me to keep the farm niggers in line. That includes you. He put me in charge, Sterling. I got to do as told."

Sterling answered softly, "Yeah, you do as told. You as much a mule as me. You Mr. Wilson's mule."

He readied himself for a whipping. Worse. Would he do it now, or come back with others? He didn't think he would shoot him, but he was resigned to it, ready. His eyes went to the white man's belt, to the chinaberry branch, to the wagon reins. Was his shotgun in the wagon? Still Clarence waited in the drive. Now it was Sterling's eye the mule avoided. Perhaps he knew what was coming even better than Sterling, for Jesup wasted no time with a weapon or a mob but hit him with his fist. The punch landed over his left eye. It laid him down on the ground. The sun hung far above him. His eyes were closed, but he could sense the sun there as the white man kicked him in the ribs and in the face, and then Sterling found that he'd turned over like a gopher tortoise, like Ketty; like the animal he was, he protected himself. He braced himself for more, and when none came, he looked up. He could open only his right eye. Through it he saw Jesup chasing the wagon down the road. Clarence had got spooked and fled.

That was what he would do, Sterling thought. He would flee like the mule he was.

He limped to the shack. Ketty was making coffee at the stove. Nancy sat on the bed, sucking her fingers. He went past them both and tore down the sheet Ketty had strung up. On the sheet he threw everything that was his in the shack. Then he tied up the ends and hoisted it on his back. Ketty had turned her back to him and now he would turn his back to her. It wasn't he who was left on the farm, he saw. It was he who was meant to leave.

He bent down to the baby on the bed, meaning to give her a kiss, meaning to whisper to her low, so her momma couldn't hear, "I'd take you with me if I could." Gently he tugged her fingers out of her mouth. Then he saw it wasn't just her fingers she was sucking on. She had something in there, tucked in her gums, an acorn or rock or marble. He fished a finger into her tongueless mouth and felt it. He couldn't get a hold of it. She gagged. She fought him with her little teeth. He beat on her back, hard, twice, and then out came the object, slick with drool. A pearl.

She was fine. She hadn't swallowed it. But in his face she saw his fear, and she cried.

TWENTY-ONE

OLIVER RAWLS SPENT THE FIRST MONTH OF 1931 PREPARING for a wedding and a funeral. Which would come first was the question only God could answer. The wedding had been set for the last day of January, a Saturday, at least in Elma's head, for they kept the plans private, in their letters, lest the reverend's wife at her father's country church loosen her tongue and get word into town. Oliver had suggested that they might elope—go to Savannah or Jekyll Island or even Florida, and make a honeymoon of it. There would be no stopping a wedding that way. But Elma wanted it done at Creek Baptist, where she'd gone since she was a girl, with the eyes of the whole congregation on the dress she had sewed. Even if Oliver's mother did give a blessing, she would have insisted on First Methodist in town, and that was one of the reasons he had not yet told her. He took the lead on the plans, ordering flowers from Bell's under the name "Dr. Rawls," ringing up a stationer's in Atlanta to print the invitations. It was a shop he'd passed on Pryor Street between the room he rented from a widow in Five Points and Torrence's Lunch Room, where he'd eaten not lunch but breakfast and dinner every day, two fried eggs and a coffee for fifteen cents, and oysters and a

Coca-Cola for thirty-five cents. Every day, at a desk in the window of the stationer's, a woman with red-painted fingernails filled envelopes with calligraphy. From behind his spectacles he saw her with one eye, his right; the other looked out at the street. He watched the women on the sidewalk and the waitress at Torrence's and the widow herself through the same right eye, not committing to them his full sight, for the risk it might involve, that he might see them, love them, want them, that he might not be wanted in return. He cast his left eye across the traffic, stepped onto the streetcar—this was difficult to do, but he'd learned how, balancing his cane on the platform with one hand and hoisting his bad leg up with the other—his mind's eye busy with the paisley landscape of platelets and cells, mapped with them like the map of the city, its squirming, circuitous streets. Six years he had been in Atlanta and still he carried a map of the city in the breast pocket of his coat. In that pocket he carried also a handkerchief bearing his initials, a gift from his mother; a Vulcan ink pencil, a gift from his father, which stained the handkerchief; a pocket watch in a hunter case; a tin of throat lozenges; and, in his last days in Atlanta, an envelope containing a crescent-shaped lock of Elma Jesup's red hair, tied in a grosgrain ribbon.

———————

It was the dead man who had first captured his attention. No spleen at all, his father had said, just an empty cavity under the stomach, as though someone had gone in and stolen it. Oliver thought maybe someone had. What he would have given to see that man, to study on him. So he had listened to his father's proposal, he had agreed to meet the mother of the miraculous twins, because he thought it might help him to understand the disease so mighty it had swallowed a man's organ whole.

Then he had watched her come through the door of his basement office with one eye, then two. It had taken both his eyes and two more to see all of her, and then to take in the house girl—Nan—and then one baby, then the next. In their faces, he had seen all of Florence. They even smelled like home, like lye soap and wood smoke and Cherokee roses, like country air. The girls stood together, shoulder to shoulder, even the babies joined with them behind an invisible fortress. They were accustomed to being looked at; they were guarded against it. Among the four of them, Elma was the only one capable of speech, and yet even as she greeted him, it was as though she wore her companions' silence as a kind of shield of her own.

That Nan was to follow Elma and the twins—still he thought of them as the twins—was understood. She was the maid, the nanny, the mother of Wilson; she might as well have been Elma's sister. Already he felt a kind of reverent love for her. Like Juke Jesup he had been called a nigger lover more than once, but for the work he did on a Negro disease, not because he liked to get in bed with them. He did love Nan, but in the same way he loved Wilson—as a child of God. She was neither girl nor woman to him. He didn't like to know he felt this way about her. He supposed it had something to do with her being dumb. He liked the idea of loving a Negro. He liked the idea of marrying one. The concept, what it meant; it was like marrying the earth. It would be the only thing that might kill his father faster than marrying the barefoot daughter of a bootlegger.

His first thought—stupid, unthinkable, and yet he'd thought it—was to claim the twins as his own. He had been riding home from work that Monday evening, after his father had left with the girls, and as the streetcar careened down Virginia Avenue, the colored women standing at the rear of the car while he sat, women who had worked twelve, fourteen, sixteen hours for white families in Inman Park, their grocery bags swaying with each turn, he thought of Irene, the maid his family had employed since he was a child. And he thought of those two girls, how they were returning home to keep their own house, resigned to raising their children as bastards, and he wondered why he couldn't be father to them. He was a man of medicine: he knew that it was possible for twins to have two fathers. It wasn't magic; it was science. But what kind of life would they lead? They were going to be raised under a story their mothers told: why not improve the story? He would claim that he and the girl—Elma—had had an affair. He would claim Negro blood in his family line. Who was he to know there wasn't some, somewhere over the last century or two? He would save the children from a life of shame, and bring shame to his father. Two birds.

But then—no—the streetcar had turned onto Rosedale; the women swayed—he would have to admit that Elma had lied. That she had covered for her father. That an innocent man had been lynched. His lie, kind as it was, would implicate the girl.

But by the time he'd stepped off the streetcar, he was already implicated. In his mind, he had already married her. That was what he would do, then. He would marry her, if she would have him. Wouldn't she have him? Wouldn't she be grateful? He would be a stepfather, if not a father. He would be a husband. A husband and a stepfather. Was there anything more noble? He walked the two blocks to his door, the words following the gait of his good leg and his bad: husband, stepfather.

Now he shifted himself from his childhood bed into his old wheelchair, the one that stayed here in his parents' house, its wicker weave rotten with holes. His father still called it an invalid chair, a phrase Oliver detested. He rolled into the kitchen and toasted two slices of bread and halved an alligator pear and settled it all in a breakfast tray across his lap. Then he delivered it to his mother and father in their bedroom. He had been born in this room, on this four-poster bed. His father had delivered all six of his children here, and now he was dying in it.

Five of those children were married with children of their own, and all of them lived in far-flung Southern cities bigger than Florence, which made his father proud and his mother lonesome. That he, the youngest child, the bachelor bound, depending on the day, to crutches, cane, or wheelchair, was the one called on to care for his aging parents, struck Oliver as unreasonable. But his father had said, waving his hand, "You're the one who doesn't want to be treated like a cripple." Three years before, for Oliver's first visit to Warm Springs, his father had driven his new Plymouth Phaeton all the way up to Buffalo, New York, to have it outfitted with hand controls so Oliver could learn to drive, at a cost he liked to bring up whenever he wrote a check to pay for the installments. It was a Phaeton like Governor Roosevelt's Phaeton, in licorice black.

His mother claimed to be improving. Heartened by the visits of her children and grandchildren at Christmas, she had risen from bed, dressed, even gone to the nine o'clock service at First Methodist the first Sunday of the year. When Oliver brought in the tray, she scrambled awake and patted her night bonnet and hung both legs over the edge of the bed. She would take her breakfast in the dining room, for she was well, she was well, she had just needed rest.

Manford was not well. The flu had given way to an unpleasant case of pneumonia. He could barely sit up against the pillow without help. Oliver held the glass of orange juice to his lips and tipped it back, as he did every hour, according to the Gerson Therapy. The old man said, "Curse the cotton-picking orange and the juice from it."

"The cotton-picking orange is the only hope you have left."

"Nonsense. I need rest."

"You need minerals to fight the toxins. Max Gerson—"

"Curse minerals and curse Max Gerson."

"Max Gerson is a revolutionary in Germany. Tuberculosis will be a thing of the past once—"

"Don't talk about the diseases that will be cured when I'm dead. An old man doesn't need to hear about the future. An old man needs bacon and a cup of black coffee."

"Max Gerson recommends a coffee enema. It could be arranged."

His father shook his head, disgusted, then winced. Even shaking his head brought him pain. "Irene wouldn't do this to me," he said.

Oliver was struck silent. His father had not mentioned her name

since Oliver had been home, though her absence was everywhere. She
had been with the family since before Oliver was born. Every day,
Monday through Saturday, she had cleaned the house and prepared
the meals and, when he was young and still recovering from polio,
cared for Oliver (for a time they had hired another cook, Glory, so
Irene could tend to him round the clock), and then she had walked
the two and a half miles back to the Fourth Ward, where she cleaned
her own house and prepared her own dinner (after a time, she was a
widow, her husband having died of a mysterious illness) and cared
for her own daughter, Daisy. When Daisy got sick, and then sicker,
Irene brought her with her to the Rawlses' house, and Oliver's mother
allowed her to lie on a cot in the back room, provided she stayed out
of sight. It was the room Irene stayed in when she needed to stay the
night, and some nights, when Daisy was in too much pain to move,
and Oliver's mother relented, they both stayed. In the back room
Daisy drank bone broth and played with a colored doll named Lola
(Lola was also sick, and had a feather pillow for a bed), and watched
through the little window as the cardinals visited the crape myrtle in
the backyard, their breasts the same red as the tree's blossoms in the
spring. Doctors were just becoming familiar with sickle cell disease
back then. Even Oliver's father didn't know what was wrong with her
at first. He'd missed the mass, which was hidden under her ribs. It
was Oliver, once he'd gone away to medical school, who had matched
her symptoms and brought Daisy to Atlanta for tests, and said as
likely as not, the way the disease was passed down, it was what had
killed her father. By then her spleen was swollen, the doctors believed,
to twice its normal size; to save the girl's life, it would have to be
removed. But Oliver's father didn't trust the doctors on the colored
ward at Grady. He cared for Daisy—he didn't want a stranger opening
her up. So quietly he'd brought in a white colleague from Macon, not
an expert in sickle cell but an expert surgeon, and his father believed
Irene should consider herself grateful. Because it wasn't every day that
colored folks were given the highest standard of care, she was to be

quiet about it—he didn't need every Negro in the Fourth Ward coming to his office asking for his organs to be operated on. Oliver didn't like the idea, but he hadn't even begun his residency—the care was out of his hands. He had been in a classroom in Atlanta, two hundred miles away, when the surgeon had taken out Daisy's spleen—"heavy as a flank steak" was how Dr. Rawls later put it—and she died of a hemorrhage, at ten years old, on the metal table in the colored exam room of his father's office.

It was true that his father felt sadness. Oliver knew he did. But there was nothing to be done. The girl would have died before long, Dr. Rawls said, with or without her spleen. The surgeon from Macon could not have been held accountable, even if he'd been operating in a proper hospital. Dr. Rawls told Irene that they had done their best, and Irene said that she believed him. She kept it quiet, as she was told. Oliver had exams, but he came home for the funeral anyway, where he was the only white face in attendance, and where he could not look Irene in the eye. Irene told her people that Daisy's spleen had ruptured. She had been sick for so long, after all. But Oliver knew. He saw the way Irene moved about his parents' house, listless, without her spirit. He knew she stayed because she had no choice. Though it was true she did the job of three women—cook and nurse and maid—his parents paid her as high a wage as she could expect at any house in Florence; and his mother allowed her to take home a full service pan each evening, or from time to time a wooden spoon with a split handle, or the stump of a wax candle, which she might melt together with another candle when she got one; and his father didn't—dear God he hoped he didn't—try to get under her apron, as all the other men in the First Ward did with their colored housemaids, their wives turning away to powder their noses. They were bound by a mutual dependence, the Rawls family and Irene, and in the silent way kin sometimes were, by guilt and by grief.

Oliver returned to Atlanta and passed his exams. He might have hung his name and his hat at his father's office then, but instead he went to the office of Dr. Charles Mercer, head of pathology at Emory, and asked him for a job. There was no hematology program yet—and certainly no study of sickle cell, outside the treatment of the poor black patients who came through Grady—but Mercer let him do what he could as a technician in the pathology lab. He fooled around with slides, sampled tissues from patients at Grady, organized the specimens in the room they called the museum. In Florence, his father carried on his practice. And Irene continued coming to the house, morning after morning, year after year, until last summer, when she had left on the Ponce de Leon for Cincinnati, Ohio, where she had a sister. She had been with the family ten years before Daisy, ten years with Daisy, and ten years without her again.

Everywhere he looked in the old house, he was faced with the irrepressible memory of Irene. The gingham seat cushions she had sewn for the kitchen chairs, and the little silk tassel she had attached to the electric light chain in the front room so she could reach—she was small, no taller than five feet in the pumps she wore every day— and the burn mark on the Hoosier cabinet where she had set a hot teakettle. And everywhere, her notes. She would use the old sheets from Dr. Rawls's prescription pads, before he had added a telephone number, and affix them with a bit of surgical tape to the Frigidaire, to the front door, to whatever fixture needed attention: *Call about newspaper. Mind broken bulb. Eat chicken by Sunday.* She was left-handed, and her cramped cursive leaned back as if blown by a strong wind. After Daisy died, she began to use the notes for her Psalms. *Taste and see that the Lord is good. Cast your cares on the Lord and he will sustain you. Be strong and take heart and wait for the Lord.* Oliver believed they were instructions to herself, but now she was gone and they remained around the house in their fading blue ink like so many unfilled prescriptions. Did his parents leave them up because they couldn't bear to take them down, or because they'd never really seen them, as they'd never really seen her?

When he had asked his parents if they would consider hiring new help—a maid or even a nurse, who could help them wash and eat and get about—his father again waved his hand. He had survived in his own practice for thirty-nine years without need of a nurse, he said; he did not need one now. He did not need anyone who was not Irene, was what Oliver concluded.

His mother spoke of their move to his sister's in Savannah as though it was a temporary arrangement, until their "lungs cleared." There was nothing like the pure salt air of the sea—he knew this better than anyone—but he didn't know if his father would even make it to Savannah, and he knew she couldn't carry on here, not without his father, not without Irene. The Christmas tree Oliver had put up was shedding its brown needles. The leaf was still in the dining room table, every chair and stool and piano bench in the house marshaled around it, as bloated and empty as when his brothers and sisters had stood and walked away from it for the last time.

It was the sixteenth of January, his twenty-seventh birthday. His parents did not remember, and he did not remind them.

And yet he saw in his mind's eye another family gathered around the table—Elma and the children, whom he would raise—but not claim—as his own. It would be their stockings hung on the mantel next Christmas. Nobody in Florence—or in Atlanta, for that matter—would understand. His parents would not understand, and so he had not told them. He was a young man with a bright future, a promising practice, if he took it. He'd been, like all of his siblings, to college, and unlike all of them, beyond it, to one of the finest medical schools in the country. Even Elma did not understand—why was he leaving his life in Atlanta, his research, his livelihood, to marry her?

You are right to be wary, he wrote to her. *You have been taught to distrust. And it is true I am leaving much behind. But I feel God is calling me home.*

He did not write that his own oak dining set, purchased from Rhodes on the installment plan, had been hauled away last month after three months of failing to make a payment. It was built in the Flemish style, with a checkered inlay that Oliver thought would make a nifty chessboard. It had been a foolish purchase. No one but he had sat at that table, aside from the widow from whom he rented his room, the only room, it seemed, in all of Atlanta that was on the ground floor. She invited herself for tea on Sunday afternoons—he had the back half of the first floor, with an entrance to the back porch, and another, the one he thought of as the widow's entrance, that opened out onto her front hall—and she came through this door and talked at him about her dead husband, what a handsome man he'd been and she what a comely girl, and her grown son Leonard, who lived with her still upstairs, and her lap dog Kitty. Last month she came to his room and saw that the table was gone, and he explained that it was being refinished. When she came again the next Sunday, he did not answer her knock. He did not want to see the truth settle on her face, the cold pity in her blue, teary, heavy-lidded eyes, which on Sundays she painted with rose shadow. The next week, Rhodes came for the chifforobe. And then the next week, the Monday before Thanksgiving, Elma Jesup walked into the hospital and into his mind and stayed there. His room was now near empty, empty of everything but his wheelchair, which he liked to drape with his suit when he removed it, as though by dressing it up he might camouflage it, and the bed, which sat in the middle of the room like a beached ship. But Elma filled it. She filled the room and she filled the bed. When he lay down in it, she rose up into his mind. He saw the Negro girl's breast and Elma's face and he was confused. He tossed in the bed. In his dreams, waves crashed around it. He dreamt he was back on the floating hospital. He dreamt Elma was his nurse, and that Irene was, and Nan. As he did too often, he dreamt of Daisy, her little body split open, her spleen blooming with crape myrtle blossoms. He got out of the bed and slept on the floor, hoping the girls, all the girls, would stay in it. He woke and dressed and went to the lab, but there was no work for him there. There was no money. He was typing a letter to Elma when his advisor came in, Dr. Mercer, and perched at the edge of his desk and told him that his work would be over by the end of the year. It was not a surprise but it was a blow. The funding on the latest project was dry, he said, dry as the dust in a mummy's pocket. Oliver was the most junior researcher on the team, the only one with any interest in blood. There was a depression on and no donors wanted to spend their precious nickels on Negro research. He could keep his desk at the university, but there was no telling when he'd be on the payroll again. Mercer said Oliver had his sympathies. When he was gone, Oliver sat for a moment. Then he typed to Elma, *After a good amount of thought I am beginning to consider my father's offer.* There was no need to stay. He packed up the desk and brought the typewriter to his rented room and laid it on a pillow on his lap, and sat in bed typing to her. He did not answer the widow's knock. For three days he didn't leave his room, not even to take his meals at Torrence's, for he had six dollars to his name. He ate only baked beans and pork rinds and his own pressed coffee. He went only as far as the mailbox, while the widow walked Kitty, to mail his letters. The widow would not cease her knocking, the sound became like the barking of her inane little dog, to which he had grown deaf. When finally she turned her key in the door, he did his best to leap from the bed and knot the belt of his robe and block the room with his body, but in his haste, his cane clattered to the ground, and there was no other furniture left on which to lean. "Dr. Rawls," she said, "you're late with the rent," and the gentleness in her voice was almost too much to bear. He looked at her with one eye, looked around the near-empty room with the other. He leaned on the foot of the bed. "That is a fine bed, Dr. Rawls," she said, looking beyond him. Now he looked at her with both eyes. She might have been a beautiful woman in her youth, but now she was stoop backed, so that he could see the part in her dark hair where her pink scalp gave way to white roots. He waited in the doorway for the humiliation. It would be worse than the call house he had frequented on Cain Street, if "frequented" was the right word for the three times he had visited the place, because the girls there were a half mile short of pretty—fat or flat-chested, or the one with the whiskers on her chin and eyes so far apart she was like a catfish, never meeting his own eyes, which was fine by him—but they were not old. He closed his eyes now and waited for the widow to make her move into his room. He would do what he must do, what he could do, and she would end up even sorrier for him. But what she said was, "My Leonard could use a fine bed like that. Is that a Simmons mattress?"

Oliver opened his eyes and found his voice. "Yes, ma'am. It's a Beautyrest, I believe. Near about new."

The bed stood in the room. In the center of the oak headboard was a carved owl that now stared at him like the fool he was. So he would be humiliated after all.

"I'll give you twelve dollars for it," she said, taking out her purse and unclasping it. "The mattress and the frame."

"I can't take less than twenty," he found himself saying.

She pretended to consider. "Well, seeing as you owe fifteen for rent, let's call it square."

He too pretended to consider. Then he told the widow that was fine. She said she'd send Leonard down for the bed when they could find help to move it, and as it came into his mind, he told her he'd be leaving come Christmas.

He did not write any of this to Elma. He did not say, *No one else would have me.*

———————

The summer of 1916, the year the boll weevil came to Cotton County, his mother and his two brothers and three sisters traveled by train to Boston, Massachussetts, to visit his aunt Josephine, his mother's sister, who had married a man in railroad stocks. They lived in a big brick house crawling with ivy, and his brothers and sisters all shared the third-floor attic, where three bunk beds were wedged between the dormer windows. His brothers turned the attic into a grand fort, hanging quilts from the top bunks, launching feather pillows like grenades from one bed to another. (This was the summer before his elder brother, Roger, went off to the real war.) In the afternoons his sisters drank tea with Aunt Josephine—hot tea from a kettle, with milk instead of sugar. And they all rode a swan boat at Boston Common and a streetcar down Washington Street and bought bathing suits at Jordan Marsh. One afternoon toward the end of summer they all wore their new suits to a public swimming pool, and jumped off the wooden diving platform again and again, except Oliver, the youngest at twelve, who to his adolescent humiliation couldn't swim. He stayed at the shallow end, holding tight to the pipe that ran round the pool and kicking, as though he was just taking a break. The next morning, waking in the bunk below his sister, he couldn't lift his legs.

Later, when it was clear that the polio in the Northeast had reached epidemic proportions, his father would say it was that swimming pool, and his mother would say nonsense, Boston was clean, they changed the water every week, and besides, Oliver was the only one who'd caught it. His mother said it was his father's office back home, where Oliver liked to play with the skeleton and the stethoscope and the children, in the white waiting room and the colored, and his father said nonsense, none of his patients had polio, there was no polio in the South, the South was hardy. His mother and father carried the argument back home with them to Georgia, where they returned at the end of August with his five brothers and sisters, for it was time for his father to get back to his patients, and time for his brothers and sisters to start school. Oliver himself was to begin the seventh grade, but instead he spent the first day of school on the Massachusetts Bay, in a bed in a quarantine room on the floating hospital. Imagine that! his aunt Josephine said. Each evening after supper she visited him when the ship docked in Boston Harbor. A children's hospital on a boat! A room of his own with a view of the bay! Oh, his friends back home would be green with envy. She couldn't get close, though. She had to stay behind the chicken wire over the door to his room, and yell through the silk scarf she wore over her nose and mouth. She yelled the news from home. His mother had written a letter. His brother Phillip had made the varsity football team. His sister Marjorie had gotten engaged. They send their love! she yelled through her scarf before she left. Her voice sounded as though she was talking into a pillow. His aunt Josephine and uncle Lars, the uncle in railroad stocks, had had a baby of their own, a girl, who had died of tuberculosis the previous summer, just before her first birthday.

From his bed, through the closed window, he tracked the day—the departure from the North River wharf, the blue ribbon of the bay unspooling, the black-tailed gulls that came to perch on the railing. His room was on the bottom floor, and from the deck two floors above he could faintly hear the delighted cries of the well children, who seemed to be there for nothing more than a day of fresh air. Nothing like salt air in the lungs, said Dr. Abelard, though the window in Oliver's room didn't open. Dr. Abelard was the hospital's sole physical therapist, a young, dark-skinned man with long sideburns and gold-rimmed glasses. He wore white cloth gloves and, like the nurses, a formidable white handkerchief over his mouth and nose. Through the handkerchief, his voice also was muffled, but he had a light, lilting accent that rose and fell like the ship on the waves. At first, there was nothing much that Dr. Abelard could do for him. He came in and inspected the warm wool bandages the nurses wrapped on his legs and massaged his calves and lifted and lowered Oliver's matchstick legs. He called Oliver "sailor" and shook his hand good-bye. Oliver had never shaken a colored man's hand before, and even through the doctor's cotton glove he'd felt a fearful thrill at his firm, smooth grip, as he'd felt when he'd first grasped a fish with two hands.

"Have you never seen a Haitian doctor before?" he asked Oliver, catching his stare. Oliver thought that, behind the handkerchief, the doctor was smiling.

He felt himself flush. "I thought you were a Negro," he managed to say.

"The Negro hails from all over the world, little sailor. I come from an island nation called Haiti, where it is too warm for your poliovirus."

"I come from a warm place too," was all Oliver could think of.

Nights were dark and lonely with the big bay beyond his window. He imagined the sea creatures sleeping under it and couldn't sleep. He got to sleeping during the daytime, sleeping through the parade of the other doctors with their clipboards and stethoscopes, who seemed to prefer that he sleep. He slept through the visits of the day nurse, who changed his dressings with the same hasty, disinterested manner with which she might make a sandwich. He woke only when Dr. Abelard came. The smell of the warm wet wool on his legs burned into his sleep, but he couldn't feel it.

After two weeks, when it was determined that Oliver was no longer contagious, he was moved to the floor above. The ward was half the length of the whole ship, with an aisle down the middle and beds lined up along either side, close enough so that two patients might reach out and hold each other's hand, and windows that opened to the sea. And in the ward were other children, more than a dozen of them. He was progressing toward the healthy ward above; soon, he told himself, he would make it to the highest level, the deck, where he might stand upright in the salt wind. He was desperately happy to be with other children, but they were all younger than he, and they spent much of the day napping, still too sick, or too paralyzed, to do much of anything. Some of them were so small they slept in cribs stacked along the wall. He tried to think of them as bunk beds, but they reminded him of a chicken coop. Most astonishingly of all, one of the patients was a Negro child, a girl of six or seven, who was learning to walk with a cane, and who was made to wear a sleeping bonnet. (And though Oliver never shared a word with her, and never learned her name—she was gone after a week, gone to the upper deck—he would years later confuse her in his dreams with Daisy.) She was on the far side of the room, but she was there all the same, lying in her bed that was like all the white children's beds, staring at the same ceiling, breathing the same air. (Her name was Franny.)

Oliver's first evening on the ward, Dr. Abelard came in with a tremendous box of books. He put them down on a table and lowered his handkerchief around his neck, which gave him the look of a cowboy. The doctor smiled and Oliver could see his tall pink gums. In the lower row of teeth, a gold cap shined.

The books, the doctor said, were for the boys and girls to keep. The children whooped. Most of them knew what Oliver did not yet know, that their things at home—their books, their clothes, their blankets and pillows and dolls—had been burned. The day nurse, who kept her handkerchief in place, helped the doctor to distribute the books. The books, he said, when he reached Oliver's bed, had been donated by Oliver's aunt and uncle. Oliver looked about for his aunt Josephine. She had come every evening for ten days, and then she had skipped an evening, and then she had skipped two.

"She's not here," Dr. Abelard said, lowering himself into the chair beside his bed.

"Where is she?"

Dr. Abelard softened the truth only a little. "She sent the books in with her driver. She's not coming today, sailor. She may not be here for some time. She sent word that she has come down with a condition of her own, and doesn't want to infect the children."

Still Oliver was looking for her. It didn't make sense—he was out of quarantine now. Now she could come to his bedside, hold his hand. "She's sick?"

"She sent word that she is sick."

"Did I . . . was I the one to make her sick?"

"No, sailor. You're past that now."

Was it better if she really was sick, or if she wasn't? To keep his voice steady, Oliver said, "You look like a cowboy."

"Do you like cowboys?" Dr. Abelard asked, smiling.

Oliver nodded. "Cowboys and Indians."

"I think we have some of them in this box." The doctor fished out a book. *The Last of the Mohicans.*

"I love that one!" Oliver said. "I read it last year."

"Ah? Well, myself, I haven't read it yet. So you can read it to me and to my friends here"—he waved his arm across the ward—"while I say good morning to your gastrocnemius muscles. In your biggest voice, please." And he took Oliver's left leg in his gloved hands and began to massage his calf.

That night, Oliver tried to put together his aunt Josephine's face in his mind. He tried to put together his mother's face. He dreamt of the pool he'd clung to, the waters as deep and dark as the bay, dreamt of being pulled down under, where fish with snouts like swords passed through the seaweeds at his feet. He woke to daylight, to the feeling of being adrift on the bed of his dream. And then he looked out the window and remembered that he was adrift, and that his family no longer waited for him on the shore.

One morning in the fourth week, he found he could wiggle his right leg. The next day he could lift it. Nothing like the pure salt sea air, Dr. Abelard said again.

The left leg, though, it stayed pinned to the bed. It was as though it belonged to someone else. It was as though his left leg had gotten up and walked away and joined that someone else's body instead.

His right leg grew and his left leg didn't. One day through the charred smell of sleep he woke to catch the look on the day nurse's face as she changed the wool dressing. It was as though she'd come across a stray parsnip left to rot and shrink in the garden.

It was the day nurse who washed him, head to toe, every other evening before her shift ended, with a pan of water and Pears soap and the same kind of wool cloths she wrapped around his legs. She folded down the sheet and folded down the waist of his pajamas and washed him as though there wasn't a roomful of eyes on him, as though he wasn't the oldest of them, and a growing boy. He closed his eyes as she washed him, so he wouldn't see the disgust in her eyes, wouldn't see his willy flinch like a kinked garden hose. *Parsnip, shrink, rot.* He could not use Pears soap ever again, and when he smelled it once as a grown man, on a girl at the call house on Cain Street, he insulted her by departing so quickly, before she'd removed a slip of clothing, that he left his cane behind in the room and had to knock again to extract it. She had made him pay double for the cane.

He wrote all of this in a letter to Elma that January, as they waited for the wedding. The pool, the hospital, Dr. Abelard, the nurse. He wanted and didn't want her to know that she was marrying a cripple. He wanted her to know the truth, the magnitude of his paralysis, the wilt and whim of his manhood. If his manhood was enfeebled, he believed, it was a result of the indignity of the Pears soap as much as it was of the polio. He wrote the story in his way, with an affinity for the word "unfortunately," for occasional, forgivable lapses into self-loathing, into self-satisfaction. If he had mailed the letter, if Elma had read it, she might have understood that he wrote in the way of a boy who'd spent many bedridden years reading Walter Scott and Daniel Defoe. But what if she didn't understand? What if she felt the same horror as that nurse, and changed her mind, and refused to marry him? What if—worse—she felt pity, and married him because of it?

He burned the letter in the same fireplace where Irene had been made to burn his clothes and his sheets and his books. Even in the letter he had burned, he could not bring himself to mention that, unfortunately, the day nurse was very beautiful. He knew this with certainty, though he never saw her full face—always she wore the white handkerchief over her nose and mouth. But she had long pink fingers and a neat blond bun and eyelashes that shuttered open and closed neatly like a baby doll's eyelashes. One evening, when Dr. Abelard asked her to take a patient's temperature, the disgust came to her face again. Her eyes snapped shut entirely, as though the request was too difficult to carry out. When she was finally able to move to the child's bed at the opposite end of the ward—it was the Negro girl's bed, the little Negro girl with the sleeping bonnet—Dr. Abelard yanked the handkerchief hanging from his neck and leaned close to Oliver's ear. "You think she might like me to wear this all the time?"

Oliver stared.

"I look more like a bandit that way." He thumped the book Oliver was reading. "Like the cops and robbers you like so much? It makes her more comfortable."

Oliver said, "Maybe she's just scared of catching something."

The doctor shrugged. "Everyone's scared. One can't be blamed."

Oliver understood, and was proud that he understood, that the doctor was diverting attention from the Negro girl, that he might borrow some of her shame. He was fiddling with Oliver's bandages now, though they were fresh and still warm, and didn't need fiddling.

"Some people," Dr. Abelard said, "some people, they like everybody to wear a mask. You must not bother with them, Oliver. Do you understand? You must keep walking forward."

Oliver nodded. And then he did see his aunt's face in his mind, not her whole face but her gibbous eyes above her scarf, full of panic, as though she were being strangled.

After Oliver had been on the floating hospital five months—five months of bandages, of stretching and contracting, of salt air and massage, of being lifted into a wheelchair, of racing the wheelchair up and down the ward, of being lifted back into the bed—Dr. Abelard fit him for a brace. Slowly, slowly, he practiced walking on crutches up and down the hall, leading with his good leg, swinging his bad one after it. He was by that time thirteen, and his left leg, which would remain in a brace for the rest of his life, was already an inch shorter than the other. The brace bolted into a new black oxford shoe, which matched a free one he wore on his right foot, plus a platform heel to make up the inch. He was one of the lucky ones, Dr. Abelard told him. His lungs had not been paralyzed. He was not confined to a wheelchair, though he would depend on one for distances. He had not spread the illness to his brothers or sisters. He had lived, unlike some of the other children who had been quarantined, unlike one of the babies on the ward, even, who one morning had not woken from her cage of a bed.

His father was the one to come fetch him. Before he did, Dr. Abelard carried Oliver up the stairs to the uppermost level, and watched him make his way across the deck with his new crutches as the gulls swooped overhead. It wasn't walking as much as dragging, it was horrid, ugly limping, a mummy's walk, but the sun was everywhere and the winter air smelled almost like the white clay along the Creek River and his tears burned in the wind. "You'll be running before long, little sailor," said Dr. Abelard. "You're going to run back to Georgia and forget about me."

Then there was his father, out of breath himself, at the top of the stairs. The sun reflected off his glasses.

"Emmanuel, is it?" his father said, nodding at Dr. Abelard but not shaking his hand. He offered neither a "Mister" nor a "Doctor," and the doctor did not remind him that that was what he was.

"Dr. Rawls, I'm pleased to meet you. Master Oliver has been waiting for you."

Oliver hobbled over on his crutches. It seemed a very long way. He was afraid that his father might shake his hand—he was nearly a man now, after all—but instead he pulled Oliver to him and he felt the leather gloves on his neck and the kiss on the top of his head, a kiss for a small child, and again his tears burned and he was glad that the wind whipped them back.

Dr. Abelard did not have a hug or a handshake for Oliver. He was smart enough to withhold them. On the train ride home, his father flipped through the papers Oliver had been discharged with, and then he stuffed them into his suitcase. "Massage? Salt air? Is this what I've been paying for for six months?"

"It was more than that," Oliver said. "Dr. Abelard—"

"Was there no snake oil? Did they not pack your legs with clay? I might have saved some money and paid a conjure woman in Georgia."

It was Dr. Abelard Oliver cried for on the train, silently, so as not to disturb his father, who had developed the habit of sleeping while sitting up perfectly straight, a newspaper held up in front of his face with barely a flutter. Oliver looked out the window at the fall colors of the countryside running alongside them. Even then, back on solid ground, he felt he might never catch up, he might never have his legs beneath him. For weeks afterward, he felt seasick, the world around him rocking.

At home, when he was back in his bed, with new starched sheets and a stiff new pillow, Irene brought him bone broth and ham hocks made by the new cook and a bit of wood to whittle. She massaged his legs, the good one and the bad, as Dr. Abelard had instructed. His father hired him a pink-faced gnome of a tutor, who would catch him up on his schoolwork while he regained his strength and prepared to return next year. Oliver would catch up so well that he would move straight to the high school in the fall, where he was the smallest boy in the ninth grade, even with his platform shoe.

For now, he lay in bed and, between his textbooks, he read the books Dr. Abelard had given him—that his aunt and uncle had given him—stories of adventure, of cowboys and Indians, of cops and robbers, of boys swinging through jungles, raiding ships, falling in love. Irene moved between his bed and, in the back room, little Daisy's. She was three years old then and already sick, her father already dead. She had seemed a healthy baby when she was born, when Ketty Smith had delivered her on Irene's bed in the Fourth Ward. Irene had paid Ketty with a sugar bowl that Mrs. Rawls had let her take home when the lid was chipped, porcelain with red and blue flowers and a silver spoon that fit inside it, though there was nothing wrong with the spoon.

Oliver knew what Daisy saw out the window of her room because it was what he saw out the window of his. The angle was different, but it was the same crape myrtle tree, brittle and bark colored the winter he returned, then bleeding red blooms in the spring. The tree made shade, the cardinals came to it. It wasn't until many springs later that he understood how silly it was, cruel, that he and Daisy had suffered alone in their separate rooms, when he might have been close enough to reach out from his bed and hold her hand, or, in his biggest voice, read her a story.

Doctoring was hard enough work with working legs. With his dead leg, leaning on a crutch with his right hand while trying to work with his left—he was right-handed; it was all wrong—his strength was exhausted performing a routine exam. In the lab, he'd had the comfort of a desk chair, but in an exam room, there was nothing to hide behind. "Why don't you sit down, Dr. Oliver?" They wouldn't call him Dr. Rawls. In the eyes of his patients, he would never be his father—he was a crippled jackleg doctor who thought he was city smart. Eventually, Oliver did sit down, and in the wheelchair he could move between his desk and the exam table without losing his breath. There was no fooling country people. They had known him when he was fourteen years old, propelling his wicker wheelchair down the sidewalk of Main Street. Now, every morning, Monday through Friday, he traveled over the same path in the same chair, from his parents' house, where years before they'd had a ramp built to the back porch, down the three shady blocks where the picket fences gave way to brick storefronts, to the office. He had never approved of his father's refusal to travel to the country, but there would be no traveling for Oliver either—the three blocks were as far as he would go.

It was a kind of relief, once he gave into it—the cold, bracing inevitability of being known. He had left the sleepwalking anonymity of the city behind. Folks stopped their cars and wagons on the street as he squeaked by in his chair. Did his mother need their girl to take in their laundry? Did they need any eggs? Could he look at Joe Junior's eyes? They were turning in again.

Manford Rawls had refused breakfast three days in a row when George Wilson came to the house. Oliver answered the door. He was tempted to tell him he was sorry, his father was too sick for visitors. But it was a Saturday morning, and he had no patients waiting for him, and he reckoned he'd best get it over and done. It was just a week to the wedding. He wanted to marry Elma without George Wilson knocking on his door. Oliver let him in. George had a kiss on the hand for Carlotta and a Bundt cake from Parthenia that their girl Mag had made. Oliver led him on his crutches to the bedroom, because there was no hope of getting his father out of bed, and set up two dining chairs at the foot of it.

"You come to pay your respects?" Manford asked. The sentence had knocked out his breath, but he took another and said, "I ain't dead yet."

George Wilson settled into one of the chairs and settled his white hat on his knee. He did not take off his white suit jacket. "I come to see if you're as sick as they say, or if you're just pawning off your patients on this poor young doctor."

"That poor doctor would do well to stop forcing his patients to drink citrus juice."

George laughed. "That what they're prescribing these days?"

Manford began to laugh as well, but a cough stifled it.

"You ain't to be replaced, Manford. That's for certain. But I'm sure he'll do fine, this young doctor, once he can figure out how to get a baby out of its mother."

Oliver regarded George Wilson, then his father.

"I sent my colored boy here fortnight ago, one of them knocked-up mill girls high in labor, I get word Dr. Oliver has taken over the practice, but he don't deliver him any babies."

Manford squinted at Oliver.

"It's not that I don't deliver them," Oliver said helplessly. "It's that I *haven't* delivered them."

"Son," Manford said, disappointed.

"I'm not schooled in your ways, Daddy. Forgive me." Oliver gripped the worn handle of his crutch. "Y'all two seem to know some clever ways to get a baby out of its mother. Almost as clever as getting a baby in."

"Son."

"I prefer to see them taken out whole."

"Son, that's enough."

"I sent the boy out to the crossroads," Oliver said. "For the Negro girl. The midwife's daughter."

"Christ," Manford said again. "George, I'm sorry."

"I reckoned she could use the money."

"I reckon so," said George, unbothered. "But I ain't inclined to invest a penny more in that farm. And I don't like owing favors to no trash."

"Jesup's trash," Oliver agreed. "But they're good girls. The midwife and the daughter. Nan and Elma are their names."

"I know their names," George said.

Oliver had felt the need to keep their names secret, in order to keep what he had learned secret, but that was silly. He hoped only that his father, in his weakened state, would remember to keep quiet about the right things.

"Imagine it," Oliver went on. "Growing up on that farm with that man. No grown folks with any sense left. Having to learn the ways of women from each other."

Manford said, "Man should have got him another wife while the daughter was small."

"She appears to get along all right," George said. "She's lucky to have what she has, that's for damn certain."

"She deserves more."

"Forgive him," Manford said. "My boy's got a liking for the redhead."

George's face seized with surprise. Oliver supposed his did too. "Suppose I do. What would you know of it?"

Manford managed to laugh. "Son, you're as transparent as an empty Coke bottle."

"She's always been a pretty girl," George said. "My grandson can attest to that."

"Have to find him first, wouldn't you?" Oliver had not planned to badger George Wilson, but he had not planned to speak to him at all. He cleared his throat. "I mean no disrespect toward you, sir. But I hold no respect for the man who ran off and left her with two young-uns to raise."

"One youngun," George corrected him. "He wasn't responsible for the other, any man with two eyes can see. And if the man who was had any respect for the girl, my grandson might still be here."

"Is that what you believe?" Oliver asked him. "That she was raped by the poor Jackson fellow? If that's so, why did you pay us to draw those babies' blood?"

George held up his hands. "You tell me. You tell me what you concluded."

"Nothing," Manford interrupted. "I told you: nothing. It was a bust. Without a sample from Jesup, that blood ain't worth two farts. Without taking blood, any one of us sitting in this room could be the father. It's in the blood, George. Even an old man like me knows that."

"Well, where's the goddamn blood, Manford. We would a had it if you'd a drawn some."

"You want to stick Juke Jesup with a needle, you stick him yourself. I can't even shit sitting up."

"I will if I have to! I got a man on the farm just to keep his two eyes on that trash. What does he see? Nothing! No one don't know nothing." Now it was George Wilson who was coughing. He coughed and coughed, then wiped his forehead with his handkerchief, then spit into it. "I know there's something no good on that farm, and the thing I hate most on this earth is seeing some slick trash like Juke Je-sup get away with it." His voice was weaker now. "Y'all don't give me no choice but to handle him myself."

"Leave the farm be," Oliver said quietly. "Leave the girls be." Soon they would be safe, he thought. He was doing the right thing, getting them off the farm. It didn't matter what became of Juke Jesup, how he was handled, as long as the girls and the twins were off the farm. "If you aren't willing to help her, to feed your own kin—"

"I help her by letting her lousy family feed off that land. Good land. Her poor excuse for a father scared my boy out of town. Pinned this whole ugly business on him. I don't know if he'll ever come home." He turned to Manford. "Been six months now. Do you know how it feels, not knowing if your boy will come home?"

Manford stared at the wallpaper. He and George Wilson had both had boys in the Eighty-Second Division. Roger had come home and String had not. But Manford was thinking about his youngest son as well. He cleared the phlegm from his throat. "I'm sorry we couldn't be of help, George."

George waved his hand. "I should have had lower expectations." He stood. From his coat pocket he took a pint bottle of Cotton Gin and set it on the nightstand beside the untouched glass of orange juice. "Even an old drymouth like you should have something to take the pain away." He rested a hand on Manford's shoulder. "Godspeed, Doctor."

To Oliver, at the front door, George said, "I were you, I'd stay a pretty mile away from that farm girl."

Oliver opened the door and looked out at the street. The January sky was a dismal gray, like an unlit milk-glass bulb. "I'm going to marry her, in fact. On Saturday." The words felt dangerously bright in the dull day, and hearing them out loud, he realized he hadn't been sure. He hadn't been sure he would marry her until he'd said it out loud, and realizing he'd been unsure, he was unsure again. He said, "I'm going to be a father to those children."

"Oh, for pity's sake." George put his hat on. "You marry the girl, you marry the father. Don't say no one warned you."

Oliver did not have the chance to tell his own father of his plans.

He had the chance, but he chose not to take it, as his father chose not to drink the gin. But on Wednesday morning, before he left for work, he rocked his father onto his side and sank a syringe full of morphine into his right buttock. "Remember the floating hospital? Remember the salt air? I know you had no mind for it then, but you got to listen to me now. Go on and float on the sea, Daddy. Go breathe deep, you hear?"

It was not enough to kill him, only enough to ease his passage. Just before eleven o'clock, while his mother sat by his father's bedside and brushed what was left of his hair—a man should go into death, she believed, with the dignity of brushed hair—Manford Rawls breathed his last rattling breath. Oliver was down the street massaging the swollen tonsils of a nine-year-old colored girl, in the exam room where his father had overseen the removal of Daisy's spleen, next door to the one where he had overseen the removal of God knew how many of George Wilson's offspring—"just tissue," he'd said, "just flesh." Things would be different now, Oliver thought. He would do things as differently as he could. He wheeled his chair home to fix his midday meal and found his mother there, still brushing his father's hair. Gently he took the brush from her. He kissed the silvery top of his father's head. Above the bed, on one of the prescription sheets, was Irene's clear-inked counsel: *Let not your hearts be troubled. In my Father's house are many rooms.*

TWENTY-TWO

THE SATURDAY HER HUSBAND PAID HIS LAST VISIT TO MANFORD Rawls, Parthenia Wilson paid a visit of her own to the county wagon. George had chosen to walk from the mill village down Main Street; he liked to feel the sun on his neck, and he liked to be seen. He was sitting at Manford's bedside when Frank drove the Buick past the doctor's porch with its grand ferns and, a short time later, past the crossroads farm, where Sara was crossing the yard, looking to borrow some sugar for a cream pie she was baking. Parthenia was bearing not pies this time but fry cakes, which Mag had cooked in hog lard and rolled in powdered sugar, and they were still warm in the box on her lap. Beside her on the seat was another box and in it were a dozen King James Bibles. In each one—because she couldn't be certain which would go to Freddie—she had underlined in shaky pencil (for she had a tremor) the verse from Acts: *Repent ye therefore, and be converted, that your sins may be blotted out, when the times of refreshing shall come from the presence of the Lord.* For good measure she had marked the page with each Bible's red ribbon, and when she reached the wagon and the rumbling trucks—for the men had made much progress, perhaps five miles' worth, from their camp in the pines—she handed the box to Lloyd Crow and said, "Have the men begin with Acts. Is there no preacher in these parts?" Mr. Crow said one had not been out, and she said she would send one the next morning, which was a Sunday. "Have the preacher start with Acts," she said. "Repentance is what the men need."

"Yes, ma'am," said Mr. Crow. "Repentance and hard work. Body and soul." He smiled as he took the box of fry cakes. "And stomach, of course."

She stood at the edge of the road, in the last stretch of dirt, the car door still open to the ditch weed. Ahead, the Straight glittered with the crystals of setting rock. The men laying it looked up over each other's backs to see the car, to eye the woman in the beaver coat. The white men allowed their eyes to linger, for they rarely saw a woman so close, and though she was old as the pines she was fine to look at, her waist trim and ladylike, even in the coat, her gloved hands like small dark sparrows. Then there among them was Freddie.

What was wrong with his eye? His right eye. It looked as though it had been sewn shut. Then he was looking back at her through the good eye. He winked it. It was horrifying, that squinty, one-eyed wink, but instinctively, she made to wink back, as one does when presented with a wink or a wave or a hand to shake. She would wink and turn her back to the men and get into the car and return home, where she would resume her embroidery, read her Bible verses, eat the fish cakes Mag was making, and then repair to her bedroom, where she would do as she had done nearly every afternoon since Freddie had gone: take the porcelain urn from the mantel, close herself in the water closet, and allow herself one teaspoon of the white Georgia clay she kept inside it. (It tasted like the farm, that clay; it tasted like the creek she'd bathed Georgie in. She'd never liked the name String. Always, to her, he'd been Georgie.) Then she'd lay a folded towel on the floor in front of the commode, kneel on it, exorcise the fish cakes and the clay both, and with the neat press of a lever, flush it all away.

She would stop, she'd told herself, when Freddie came home. She had been waiting and she had been waiting for the day when Freddie would return and she could return to life as she knew it, to meetings at the Chanticleer without Mary Minrath asking, "Any word? Any word?" And then the day had come. Sheriff Cleave had turned up on her porch with the news she had been waiting for: Freddie had been picked up in Meredith. He was alive, in a holding cell above Sheriff's own home. She imagined what might happen next: her husband would go down to the Third Ward and post bail, and their grandson would be back in his childhood bed by nightfall, and in the papers by the morning, which they would read over a large and fine breakfast. Would nothing change? She put her hand to her throat and looked out beyond the sheriff. His motorcycle was parked by the mailbox at the bottom of the steep drive. Along the mill village road, the chain gang was cleaning the ditches. If it hadn't been, the thought might not have crossed her mind.

"Does anybody know?" she asked him.

Sheriff cocked his head. "Just the two of us, ma'am. I picked him up myself. Came straight here to tell you. Thought you and George would want to know."

She told the sheriff what he was to do: go back to the jail, fetch Freddie, and deliver him to the chain gang. He was to give him a new name. He was to tell no one that Freddie had been found. She did not explain that there she could keep an eye on him, that she could ensure that he paid at least a small price for his crime.

Sheriff was confused. He couldn't do that. It was the warden's gang, for one—he didn't have any say over it. And for two, he owed it to George.

"You owe it to me," she corrected him. "My ladies of temperance would be very interested in your protection of my husband, Sheriff. They are very clever at writing letters."

She had thought he might be out there for a day or two. He would sweat. He would know what dirty work was. Surely it wouldn't take

long for a passing car to take notice of him, a mill worker crossing the
street, before all the town would know he'd returned.

She hadn't counted on her own husband transferring the gang out
into the wilderness, to ready another road. And she hadn't counted on
that squinty eye, which rendered his face, even to her, nearly unrecog-
nizable. She certainly hadn't counted on his own willingness to play
her game, a game he did not seem to know she had initiated.

It was infuriating, that wink. In it she saw all of the arrogance,
the ingratitude, the recklessness—the godlessness!—of her only son's
only son (did he know what it was to waste a life, when his father's life
had been wasted?), and her desperation to save him crashed against
her desperation to punish him further. "That man," she said to Lloyd
Crow.

"Which man, ma'am?"

"That boy in the back." She pointed, and the smile dropped from
Freddie's face. "He winked at me."

"He winked at you?"

Were he colored, she could have had him strung up in an instant.
Freddie himself would have done it for her. Had done it. Lynching was
ungodly, and trashy besides. The thought turned her stomach. She
had a weak stomach, that was the problem—she could not keep down
the sins of men.

"Who is he?" she asked Mr. Crow. Freddie was back to working
now, keeping his eyes on the road.

"Smith is his name. John Smith."

She nearly laughed.

"And what's happened to his eye?"

"Don't know, ma'am. He came to us that way."

"And how did he come to you, Mr. Crow? What is his crime?"

"His crime? He's new on the gang, ma'am. I believe it was petty
theft."

She blinked. Petty theft. Next to what he had done, it was like one
of the games he had played as a child—cops and robbers, cowboys

and Indians. They were playing games again. They had played peekaboo together when he was very small, and he was playing peekaboo
with her again. She waited for him to look up. Did he want her to play
along, or did he want to be rescued?

"I'll discipline him, ma'am. I'll find a way to keep him in line."

"No, no. Not necessary."

"I'll keep an eye on him, then."

"Does he not have an eye patch? Put an eye patch on that poor boy."

"An eye patch, ma'am?"

"I'll send one. Cover that eye. Does he mean to frighten an old
woman?"

"Yes, ma'am."

"Tell him to start with Acts," she said, and turned to go before
she changed her mind.

In the car, she did not cry. In the rearview, she watched Freddie's
silhouette stand up straight to watch her drive away. She closed her
eyes. She remembered what he'd looked like as a boy when she'd
looked in at him at night, his face still in sleep, both perfect eyes
closed, the shadows of his lashes on his cheeks. Georgie's boy. He
had been innocent once.

———————

By the time the car had passed the crossroads farm on its way back
to town, Sara had borrowed the two tablespoons of sugar she needed
for her cream pie. Elma hadn't seen her reach into the kitchen window
and take Ketty's old sugar bowl from the sill; her back was turned; she
was breading a chicken. That night Jim and Sara came again to the big
house for supper, and afterward, while the twins rattled a catalpa pod
in the cotton basket on the floor, while Jim and Juke drank tumblers
of gin and they all sat eating slices of the pie, all but Elma, who said
no thank you, Sara reached for the little sugar bowl that had found its
way to the table, making to sweeten her tea, declaring, "This baby has
got a sweet tooth!" The bowl was porcelain with red and blue flow-

ers and a dainty little lid that was chipped and a silver spoon that fit inside it, and too late Elma remembered the last time she had opened that lid, just as Sara served up the jade ring, and gasping, making a show, missed the teacup and spilled the ring and the sugar out on the table. "What in Heaven?" she asked.

Elma scooped up the ring and, holding it in her palm, blew a cloud of sugar from it like dust. "There you are!" she said to it, as though it were a tiny frog prince. "I forgot I put you in there."

"What is it?" Juke said. He'd been leaning back on the hind legs of his chair, and now he sat up and let them fall flat.

"It's a ring, Daddy. I was hiding it for safekeeping."

"Whose ring?"

"Looks like an engagement ring to me," said Sara.

Elma's heart was pounding, but she saw that there was no backing out, that there was no more putting it off. If she was going to tell her father, she might as well do it here, with Jim and Sara at the table, where he wouldn't be tempted to kick her chair out from under her. "As a matter of fact, it is." She looked to Nan, who was looking for something deep inside her teacup. Maybe a ring of her own. She looked to her father, who was squinting at the ring. "I'm fixing to get married to Dr. Oliver Rawls."

Now she slipped the ring onto her finger. It was a little loose, but it hung heavy and it caught the light of the gas lamp on the table.

"Rawls?" Juke said. He'd had a tumbler of gin and was on his second. "You gone marry an old man?"

"His son, Daddy. Oliver. He's the doctor I told you about, who's been writing me letters. He's already moved back to town, to take Dr. Rawls's place. But he don't act anything like his daddy. He's got Atlanta manners."

"Atlanta?"

"But we gone live here in town, in his daddy's house. Once his daddy ain't in it no longer."

Jim said, "Dr. Rawls don't have long, if talk is true."

"What you know about it?" Juke said to him.

Jim shrugged. "I heard talk about it at the mill."

"I don't like that old man," Juke said. "I hope the devil's warming up a bed for him."

"His son's a good man," Elma said, "and he's ready to take good care of me and the twins. Ain't any man who would take on a person in my position, and two kids to boot."

Sara weighed the statement, then raised her eyebrows in agreement.

"I didn't ask for your blessing," Elma snapped at her. To her father, she said, "It's your blessing he wants. He came calling on Christmas, to ask you for it."

"That's what he came for, uh? A blessing?" Sara put on a confused face. "His car was here an awful long time."

Elma ignored her. "He wants to do the proper thing. But there ain't been much time. His father's ill, and he's had all his patients. I wanted him to be the one to ask you, before I went around wearing his ring. It's bad luck otherwise."

"So that's what that wedding dress is doing in your closet." Sara elbowed Jim. "I told Jim I saw it hanging there and could have sworn it was lined with my own good charmeuse."

Elma felt her face burn. "Were you looking for the sugar in my closet?"

Sara took a sip of her tea. "I was looking for my charmeuse."

"You left it here in the house. Thought I'd take it as a souvenir. Souvenir harvesting, ain't that what they call it?"

Sara shook her head against a laugh.

"Y'all can snoop around in our closets alls you want. You ain't gone find nothing!"

"All right now," Jim said, just as Juke said, "What's this talk?"

"They're here to spy on us!"

Juke looked to Jim. "You a guvment man?"

"Wake up, Daddy! George Wilson hired em to learn how to do

what we do. They gone take over the farm from us." Elma was standing up now, and she lowered her face to her father's and said, "He's gone take over the still, Daddy!"

"That ain't the case," Jim said.

"That true?" Juke said to Jim. "You a scout?" He looked to Sara. "You a scout?" When they said nothing, Juke stood and slammed his knuckles against the table. The sound startled the babies, and Winna started to whimper.

"That old man trying to run me off the farm?"

"It's true, Daddy. They think they gone just sweep in from New York and take it all."

Nan picked up Winna and put a chicken bone in her mouth.

"That shack you so cozy in?" Juke said to Jim. "I was born in that shack."

Jim put up his hands. "We got no intentions of taking over nothing."

Sara said, "No thank you. We got no aspirations to take over your life."

"Shut up," Juke said to her. "Jim, shut your woman up. It's you I got trouble with."

Jim said quietly, "We didn't intend to get in the middle of nothing. We hadn't even heard about any Genus Jackson when we moved in."

They were like two shoes dropping, like two creek-filled boots dropping from a dead man's feet to the ground. Genus. Jackson.

Juke smiled. He nodded. He understood now. "Thas all right. Thas all right." He slid his chair back behind him and went to his room. When he came back he was holding the twenty-two. "I should a known better than to take in outsiders. At's what got me in trouble before." He cocked the revolver, but returned it to his side. "You think I got it in me to kill? Do you? What did you conclude, after living off my cows' titties for the last six months? What you fixing to report to that Judas George Wilson?"

"We don't want any quarrel, Juke." Jim was still seated at the table, his arm around the back of Sara's chair. "We don't plan to take nothing over. We just plan to leave."

"We're gonna leave?" Sara asked him, pleading, relieved.

Jim nodded. "First thing in the morning, we'll pack up and go." To Sara he said, "It's time to go, with the baby coming."

"Hell yes, it's high time," Juke said. "But you ain't waiting till no first thing in the morning. First thing tonight!"

Juke sent Nan to help them pack up the shack. Together the three of them carried the pasteboard suitcases to the Ford, the banjo, the bolts of fabric. The dogs followed them in and out of the shack, back and forth to the car. Juke stood on the porch watching them with the gun resting on the railing, drinking his third tumbler of gin, dipping tobacco. Elma put the babies to bed. She didn't hear Sara say to Nan, "We're gonna worry about you, Miss Nan. We'd take you with us if we could." There was no one to hug but Nan, so Sara and Jim both hugged her longer than they'd expected to.

When they neared Florence, Sara asked why didn't they stop in at Mr. Wilson's, wouldn't he give them a warm place to stay, and Jim said George Wilson was the last person he wanted to see, and they were probably the last he wanted to see too, given how they'd disappointed him. They had to get out from under him, Jim said. He was glad now they were leaving under cover of night. They had just turned north on the highway when Sara said, "Stop." She put her hand on Jim's elbow. Jim pulled over to the side of the dark road. She said, "Damn damn damn." She slammed the dashboard. "We forgot the gramophone." It was on the porch of the big house, where they'd set it the night Jim learned she was pregnant.

"Damn," Jim said.

They sat in silence for a moment. Quietly Sara began to cry.

"We'll be okay, Georgia peach."

"Don't call me that, Jim."

She wasn't crying over the gramophone. She was crying for herself, because she had lost a friend, and because she too was spiteful and hateful and full of lies. Sitting in the car at the side of the road, she wasn't pregnant. Her lie had worked—they were leaving the farm, they were moving back home—but there was no satisfaction in it.

"God, I hate the South," she said.

It wasn't what she meant exactly, but saying it helped her believe it. Later, when her feelings had hardened into something more distinct; after she and Jim had made love in every shantytown between Georgia and New York; after they'd left the Model T in her uncle's driveway, as though they'd just taken it out for a spin; after she told Jim, riding a freight home, and crying real tears, that she'd lost the baby; after they'd arrived in Buffalo and moved in with Jim's mother, who prayed every night at the table for God to sow a seed in Sara's womb; and after a baby didn't come, and didn't come, she'd look back at their time at the crossroads farm and mostly hate Elma, who had two babies at the same time, more than she had milk for, more even than she wanted.

Now Jim turned around in his seat and rummaged around in the back. Underneath the stack of suitcases, he lifted a sheet of damask fabric. "Look here." Hidden under it was a crate of Cotton Gin.

Sara laughed. Jim reached for two of the jars and gave one to Sara and took one for himself. "I'd say we're square, wouldn't you?"

———————

Parthenia Wilson did not send an eye patch but she did send a preacher. He was a small, high yellow man in top hat and tuxedo tails, like some country magician, named Teacup Clifton. He wore the hat to make himself look taller. Standing on the stump of a pine tree the men had felled, he looked, Sterling thought, like a stork on a post.

The men had sat on the tree stumps scattered around him, stumps that looked created by God for that purpose, for their wilderness church. "We worship the Lord where we find Him," said Reverend Clifton, "and we find Him everywhere. Hear His voice here in the trees! See His face there in the creek! Brothers, all we must do is open our eyes and ears! *For the Lord hears the cries of the needy, and despises not his prisoners!"* Some of the men hollered and cried along with him, saying, "Amen," saying, "I hear you, Lord!" Sterling nodded along, but he remained quiet. He did not have a heart for God. God had burned down his house with his family in it. God had hardened his woman's heart against him. God had put him in chains. All the same, he would rather sit on this stump and listen to the man in the top hat than lay down road. It was a Sunday, the first day off in the camp since they'd begun paving the Straight. Sterling's muscles ached in a way that was almost pleasant, the way they ached only after they'd had a chance to rest. The insides of his ankles, from the shackles. His back, his arms, especially the right. Yesterday, the fry cakes and Bibles; today the preacher. They were gifts from the woman he understood to be Freddie's grandmother, George Wilson's woman. And tonight, if talk was true, there would be another gift, this one from the warden.

When the preacher turned to the Bible, and spoke of repentance, Sterling did not nod. He did not think of the crimes that had brought him here to the camp, which were not crimes. He did not think of anything. But later, after the preacher left and after the midday meal, the prisoners were sent to piss out near the turkey oaks. The white men were sent first, then the colored. The eight of them stood in a silent row, their ankles chained, draining themselves into the dirt. Then they were sent to wash their hands and faces in the nearly dry creek bed. Sterling could barely see his own face in the creek, let alone God's. But staring off into the surface, staring down the hours left in the day, Sterling did think then of Ketty on Juke's bed, the pearls hailing down on her back. And without meaning to, his mind called up its picture of his parents dropping to their knees, and as they fell their names rose up—Joseph, Lucille—and his eyes stung.

He splashed his face with the cold water. He shook his head like a dog. Still squatting, he warmed his numb hands in his armpits. Maybe it wasn't God who'd put him in chains. Maybe it wasn't even white men. Maybe it was one white man. A man who'd seen to it to lynch a Negro on his farm, and then to go on playing daddy to Sterling's child. And there he lived and breathed, just down the Straight, without a care in the world.

He wanted to save some hate for the warden but tonight the warden made it hard to hate him. It was Sunday, and to keep them happy and working another week he drove into the camp with two whores in his truck. "Y'all bad boys paving a good road. I brought y'all a reward for being so good." Sterling had been with one of them, the older one, at the county camp past the mill, on a Sunday past. The one he got this time was younger, with darker skin and a pregnant belly. She wore her hair in plaits the way little girls did, the end of each plait slid into a painted stack of beads. When it was their turn in the tent, Sterling held her hair in his fist, gently as he could, to keep the beads from drumming together.

———————

Every day they paved the road a little farther. Any day now, they'd reach the crossroads farm. Crow had gotten into the habit of sending teams of four or five men out to each farm, ahead of the rest of them, with a drag pan and a wheelbarrow and a shovel and a rake. They were meant to gather topsoil to smooth the next stretch of road, for the layer that went down before the rock. Sterling had done the work on another farm and the fields had been a welcome change from the endless road. Now he had it in his head that he would be on the team at the crossroads farm. He imagined his feet in the rows of the field he'd used to work, skimming the dirt he'd turned over for six seasons. He would see Nancy on the back porch and he'd wave to her, just as if he was coming in from that field after a long day. After breakfast the next morning, when the time came for Crow to ask for volunteers, he'd raise his arm first and highest.

The white Smith had the same idea. "I'm a get me on that next farm job," he said to Sterling at supper. He kept his voice low. "Thas one a my granddaddy's farms. Figure I got some folks I'm ready to see."

Sterling did not like that idea. He didn't want any more devilment on the farm. But he just said, "Reckon I might join you. I like farm-work."

"Ain't sure if they're ready to see me," the white boy laughed.

But Crow didn't wait until breakfast to gather the team. He didn't even ask for volunteers. He came through the tent that night after the men were chained in their cots and waved his shotgun across four of them at the end farthest from Sterling. "First thing tomorrow, y'all on topsoil with Talvey. On the Wilson farm."

Sterling shot up in bed. "Mr. Crow, sir, you got need for another? I got experience in the field."

"Ain't take no expert," Crow said.

"I got knowledge about them mules. You gone use Mr. Wilson's mules, y'all should know they unruly."

"What you know about them mules?"

"I only heard they unruly, sir."

"You the unruly one, Sterling. You missing the warden's ways?"

"No, sir."

"Then you speak when spoken to."

Sterling couldn't sleep. He lay on his back, the chains heavy on his ankles. In all his years of sleeping on boxcars and plank bunks and flimsy corn-shuck pallets, he had taken for granted the miracle of sleeping on his side.

He thought he'd imagined the scene every which way, but now he had to readjust the picture. So he wouldn't set foot on the farm, but he'd pass it. It would be the front porch, not the back. The girls would be out there again with the babies, and he'd call out to them. That much he knew. He wouldn't let the wagon pass by again without call-ing out. It would be worth the Georgia rack, if that's what it came to. But Nancy wouldn't recognize him. But Elma would. She might. But the girls might not be home at all. They weren't there the time he'd left the flowers in the mailbox. Where might they be? They might be inside. It was winter, cold. The thought of passing by the house again without calling out to his daughter made his breathing jagged. Above him in the tent, he could see his breath in the air. That was how cold the night was.

The next day on the road his body was slow, drained of sleep, and Crow said, "What's got you, Sterling?"

He said, "I'm sorry, Mr. Crow. I got a sick stomach. I think it was them lard cakes."

Back at camp at the end of the day he complained of it again, and though it wasn't time for the privy, Crow let him go with the white boy named Smith and a ball and chain. Pissing was to be done in turns, but at times their bowels called them together. "Y'all go play your little-girl games." Talvey, the shotgun guard, stood a few yards off with one of the hounds. Sterling kept his voice low. It was the only time they'd been alone since they'd first shared the privy, and he was worried it might be the last. He said to the boy, "You ain't got the farm job."

"Naw. Thas all right. Farmwork's for niggers."

"Thought you was ready to show your face."

"Getting readier every day. Tired of paving that gotdamn road. Thas nigger work too."

"You ain't gone be doing no kind a work for long. When you out a here, you gone be living fine."

"Who said I'm going anywheres?"

"If you as rich as you say, your granddaddy gone come pick you up from the warden hisself."

"You reckon?" His face was more serious than Sterling had ever seen it.

"Sure."

"I don't know. I been in hot water plenty, but not this hot."

"If Jesup's the one done it, then you ain't got nothing to worry about, now do you?"

"I reckon not. My grammy's sore with me, though."

Sterling waved his hand. "She be making you flower crowns before long."

The boy tried to chuckle.

"Longer you stay here, the longer Jesup go free. Thas the way I see it."

"Jesup was the one who told me to run! I weren't thinking straight. I just knew my grammy and granddaddy would be sore at me. Bringing shame on the family. I ain't no war hero, thas for sure. I ain't never been good enough for them."

"Son, you on the chain gang and you got kin delivering you fry cakes! Thas more than any of us got. You be out a here soon, and you be fine. You tell the law what Jesup done. They'll believe you. You're people. He should be the one on this road gang."

Sterling allowed himself the fantasy of Jesup in chains.

"I reckon it's time," the boy said. "We fixing to come up on the house soon, one way or another."

"I got to ask a favor a you, son."

"What's that?"

"I got to ask you to deliver a message for me. Case I can't deliver it myself. Case I don't make it out."

"A message to who?"

Sterling brought his voice close to the boy's ear. "What if I told you we got friends in common?"

———————

So again the tar paper shack was empty. Nan wore a pair of her mother's canvas gardening gloves to sweep it out, and a head wrap, low enough to cover her ears. But the gloves had been eaten with holes by pickleworm moths and through them the broom burned with cold on her hands. She did not waste wood on a fire. The stove sat cold and squat, as though it was trying to gather its own warmth. Used to be she would daydream about moving back into the shack with

Wilson. They would smell the grits and coffee and share the narrow bed. But soon Elma and Juke would be gone from the farm—Elma to marriage, Juke to she didn't know where—and someone else would be stationed there in the shack. Nan supposed that if she hadn't stolen that ten dollars, Mr. Wilson might have seen it was Juke he had issue with. He might take pity on her still and let her stay. Without Juke there, the farm might become again like a home to her, the only home, after all, she had known.

But then—she swept on—if she stayed, she'd be without Elma. Was the farm her home, or was Elma? Or could she and Wilson make their own home together anywhere, alone?

And—what was she thinking?—if she stayed, she would be without Wilson. Wilson was her home. There was no way she could keep him with her, not apart from Elma, unless the world knew she was his mother.

She knelt to sweep under the bed. There was nothing under it but dust bunnies, but still she felt as though someone were there in the room with her. The air in the shack was still scented with Sara's Agua Florida. But under it was another smell. Lavender soap; gin; Genus's chalky, silty skin, the palms of his hands blistered as bark.

She leaned the broom against the wall and knelt next to the stove. Carefully she lifted the loose floorboard, and another, beside it, she'd loosened herself. Genus's corn-shuck hat was pressed there among the other hidden things, its brim folded tidily, like the wings of a roosting bird. She reshaped it with her hands and placed it like a golden crown on her head. Over the head wrap, it fit snugly.

A dog was barking in the north field. It wasn't Castor or Pollux. And there were men's voices. She risked moving to the window. A boy was pushing a wheelbarrow down the turn row. He was wearing prison stripes and a striped knit cap. She craned her neck farther. Three other men were hitching a contraption behind Clarence, and Castor and Pollux were circling them like sheep dogs, smelling their boots. They weren't in chains, but on the other side of the fence, a

skinny white man with a shotgun and a bloodhound was biting off
a tobacco plug. "Good dog, good dog," she could hear one of them
chanting. She looked sideways at the one with the wheelbarrow, a boy
who looked no older than she was. His shoes were several sizes too
big for him, and his pants sagged at the ankles and waist.

She wanted to step out of the shack and call to the dogs. Come
here, you fools. Leave those men alone. She wanted to tell the boy it
wasn't the dogs he had to fear. She wanted to tell him, Pick up your
pants and run.

————————

Elma was on the back porch with the babies watching the men in the
north field when the barefoot boy on the bicycle came to deliver a letter. Juke was in the barn and Nan was in the shack. The dogs were
so interested in the prisoners that they didn't look up when the boy
came around the back. She gave the boy some corn pone to take home
with him, then settled on the porch with Wilson in her lap (thinking,
Folks are watching, show him love, thinking, *I do love him!*) while Winna
rolled about at her feet. The letter was from Oliver and she opened it.
Wilson grabbed onto a corner of it and got it in his mouth, and she
tugged it back. "Bless God," she said to the baby, bringing the letter
close to her eyes. "Dr. Rawls went and passed on."

For Elma the news was bittersweet. It meant that her new life in
town could begin. It meant sorrow for the loss of a man who'd shown
her kindness. But there was sorrow for herself too, and a sick, runny
panic, like a bloody nose that wouldn't clot, because the letter said
that the funeral would take place on Saturday, the last day of January, and that their wedding would be postponed. Elma said the word
aloud—"'postpone'"—and laughed. He was sorry, Oliver was, but he
needed time to mourn with his brothers and sisters, who were all returning to Florence for the funeral, and his poor mother, whom in her
weakened state Elma's presence might distract. Elma put down the
letter. "'Distract,'" she said bitterly, and tried again to laugh.

How to postpone a wedding that was days away? The invitations, at last, had been mailed, and the news had traveled across church and into the country and all the way to Augusta, where it had already reached Bette Hazelton. She had indeed gone to live with her sister, but still owned a fine stack of gold leaf stationery, on which she sent her congratulations. How wonderful, she wrote, that God had seen to it to bless the poor children with a proper father! Elma went to burn the note in the stove, and then her pride stopped her, for they were the words she had wanted to read, and why pretend otherwise?

She hadn't even kissed him yet. That was the thought that was stuck in her mind as she rocked on the porch. On Christmas Eve, he had held his sticky hands to her breasts and then inspected them through his glasses like a young boy playing doctor. Then he had buttoned her shirt and put on his coat and hobbled on his cane to the door.

How little he must think of her. It wasn't enough that she was the daughter of Juke Jesup. She'd had to make a show of it, dressing up like trash, then stripping for him like a whore. She had wanted to use what she had—because what else did he want from her?—to make him hers, to seal their union before he, like Freddie, slipped between her fingers. But she had been wrong. Couldn't she have worn a dress? Couldn't she have made him coffee? That was the kind of lady Oliver Rawls wanted to marry. He had seen what he needed to see and he had left, and though his letters still came, now they said "postpone" and "distract."

The screen door of the shack slammed and Nan came across the yard. She made to take Wilson off her lap but Elma gave a tiny shake of the head and Nan stepped back. Nan cocked her head toward the men in the field and opened her face to Elma like a question.

"They from the chain gang," Elma said. "They just borrowing some dirt for the road." She told Nan the news about Dr. Rawls and the wedding and the funeral, and Nan put a hand on her shoulder.

"Too cold for rocking," she said, and bundled both babies and carried them inside. Nan drew the curtains and closed herself in the pantry to nurse Wilson. Elma stoked the fire and stirred the stew and after Winna scratched her own cheek till it bled, she sat the baby in her lap and trimmed her nails while she nursed her, first her fingers, then her toes, singing This Little Piggy and tickling her pinkies, and Winna pulled off her nipple to laugh. Then she fit the baby's hands and feet with socks and put her in the crib for her nap. When Nan was done nursing Wilson, she put him down too. They covered the babies with their blankets and for a minute they both stroked their backs. At six months old, they nearly filled the crib. Juke would need to build a bigger one, or maybe it was time for them to each have a crib of their own.

"I ain't gone get left again," Elma said. "I ain't gone lose another wedding."

There were times when she wanted to talk to someone who could talk back. She went to find her father in the barn, where he was sitting on a stump hammering at an old iron horseshoe, a near empty tumbler of gin at his feet. There had been no horses on the farm since George Wilson had lived there, and the horseshoes were as old as Juke himself. Juke had tossed them with String as a boy and he had tossed them with Jim, and for years they had hung on rusty nails on the wall of the barn, alongside the shovels and rakes and hoes, waiting for their true purpose. Now he was bending them to the longer, narrow shape of the mules' feet, which (much like the feet of the barefoot children on the farm) had gone entirely without shoes. There was no need for a mule to wear shoes over the gentle clay terrain of the farm, but Juke intended to walk them off the farm with him. No matter that they belonged, Mamie and Clarence, Archie and Jo, in the eyes of the bank and the law, to George Wilson. In the eyes of God, they were Juke's. It was he who had fed them and loved them and shoveled their shit. And it was he who would load them up and walk them down the

Twelve-Mile Straight, burdened with a load unlike any they'd carried before. Between the truck and the four mules, he believed he could carry the still.

The barn door swung open and his daughter stalked in. She was wearing her chore coat and his own newsboy cap and carrying a letter. "Dr. Rawls went to be with the Lord, Daddy." As she might tell a young child to keep him from crying.

"That so," Juke said. He looked up from the horseshoe, then hammered it twice more.

She put her hands over her ears. "It is," she said. "The funeral's Saturday."

"You ain't going."

"No. I don't care to."

"I don't like that man."

"We're still having a wedding, Daddy. We just gone move it some."

Juke hammered. Elma sniffed.

"What you doing with them horseshoes?"

He was in no mood to talk about his plans. He had very little idea how to attach the shoes to the mules. He might hurt them. He would have asked the McArdles for help, for Old Abe McArdle used to have a mare, but last year he'd had to sell her, hoping to keep up payments on the farm. George Wilson had bought it from him, in fact, hadn't he, making a show of his magnanimity. But the money hadn't been enough and just before Christmas, the bank had foreclosed on the farm and auctioned off the land and the house and the farm equipment, down to a box of nails, which Juke himself bought for a penny. He hadn't needed the nails, but he'd felt it was something he must do. Well, he'd left Abe with a jar of gin before he'd piled his family and what was left of their belongings into their wagon and followed their last mule east to town, the five children walking alongside the wagon in their bare feet, whipping branches at the dirt road.

"Just hammering," he answered.

Now that road was being paved. He could hear the roar of the trucks down the Straight, carrying the gravel they'd shipped in from Macon. And now a team of unchained convicts was using his own mule—*his* mule—to rob his field of the soil that eroded more with every season, as though there were enough to give away for free. George Wilson had offered up the soil, and what could Juke do about it? Hank Talvey had sidled up on his horse and said, "Howdy, Mr. Juke," not taking off his hat, not stepping down to shake his hand, just looking down at the top of Juke's head. "We'll stay out your way." Talvey had a taste for gin but for all Juke knew, he was getting it straight from George Wilson now. For all Juke knew, Talvey was running Juke's own gin himself. One day Juke had been at the warm center of George's circle, but when he wasn't looking the circle had shifted and now he was standing out in the cold with his pecker in his hand like Abe McArdle on Christmas. Soon there would be new men in his field, if not these prisoners, then other men George Wilson would buy off the chain gang for a song. He was already gone.

"They fixing to be here long, Daddy?"

She'd left the barn door open and through it they could see the men in the distant field. "Two, three days, I reckon."

"We could play them some music on the gramophone."

"Don't got no colored records."

"It don't matter, Daddy. Music is music. Makes work go easier."

"They ain't supposed to have it easy. They's convicts."

He wondered if he'd have to wait for the road to be ready before leaving. Could be weeks until it got all the way to town. Traffic was closed a hundred yards on either side of the roadwork, so no one could get in or out anyhow. Taking the new road to the state highway would mean a swift, smooth exit. But if he didn't want to be seen, it was the back roads he'd have to take. He'd head north, to Georgia's piney mountains. That was the place for him, the place where String's cousins had had a still of their own. He'd dig up the jars of money he'd buried in the ground. It would be enough to take him to where he wanted to go.

He'd considered going to Carolina, where his father's people still had a fishing camp along the Catawba River. His great-grandfather had been a Catawba Indian. Juke never knew him, and his own father, Ernest, had fled to Georgia when he was fifteen. Juke did not want to return to a family he didn't know. He would leave, like Jim and Sara, under cover of night. He would keep going north until he found the right place. He would know it when he saw it. He'd see it from the road—a gently sloping ravine dense with pines, dense enough to hide a still and a new cabin he'd build from the pines themselves.

It was a peaceful picture. It was a peaceful life he wanted. He would work for himself. He'd get out from under George Wilson's thumb.

He wished only that he'd have a companion. Someone to warm the bed beside him. He thought of one of Easter Moore's daughters, who had kept him warm for several nights in the Easter Hotel. He did this so he might not think of Nan, which might keep him also from thinking of Wilson. But half of his mind, the half that was drunk at ten thirty in the morning, was already thinking of Nan there with him, on the porch of his new cabin in the piney ravine in north Georgia, hanging a wind chime she'd made, and there was Wilson on her hip, reaching to play with it. And then he saw there in that half of his mind—he was drunker than he believed—that Nan wasn't Nan but her mother. It was Ketty he was picturing, a baby on her broad hip.

He shook his head. It was not possible to live as man and wife with Ketty because Ketty was colored and Ketty was dead. He could no more live with Nan and Wilson.

But perhaps if the cabin was deep enough in the woods. Perhaps if the pines were dense enough.

"You all right, Daddy?"

His daughter lowered herself to the stump beside him. The barn cat came and threaded itself through her legs.

"What about the children?" he asked her, resuming his hammering. He could not say Nan's name aloud. "Where will they go?"

"Course they'll go with me and Nan, Daddy. To Oliver's."

She read the surprise on his face.

"Nan's coming with me, Daddy. Yes. Of course she is."

The hammer came down hard on his left thumb. He leapt up and yowled, upsetting his tumbler of gin. The barn cat took off. He picked up the hammer with his right hand and threw it at the barn wall, knocking two of the hanging horseshoes to the ground.

"Good Lord! You all right, Daddy?"

What kind of fool was he? He would never get the goddamn horseshoes on the mules' feet. Even if he did, those mules would never be able to carry that load, unseen, along the back roads. He couldn't even read a map.

"Good Lord, yes! I'm sure fine! Just getting chased off my own farm! Just getting left by my own daughter! My own son!"

"Daddy—"

"Ain't no one to hear but convicts," he said. "Let em all hear! He's my son and he's gone be living fine in town without never knowing his daddy."

She whispered fiercely, "You should be glad he'll be living fine, Daddy."

"You think they'll take kindly to darkies living with you in town?"

Elma shrugged. "Folks in town got colored help living with them."

"What about Wilson? You gone play him off as the help too?"

"We don't want to play no one off as nothing, Daddy. That was your idea."

Juke waved his hand in the direction of the fields. It was barley he was growing for cover that winter. June and Anna liked the barley; April and Margaret favored the rye. "Ain't like the country. Out here you can do what you please."

His daughter was looking at the ground. Now she raised her eyes and they found his. "That's why we're leaving," she said quietly. "So you can't do what you please with us no more."

Juke looked around for something else to throw. He picked up the horseshoe he'd been hammering and hurled it at the wall with the others. Another fell to the ground with some other tools.

They sat in silence for some time. In the field, the drag pan had come loose from Clarence and the men were set on fixing it. Juke didn't jump up to help. He wiped his mouth on the sleeve of his coat. Now that his hands were empty the cold came to them.

"That groom of yours know who Wilson's momma is?"

She was sitting with her hands between her knees, avoiding his eyes now, his cap slipping down over her forehead. She looked like the little girl she still sometimes was. "He ain't my groom just yet. He knows what everyone else knows."

He wasn't as drunk as she thought. He had mind enough to suspect she might be lying. Could be she was protecting her young doctor, who was in turn protecting her. What other bond might they share? He was surprised to feel his own relief, and he wasn't too drunk—he was just the right amount of drunk—to see how fiercely she was protecting the secret he'd forced upon her. Was it more fiercely, even, than he was protecting it? Because now what she wanted was to live in peace and quiet, unbothered, with the family she loved, which evidently did not include him.

He tried something. "He don't know?" He stood and made his voice big. "He don't know that it's *my son* he's fixing to raise?"

Elma leapt to her feet. "Daddy, hush!" She went to the barn door and slid it closed.

It was an instinct now, ingrained in her. She would do anything to keep the truth hidden. It was she the lie served now.

The men were too far to hear. No one was around but Mamie, who was shuffling her feet in her stall. The ruckus had made her nervous. Juke felt the cold reach his head, and the half of him that was still drunk stood up with him and shook itself sober. What kind of fool was he? He couldn't leave the farm. Those mules, those cows, those fields—they belonged to him. They were his birthright.

"So y'all gone just leave me, then. I see how it is. Old man always gets left behind. I worked these fields forty years. Then in one week I lose the farm and the only kin I got."

"Daddy, we'll just be but six miles down the road."

"Weren't enough to lose a momma to childbirth. Had to lose a wife to childbirth too, same week I lose my daddy. One week, I tell you. Now everybody else gone leave me too."

"Where you gone go, Daddy? What you gone do?"

He reached down and began to collect the horseshoes. He collected the auger and the hoe and the drawknife and hung them back on the wall. In the stall beside them sat the rusting disk harrow Elma used to love to ride in his lap. Above it hung String Wilson's old bamboo fishing pole and a slingshot he had carved for Juke, the rubber band long gone. Juke had hoped that one day Wilson would play with them. He had hoped that he would sit in his lap on the harrow, that he would watch him grow tall on this farm. It had been worth killing for, not long ago, the thought of his own son plowing the fields beside him. Beside the fishing pole and the slingshot, beside the hoe he had beaten Genus Jackson with, was the hay sickle he had used to cut down his body.

"I'm staying right here."

"Daddy." Elma was helping him hang the horseshoes, and now she crossed her arms. "You know what Jim and Sara said. We ain't wanted here no more."

Juke waved his hand dismissively. "I ain't gone let an old man scare me oft. He wants to push me off the farm, he's gone have to come talk to me and my shotgun."

"Daddy."

"I given this farm everything I got. I made this farm bleed gin. Ain't no one else can do like that. Old man knows it." He thought of what George had said the last time he'd visited the mill: *Why blind myself?* George needed Juke as much as Juke needed George. "He like to talk. He like to stick his chest out and throw his money around. He want to cry about his no-count grandson running oft, ain't on my head. I ain't as yella as Freddie. His daddy would roll over in his grave, if he knew how yella his son turned out. I ain't gone run oft. I made this farm bleed. I intend to keep on."

Elma shook her head. "You crazier than a rat trapped in a tin shithouse."

Juke smiled. It was a favorite phrase of Ketty's. "That a way for a lady to talk?"

Elma stood. "I may be fixing to be a wife, but I don't intend to be no lady."

"Ain't no shame in it," Juke said.

TWENTY-THREE

THE LAST TIME IT HAD SNOWED IN COTTON COUNTY WAS THE day a white woman had been lynched in Meredith. It was near the end of the last December of the previous century, and the snow had come and gone in less than an hour. Juke Jesup was eight years old and it was his first lynching. He didn't know you could string up a woman, and a white one. She was more girl than woman, fifteen, from a family of wandering halvers-hands new to the county, and she was pregnant, made so by the country doctor in Meredith, or so she'd said. The doctor was a grown white man with a wife of his own, and the girl's brother had gotten in a quarrel with him and killed him with a jam knife, left it sticking out of his neck. The mob had gone after the brother but he'd run off, so they went after the girl instead and killed her with the same knife. When they strung her up in her nightgown from the barber's pole next door to the doctor's office, the knife still stuck out of her rounded belly like a flag planted on a hill. That was where Juke had seen her when the snow started to fall. His father had waked him up in the early hours of morning so they could join the wagon heading over the county line to see her. A Negro was one thing. If you were woken to join the mob, you might, or you might turn over and go back to sleep. But a white woman—that was something to see. The town square was crowded with more people than Juke had seen in one place before. His father put him on his shoulders so he could get a better look. The snow came as the morning broke, so it seemed the day was darkening before it began. The flakes fell on Juke's head and on his father's and on the girl's, and on her face and shoulders and the tops of her bare feet. Juke thought she looked cold. "Is it cold when you're dead, Pop?" he asked, and his father said, "Not where she's going." By the time they returned to the farm, the sun was shining and the girl had been taken down from the pole like the laundry and the snow on the ground had vanished. It was as though the night had not happened at all.

Manford Rawls too had seen the snow and the girl, and he had been haunted by her. It was no way for a white girl to die. But the doctor who was killed had been his associate. He had gone to see the dead girl and he'd gone to the doctor's funeral, but afterward and for the rest of his life, he no longer went on country calls. He did not want to adopt the other doctor's reputation. (As it was, he did not like going into the country at night, where he'd once gotten lost on a dark dirt road. He'd told no one that he'd had to wait in his wagon until morning's light to find his way back to town.) Dr. Rawls did not have relations with anyone but his wife, but the country people who had no way of traveling to his office in town became sick with typhoid and tuberculosis and syphilis and some of them died.

Manford Rawls was buried on a Saturday at Florence Baptist. The patients who attended his funeral were the patients who had lived. Some of them brought the children the doctor had delivered, and some of the children brought their children, Johnny Manford and Billy Manford and Jimmy Manford. The mothers of Cotton County did not think Manford made for a good Christian name, but they thought it made a fine middle one.

It wasn't snow on that day but a pebbly rain that fell just long enough for the procession from the church to the cemetery. Sheriff Cleave was there; Judge Jeffords was there. Q. L. Boothby, who had served with Dr. Rawls on the board of the Roosevelt Warm Springs Institute for Rehabilitation, was there from Macon. The Jesups and the Wilsons were not there, though the day before, Parthenia Wilson had sent Frank to the house with a boxwood wreath his sister had woven. By the time the doctor's three sons and his one living brother had lowered his casket into the ground, the rain had ceased. He was a small man, and they carried it without much trouble.

Down the road some six and a half miles, the road men from Macon sat in their trucks, cigarettes hanging out the window in the rain. Lloyd Crow too had collected his men into the wagon until the rain passed, because road didn't lay down right when it was wet. They lay on their backs in their bunks. They were grateful for the rain—everyone by then was grateful, so badly did the county need rain—but Crow was not. George Wilson wanted the road paved clear to the mill village by the end of February, but it had rained for most of three days last week, one gully washer after another, and they were behind schedule now, and Wilson was not a man he aimed to disappoint. Crow had his mind on the crossroads farm, which he knew to be halfway between camp and town. Once they crossed String Wilson Road, they'd have more behind them than ahead. And maybe the man with the banjo would be on the porch, and maybe he'd play "Ain't Misbehavin'" again, and Crow would let his men rest their eyes on the women for a while, the redhead, the Negro, the brunette, who had Indian in her, he thought. The men were tired and cold and so was he. It was hard for him to believe that there'd been a lynch mob on that farm just a few months ago, and so he didn't believe it, not really. Instead his mind saw the brunette clapping on the porch, her flat black shoes tapping the rhythm on the steps, her long black braid bouncing down her back.

———————

When the gang finally approached the crossroads, it was a whole Saturday later—the sixth of February, ten thirty in the morning. Now a cool platinum fog lay thick over the road. Crow sat at the head of the wagon and inched it forward. Behind him, the gravel trucks groaned, and behind the trucks, the men laid the rock. Crow dozed, and so did the horses. Then they inched forward again. The warden liked to talk about a prisoner who'd escaped from the gang under cover of fog: if you were going to run, now was the time. Be vigilant in a fog, the warden warned. But the fog made Crow sleepy. He was half-dozing when he opened his eyes and saw the mailbox of the crossroads farm poking its black head through the fog. He sat up straight. He was awake now. Gave the horse some leather. The men were somewhere behind him in the fog, and he prodded the horse twenty yards forward. He heard Talvey on his horse call, "Crow?"

Even in front of the mailbox, he couldn't see but halfway down the driveway. The fog was so thick you could cut it with a knife and spread it on your toast. He hopped down from the wagon and tied the horse to the mailbox and grabbed his shotgun and called the hounds. They followed him up the drive. It was hard to believe, at ten thirty in the morning in a fog, that there might be a man on the porch playing a banjo and a girl dancing to it. He heard no banjo. But he was eager for a diversion. Some refreshment. Just before he reached the steps, two dogs darted out of the fog.

They were all on each other before he saw them. Two dogs and his two. He yelled for his two to get back. He yelled for Talvey. He saw a yellow coat, a black tail. He put his hand into the fog to draw one back and felt teeth. He thought of the rabid boar that had been found in this part of the county. He thought of his men, who could be running off now in the fog. He thought if he hadn't gone up this blasted drive, listening for the imaginary siren of a black-haired girl, he wouldn't have been caught in a cloud of four snarling dogs. He put himself in the middle of them, and then they toppled him, and when the yellow one was on him, he fired his shotgun.

That scattered them. Talvey was there then and hopping off his horse. He had a little of the dried groundhog meat in a sack and he called the hounds with it. The black dog was gone and the yellow one was on the ground, and blast if Crow hadn't shot it dead. He put his hand back into the fog and felt blood on its neck. The shotgun had made a good mess.

"Goddamn of a sumbitch!"

Talvey had the hounds wagging their tails now. "Ain't no worry, Crow. That dog was a danger. Them dogs as mean as their daddy."

"Sumbitch."

"We could roast it. I ate me a coyote before."

"Sumbitch, Talvey! Get your ass back to the wagon and lock them dogs in it."

He did not want to go into the house. Juke Jesup would not be pleased to see his dog was dead. The warden wouldn't be pleased to hear it, either. He looked around. He could leave. He could run off himself into the fog. No one had come running when they heard the shot. The farm looked all but abandoned.

He looked again at the dog on the ground, as much as he could see of it. If it weren't for the blood, it might have been taking a nap. Blast if he hadn't had a yellow dog as a boy.

He climbed the steps. The porch was empty but for a couple of rocking chairs and, on the plank floor, a silent gramophone. Crow put his hands on his hips and eyed it. Then he walked down the breezeway and knocked on the door to the left. He knocked on the door to the right. He thought he heard a baby crying inside, but he was listening too hard, listening still for some music in the day. He turned and went back to the gramophone and, squatting, placed the needle on the record. From the road, his men could hear the tune. It was too bright for a funeral hymn, but Crow played it again and again as the men dug a grave for the dog under the cottonwood tree and buried it and marked it with stones. Together it took them only an hour, but it was another hour they were behind.

By the time morning gave way to afternoon, the sun was spinning its spokes of light through the gray. As the fog burned off, you could see the first of the purple martins just returning to nest in the gourd tree, and the purple martins could see clear to the crossroads, where a black Labrador was climbing out of the ditch. She'd been scrambling between the road and the creek for more than an hour, her nose and tail both skimming the ground, first heading east, beyond the crossroads, then changing her mind and turning around toward home. When she came up on String Wilson Road in front of the crossroads store, her coat was stuck with cockleburs and dripping with creek water. Jeb Simmons, who'd gotten up from his chair on the store porch to help direct traffic, said to no one in particular, "Mr. Juke's bitch took her a bath." Now that the road crew had reached String Wilson Road, which was paved, they'd had to cut off traffic all four ways in order for the men and the wagon and the two horses and a gravel truck to cross it. Across the intersection, Drink Simmons was doing the same. He wished he had a flag to wave. A line of cars was piling up and folks were honking. Drink went to each of their windows and said, "Sorry, Mr. Joe," "Sorry, Miss Sadie. Them boys got to get acrost. We'll let you through directly."

Then a Coca-Cola truck fixing to make a delivery at the crossroads store got a back tire stuck in the ditch trying to turn around, and when it tried to climb out, the other back tire got stuck, and the truck fell ass down in the ditch and the back doors opened and case after case of Coca-Cola came tumbling out. The driver hopped out and started cussing. The angle was such that neither of the big gravel trucks could drag it out. So the truck sat there in the ditch with its headlights shooting through what remained of the fog while Jeb Simmons went to borrow some rope from the crossroads store, which held up the traffic more. While they waited, the chain gang turned around and made its way back across the road and all the while the black dog trotted alongside them, wagging, barking, confused. She recognized the smell of some of the men's boots. They were caked with dirt from her farm. Then she trotted ahead to the wagon and all at once she smelled Lloyd Crow and gunpowder and the two hounds, caged inside, and she barked and darted sideways and skedaddled down into the ditch on the opposite side of the road, in front of the church. The hounds barked back. Her nose had never been so full. And now underneath the rising fog she smelled what she had nearly given up looking for, and she scrambled back up to the road and up the brick pathway to the Creek Baptist Missionary Church, her paws leaving white clay prints behind her.

Along the path, the congregation was spilling out the open doors, and the dog, wagging her tail, smelled each of their fine patent leather oxfords and worn farm boots, for today, a Saturday, the church had called together town and country folks alike. "Git!" the folks said. Someone was distributing a sack of rice, pouring a few grains into each of their open hands, and they thought it was the rice the dog was after. Among them was a photographer for the *Florence Messenger,* and though he was there for the society page, he turned to aim his camera at the intersection, where twelve men were now playing tug-of-war with a two-ton panel truck. Behind them, unspooling westward, six miles of gravel road glittered. When finally the men hoisted the vehicle out, the driver gave them each a bottle of Coca-Cola, and of course it was the best bottle of Coca-Cola any of them had ever had, the bottle they would remember on the hottest and driest days to come. Then Talvey moved them across String Wilson Road again to let the traffic pass. They were only halfway to town, but they walked with pride, their chests leading them, as though already they were crossing the invisible tape of a finish line. They had paved that road. They had moved that truck. They had not had so many eyes on them for a long time. The photographer's camera clicked, and they lifted their faces as they drank from their bottles, the sun, now bright, catching the green, misty light through the glass.

————————

Elma Rawls, for that was who she was now, was not carried across the church threshold by her husband. She might have been able to carry him. When they appeared in the doorway side by side, Elma carrying a paperwhite bouquet, Oliver clinging to Elma's elbow ("I'll be your cane," she said), the newspaperman's camera turned back to the church, and the congregation clapped and cheered and tossed the rice in the air. It rained down on them over the path. It landed in the bouquet and in the hem of Elma's dress and in her eyelashes. The fog was no thicker now than the steam from a kettle. Through the fog, through the falling rice, she saw the men in stripes who were standing across from the church on the other side of the ditch, finishing their drinks. *Goddamn*, was what she thought—she did not want convicts at her wedding. Then she saw the twelve men's eyes turn to her. She saw all of them without seeing any of them. She too had not had so many eyes on her for a long time. The babies were home with Nan. The men weren't looking at the twins but at her. She wasn't the Whore of Babylon, she wasn't Mother Mary in a chore coat. She was an eighteen-year-old woman in a McCall's wedding dress, and she'd just married a doctor, and that was what they saw. Go ahead and look, she thought.

Then there was Pollux panting at her feet. The dog nudged her wet snout into Elma's dress. Elma pushed her away, trying to laugh. *Goddamn*, she thought. "What you doing out here? You been in the creek?"

Behind her, her father came through the doors and Pollux set to panting and wagging her tail and burying her wet snout in his knees. "Get on home, girl. You ain't been invited."

The dogs didn't wander far off the farm. They never wandered off alone.

Lloyd Crow came over on his horse and said, "Pardon, Mr. Juke.

I got to speak with you." He got off the horse and led Juke around the side of the church. Again the traffic heading north and south was passing by like any day. The sack of rice was emptied.

Elma thought, What now?

If Castor hadn't been shot by Lloyd Crow, or if it had rained for two days instead of three, the crew might have been past the church by the time the wedding let out. If Sterling had known, while he dug a grave for the dead dog under the cottonwood tree, that his daughter hid in the pantry not ten yards from him, two babies bundled to her chest, she would have been the one he called out to. Instead it was Elma's name he said. He was not much more than ten yards from her too. All at once she heard his voice and remembered it and realized she had forgotten it. She saw him. He stood at the edge of the road in the middle of the chain. He couldn't move any closer to her without taking the whole gang with him. He was waving his bottle. He had a clean-shaven face.

To Oliver she said, "Good Lord. That's Uncle Sterling."

What could she do but wave back?

That might have been plenty, that might have been a full wedding day, enough for folks to talk about. She picked up the hem of her dress and made her way down the path to the edge of the ditch. She did not want to get her shoes dirty, but what did it matter now? Nothing was the way she'd pictured it.

She held the bouquet above her brow, looking across the ditch through the last breath of fog. "Uncle Sterling, is that you?"

And then, from a short way down the chain, a voice said, "It sure is. Uncle Sterling, you fixing to introduce me?"

She stopped short before she slid down into the ditch.

"Howdy, Miss Elma."

The man was smiling at her. One of his eyes was squeezed shut. He wore a striped knit cap low over his brow, and now he took it off and she saw the peeled, pale onion of Freddie Wilson's face.

"I got a riddle for you, Elma. Why did the chain gang cross the road?"

Oliver was at her elbow now. She'd left him without a cane, and he'd found his way to her, and now he was the one holding her up straight.

Freddie lifted his bottle of Coca-Cola. "To get to toast the bride."

III

TWENTY-FOUR

THE FIRST TIME HE FELL IN LOVE?

Warm Springs, summer of 1927. Not so long ago. He was twenty-three years old. He was in love with the place first. The dark-shuttered inn with its ship-mast turrets and bell-shaped porches, like some overgrown Japanese fortress; the silver, silky-skinned swimming pool (where now he was not the only one clinging tight to the edge); the acres of rolling green lawn. It was the kind of grass that called for picnic blankets, and on sunny days for lunch they were wheeled outside and lowered from their chairs to the ground. There were chicken legs and lemonade and watermelon, and the children—there were many children—spit the seeds in the grass. In the afternoon there were Bunko games on the porch and there was a radio playing Fiddlin' John Carson and there were women in sun-hats and bathing costumes and children shrieking and splashing. At night the lovebirds—there were many lovebirds—snuck out to the lawn to lie beneath the loblolly pines and gaze up at the stars in the silky-skinned sky, the picnic blankets still rough with bread crumbs beneath them.

What was her name?

Well. He never knew her name. She had no name.

What? Did he never kiss her? Did he never take her to the lawn under the stars?

Well—Oliver shifted on the edge of the bed—there was no one to kiss, no one to take. Everyone was taken. There was just the place, first and last. There was the lawn and its lovebirds. He wanted to be in love under the stars, but all the lovebirds already loved each other.

"Oliver, I think you're playing with me."

"I don't mean to. I meant to tell you a story, like you asked for."

"I meant a real story."

"You're asking if I been in love. I wanted to be. If it was to happen, that's where it would have happened. Everything was in place."

"And now?"

The bed was the biggest either had ever been in, with four feather pillows each the size of a winter hog, and a gold damask duvet that was still made up beneath them. They were on the bed, then, not in it, sitting with their legs hanging over its edge, and whether they would eventually be under the bedclothes, whether they would be kicked to the end of the bed, to the floor, whether the Hotel Chanticleer's chambermaid would need to gather them up to wash or could just smooth them out in the morning, neither of them was yet sure.

"Now," said Oliver, "I'm in love with a redhead who walked through my office door. When nothing was in place."

Elma felt the blood rush to her cheeks. She didn't know if he meant he had never been in love, or had never made love, and if she preferred that he had never been in love, or never made love, before her. "Saving yourself for me, is that what you mean?"

Oliver gave a nervous laugh. "I suppose it is."

"Well, I never was in love." Quickly she added, "Not before."

She could sense him putting together the right words. "Not with Winna's father?"

"Oh, no. Lord no."

"I intend to be a father to her, you know. Winna and Wilson too."

"I know you do," she said, and tentatively she patted his knee. They hadn't touched each other since that afternoon, when she'd helped him stand in front of the church. They had both been so embarrassed by it, his stumbling helplessness in front of Freddie, her straining to keep him steady while someone fetched his cane. She'd never been more confused, holding her new husband straight with one hand and straightening her hair with the other while the man who was supposed to be her husband looked laughingly at them both. In her arms, Oliver had felt like a store mannequin falling over at the waist, and now as she patted his knee—he didn't flinch—she felt again that dead doll weight.

"You can't feel that, can you?"

Now Oliver was the one blushing. He shook his head.

"This one"—gently he took her hand around the wrist and drew it over his lap and dropped it onto his other knee, his right one, the one farthest from her—"this one I can feel."

Through his tweed pants she could feel the sharp skull of his kneecap, and under her thumb, the twitch of his thigh.

She drew back her hand. She remembered the last time they'd been in—on—a bed together, how foolishly she had thrown herself at him. She would not make the same mistake. She would behave like a proper bride on her wedding night, if there was a way tonight to salvage propriety. She would wait for her husband to remove her dress. Now at least she was wearing one.

But Oliver, she was coming to see, did not like to take initiative. He liked to ask her which way she liked things. Did she want the reverend to read First Corinthians? (She did.) Did she want to invite his mother? (She did, though she'd left for Savannah early, to avoid the wedding, Elma thought, leaving the house on Main Street empty. None of his family had attended the wedding, not a cousin.) Did she want Wilson to sleep in the same room as Winna, or the same room as Nan? (It was his house. He could decide. Didn't he know that sometimes a girl wanted someone else to decide?) It was that freedom she'd craved, after so many years locked in her father's house, and yet she didn't know what to do with it; it made her feel unsteady on her feet, as though at any time she could make the wrong choice, and she would fall and take them all down with her.

Did she want to stay the night at the Chanticleer, after all that had happened that day? It wasn't a real honeymoon, he'd apologized—he liked to apologize—but he'd thought it would be a nice surprise, a quiet place for them to spend their first night together as husband and wife. But if it was too much, if she wanted to go home to the farm, or to the house—whatever she wanted.

What she wanted was to lie down on the gold damask duvet, which was exactly as fine as she'd imagined, while her new husband climbed on top of her and pounded back the disgrace of the day, the disgrace of the year.

And so here they were. There was the wingback armchair. There was the fire sputtering in the fireplace, their own fireplace right there in the room. There were the electric sconces, two of them above the bed. Part of her wanted to turn them off so she might sit unseen in the dark, but she liked the soft, yellow light they cast on the dark ribs of the wallpaper, like sun on the ripples of the creek. She sat with her hands in her lap.

"Elma Rawls," she said aloud, trying it out.

"What?"

"Elma Rawls." She looked at him. "Gone take a while for me to get used to that."

"Elma Rawls," he said, "it's going to take both of us a while to get used to this."

"Used to what?"

He cast his arm back over the bed. "To being married." A bead of sweat skated down his temple. "It'll take time, I reckon. We can take our time. If that's what you want."

"Are you asking me what I want?"

"That's what I'm asking."

"I want to lay down," she said.

Oliver braced his hands against the edge of the bed and lifted his torso and swung it back and to the right a foot, toward the headboard. It was so warm in the room that he'd taken his suit jacket off, and through his shirt she could see his biceps tense. His arm muscles were well-formed—from years of carrying his weight on his crutches, she would learn—and he had a certain dexterity, didn't he, a contained kind of comfort in his own body, as though it were a jalopy only he knew how to drive. Steadily he pushed back one more time, lifted his left leg just above the knee—she shifted down the bed to give him room—then pivoted his waist, cranking both legs onto the bed with his right, so that his body lay before him now. He arranged his arms behind his head, settling into the pillows. The underarms of his shirt were dark with sweat.

"Been a long day," she said, slowing herself down, because she felt that she might hurtle forward if she let herself.

"You must be tired."

"I am tired."

He patted the bed beside him. "Come on, lay down and rest, Elma Rawls."

She looked at the great expanse of the bed. "You got to take your shoes off first, Oliver." They were both wearing their shoes and she realized how sore her feet were, how pinched her toes. She began to take off her heels, unbuckling the straps and standing them up on the floor at the foot of the bed.

He looked down at his feet. His face was figuring out what to do.

"You must want to take your shoes off, Oliver, after such a long day."

"I do. It's just . . . it ain't so easy."

"Let me." She reached for his left foot, and he pulled back his right one.

"Wait."

"What is it?"

"Can you . . . can you get me my jacket?" He pointed to the table, where his cane was propped against the armchair, and over the chair, his jacket. She handed it to him. It was heavy, and from the inside pocket he took a silver flask. "Do you mind if I have just a taste? It helps, sometimes, with my nerves."

"Oliver Rawls. You got something up your sleeve?"

He laughed. "I don't drink much, I promise you. If you mind, I won't—"

"I don't mind," she said, though she did, though she was thinking now of Freddie and of her father, the two men she didn't want to be thinking of on her wedding night. "That's not—gin, is it?"

He shook his head as he took a sip. He downed it quickly, as though it were cough syrup. "Whiskey."

"What's whiskey taste like?" She remembered the way the gin had made her head light and liquid when she was in labor.

Oliver thought. "Strong."

"Can I try it?"

"It's very strong, Elma."

"You saying I can't handle it?"

"I think you could handle just about anything."

"Hand it over, then."

He did and she took a sip and her throat burned and tears came to her eyes, but she put on a face like she'd just had a sip of Earl Grey.

"Do you like it?"

She said, "It tastes like axle grease."

He laughed. "I told you it was strong."

"Give me some more."

"Elma."

"Give me some more!"

He handed it over. She took another swig. It was like the terrible, wonderful sting of dunking her face in the cold creek.

"Look like you the one with something up your sleeve."

"No." She returned the flask to him. "I don't drink, either."

"Really? With—?"

"Never. I hate the stuff."

"Me too," he said, and took another sip.

"Is it helping? With your nerves?"

He sighed. "It's my leg." He knocked on the left one, and to her surprise—was she drunk already?—it made a sound, a metallic thump.

"Does it hurt?"

"No, ma'am. Can't feel a thing."

Carefully he lifted his pants leg from the thigh, and at his ankle she could see the place where his shoe, which had a thick platform heel, like a woman's house shoe, was bolted onto what looked like a metal brace. A brace, then. It was why he walked the way he did. All at once she was flooded with the relief and dread of understanding. That shoe was like an ugly baby (yes, she was drunk already, or half drunk; she could feel the whiskey spreading its wings across her chest); it was like a baby with a harelip, or one of the tiny, hairy babies at Coney Island. Gathering her courage, like she was set to take another shot, she took his shoe and cradled it and lowered it into her lap. Oh, she was glad for the whiskey. She eased the pants leg up farther, and he let her. The brace was fitted on either side of his calf, which was pale and skinny and nearly hairless, like a boy's. She looked at his leg. She didn't dare look him in the face. Her own face was flaming. Quickly, like she might touch a stove to see if it was hot, she touched his shin. "Can you feel that?"

Then she did look up at him. Her husband's eyes through his glasses were warm and faraway and silver. He shook his head.

She crept the pants leg up farther, until it was bunched above his knee. Up went the brace, as far as she could see, farther. She touched his kneecap, more confidently this time, like she might touch the stove after being reasonably sure it wouldn't burn her. "That?" she said.

Again he shook his head. He swallowed. He was thinking, she

thought, that she might keep her hands moving in their upward direction, and she was thinking she might do the same. And thinking
it, she lost her nerve and dropped her hands to his calf. She rubbed
her palms around it, first gently, then more vigorously, her knuckles
knocking against the brace. She thought suddenly of Winna. How
she would jog Winna's legs, pressing her knees against her chest
when her belly was upset, and then her constipated baby was in her
head when she was supposed to be making love to her husband. Her
brain felt loose. Winna and Wilson were with Nan. Nan would nurse
her. Elma's breasts were full but Winna hardly nursed at night anymore; Winna would be fine. Nan was at the new house, Dr. Rawls's
house. Oliver had already hired a man to move what little they would
bring with them—the crib, the rocker, their clothes, some books, the
sewing machine—and Oliver had decided, because Elma wanted him
to decide, she couldn't decide anything else, not today, that the man
should go on and move Nan too. And although Juke was no longer
there, though he had, over the course of the long afternoon, been
escorted by the sheriff to the jailhouse, Nan would be safer at the
house in town. She was safe. She could stop worrying about Nan.
Who was she to think Nan needed her?

It was her father she was worried about. What kind of bed was he
sleeping on tonight? How long would they keep him?

She shook her head. The whiskey was making it hard to keep
her mind where she wanted it. Oliver's eyes were closed. He looked
pleased, though if he couldn't feel pain, she reasoned, he couldn't feel
pleasure. She was kneading his dead leg roughly, like a firm dough.
What was she doing? It was easier at Christmas, when she had decided to be a tramp. It was easier before that, in Freddie's truck, when
she had no choice but to be a tramp, when being a wife was a far-
off promise, and all the things that would happen had not happened
yet. She was massaging Oliver's calf and thinking of Freddie, that
first time, how she had not even had to decide to take off her drawers, how he had yanked them aside and sat her down on his lap, her

spine wedged against the steering wheel, her breasts mashed against his liquor-hot mouth, without need for the pillow talk that was now, she was learning, the harder part, the husband-and-wife part, the part she would have to do for the rest of her life. It was that hungry, wordless part she wanted now, the part that was like the liquor, fast and painful, in and out.

"Oliver?"

He opened his eyes. Her hands paused on his leg.

"What *can* you feel?"

She thought she saw the crotch of his pants pulse. It rose and fell and was still. But her brain was loose and the smoke from the fireplace was making her eyes water.

He tapped his left thigh just below the groin. "Here up," he said, "I can feel everything." He adjusted his glasses. "But I can't *do* everything."

She nodded. "I see," she said, but she didn't see.

"Do you want to? See?"

She blinked. "See what?"

"My leg. Everything. Whatever you want."

"Are you asking me what I want?"

"I want to be honest with you. I've—I've seen you. It's my turn. I don't want to hide anything from you, Elma."

She shook her head.

"No? You don't want to see?"

"No. I mean, no, I don't want to hide anything, either."

"No," he agreed.

"Let me." His foot was still cradled in her lap. She had grown used to it.

"There's a pin through the bottom. You just—kind of push and pull. To release it."

She struggled with it a moment.

"You need both hands."

Then she sprung it loose and the brace fell slack. She untied the shoe and pulled it off his foot. She untied the other one. She put the shoes on the floor beside her own.

There were three leather straps. One across the calf, one just above the knee, and one around the upper part of his thigh.

"It's easier to take the trousers off first," he said.

She put her hands in her lap. "Shall I turn off the light?"

"No. Leave it."

He loosened his belt and without being told she began to slip the trousers down, first unbunching the left pants leg, then drawing them both around and over the brace and off. She did this slowly, carefully, as though removing a drop cloth from an antique piece of furniture.

His legs lay before her like two buttered noodles. One leg was a good two inches shorter than the other. His shirttails covered his shorts. His eyes were closed and his face was turned, as though he were the one seeing them for the first time.

"Oliver? You all right?"

"Never let anyone do that before."

"It's all right, Oliver." They weren't so awful, were they? Did a man need legs to be a man? "It's all right," she said again.

The first two straps she unbuckled wordlessly and without help. It was a puzzle, one she could solve, a place to focus her mind. Out of the corner of her eye she thought she saw his crotch move again, but she kept her eyes on each buckle, each clasp.

The last strap was laced instead of buckled, like a woman's corset. Elma had never worn a corset before and she felt queasy unlacing this one. It was a puzzle, she told herself, a knot to untie. Her fingernails were long and she scratched his thigh and she apologized.

"No, no," he said.

"It's all right," she said. "It's all right."

And then the last strap was undone and she could lift his leg out of it. "Does it hurt?" He shook his head. She thought of the feeling of lifting a log down by the creek. The kind you expected to be heavy but instead was hollowed out. She turned to rest the brace in the chair, and it slipped and she rearranged it, and then the cane slipped and she rearranged it, and when she turned back to the bed Oliver had unbuttoned his shirt and removed it and then he removed his undershirt too. He blotted his face with his undershirt and dropped it to the floor. Now he was in his shorts, very clean, very white shorts. She tried to keep her eyes on his arms, his very strong, very white arms, the dark hair on his chest. The legs weren't so awful, were they? So terribly awful?

She took the flask from the nightstand and took another sip and shook her head with the heat of it. "I finished it," she said. "I'm sorry."

"No, no," he said.

She sat on the edge of the bed and he unfastened the buttons on the back of the dress, eight pearl buttons she had sewn on by hand. They had been buttoned once—Nan had dressed her—and now they were unbuttoned, and they would not be needed again. She was sorry to take off the dress, but she did. The whiskey was just enough to help her drop her slip and brassiere and drawers to the floor in a puddle at her feet. She watched her husband watch her. To keep her hands busy she removed the pins from her hair, which was falling from its twist. He said, "I didn't think you could look more beautiful than you did in that dress."

She could feel her cheeks blushing with the whiskey. She wanted to be under the bedclothes—it was what married people did, wasn't it, they did what they did under the bedclothes—but she couldn't imagine how they might get under them together, how she might have to help lift them out from under his body. So she lay down beside him on top of the gold duvet. The feather pillow floated up around her ears. She felt a sad, futile longing for the pillow, for its weight on top of her, her legs around its great mass. Her red hair was kinked from the bobby pins and it lay in waves over her breasts, which were full of milk. She prayed they wouldn't spill.

Quietly Oliver shimmied out of his shorts. She sat up on an elbow to help him, but he didn't need help. It took him some time.

She had not lain down next to Freddie, other than in the bed of his truck, where there wasn't room to stretch out flat, let alone to study his manhood. It had been dark, the headlights off and the moon dull, everything quick and cramped and confused. It was Genus's manhood that hung in her mind.

Oliver's manhood was like a little white sleeping mouse. Every once in a while the mouse would twitch its tail in its sleep. Part of her wanted to reach out and pet it. Part of her wanted to leap from the bed.

Oliver spoke to the ceiling. "We make a fine pair."

"Oliver," she said, though she wasn't touching him, "you make a fine man. You're a fine man." He was fine, wasn't he? He was fine.

"I'd like to do everything. I would. Maybe I can."

"You're fine, Oliver," she managed. "You're a good, good man."

He gave a pitiful laugh. "A good man." He looked at her, suddenly desperate. He took her hand, and between their naked hips their wrists were pressed together and she felt the blood coursing through his veins. "I want to. I promise. Maybe someday I can."

She drew her hand back, laid it on her stomach. "But not tonight," she said. She meant it as a question.

"Not tonight, darling."

She understood he didn't want to try and fail. Not on their wedding night.

"No," she agreed. They lay there for a few minutes, breathing deeply, the firelight making shadows on the wall. She sat up a little and then lay back down, just to feel her head sink into the pillow again.

"You can change your mind," he said.

She turned her head to him.

"I'll understand. If you want to go back to him. Now that he's back. Now that you've seen me for what I am. If—"

"Oliver, what? Go back to who?"

Neither one of them had said his name. "Freddie Wilson."

Elma sat up. She looked down at her husband. "Good gracious, Oliver! I hate that man! Don't you understand? I hate him!"

Oliver gave a meek nod. "All right," he said softly. "I'm sorry."

"I hate him," she said again.

"I've tricked you. I didn't mean to, but I've tricked you."

"No," she said. "No, you haven't." But she did feel tricked, she did feel deceived, and now she felt angry—angry for his apology, his adoration.

"It's your choice," he said. But he was wrong. She had no more choices left.

He looked at her hopefully. The fire flashed whitely on his lenses.

"Enough looking," she said, and snatched the glasses off his face, and now there was nothing more to take off.

TWENTY-FIVE

Macon Telegraph, February 8, 1931

FUGITIVE RETURNS TO COTTON CO.

F. Wilson In Custody Under False Name

SECOND SUSPECT CHARGED IN JULY MURDER

FLORENCE, Ga., Feb. 8— The Cotton County Sheriff's Department is conducting a review of a "cold case" after a fugitive from the law, George Frederick "Freddie" Wilson III, was discovered Saturday in Cotton County custody under a false identity. The 20-year-old former foreman of the Florence Cotton Mill and grandson of mill owner and planter George Wilson was wanted in connection with the July 7 murder of Genus Jackson, after which he fled from the county. A second suspect, John "Juke" Jesup, was also taken into county custody on Saturday.

On November 4, Wilson was arrested on charges of petty larceny for stealing "a rooster, a pumpkin squash, and a pair of overalls off a clothesline" from a farm in Meredith. The fugitive had brought himself to Dr. Aldus DeMille for multiple lacerations after the rooster had apparently pecked both arms, his neck, and his right eye. "That bird nearly pecked the eye clean," said Dr. DeMille. "He looked like he'd been sorting wildcats."

When the doctor grew suspicious of the patient's erratic behavior, he reported Wilson, who had presented himself as "John Smith," to Deputy Sheriff Herman Flood, who assigned him three months on the Cotton County road gang.

"He was right under our nose," said Sheriff S. M. Cleave, who'd been away on a hunting trip at the time. "But we had no reason to suspect him of nothing other than being a farm beggar. No one couldn't hardly recognize him with his eye clawed out."

Wilson managed to serve twelve weeks on the road gang under the false name before he was identified while paving Twelve-Mile Road near the intersection of String Wilson Road by Mrs. Elma Rawls, née Jesup, 18, Wilson's former fiancée. Chain gang guards held the crew of convicts near Mud Turner's crossroads store while word was relayed to Florence. Sheriff Cleave and Warden Mississippi Barnes shortly arrived at the crossroads in caravan.

In July, Jackson, a Negro, was determined to be hanged from a gourd tree on the crossroads farm owned by Wilson, Sr., before his body was dragged some six miles to Florence's mill village. Jesup, the sharecropper who hired Jackson as a wage hand, accused Wilson of the murder, citing retaliation for the rape of Mrs. Rawls.

But Wilson turned the tables on Saturday, claiming to authorities that Jesup was the one responsible for Jackson's killing. He reported to the sheriff that Jesup had threatened to kill

Wilson's newborn daughter, Jesup's own granddaughter, if Wilson refused to leave town and "take the fall."

Jesup protested, denying the charges vehemently. Witnesses to the events described his behavior at this point as "ornery" and "heated up." He repeatedly threatened both Wilsons, calling them "yellow scoundrels."

Jesup was taken into custody and escorted to the Cotton County Jailhouse in Florence on charges of public intoxication. Sheriff Cleave released a statement later that evening that Jesup had been indicted on charges of Jackson's murder. Jesup's bail hearing is set for Friday.

"What's important is that the people of Cotton County are safe and sound," Sheriff Cleave stated. "We're going to hear the matter out."

Sheriff Cleave and Warden Barnes both declined to speculate on whether the crime against Jackson would be reclassified as a mob killing, or if others would be charged. After a three-year hiatus, the state of Georgia recorded six lynchings of Negroes last year.

Q. L. Boothby contributed to this report from Florence. See Editorial, 2B.

TWENTY-SIX

WHEN THEY WERE YOUNG, JUKE AND STRING HAD PLAYED the games farm boys play. One game they called jailhouse. The jailhouse was the chicken coop. One of them was the jailbird and one was the guard. The guard brought the jailbird bread and water on a tray. The jailbird threw it at the guard and tried to escape. The guard shot at the jailbird with his stick gun. "He's fleeing the coop!" The chickens scattered and pecked. The jailbird was clever and low-down, but most times you wanted to be the guard. The jailbird got chicken shit on the knees of his dungarees and stunk to Heaven till he was made to scrub in the creek.

What Juke felt in the jailhouse now was bored. For two days, other than the few hours Wolfie Brunswick was there to dry out, he was the only one in the cell. Second day they'd given him prison striped pants and a denim work shirt. They fed him all right, the same cook who cooked for Sheriff and his woman downstairs, fatback and cracklin' bread and black-eyed peas. He had peace and quiet to piss and shit as he pleased, and when the deputy left to piss and shit himself, Juke would sit on the porcelain toilet just to have something to busy himself with, just to sit and to listen to the flush. Regular meals and a toilet that flushed. It was more than George Wilson would have for him.

He hadn't had a drink since Friday. That was part of it. Public intoxication, Sheriff said, but he'd been sober the day of his daughter's wedding—he didn't drink before church—and he was sober now, so sober he could see out the corners of his eyes the hairs growing on his own cheeks, rusty gold in the light that came through the bars of the window. He needed a shave. A shave and a drink. He scratched at his jaw.

His hands were sore where he'd slammed them against the bars and still there was blood dried in his knuckles and he wondered had he broken some bones. He had already cycled through a good deal of his rage on Saturday afternoon, and then on Saturday evening Sheriff had come up and told him the county was charging him for what happened on the farm in July, and then came panic, followed by disbelief, followed by pleading, and then Sheriff, though he'd retired downstairs by then, had gotten what was left of his rage, the low-down Judas chickenshit he was, and a yellow scoundrel as well. Then he was tired and he slept for a long time, and Wolfie Brunswick came in and out of his dreams. They kicked Wolfie out when he was dried out. And then Juke woke up, the sweat dried all over his skin, like a new skin, like a snake skin, and he realized that was what he'd done too. He'd dried out.

Friday was what he was waiting for. Friday he could post bail. But the only man who could post bail for him, the only man who once would, was the man who'd put him in jail in the first place.

Late Monday night, footsteps came up the stairs. They were struggling footsteps. There were two cells that Juke could see, the one he was in and the empty one next to him, which was for white women, the deputy told him. There were three cots in his cell, along the three walls that weren't the door. The front and the left side of the cell were bars, and the one on the right was concrete block with a window, and the one behind him was another concrete wall, and from behind this wall he could hear another cell door opening and closing. He could hear a woman crying. He suspected it was a colored woman and it was, he could hear her crying a drunk, muffled, protesting cry.

"What's that woman here for?" he asked the deputy quietly when he saw him next.

"What you think? Hustling."

"Where at?"

"Where you think? Down along the tracks. Front a Young's."

The deputy was plump as a groundhog, with a groundhog's wide neck and upturned snout and long yellow teeth. His head was large but his hat too large still. It was a police officer's hat. Juke supposed that was what he was. The deputy returned to the wooden chair where he sat by the door and removed the hat. Under it, sitting on top of the man's bald head, was a sandwich wrapped in wax paper. Juke laughed. "Got you a sandwich?"

The deputy picked it up, returned his hat to his head, and unwrapped the sandwich. "Barbecue. Can't go down to Young's without getting me some."

"Smell good," Juke said. He had eaten that barbecue. He could taste it now.

He watched the man eat. The woman's crying had quieted.

"What's your name?" Juke thought to ask. He was lonely and he was bored.

"Flood. Herman Flood."

"You enjoying that barbecue."

Herman Flood's mouth was full of it. He grunted.

Juke could taste it. He could taste the barbecue and the corn liquor and the girls. He wondered if the woman on the other side of the wall was one of them. If he knew her, if she knew him.

Eventually Juke slept. He dreamt of Clarence and Mamie, Archie and Jo, shipped off on a truck for dog food. Elma was helping load them in the truck. The man driving was George Wilson, but George

Wilson when Juke was a child. He dreamt of Lefty buried in the cold ground, and Castor buried in the cold ground. He dreamt of String the Indian chief with a crown of chicken feathers. He dreamt of String the Negro painted in tar. They were different dreams or all one dream. He had been drunk a long time and now he was not. He felt the memories float up to the surface like bloated, wide-eyed fish.

He sat up on his cot, awake. Lefty was buried, Castor was buried, and his money was buried. Mason jars of it, dollars and coins, ten years of money paid to him by George Wilson. It was all buried on the farm. How much was there?

Slowly he came to recognize the sound of someone singing. It was night still, or early morning. The streetlamp outside the window laid yellow light across the floor of the dark cell. Herman Flood was not in his chair by the door. The voice was coming from the other side of the wall. It sang *Sometimes I feel like a motherless child*. That was what his mind, half sleeping, told him. The voice sounded like it was made of paper and cloth, that it was stitching together bits of rag and wiregrass and bark.

His mind told him to lie down again, to return to his dreams, which was the closest he could get to being drunk. But another piece of his mind was keeping him upright in the cold dark cell, listening. His ears waited for the next part of the song. From the murky place of his dreams, he felt each word float up to the surface, and he remembered each one just as she gave it breath.

Sometimes I wish I could fly
Like a bird up in the sky
Closer to my home.

He was singing under his breath, and then he was singing more loudly.

The voice on the other side of the wall stopped. Her name was Lorraine.

"Don't stop."

His wet nurse must have sung it to him as she rocked him to

sleep. He didn't remember her name (it was Abigail) but he could al-most remember her face, the voice that was something like a mother's.

"Please don't stop," he said.

————————

Tuesday he slept the day away. He tried not to eat because he didn't want to shit, not with the woman listening on the other side of the wall. But he was hungry, so he had supper and then slept some more. He dreamt of Sterling appearing like a ghost on the chain gang, and Freddie's eye swallowing itself. Was that part a dream? He dreamt of Wilson. Wilson was filthy, his body tarry with mud, his hands and knees red with ant bites. There were government men coming for him because he'd been let loose on the farm, roaming around in his diaper, his diaper full of shit. Juke woke and sat on the toilet and let the black-eyed peas run through him. He was grateful now that the woman wasn't singing, or crying. He hoped she was sleeping. He sat on the toilet and he cried without making a sound.

It was just Nan left on the farm now. For all he knew she'd let the babies loose just like her momma had done.

Or was she in the doctor's house by now? And if she was at the doctor's house, who was feeding the animals? Who was milking the cows? Were they let loose to pasture with the twins?

When Herman Flood returned to collect Juke's empty plate, Juke stood and made to talk to him.

"Can't I get word to my kin?"

"I done told you. You can see your kin Friday."

"But can't I get word before the hearing. It's about the bail money."

The deputy laughed. "You ain't got enough kin to make no bail."

"What you know of it? How much is it?"

"I ain't the judge, Mr. Juke, but I reckon it's a pretty penny."

Juke sat down on his cot. He pictured Elma shoveling up the jars. He wouldn't be able to tell her where they were. The only map he had was in his mind. Maybe there was no one left on the farm to dig them up. Then a terrible question came to him. He wondered would Elma dig up the money for him if she could. Would she want him home, or would she leave him there to rot.

"I been thinking. You saying kin can't come to see no prisoners, or is it my kin ain't been to see me."

"Ain't no one allowed to see you. Sheriff don't want it that way. Sure enough not no reporter from no city rag."

Juke stood again. "Who's that."

"Macon man. Sheriff showed him the door."

"He come to talk to me?"

"Sure enough. Yestidy."

"Hell! What if I got something to say?"

"You can say it on Friday."

Juke tongued the empty ditch along his gums. His teeth were so dry they ached. "That's all right."

The deputy turned to go, taking the tray with him.

"I need me something to chew, Herman Flood."

Herman Flood grunted.

"Some tobacca. I know you got some. I seen you chew it." The deputy was halfway across the room and fading with the evening light. "I know you drinking with the sheriff, Herman Flood. That's my Cotton Gin, you know. That's my gin you drinking while I rot in this cell."

The deputy's key chain jangled from his belt.

"Even Sheriff ain't come up but once. Why ain't he come? I'll tell you. He's a Judas like the rest. Ain't got the guts to look me in the eye."

The deputy turned as he reached the door.

"I know you got you some barbecue under that hat, you yellow belly!"

Herman Flood lifted his hat, as though to say good night. There was nothing under it but his bald head.

Wednesday—or was it Thursday already?—it was Wilson still fixed in his mind. Wilson was still painted in tar but now he had no ears. Castor had chewed them off. In their place were chicken feathers. The chicken feathers were on fire. Juke woke slapping at the scar on his arm, putting out the flame of his dream.

"Herman Flood. Mr. Flood!" He stood and rattled the bars of the cell. "I weren't never hurt no baby."

Herman Flood was not in his chair. Juke could feel the woman's silence on the other side of the wall, a silence built of paper and cloth.

"That scoundrel Freddie Wilson say I was set to hurt a baby. Winna Jean. Ain't never put a hand on her. Neither a them babies."

Then the silence was gone and in its place was a sound close to crying or singing, but it wasn't crying or singing. Juke hushed. He hushed, hoping the woman might take up her singing again. He hushed a good while, listening. It was dark in the cell and the streetlight came in the window and fell over the deputy's empty chair.

Then he heard the sound of coins jangling, or keys. Was he hearing things? He could hear the hairs growing on his face. He clawed at it.

"Mr. Flood? You there?"

The white cotton dust on Jessa's feet, and the white snow on the pregnant whore's feet, and him, Juke, swimming through a creek of chicken feathers, their quills in his nostrils, in his eyes and ears. Waking up coughing them up. He slid from the cot to the concrete floor and he crawled to the bars and he beat his head on them until all that his mind contained was the pain.

"Quit that bulling around," Herman Flood said. A man was with him, short, muscled, in dungarees and handcuffs. Flood let him into the cell and uncuffed him.

Juke rose up to his knees. A white band pressed over his vision. Through it he could see the man flex his bare arms. The hair on his arms was dusted with white lint. Cotton.

Flood was already gone, his key chain jangling behind him.

"Bob Pruitt," the man said, and held his right hand out to Juke. The hand looked strangely small, a rough little hoof of a hand, and it took Juke a moment to count a finger missing, the pinky.

"Jesup." Juke took the hand and Bob Pruitt helped him to his feet. Juke's head swam with pain. "Juke Jesup. Like for the juke in town."

"I know who you is. You and George Wilson run the blind tiger."

Juke winced. "Ain't no one left blind to it, I reckon."

Bob Pruitt had been a carder at the mill until that morning, when he'd been discharged by George Wilson. "We got us in a quarrel, you could say. Didn't want it that way. Newspaperman came yestidy. Asking what happened to my boy. That's Denny. My son. Ain't but twenty-two. Young man, strong. I worked in that mill since the year he was born. I know what them machines can do." He held up his right hand. "But I never seen nothing like what happened to Denny. You hear what happened Monday?"

"What's today?"

"Thursday."

Juke shook his head and the pain rose to his eyes.

"You been in the mill? You seen how high them ceilings is in the card room?" Pruitt raised an arm in the air.

Juke nodded. "My woman was a spinner."

"Denny was running one a the card machines. Like any old day. That machine been acting up for weeks. I know 'cause I'm the one fixes em. I oiled it and oiled it within an inch of its life. I told the new foreman, Mr. Richard, it got no more life left in it. Finicky, is what I told him. Liable to eat it a whole hand. Mr. Richard told Mr. Wilson, but Mr. Wilson don't do nothing. And first thing Monday morning, me and Denny go in and turn on all the machines. You know what it's

like on a Monday morning in the mill? Your lungs has had all weekend to clear out. You go in Monday morning and you can't hardly
breathe, all the wet hot cotton in the air about to choke you. Denny's
lungs ain't been good as it was. He was having him a coughing fit.
He weren't paying good enough attention. He turns on his machine
and I'm over acrost the room. Alls I see is Denny get throwed up to
the ceiling. He would have gone clear up to Heaven but them rafters
busted his head and spit him down to the floor."

"Holy Lord. It kill him?"

"Just about. Busted his head. Broke his arm and his pelvis and
most a his ribs and smashed up his face. Mr. Wilson say he'll pay his
hospital. Ain't that big? He'll pay his hospital. Boy's in a body cast."

"Well, holy Lord."

"How my to feed my family? My woman had to leave her machine
to tend to him. Then I got two kin ain't getting no pay. And now I
ain't gone get no pay neither, 'cause I'm here in this cell with you."

"Of all the lousy, low-down, scoundrel—"

"Mr. Richard I ain't got a quarrel with. He done what he could."

"He's foreman now?"

"For now he is. But ain't no telling how fast Granddaddy will put
Freddie boy back in it, now he's home."

Juke was sitting on the cot and Bob Pruitt was standing. The
band of light over Juke's eyes was loosening. He had the sense that
nothing had changed and everything had changed. Freddie was back.
He'd be off the chain gang and back in the mill by Monday. And Juke
was in this cell, and no one would come and get him out.

"I ain't even tell the paper half of it," said Bob Pruitt.

"What paper?"

"*Testament*. Fella named Boothby, with a smoking pipe, come into
the village yestidy. I told him all about Denny. You bet I did. I showed
him his pictures. Denny liked to draw pictures. He had a man take a
picture of Denny's pictures. And they went back to Macon and took

more a Denny in his hospital bed. They put it in the paper and Mr. Wilson see it this morning, and that was it. He wouldn't have no one talk against him in no big-city paper."

Juke was thinking of the way Bob Pruitt was talking about his son, the way he could take up for him in the papers, and he was thinking about Wilson, the way he could sit up tall on his shoulders now and hold on to Juke's forehead, right there where that band of light was cooling, and Juke would hold his small socked feet, but no one knew he was his daddy, not even Wilson himself.

"Why you telling me all this, Bob Pruitt? Don't you know I been in deep with George Wilson? How you know I ain't one a his scouts?"

Bob Pruitt sat down on the cot opposite Juke's. "Everyone know Mr. Wilson cut ties with you, Mr. Juke." He said it kindly, like he didn't want to disappoint him. "Way I figure it, it's been coming a long time. Seem like half the hands aspire to be Klansmen. Other half love your gin too much. Aspire to be drunkards. No offense intended."

Juke shook his head.

"He got a new man making whiskey for him out west a town."

Juke opened his mouth to speak, then closed it. "Whiskey," was all he could get out.

"Out in them piney woods. Why you think they paving the Straight?"

Juke focused his eyes on the man's right hand, the severed finger. The finger was lost and the hand went on being a hand.

Cut ties. *You and George Wilson run the blind tiger.* They'd run it in the past, is what he'd meant. His time had come and gone.

"I know it," Juke said. "But I'm the one cut ties. I give up the moonshining. I told George Wilson I'm through."

Maybe he was through, he thought. Maybe he would give it up. Making it, drinking it. Look how it had poisoned him. Look what it had gone and done.

"Well, I reckon his ties is cut with both of us. Reckon he put us both here."

Pruitt was looking down at him. He could see it in his face. What this linthead must think of him, banging his head against the wall like a madman. All Juke had wanted was a body to talk to, and now there was one in front of him, thinking he knew him up and down.

"Tell you what," Bob Pruitt said. "Someone ought to kill George Wilson dead."

Juke grunted. He didn't know if the man was trying to trick him or cheer him up.

"You the one to do it, Juke Jesup. Ain't you the one who killed that darky boy on his farm?"

Juke looked to the concrete wall. It was early afternoon and the gray paint was silver in the light from the window. He thought he heard a sound from the other side, the sound of flat shoes on the concrete floor.

"What you know of it?" Juke said quietly.

"I seen him come into the village." Bob Pruitt lowered his voice. "I was too late to get me any good parts. But I got me a piece a his union suit. Carry it with me when I can."

Before Juke could tell him not to, the man drew a square of cloth from the pocket of his dungarees. It was the size of a handkerchief and stained red with blood.

"Lord's sake! Put that away!"

Pruitt smiled. "It's right ugly, ain't it?"

"Put that trash away."

"Ain't you keep nothing from him? Bring back that killing feeling?"

"Shut up, fool. You ain't know nothing about it."

"You saying you ain't did it?"

"I don't like the way killing feels," Juke said.

Pruitt smiled, pocketing the cloth. "Then you saying you did."

"Freddie Wilson done it," Juke said softly.

"Low-down dog," said Bob Pruitt. "It's Freddie Wilson ought to hang, then. Freddie and his granddaddy. Doubleheader. That's a sight I'd like to see."

"Hush, if you don't mind. I got a headache," Juke said.

"How long you been here?"

"Five days." He lay down on his side and closed his eyes. "Feel like five years."

Bob Pruitt lay down on the cot across from Juke. Juke slept but Bob didn't. Around six o'clock, end of the day shift, Mr. Beau Richard came to bail him out for fifteen dollars. No hearing, just fifteen dollars paid in Sheriff's parlor. Sheriff gave five of it to Herman Flood and sent him to Young's to fetch them corn liquor and barbecue. When Juke awoke, Bob Pruitt was gone.

"Bob Pruitt?" he asked the room.

Night had fallen and he could feel the woman breathing on the other side of the wall. He could feel her silence made of newspaper and ragged bits of apron.

"Herman Flood?"

He could feel rather than hear the woman's voice rise up against her silence, and then he heard a jangling of keys. Then he heard a sound like the slam of a screen door. She cried out.

"Herman Flood! What you up to?"

They were struggling sounds. There was nothing to drink to drown out the sound. "Herman Flood! I hear you, Herman Flood!" There was no pillow to put over his head. He kicked the bars of the cell. He slipped and fell. He crept to the toilet. He put his head inside and flushed it, and for a moment the sound flushed out all other sound.

When he pulled his head out of the bowl Sheriff was standing before his cell. Juke's face was dripping wet. He slicked back his hair. "Sheriff."

"You crazier than I thought, Juke Jesup." Sheriff's shirttails were undone and his face was flushed.

"Where's Flood?"

"Ain't no one here but me."

"That woman. You been in her cell."

"You know that nigger gal? You want some a her?"

Juke wanted to spit. His face was wet but his mouth was still dry. He wanted a drink and he wanted a fight. He wanted to pound the sheriff to the ground. He thought he'd been on their side, but now he was sober as a baby and he saw the truth: he was on the other side. They were all against him.

He's fleein' the coop!

"You crooked, Sheriff. You crooked as George Wilson."

"I'm crooked? You a straight shooter now, Jesup?"

"Suppose I am."

Sheriff chuckled. "Well, that's good. 'Cause I got a surprise for you, Mr. Juke. I been out to the crossroads farm today. Got a look around."

Juke stood and gripped the bars. "That right?"

"Had some friends with me. George Wilson. We had a look-see."

"Had you a look-see. That right."

"Yes, sir."

"Ain't seen nothing you didn't know about already."

"You'll hear all about it in time. Tomorrow, reckon."

"You crooked, Sheriff. You the most low-down of us all."

"That right? More low-down than you, Mr. Juke?"

"Go to Easter's. You want a nigger gal, go to Easter's and pay."

"That what you do? Before you kill a nigger, you like to pay him first?"

Sheriff came a step closer and his face came into the light. His mustache was dark with tobacco and spit.

"Nigger lover don't like it when he's locked up and can't have none of the fun."

———

With the sheriff gone the woman's silence was in the room with him, thin and dry, like a rag stiff with blood.

He wanted her to sing. She didn't sing. So he sat down on the cot and closed his eyes and he sang it himself, loud and full, the notes fill-ing his lungs. He pretended they were singing it together, stranger to stranger, through the concrete wall. And as the words appeared on his tongue, he heard not his nurse's voice singing them but Ketty. Ketty at the creek, Ketty at the stove, Ketty in his bed, singing,

Sometimes I feel like I'm almost gone
Sometimes I feel like I'm almost gone
Sometimes I feel like I'm all alone
A long ways from home.

TWENTY-SEVEN

B UT BEFORE THAT, FIRST THING SUNDAY MORNING, THE DAY AF-
ter Elma Jesup married Oliver Rawls, the day after Sterling
Smith and Freddie Wilson appeared on the chain gang,
Nancy Smith had nursed her son in the house at 52 Main Street. She
wore her nightgown and her head rag—her hair was longer now, just
full enough to plait and wrap—and a pair of bedroom slippers that
had been left behind in Carlotta Rawls's closet. The picture window
in her new room, the back room, was south facing, and though over
the distant fence she could see the busy chimneys of the neighboring
street, she saw no other windows. The only other soul who could see
her was the cardinal in the crape myrtle that stood in the backyard.

The morning sun poured through the window where Pollux, on
the rag rug, and Winna, in the crib, still slept. Winna would have her
own room in time, her own crib, but Nan had wanted both babies
close that first night. She had woken twice, heart pounding, disori-
ented in the dark, and having located them in their crib like their
constellations in the sky, she went back to bed, satisfied. More disori-
enting than the dark was the light she woke to. There were no roosters
to announce the dawn, no cows to milk, and the only breakfast she

had to make was her own. She was hungry, she realized. She walked
now, nursing Wilson still, the neck of her nightgown pulled low, to
the kitchen. It was cooler there, cold—she would have to build the fire
back up—and when she opened the refrigerator, the cold drifted out
at her like a wind. Wilson shivered. She closed the door. On the front
of the door—the whitest white she had ever seen—was taped a doctor's prescription sheet, where someone had written, *Be strong and let
your heart take courage, all you who put your hope in the Lord.*

She opened the refrigerator again. Out poured the cold air. Wilson pulled off her breast. She wrapped him in his blanket and shivered, teaching him *cold*. The two of them stood thrilling in the draft
for a moment, staring into the foggy eye of the Frigidaire.

There were milk bottles stacked in rows and a bundle of parsnips
and a bottle of Heinz tomato ketchup. In a wire basket hanging from
a shelf, hen eggs, a dozen at least, loose and cold, like river stones.
She sat Wilson on the floor, his blanket puddled around him—they
were black and white tiles, and the part of her that was still fourteen
and not yet fifteen wanted to hopscotch the squares—and lifted her
nightgown and put three eggs in it to carry. She walked the eggs to
the stove. She hummed a song she made up as she walked. Wilson
followed her with his eyes. He followed the song, his ears awake to
the new sound. She couldn't remember the last time she'd heard it
herself. At the stove she set the eggs in a pan and looked around for
wood. She looked for matches. She opened one of the oven doors. She
opened the other. Then she tried pressing one of the dials below the
stove. She gave it a pinch and a turn. She heard a click. In a moment,
one of the ash gray spirals grew orange at the edges. She gave a joyful yelp. In a moment more, the burner glowed red. She clapped her
hands. She hovered her hand over the electric flame, feeling its heat.

And then Wilson was clapping. Seven months old, sitting on the
floor in his white cotton nightgown, he offered up his first applause.

Nan gave another gasp. She laughed. She clapped. She went to
the baby and she knelt on the floor. And then she cried.

The day before, the day of the wedding, seemed far off now. From the place she'd hid with the twins, she could hear but not see the dogs barking, and then the gunshot, the music on the porch, and later, though she still didn't dare to leave the pantry, the truck wrecking in the ditch at the crossroads. She had never been to a wedding before, and she wasn't sure which parts of the ruckus were coming from the church. A long time seemed to pass before the knock came at the breezeway door. She seized up, gathered the babies onto her lap. The knocking continued. After a few minutes, a little voice hollered, "Miss Nan!" And worried that something had happened to Elma, who should have been home by now to feed Winna, Nan stood and went to the door and opened it.

It was little Lucy Cousins, wearing her Sunday clothes. Her shoes were muddy and her freckled face was red from running in the cold. "Miss Elma said to fetch you. Your daddy's come home."

Nan squeezed her eyes shut. The words were like too much sunlight. It was dark in the house, and it took a moment for her eyes to adjust.

She found shoes and her chore coat, bonnets and booties. She strapped the babies into the little red wagon with a quilt, leaving the sacks of flour there to brace them. She looked at her reflection in the diamond-shaped sliver of mirror hanging beside Elma's chifforobe. She adjusted her head wrap. She hadn't washed since Tuesday but there was no time now.

As she followed the little girl down the road, pulling the babies behind her, she paged through a book in her mind, a book of pictures she had conjured of her father, her father working in the steel mill, her father dropping a Buffalo nickel in an envelope, her father's bristly mustache, which smelled like pipe tobacco and almond oil. She had long had a picture in her mind of his homecoming: he would come up the driveway in an automobile, a Pontiac or a Chevrolet, with a license plate that said MARYLAND. The dogs would go out to greet him first and she'd step out onto the porch. He'd be wearing a Sunday suit and a wide-brimmed hat, which he'd tip up to get a better look at her, and then he'd take off the hat and hold it over his heart, and his eyes would see and see her. And then she would know. She would recognize him. She would recognize her own face in his.

But she knew that nothing happened the way you imagined it. That was how she knew it was real. The road was freshly paved, as though it had been laid down for this walk. It was smooth and still a little soft under her feet, the chalky smell of compressed rock still burning through the low-lying fog. Up ahead she could see a cluster of vehicles at the crossroads store. She could hear Pollux barking. Folks were milling about on the porch of the store, drinking Coca-Colas, playing checkers, as they sometimes did after church, but there were more of them than Nan had ever seen, spilling nearly into the road. Her heart was beating fast now. Parked among the cars and trucks was the sheriff's motorcycle.

"Nan!"

Then there was Elma in her wedding dress, pushing through the crowd. She was wearing a worried face, but as she reached Nan she seemed to remember that she was happy. Nan felt the eyes of the crowd turn to her. It was as though the eyes of the crowd followed Elma's eyes.

"You're not gone believe it, Nan. Your daddy's come home." She reached for Nan's hand. On Elma's ring finger she felt the sharp weight of the jade ring. Elma pulled her closer and whispered in her ear that he was on the chain gang, that so was Freddie, that Freddie was why all the people were there. "It's all right. You won't be able to get close to him. But come on over and meet him."

Elma led Nan, who led the twins in the wagon, through the eyes of the crowd. There was Mrs. Cousins and there was Mr. Simmons and there was Dr. Oliver, sitting at one of the tables to rest his leg. There at the corner of the store was Juke, talking to the sheriff. He was making a ruckus but he stopped as they passed. They all stopped. Fell quiet. They all parted for their little train—Elma, Nan, the wagon. And though she was still filled with fear, she felt the power, the protection, of the hand that led her. There was an awe in their eyes as they watched Elma go. She was the bride today, yes, but she had long been bride to the town. They had hailed her, they had followed her every word. They had believed her. This was what Nan saw. And she remembered the day that Elma had earned their deference.

Around the corner of the store, which had fallen into shade, the chain of men leaned against the east wall. Some were drinking Coca-Colas. Some were smoking cigarettes. They chatted quietly, as though waiting in line for a picture show. She scanned their faces. She didn't recognize him. He could have been any of them.

"Warden," Elma said to another man in uniform. "I got my chore girl here. That's her daddy." She pointed to a strong-shouldered man in the middle of the chain. "Uncle Sterling!" She waved. "Warden, could she stand and wave?"

The warden said nothing. Just stared. Nan hoped Juke was watching too. The man was leaning against the wall, smoking a cigarette someone had given him. A tin cup and a spoon hung from his belt; a handkerchief hung from his back pocket. When he saw her, he dropped the cigarette in the dirt and stomped it out and stood up straight. Nan stood up straight too. He was wearing a hat, not a wide-brimmed hat but a striped knit cap. He didn't take it off. Just stared. His face was clean-shaven, his long sideburns silvered.

She was feeling brave. So she lifted her hand and waved.

He waved back.

"Hello, Nancy," he said. "You a sight for sore eyes."

———

She had mostly stopped crying, was holding Wilson on her hip and watching the water boil, water she had procured by turning a faucet in a cast-iron sink. She was reaching her hand toward the burner and then pulling it back, teaching him *hot,* when a sound filled the room. It was like the squawk of a monstrous crow. It came again. No, it wasn't like a crow. It was unlike any sound she had heard before. Pollux came into the kitchen, tail up, barking, nails clicking on the tile floor. The sound came a third time, and she saw on the wall the black instrument rattling on its hook—yes, like a crow on a branch, struggling to open its wings. Haltingly, she moved toward it. It hung on the wall above the table. It rang again. It was ringing. She stopped some distance from it and listened to it ring, six times, seven. She put her free hand over her ear and looked at Wilson, whose eyes were wide. And she taught herself the word as she would teach him if she could—"telephone."

––––––––––––

She had not been at the crossroads when Juke had been hauled away. She had left first. Mac Burnside, the colored man Oliver had hired to move the furniture, had driven Nan and the twins and Pollux—for Pollux was more house dog than farm dog, Elma reasoned, and couldn't be left alone, not without her mate—to Dr. Rawls's house in town. They had almost reached town, the place where the still dirt Straight became Main Street, when the sirens came up behind them. It was the sheriff on his motorcycle, kicking up dust. Mac Burnside pulled over to the right, nearly to the ditch. The motorcycle passed them on the left. Behind it was a patrol car, the warden driving. All the times she had seen the lights of a siren in a rearview mirror, all the times she had heard that motorcycle come up behind a country wagon when she was out on a call, her heart backed up in her throat. But this time was different. In the backseat of the patrol car—she could see him as it passed—was Juke. She watched the car recede far ahead of them before Mac pulled back onto the road. In her dress pocket was a key to the front door of the doctor's house, and she squeezed it.

Now she was inside the locked house and the telephone had

stopped ringing. The kitchen was as quiet as it had been loud. It must have been a call for Oliver, or for Mrs. Rawls, someone who didn't know she'd left for Savannah. It wouldn't have been Elma or Oliver. They knew she couldn't talk back. But maybe they had a message for her, and they thought if she lifted the receiver she might be able to listen. Maybe they'd been held up at the hotel.

But maybe it was her father. Maybe he had a message for her too. Or maybe he didn't know—was it possible he didn't know?—that she had no way of answering the phone.

The ringing had woken Winna. Nan brought her to the kitchen to feed her what milk she had left. Still the sunlight filled the room but the ringing phone had cut through the calm. She boiled the eggs and ate them and had enough left to feed to Pollux and to the babies. Wilson spit the egg out but Winna was licking the last bits off of Nan's fingers when the phone rang again.

She didn't sit around and wait for it to stop. She left Pollux to bark at it and gathered the babies and hurried them to the back room. She shut the door. She busied herself by changing their diapers. She hummed the same tune, more loudly, to cover the sound. When the ringing stopped, she felt her breath return to its normal pace. She pointed out the window to the cardinal in the crape myrtle. She tapped the glass. She found a brown-skinned cloth doll with black yarn braids—where had it come from?—and she danced it for Winna.

Another bird came to the branch. Nan looked up, seeing it out of the corner of her eye. Under its gray wings it hid a yellow belly. A kingbird. Wasn't it? It stepped toward the cardinal. It spoke a few words of a song. The cardinal spoke back.

Furiously Nan thumped the glass, and both birds scattered.

———

When the knock came on the door—a heavy knock, the kind that was made with an iron knocker—she was ready for it. The dog bounded to the door and barked back at it. It wasn't Oliver and Elma come home; that much Nan knew. Oliver wouldn't knock at his own door. It was someone come to take her away, or to take the babies away, or both. She had had one night in the house, a few safe, sacred hours, and already she could feel her future self looking back on them with longing.

She was resigned to it. She wouldn't hide anymore. She put the babies together in the crib and she closed the back-room door. She was in her nightgown still. At the door she took the chore coat where she had hung it and pulled it on. She took a broom from the closet. She was just a house girl with a broom. But if it was someone come to hurt her, she would have the broom and she would have the dog. And then the familiar fear came to her, the feeling of opening a door to the unknown, and she allowed herself, hand on the knob, to admit its source: that it was Juke at the door. That it was Juke's voice on the phone, come to find her.

She dropped her hand from the knob. There was a small hole in the door, just above her eye level. A peephole. She stood on tiptoe and peered through it. On the other side was Sheriff Cleave, standing on the porch.

She was so relieved it was him—not Juke, turned loose from the jail—that she unlocked the door and opened it.

The morning was as mild as it had seemed from inside. Yesterday's fog was a memory. Down the porch steps, in the little paved driveway, the sun glared off the motorcycle's mirrors.

She held the dog by the collar, letting the man look both of them up and down. She remembered that, in the big house on the morning after Genus was killed, he had been polite. Now he said, "You the woman of the house?"

It was a joke. He was playing. Nan could only shake her head.

"Is the woman of the house home, child? Or Dr. Rawls?"

Again she shook her head.

"I know you ain't got no voice to speak of. I seen you yestidy out at the crossroads store. And I remember you at the farm. You remember that day, girl?"

She nodded.

"You look like you seen a ghost that day."

The sun was bright and she shielded her eyes from it. The door stood open and she stood just inside it, the dog sniffing the air but still now at her side.

"I been ringing you up all morning. I guess you ain't know how to use no telephone." He was all business now. It was no fun, she supposed, playing with a girl who could only shake her head and nod, who couldn't even say, "Sir." "Neighbor ring up the station, say she seen a colored girl up in the doctor's house. Ain't no one ever seen her in this part a town, she says. Ain't no one else about, no woman of the house. No man."

Nan held tight to the broom with her right hand. The left hand, the one shielding her eyes from the sun, grew heavy.

"You got them babies with you, child?"

Nan waited a moment before she nodded.

"Gemini twins." He chuckled. "Mr. Juke's over in the jailhouse. You know that?"

She shook her head. She didn't know why.

"Oh, yes. He's fixing to be there till Friday at least." He whistled off into the yard. "Got him in some trouble. Related back to that night I been out to the farm. Ugly night. We getting to the bottom of it." He looked back to her sharply. "I know you got no voice to speak of. But if we put you on the stand, if it come to that, if you were called to the stand, you'd have to indicate. Yes or no. You'd have to give an answer best you could. You'd be under oath, child."

Nan stood frozen. She indicated nothing.

"Just 'cause you got no voice don't mean you get out of answering."

She gave a small nod to satisfy him.

"You can say a whole lot with yes or no. Like this. Less try. How many hours you gone be all alone here in this house?"

She paused. And then she shook her head.

"No, you ain't answering? Or no hours?" He was smiling now, playing again.

"You know how to count? You know your numbers?"

She nodded. A maid didn't read but she was expected to count to cook.

"All right then. No hours. Spect them newlyweds will be home from their honeymoon soon. Spect they had enough honeymooning. Don't take long for some folks. Not even one hour."

He was a short man. They stood eye to eye. She might be able to get the handle of the broomstick in the fleshy place under his chin.

"All right then." He'd made up his mind about something. "Tell Dr. Rawls if he's smart he won't leave no strange colored girl alone in a house in the First Ward. This here is a courtesy call. Lucky I ain't bringing you to the jailhouse. Folks ain't take to outsiders this side a town."

Nan took a step behind the door, ready to close it. For the first time, she noticed that the ferns, the grand ferns that stood on the pillars of the porch, had grown brittle and brown.

"Draw them curtains," said the sheriff. "Lock that door." He spit on the porch. "You ain't never know who'll come around here."

But then Oliver and Elma came home, and mostly they were bright and busy days, their first days in the house, the three of them finding their patterns, their places. Nan showed Elma how to work the sink, the stove, where the electric light switches were, and Elma pretended that she knew it all, and Nan felt sorry for her, for having to dull her own delight. Nan bathed the twins every morning, and took a bath herself, the water rushing out of the faucet as hot as if she'd boiled it. Winna cut a new tooth on her new doll's yarn braids, and Wilson clapped for her. Along the fence in the backyard, Pollux dug a dirt patch in the sunny grass. They took to calling her

Polly. With Castor gone she didn't seem to need her whole name anymore.

On Monday Oliver returned to work. At noon the girls came to listen for Polly's bark, and then the wheels of the wheelchair on the back-porch ramp, and then they all sat down together for a meal Nan had made, and then again for supper. Nan did most of the cooking and the cleaning; she was happy to have no yard chores; she slept well. She slept in the bed in the back room where Irene Douglass had slept with her daughter, Daisy. Still the twins slept beside her in their crib, where she could get up and see them if they needed her, or she needed them. All night the quiet rush of traffic passed by. A light from the street reflected off the white fence and filled the room like the moon.

In the evenings, after the babies were asleep, Elma and Oliver sat in the front room, still bright with lamplight, and Elma read Carlotta Rawls's old issues of *McCall's* and *Woman and Home* and Oliver read the newspaper while the radio played. They listened to the news until the news got bad, and then Oliver changed the station to jazz, which Elma didn't care for, and then he changed the station to fiddling. Nan hurried through the dishes and set up the ironing board between the kitchen and the front room so she could listen while she ironed. One night Oliver turned and turned the dial until he could find the voice of a man he said was the governor of New York, a man who spoke like Sara and Jim, but even taller, tighter—*New Yawk*, the man said, his name was Roosevelt, and he was talking that night about coming to the aid of crippled children, he was saying, "as some of you know, I walk around with a cane and with the aid of somebody's arm myself." Oliver's newspaper was closed and he was sitting at the edge of the leather chair with his elbows on his knees, listening. This was what he'd been turning and turning the dial to find. "And so this great movement across the United States is spreading like wildfire," said Roosevelt. "Down at Warm Springs, Georgia, where I go every spring and autumn, we have what is one of many active expressions of this idea. Down there we take care principally of children who have had infantile paralysis, and the treatment there is not a treatment of operation but is primarily a treatment of trying to restore the muscles through swimming and exercising in warm water." At this Oliver reached over to touch Elma's knee, wanting her to listen but not wanting to miss a word himself. She was looking at her magazine but now she half-lowered it and raised her eyebrows and nodded. "What we want to do is to get about," Roosevelt said. "And what we want to do, most of us, is to consider ourselves normal members of the community." Oliver took off his glasses and polished them on his shirt, as though clean lenses might help him to hear more clearly. "We who have been crippled are not in any way different from the people who are not crippled; we are the same kind of human beings."

When Roosevelt was finished, Oliver sat stunned for a moment, and then he stood up with the aid of his cane, as though cured by the address, and began to praise Franklin—he called him Franklin—as though the governor could hear him through the radio. What he had done for children, for crippled people, the sick, Oliver said—well, it was brave and it was unprecedented. He began to talk about what the man had done at Warm Springs, a place Oliver had been three times, but never when the governor was there. By then Elma had returned to nodding at her magazine. Nan had the sense she had heard it before. He was talking, then, not to the radio and not to Elma but now to Nan, who stood ironing and listening. He began to sway unsteadily on his feet, and Nan knew it meant he was tired, and knew he did not want anyone to catch him. He found his balance on his own. By now he was looking at her with the same intensity with which he'd just listened to the radio, and she was looking at him. They both stood in the stillness of the silenced speech, missing the voice, wishing it would go on. Was she too a cripple? Was that what she was? They were both wondering it. The way the governor had talked, it was something she almost wanted to be, a word that would explain what she was missing, that would join her with others who were missing something too, others that included her and Oliver in one sentence, one breath. Nan coasted the iron back and forth, steadily, not wanting to stop.

Elma flipped the pages of her magazine. "I reckon he's got fine things to say," she said, "but I don't like his voice. Sound like he being strangled."

———————

Elma spent the week going to town, to the dime store, to Pearsall's, to the Piggly Wiggly. First place she went was the department store, Cantor's, where she bought a buggy big enough for Winna and Wilson, so she wouldn't have to carry them in the wagon. She pushed them back and forth to town, letting folks slow their cars to watch her on the sidewalk. She bought a pair of patent leather heels and a good spring coat, and three new dresses, and rouge and red lipstick, which she wore breakfast to supper. She walked the packages home if she could manage them with the buggy, or she had them delivered. For the babies she ordered two wooden high chairs. For Oliver she bought two new silk ties, one red and one blue. For Nan she bought caramel milk rolls and a children's book called *The Wonderful Wizard of Oz*, which Nan did not need to hide but hid anyway, and which she loved despite herself.

On Thursday afternoon Elma came home in a dark mood, struggling up the ramp with the buggy, Wilson fussing in it. In the parlor—Elma used the word "parlor"—she handed him to Nan and shook off her coat and each set about nursing her own child. There was a comfort in this that they didn't need to acknowledge. They had settled into it, Elma on the sofa and Nan in the rocker they'd brought from home, the curtains drawn and the fire spitting.

"That's it," Elma said to Winna, "that's all you're getting from me, darling." She was looking at Nan now. "This here's the last milk I got for these babies. Both of them. I'm tired a rushing round to feed them, full a milk. They old enough now to drink cow's milk. Lord knows we got enough bottles of it. Lord knows it was enough for me."

They sat in silence. Nan was thinking of her mother running Elma out to the cows to suckle from their udders. That was how the story went. She was wondering how that could be the same woman who had cut out her tongue, keeping her from suckling.

"You can feed them if you want to. I ain't gone stop you. You want to?"

Nan nodded. She didn't want to stop nursing Wilson, not ever. She would feed Winna too if she had to. But Winna would eat anything. Winna didn't need her.

"By all means. I ain't gone stop you. Me, I'm done. I'm tired of being no milk machine. It's fine for a farm. We in town now."

Wilson was sitting in her lap, legs straddled around her belly, his hands around her breast like a jug.

"I was thinking. We can say you a wet nurse. If folks come by. Might be easier. In town it might be different. No one much knows you in this part a town. We can say you the wet nurse, you feed both my babies."

Wilson gave a little bite—he had four teeth already—and Nan pulled back.

"I know—you had to be pregnant to be a wet nurse. We could change the story. We could say you had a baby that died."

Nan stood now, pulling her dress closed, holding Wilson to her neck and burping him. She gave Elma a stern look.

"What you looking at me that way for? I don't want it that way. I thought it would be easier for you."

Elma took Winna off her and buttoned up her own dress. "Now, that's all, darling." She sighed. "I don't know what I'm saying. Ain't nobody stopping by. We been here five days and not one neighbor stopped by to say how do you do. Ain't no one brung us a casserole. We seen more folks in the country!"

Elma put Winna down on the rug. Winna rolled onto her back and then her side and then hefted herself up on her forearms. She was set to crawl any day.

"I just come from the beauty shop down on Pearl Avenue. Estelle's. The one with the parasols painted on the window? The umbrellas?" Elma stood with her arms crossed, looking toward the cloaked window and the street beyond it. "I come in there with the babies in the buggy, brand-new fine buggy, both of em asleep. Well, Wilson's asleep and Winna's just lying there quiet chewing her doll, ain't doing nothing. Perfect babies. I wanted to get my hair done up in a bob. Not real short but just curled to look short? Like Carole Lombard?" She piled her hair up to show. "I figured I'd look fine tomorrow at the courthouse and it would keep through church on Sunday. You know what that lady told me?"

She waited for Nan's silence.

"She says, 'We don't allow babies in this beauty shop.'"

She dropped her hair and it fell around her shoulders.

"I says, 'These here are my babies, they are twins, they are quiet as can be, they're sleeping in their buggy, I simply want to get my hair done up.' Lady says, 'No, ma'am, I'm sorry, there are no children allowed in *this establishment.*' Says, 'It's policy. Leave em with the help.' I say, 'Let me speak to this Estelle, if you please.' She says, 'I am Estelle'! I say, 'Well, Miss Estelle, if it's your policy, you can change it, can't you now.' I say, 'My name is Mrs. Elma Rawls and I am the wife of Dr. Oliver Rawls, and these are my children, and they won't do none of your fine customers no harm.' Now they're all looking at us. There's a whole herd a old ladies with their heads in them domes, looking on." Elma took a deep breath. "And Estelle looks into the buggy like it's a pit a rattlesnakes. She points to Winna and says, 'This child can stay.'"

Nan felt Wilson's warm breath on her neck. He had fallen asleep.

"I say again, 'I am their mother.' And she says—do you know what she says?" Here Elma's voice choked. "She says, 'You ought to be ashamed of yourself.'"

Nan closed her eyes for a moment.

"I says to her, '*You* ought to be ashamed of yourself!' And push that buggy out the door. The door's closing and I says, 'This the ugliest beauty shop I ever seen! Y'all look like a herd a ugly cows!'"

Nan stood and rocked Wilson back and forth.

"I woke up Wilson hollering like that. I think neither one of em had a good enough nap. I'm sorry."

Winna rolled onto her back again and kicked into the air. Elma stepped over her and crossed the room to Nan. She let Elma reach a hand over and pat Wilson's back.

"I'm sorry, honey. I'm worried sick about tomorrow. I'm so worried I can't eat. I ain't eaten since yesterday."

It was the closest they'd gotten to talking about the hearing. All week long they had fussed and fancied, carrying on like they had no cares. They were playing house while both of their daddies were in prison, Nan's in chains and Elma's in the jailhouse. Nan didn't hold it against Elma, not that part. What else were they to do? She hadn't eaten since yesterday, either. She might have put the leftovers in the Frigidaire, but she'd fed them to Polly instead.

That evening after supper, Nan went to slide her plate into the dog's dish and Polly didn't come.

Elma and Oliver called for her out the back door, out the front.

"Polly! Pollux!"

Along the back fence, the hole she'd worn in the grass was dug deep.

They piled in the car, all of them. Oliver wanted to drive through town first, but Elma wouldn't let him holler out the window. She said it wasn't proper. They tracked through all of the First Ward before Elma convinced him to go out to the farm. None of them wanted to do it. It was dark by then.

But Oliver turned the car around and they drove slowly and in silence, the headlights creeping along the road. A half mile before the crossroads, the tires bumped up to the paved road, and they all felt that they had crossed a body of water to an island, a narrow strip of land with wilderness on either side. Oliver and Elma lowered the windows and called out, "Polly! Pollux!"

None of them had wanted to return to the farm, but there it was, inching toward them in the headlights as Oliver turned into the drive. There were the porch steps and there was the barn, there was the shack. The farm had been abandoned for less than a week, but from the car they could see the weeds that needed hoeing. The girls stepped out of the car. Nan had grown up on this farm, under these stars. She was not afraid of the dark. And yet she went into the yard as one went into a burning house.

She knew how God liked to take some things in order to grant others. So she made a bargain with Him. He could keep Pollux if it meant she never had to set foot on this farm after this night. Then, in case that one wasn't strong enough, she made another. God forgive her: He could keep her father a prisoner if He kept Juke too.

Elma called. Nan clapped. Oliver stayed with the babies in the car. The old pregnant sow came wriggling out from the under porch, her belly dragging over the ground, not like a dog smelling her master but like a pig looking for scraps. Still, Elma went to her and, Nan was surprised to see, knelt down to give her a rub under the chin. "You seen Pollux?" They moved past the well, into the garden, called hello to the cows and the mules in the barn, the chickens and guineas in the yard. Elma counted them with their lantern. There were two chickens missing, but the rest were there. They collected the fouled eggs to feed to the sow, but whatever neighbor George Wilson had hired to look after the animals was doing all right. Nan half-expected him to come out of the shack or the big house and spook them. Someone or something was different. She had the all-overs.

When they'd walked the north field and the west, they came around to the oaks down by the creek. Nan couldn't see much but she could hear the creek trickling along. Elma was holding her hand and she held it tighter now. Nan could tell by the wiregrass at her ankles that they were on the path to the cabin. They had never been there together before, and her feet held fast to the ground. Elma pulled her. "Nan, come on!"

Castor and Pollux used to go down there in the summer and lay in the cool shade of the oaks. Maybe that was what she was feeling, Pollux down there in the dark. She closed her eyes and let Elma pull her through it. And then under her feet, even through her shoes, she could feel the path change. The dirt was furrowed. Elma must have felt it too. They knelt together and Elma held the lantern close to the ground. They were tire tracks. The tires of a tractor, or a truck. They ran their fingers over the dirt for a moment. Then they stood and made their way to the cabin.

The cabin door stood open to the night. The single window was shattered. Inside, the cabin was near empty. The barrels, the copper pots, the mattress, all of it was gone. On the dirt floor, two empty jars lay on their sides, glass eyes staring back at them. And in the stump where Nan had once sat, an ax stood.

Then came the sound of scrambling through the woods. The dog barked, making them start. It was coming from the creek. They tore out of the cabin, hand in hand, and out of the dark jumped Pollux, wet with creek water, and then they were wet too. "Polly, you dumb wet fool!" Elma got ahold of the dog around her neck and together they all bounded back toward the car. Nan couldn't get in it fast enough. Polly jumped in the back with Nan, licking the babies, all of them panting.

Oliver said the dog was so wet she must have swum the whole way to the farm. "I wonder if she was looking for home, or for Castor," he said, turning back onto the road.

Elma didn't say anything about the still. Not yet. She looked toward the place where the empty cabin stood and said, "Or for my daddy."

Nan, she looked west, where the black road led out to the pines, where her father was falling asleep in the county camp. She wondered if it was too late to take back her bargain. God had seen no use for Pollux after all.

"She's confused," Oliver said. "She don't know where home is yet."

Nan wasn't set to go to the courthouse. Elma and Oliver would go, and Nan would stay home with the babies.

But Friday morning, Oliver opened the newspaper. On the front page of the *Florence Messenger* was a picture of the still. Sheriff Cleave and George Wilson were there, along with six or seven government men. They'd hauled out the equipment and posed it in front of the cabin. Most of them stood with a foot on a barrel, shotguns cocked across their laps, like hunters on a safari with their trophy kill. Sheriff Cleave managed to get his motorcycle in the picture. Looking at the picture, you wouldn't know that the shotgun in George Wilson's hands, a Winchester twelve gauge, had been retrieved from the cabin itself.

They all sat around at the kitchen table looking at the paper. Elma read it out loud, for even Oliver didn't know that Nan could read it herself. She read it with her hand over her mouth, and every few sentences, she had to stop and take a breath, or ask Oliver what something meant. "What's an arraignment?" "What's bond?" Oliver said arraignment, bond—it didn't matter. The country courts did things the way they wanted, all at once if they liked. Freddie Wilson got his own article on the same page; it said his bond would be set on the same day, that day, Friday. It was in that article, in a small paragraph at the bottom, that Elma read Sterling Smith's name, and had to stop. She looked up at Nan. "It says your daddy's gone be in court today."

It was a fine morning, so they walked down to the courthouse together, Oliver on Elma's arm, Nan pushing the buggy behind them, like a family out on a stroll.

Inside, they had to split up. Elma didn't want to face the same thing she'd faced in the beauty shop, so she let both twins go with Nan in the back. The courtroom was the grandest room Nan had been in, grander than the movie theater with its colored balconies, the ceiling dripping with chandeliers. The ceiling made her dizzy, so she closed her eyes until the room filled with bodies, more bodies than she had accounted for. It was not a trial, as far as she could tell, as far as Oliver had told. But the room filled with bodies, white bodies, and then the bodies stood as the judge filed in. She stood with them. They sat. She stood long enough to see the back of the men's heads at the front of the room: at one table, Juke; at the other, Freddie Wilson and her father. They all wore the same striped prison pants and denim work shirts. She couldn't tell if their legs were in chains but she thought their hands were in cuffs in their laps. Other men's heads were between and among them. Just before she sat, her father looked over his shoulder, toward the back of the room. She could not catch his eye. When she sat she couldn't see any of them but the judge. She prayed the babies would stay quiet, so she might be as invisible to the bodies as they were to her. As far as she could tell, she and Wilson and her father were the only colored bodies in the room.

The judge's head was as white and bald and pointed as an egg. He wore spectacles low on his nose. He said some words Nan didn't understand. Then he called Juke to stand, and Juke stood at his table. Again she saw the back of his head. She could not see Oliver's head or Elma's.

The judge read from a piece of paper before him. "Juke Jesup, Cotton County has charged you with one count of murder in the death of Genus Jackson, one count of blackmail, one count of public intoxication, and seven counts of the manufacture of distilled spirits."

A wave of voices rose and fell. The judge used his gavel.

Juke said, "Seven counts, Your Honor?"

"You have a right to a lawyer. Do you need a lawyer appointed you, Mr. Jesup?"

"No, sir. They gave me one, but I sent him on home."

"You sent him home?"

"He weren't but twelve or thirteen years old, Your Honor. He look like the ink still wet on his law degree. You gone give me a snot-nosed baby for a counselor, I reckon I can defend myself better, with a hand tied behind my back."

"Is that right? How do you plead, then, Mr. Jesup?"

Juke cleared his throat. "Is it just guilty or innocent, Your Honor?"

"Yes, Mr. Jesup."

"Then I plead innocent."

"To all counts, Mr. Jesup?"

"Yes, sir. All counts."

A voice called out, "Someone get that man some counsel."

The judge followed the voice with his eyes. "Mr. Boothby, you got an objection to share with this court?"

A man in a front row stood. "Pardon me, Your Honor. I'd like to see the law carried out fairly. No one wants to see a trial of this magnitude miscarried because a country fellow goes undefended."

"Do you wish to act as his counsel, Mr. Boothby? You already acting as judge and jury in that paper of yours."

"I'm no lawyer, Your Honor."

Sheriff Cleave stood and said, "Pardon me, Your Honor. The prisoner has been advised of his rights. He was appointed a lawyer."

Mr. Boothby sat down and the sheriff followed.

"Juke Jesup," said the judge, "get you another lawyer if you desire one before you return to this court for your trial. Date set of April 23, 1931."

"Yes, sir. I don't reckon I'll need one. What I got to say I can say on my own."

"Have you got something to say for yourself?"

"Yes, sir. I didn't do none of those things. I ain't a killing man. I wouldn't kill no Negro. I wouldn't hurt no baby, like that man say." He pointed to Freddie. "I stand before you sober as a baby myself. I'm a lover of Negroes, sir. I feel I'm being persecuted for my love of Negroes."

Another wave of voices. Again the judge used his gavel.

"I been talking to God about it, sir, and I find the only way about it is to tell the truth."

"This is not a trial, you understand, Mr. Jesup. You'll have your trial in due time, with a lawyer present."

"Yes, sir. I can't wait that long. I aim to tell you that I didn't kill no Negro. I got no reason to. That Negro you say I killed, he weren't the father to no baby."

There was barely a murmur of voices. No one wanted to miss what was said.

"You're referring to Genus Jackson," said the judge.

"Yes, sir."

"And the mulatto child."

"That man didn't rape my daughter, sir. He ain't the father and my daughter ain't the mother. He's my child, sir. I stand before you and before God and say he's my child. And the mother is my house girl, Nancy Smith."

Nan closed her eyes. If she couldn't see them, they couldn't see her. If she held her breath, they couldn't hear her.

"Mr. Jesup, you aim to tell me a man was killed and there was no rape?"

"I never said nothing about no rape myself, sir. My daughter never did neither." Again he pointed at Freddie. "It was that son of a bitch who said it, and who done the killing."

"You aim to tell me we're sitting here in this courtroom because you was dallying with a housemaid?"

"I won't say dallying, sir. My daughter, she took on caring for the child. The mother's but a youngun herself, and can't form words. She don't got a full mind to care for no child alone. That's my child."

"Mr. Jesup, this is not a custody trial. This is a bond hearing. Do you know the meaning of 'hearing'?"

"Yes, sir. I believe it's my time to be heard out."

"Mr. Jesup—"

"I just aim to lay it—"

"Mr. Jesup! The charges stand!" The judged knocked his gavel. "You got more on your shoulders now than when you walked into this courtroom. I advise you to hold your tongue until you have a lawyer to hold it for you. But I am obliged by Cotton County to set your bail, as specified, at two hundred dollars."

Nan sat frozen. She would hold her breath until she saw Juke carried back to jail again.

Juke was quiet for a moment. Then he began to laugh. "Mr. Judge, you might as well go ahead and string me up. I won't have two hundred dollars if I live two hundred years."

Down in front, another man stood. Nan could see only the shoulders of his white suit and the back of his white head, but she knew it was George Wilson.

"Your Honor, I'll post bond for Mr. Jesup."

"Mr. Wilson?"

"I'll post the two hundred dollars. He works a farm of mine, Your Honor. I need Mr. Jesup on the farm, where he can do some good. I been paying a pretty penny to have the land tended in his absence."

"Mr. Wilson, you are entitled to do with your money what you please."

From there, nothing much mattered. Nan listened to the rest of the hearing as she'd listen to a radio in a distant room.

"If you please, Your Honor, I aim to pay the bond on two other men in custody of the court."

"Mr. Wilson, I like to finish one matter before I carry on to the next. But if the matter is related, I will hear it. Who are the men, Mr. Wilson?"

"My grandson, Frederick Wilson."

The judge read from another paper. "George Frederick Wilson the Third, please stand."

Freddie stood.

"Naturally you desire to see your kin free, Mr. Wilson. But Frederick Wilson has no bond. He was sought not on formal charges but merely on suspicion of accessory. As of today, February the twelfth, 1931, he has served his sentence of three months in Cotton County. The county holds no other charges against him."

"He's free to go, Your Honor?" George Wilson seemed as surprised as anyone else in the courtroom.

"For the time being. I release him into your custody. I advise you to keep a close eye on him."

"Thank you, Your Honor."

Freddie sat.

"The other man, Mr. Wilson?"

"The other man is Sterling Smith, Your Honor."

"Sterling Smith, please stand."

Sterling stood.

"What business do you have with this prisoner, Mr. Wilson?"

"He worked the same farm for me, Your Honor. He left the county some thirteen years ago owing me a debt. I aim to see it paid."

"Thirteen years is a long time, Mr. Wilson."

"A debt is a debt, Your Honor. I will post his bond, if you please."

"You are entitled to do with your money what you please, Mr. Wilson. I will release him into your custody, not on a bond, but on a fine to recompense the expenses of the county. That amount is thirty dollars."

"I will pay thirty dollars for him, Your Honor."

"Very well. I advise you to keep a close eye on him. On the three of them."

"I aim to, Your Honor."

"Any other prisoners you'd like to take off the county's hands, Mr. Wilson?"

"No, Your Honor."

"Then God help you, sir, and God bless this court. This hearing is adjourned."

———————

She had stayed to see her father. Her hopes had been exceeded: he was free.

But before the judge had struck his gavel the final time, she had pushed the buggy down the aisle, into the long, endless, marble lobby, and out into the sun, holding her hat on her head to keep it from flying loose. She pushed the babies home and she locked the door behind her. Already the black telephone was ringing.

TWENTY-EIGHT

THE WEEK AFTER THE HEARING, THE TWINS FELL SICK WITH something like the flu. It started with Winna and soon Wilson had it, fever and rashes and a cough that kept the house awake. Nan thought Winna wasn't taking to the cow's milk that Elma had started feeding her in a bottle. She couldn't keep it down. Elma worried it was whatever virus had sickened Dr. Rawls and his wife and the rest of the town, trapped in the stale air of the house. But none of the grown folks got sick, and Oliver said it was the kind of late-winter illness that all babies got, that they would be stronger for it in the end, that it would pass. The winter had indeed and at last come to roost, a cold fog settling over the wiregrass country for a week. It was the kind of weather that would make most folks want to stay inside, and that was what Nan and Elma and the babies did, as Oliver came and went.

When he wasn't there, they ignored the knocks on the door. It was a kind of thrill. More thrilling was the ingenious idea Elma had to simply remove the telephone from its hook, which prevented it from ringing altogether. It did give a plaintive tone at all hours, and at first it drove both girls mad. The dog howled and rolled on the floor. They tried to put the radio on to cover the noise, but the only program they got clear during the day was the local news, and that was far worse. Before long they found they got used to it. It was like the sound of the wind, or the teakettle whistling, or the steady hum of cricket frogs. It was a force that kept other sounds away. When Elma finally had the idea to drape a coat hanger over the hook, and her new coat on it, they'd been indoors for three days, and the knocks had mostly ceased. The coat hung there on the kitchen wall, tricking the telephone silent.

When Oliver was there, he answered the door and sent folks away. The sheriff, despite Nan's fear, didn't come again. They were reporters, mostly, and neighbors come to pry. The Dampiers and the Cavanaughs and Mrs. Stovall, the neighbors who shared the party line, came to complain of the Rawlses' code ringing at all hours of the day. Long, short, long, long. Wasn't anyone there to pick up the phone? Did they need a secretary? Answer the ring, or they would! It was worse than when the twins were born, and now it had followed them here to the house in town. Elma blamed herself for wishing a neighbor might bring a casserole by.

It was Juke's knock Nan most feared, and it was Freddie's knock for Elma. Both men were free now, free to knock on any door they pleased. Nan and Elma felt safer when Oliver wasn't there to open the door. He meant well. But what protection was he?

He knew himself what little he could do. When he'd returned to Florence before Christmas, when his father was still alive, his waiting room had been full. Slowly his patients had been dwindling, and now, after the hearing, they'd dropped to half their number. One evening, coming home for supper in his wheelchair, a man driving a pickup truck veered his car toward the sidewalk. The wheel of the truck came within inches of the wheel of the chair. Just as quickly, the truck jerked back onto the road and sped off.

It wasn't a green Chevy. That truck Freddie Wilson had abandoned under a bridge in Jeff Davis County not long after he drove out of town. But Oliver read the plate number. He repeated it in his head as he wheeled himself home, and when he got there and found his wife's coat hanging from the telephone, he lost his nerve. What would the sheriff do, if he reported it? It might have been the sheriff who'd tried to run him off the road.

He didn't tell the sheriff and he didn't tell Elma. Instead, every morning, he drove the three blocks to the office. He didn't come home for the midday meal. He told Elma if she needed him to call.

Problem was, when he didn't come home for dinner, he couldn't collect the mail, which Mr. Horace delivered like clockwork every day between twelve and twelve thirty. The dog rose to sniff at it as it fell through the slot and onto the mat.

One evening he came home and Elma had opened a letter from the bank. It had the word "foreclosure" in it. She showed him with a painted fingernail.

"You've opened my mail."

"It's addressed to Dr. Manford Rawls."

"That's right. I've taken over his mortgage. He ain't going to open this letter, is he?"

"I reckon not. But I reckon I'm alive as you."

"You may open any envelope with your own name on it, Elma."

Elma blinked. She put the fingernail in her mouth and nibbled at it. They were both remembering the letters she'd sent to this address. The distance from the farm to the house had seemed a long one, as long a distance as then to now.

"My mistake," she said.

All the banks were threatening foreclosures. That was what he told her. They were all bluster. "Only man more frightened than a man who owns a house is the man who holds the note on that house."

The next day he came home and the mail was still on the mat. She hadn't even picked it up. He stepped over it. It piled there for three days until finally Nan collected it and put it in the basket on the table.

———

It was the middle of March before the Twelve-Mile Straight was paved, two weeks later than George Wilson had ordered it, but the road gang was two men shy. The people of Cotton County drove up and down it for no other reason than to take a drive in the country air. By then, the week of winter had passed and the air smelled sun baked again, the pear blossoms, the cherry blossoms already blanketing the sidewalk of Main Street. In the country it was beardtongue and bee balm and bird's foot violet rushing into the open windows of the cars, and no dust, no clay in their tires. No matter that the road still dead-ended. There was no reason to visit the county camp, except to see where Freddie Wilson had been hiding in plain sight. The whiskey operation George Wilson had established was not in plain sight; it was buried in the pines deeper yet; he himself had only been there once, on a horse borrowed from Lloyd Crow, though Lloyd Crow knew nothing of George Wilson's purpose, knew only to say yes when asked. The cars approaching the end of the road caught sight of the distant tents under the pines and then turned around, so many times that they wore a roundabout path in the scrubgrass ditch.

On the way back to town, they took another look at the cross-roads farm. Some saw Juke Jesup behind a mule and a plow, ready-ing the west field for corn. "Fool's back to plowing like the rest of us." Some went on and said more, the white sharecroppers and their sons and wives, the folks in the mill village. "Got him an outside child. Mulatto boy. Drinking nigger juice all these years and it finally ketched up with him."

Some saw the Negro behind the other mule, the older plow, readying the west field for cotton. They didn't know who he was. They only said, "That man got a death wish."

At Estelle's beauty shop on Pearl Avenue, the women with their heads under the heated domes said, "That girl try to come in here other day."

"Try to tell me that child was hers. Try to say they Gemini twins!"

"Mildred believed it."

"You believed it yourself. You said it was a miracle."

"I said it's possible. I read a science book on it. I didn't believe they was twins. Just look at them!"

The men who knew Juke Jesup, the ones who had been there under the gourd tree, didn't care who was daddy to what baby. They sat in their open truck beds and said, "Y'all seen it same as me. You know it was Mr. Juke put that poor mule under him."

"Yeah, but it's Freddie cut him down. Y'all seen it."

"Ain't matter now. Mr. Juke been charged and Freddie boy free."

"Mr. Juke get all charged up. Ain't right."

Some of the ones who'd been there, others, didn't talk about it at all. It had been out of the papers for months. That was how they liked it. Now it was back in.

With Nan in town now, colored folks didn't have much reason to go all the way down the Straight. But those who passed the farm didn't say the word, either. They said quietly, after they were a good ways past, "Guess Mr. Juke got what coming to him. Had it coming to him ten ways."

"Ain't got it yet," they said. "Ain't been tried."

Ezra and Long John and Al hadn't worked on the farm since harvest. Al's wife, Cecilia, said to him, "Mr. Juke's gal crying wolf after all. Think she fancy with her lying mouth. I told you that girl crying wolf."

"You didn't either," Al said. "You and Ezra and John say he found him the wrong white girl."

"Well, he did now, didn't he."

"Poor child of God," Al said. "Ain't killed for nothing but to cover Mr. Juke."

"Tell you what, you ain't gone back to work on that farm."

"Ain't Mr. Juke's right to call on me no more. He's George Wilson's nigger now."

———

It was gossip because Nan and Elma would confirm nothing to the
press, not to the gossip columnists, the society pages, not to Q. L.
Boothby, though not because he didn't try. Nan and Elma did not answer the telephone and did not answer the door. They would neither
confirm nor deny.

At the Florence Cotton Mill, where Freddie Wilson had been re-
instated as foreman, they were sending the press away as well. Beau
Richard had been demoted to second foreman, a job George Wilson
created on the spot; he said the job had been interim foreman, but
as a matter of goodwill, he'd extend his salary. The job of the second foreman, Beau Richard learned, was to stand in front of the mill
with a shotgun and turn the press away. He had a thing or two to tell
the newspapermen who came and aimed their cameras at him, but
he'd seen what happened to his friend Bob Pruitt and so he held his
tongue.

At the crossroads farm, Juke Jesup did not invite the reporters to
sit on his porch. He did not offer them gin. Was it true that there had
been no rape of his daughter?

"You the law?"

"No, sir. I'm from the *Albany Times*."

"Then I got nothing to say I ain't said already."

Some of the papers noted another fellow on the farm, a broad-
shouldered Negro who kept quiet in the field. Nobody recognized
him any more than they'd recognized Genus Jackson. Some of them
looked into the court papers. Name was Sterling Smith. But none of
them put Sterling Smith and Nancy Smith together. They saw the
smoke coming out of the chimney in the little shack.

———————

The folks from Rocky Bottom and the Fourth Ward, they didn't have
business out on the Straight, but the truth was, they didn't call on
Nan anymore, even in town. She was closer now, six miles in, more
likely to get to a quick-birthing mother. But they didn't want to knock

on the door of the doctor's house, not after all that was said about her. Some weren't sure she was in there. Some thought, even if she was, they didn't want to get mixed up in all that. Girl had gotten too close to white folks, and they'd poisoned her, poor child. Wasn't her fault. But they didn't trust her to deliver their own child now. They wanted a clean colored girl, hands like her mother's, steady, smart.

One night a father went looking for her at the farm, not knowing she'd left for the doctor's house. He was part Creek; he lived in a cabin in the Indian village in Meredith; the news hadn't gotten to him yet. (Even if it had, he didn't care for news. He was not a superstitious man.) It was the shack door he knocked on in the middle of the night, and Sterling opened it.

"I believe it's my daughter you looking for. She ain't here. She stay in town now."

"Whereabouts?"

"She deliver your child before?"

"No sir. Her mother did. Five-year-old boy. Three-year-old girl."

"That's my woman did that. Ketty."

"That's right."

"Tell you what. I'll go with you. I'll take you there." He held the door open while he took his hat and coat off the hook by the door, and he followed the man to his horse and jig. The five-year-old boy sat holding the reins.

It was close to one o'clock in the morning when they reached the house on Main Street. Everyone was in bed. But the part of Nan that still lived in the country, the part that was still midwife and always mother, lay near the surface of sleep. She heard the horse slow to a stop even before the dog did, and by the time the knock came and Polly was barking, Nan was up on her feet. The babies slept on, but Oliver and Elma appeared at their bedroom door. Someone put a light on. The knock came again, louder. It wasn't the *Florence Messenger* calling, not in the middle of the night. It was Juke or it was Freddie or it was the law.

"It's Sterling!" came a voice through the door.

Nan looked at Elma. Their eyes went wide with relief.

"Well, let him in," said Elma.

Oliver opened the door. There was Sterling and the Indian father, whose name was Footsie Davis. They both took off their hats.

"Sorry to bother you folks so late," said Sterling. "This father got a need for your services, Nan."

It was determined that Nan would go, and that Sterling would go with them. But Oliver said they'd better take the car, if it was the third child coming and they were headed all the way to Meredith. They'd better take the car and Oliver had better drive it, for it was a funny car with hand gears, and besides, he might be needed to help.

They drove out under the half-moon, Sterling, Footsie Davis, Oliver, Nan, the child Ketty had delivered, whose name was John. The horse, whose name was Willie J, the J standing for nothing, stayed behind with Elma and the twins, yoked to the pear tree in the front yard. They'd left fast and Nan had forgotten a coat, so Sterling, in the backseat beside her, offered his. She nodded, though she wasn't cold. He draped it around her shoulders. There. They'd found a way to talk yet. They were like a courting couple, Oliver thought, looking in the rearview, and then he raised his voice as he spoke to Footsie so they might have some privacy.

It was an olive army coat issued by Cotton County, still stiff, but it smelled like him, musky, and like the wood smoke of the shack. Was it her father she was smelling, or Genus? "You so popular," he said, "I got to come see you in the middle of the night, just to get an appointment."

Nan smiled.

"I been trying to see you. Since I get out. But longer than that, I mean. I been trying to see you since I heard what happened to your momma."

Nan's smile turned confused.

"Since before that, even. I wanted to send for you. I'll tell you about it all sometime, if you'll let me."

Nan nodded.

"All right then. I got a lot to say. Got a lot to ask." He closed his eyes and turned away. He pinched the bridge of his nose. "Reckon we got to figure that part out. We take it slow." He clapped his hands, one clap. "All right! I'll start with something small." He leaned over and shielded his mouth with his hand. "This here the first time I been in a automobile. Not counting no police wagon."

He had her smile back.

"That's our first secret. You and me, girl."

She was thinking of the bargain she'd made with God. She thought maybe she could accept Juke's being free if it meant her father was free too, in the backseat of this car with her on this night.

"Look like it's tomorrow now. Look like you got a birthday, girl." And Nan realized it was true: it was tomorrow, and it was her birthday. She was fifteen. "Look like you ain't the only one come into the world today."

At the cabin, the men watched her from a distance. It was a one-room house, the mother on the only bed, one child in it with her and another coming fast. It had been a good thing they'd taken the car. It had been needed more than Oliver, who helped only to catch the baby, and only, he knew, because Nan let him. It was as though the baby, another girl, was Oliver's own child; that was how glad he was to catch her. All of the men cheered, and the mother, whose name was Eluhu, wept with joy and relief. The little boy John fell asleep at his mother's feet. The little girl, whose name was Ketty Ann, fell asleep at her mother's side. The mother declared that the baby would be called Nancy Mae. It was the first time a baby had been named for Nan, though only she knew that. All of the men cheered again. And then the mother ordered all of them out.

TWENTY-NINE

OLIVER'S FATHER HAD TAKEN HIM AND HIS BROTHERS ON weekend hunting trips when they were boys. Growing up in the house on Main Street, they'd had a rifle and a couple of shotguns and a mess of pellet guns and a little antique Remington derringer they used to fight over. Oliver believed his father did what any father in the South felt it was his obligation to do, but they never brought home anything much other than rabbit and quail, once a skinny buck more trouble than it was worth, and after Roger went to the war, they stopped hunting. When Manford took ill, Oliver had found the pistol under his pillow, and he'd been seized by a sudden fear that in his fever and pain his father might accidentally, or not accidentally, find use for it. He'd gathered up all the arms and brought them down to Honest Earl's Gun and Lock. He needed the money, truth be told. He made out well, and it was a good thing he had, seeing how his new wife had taken to the shops in town.

But now Freddie Wilson and Juke Jesup were free and he was sorry that the guns were gone. He thought about going down to Earl's to see if the derringer was still there. A man in his condition should not be in this backward county with no pistol. What would he do if

Freddie Wilson came to the door and demanded to see his daughter? Or if Juke demanded to see his?

"Maybe you ought to get a gun," Elma said one night as they got into bed. It was the bed his parents had slept in and now it was theirs. Their marital relations were inadequate enough as it was. What did not help was sleeping in his parents' bed.

"What need do I have for a gun, Elma?"

"What need? If Freddie shows up he's gone have one, that's what need."

"I can defend myself—I can defend you all—just fine without need for a gun."

Elma took some hand cream from the nightstand and began wringing her hands with it.

"Where'd you get that?"

"This?" She held up her hands. "Brought it from home."

He nodded. "Haven't smelled it before. Smells nice. That eucalyptus, or—?"

"Think I got it from Cantor's?"

"No, no."

"I know better than to spend your patients' fees on hand cream at Cantor's. You don't need to tell me twice."

"All right now." He was lying on his back in his twill night pants and no shirt, because Elma had told him she liked his chest bare and he believed her. "Bring that eucalyptus, or whatever it is, over here."

She inched closer to him. She was fresh from the bath and her legs were smooth and her hair was wet on her nightgown. Her breasts were smaller now that she'd stopped nursing, her cleavage less steep, though he didn't dare say he noticed. She laid a sharp-smelling hand on his chest.

"I aim to make you happy," he said. "I aim to keep you safe."

"I know you do."

"Best way to keep you safe is to keep you in this house. And I can't make the note on this house if you're spending money on—"

"I *know*, Oliver." She pushed away.

"All right then. I'm sorry."

She sat up and rubbed her eyes with her oiled hands.

"I'm sorry," he said again. "This isn't what you hoped for. *I'm* not what—"

"Oliver. Please."

He reached for her hand and pulled it back to him. "I wish I could take you somewhere fine."

She gave a long sigh. "Somewhere we could hide," she agreed.

"A proper honeymoon. A beach somewhere. When all this is over—"

She pulled back again. "When all this is over? When's it gone be over?"

He sat up a little. He had let himself get excited. "Well." He folded his hands over his lap. "The trial, I guess. I guess we'll wait and see."

"And what will we see? If my daddy goes back to jail?"

"For one."

"And if he does, what? All this will be over? My daddy on the chain gang, and Winna Jean's daddy living in his castle down the road without a care for her, and she'll just grow up thinking everything's fine, everything's nice, 'cause she got a little picket fence to hide behind?"

"I'm her daddy, honey. I'll be her daddy."

"I know, Oliver! I know!"

"You want Freddie to come knocking? That what you're saying?"

"I don't know, Oliver!" She looked at him. They both seemed surprised to hear her say it. "I don't know. I want him to care about his daughter. I want her to be able to . . . I want her to have—"

"You want her looked after. The way a Wilson could look after her."

She gave a half nod, half shrug.

"But me," she said, "I don't care if I ever see him again. I hope I don't."

Oliver reached out and stroked her knee.

"It's okay if Freddie don't take up for her," she said. "That's all right. I'd be scareder if I was Nan." Her voice had been hard but now it fell into tight little sobs.

"Elma . . ."

"It ain't about Freddie. 'All this,' like you say? It ain't about Freddie or Winna Jean. They'll be fine. It's Nan I'm scared for."

"You're worried that—"

"That he'll come for Wilson is what I'm worried about! If he don't go back to jail . . ." She took a deep breath. She whispered, "I'm afraid he'll come for Wilson."

Nan was in the back room with the babies and their bedroom door was ajar. Oliver started to stand. "The door," he said.

"I'll get it."

Elma stood and closed it.

"Thank you," he said. "Now listen. Your father won't survive that trial. Not with all that's pinned on him, not with George Wilson behind it. Wilson will be safe here with us. I love him as much as your father claims to. I'll be a father to him too, a real father. That hasn't changed just because your father, speaking in tongues, drunk as a skunk, claims him in some country court."

"He wasn't drunk. I ain't ever seen him less drunk."

"And now that the truth is out, we don't . . . we don't have to live under that burden any longer."

"That burden."

"You know what I mean, Elma. Of course it was a burden. For all of us. The children aren't twins. Fine then. Everyone knows. They'll still be kin of a kind. They still *are* kin."

"I hear you, Oliver. You're trying real hard with your scientist talk to make 'all this' make sense. So you can keep telling yourself you married me for a reason."

"I married you for many reasons."

"All right then. One of them was to help me keep a secret. That secret ain't a secret no more."

"No. None of us expected it to go this way. But we'll make the best of it. That's why the vows say, 'For better or f— '"

"Oliver. Oliver! There ain't no 'better.' Maybe for you, there is. You ain't got to give up nothing! You ain't got to be a lady in this town, like Nan and me, for the rest of our lives, while this town looks at us like . . . like we're devils!"

"You think I ain't had to sacrifice anything? My livelihood?" His voice broke. "My family?"

From the back room came the sound of one of the babies crying. Wilson. He was beginning to tell their cries apart. Winna's infection was clearing but Wilson was still sick, and he'd been crying off and on in the night. "I know you have, Oliver." Then came the dog, matching her whine to the baby's.

"Darling. You ain't a devil. I don't care what some country trash say. I'll defend you to every one of them."

"I'm party to it. What's that word the judge used? About Freddie? 'Accessory.'"

"Elma. You're an accessory to nothing."

"I'm accessory to the devil. And, 'darling,' so are you. You know what you married into?"

"'Accessory to the devil' is not a law term, Elma. They aren't gone charge you with nothing."

"They might put me on the stand. Against my father. I'd have to talk, if they put me there, wouldn't I?"

"Well. I suppose you might."

He tried stroking her knee again. She closed her eyes. There were tears on her cheeks. "I'd tell the truth, if they asked me. I'd say Genus was a good man who got killed for nothing."

"All right now." He tapped her knee. "Listen. It's no good to guess what might or might not come. We're making ourselves crazy with all this."

"Did you know that Nan loved him? And he loved her, Oliver."

"Nan?" He ran his hand through his hair. His stomach felt a little sick suddenly. Did he not like to think that Genus was a real man, who was loved? Or did he not like to think it was Nan who loved him? "That's ridiculous," he said. "She's a child."

"They were in love, Oliver. That was love. I saw it myself."

"It's late, darling."

"I saw them in the creek one night. I still see them when I close my eyes. It was the devil called me down there, I knew it even then—"

"Enough, Elma! Enough with all this! It's over. There's nothing to be done."

Elma looked at him sharply. "'All this.' He's dead, Oliver. It won't ever be over."

THIRTY

H E'D LEFT THE FARM IN THE SUMMER, LAYING-BY TIME, AND IN his mind it had laid by for more than thirteen years, the cotton never ripening but growing a little taller every day, as his child grew taller every day.

Now it was spring and the cotton had long been leveled. The land lay flat and sun scorched, dry as a gopher tortoise's back. The black ruins of a shack stood out near the barn, not a shack that had fallen over with age but a young one burned down, some of the pine logs still round and strong as a man's leg. There were azalea bushes planted in new flowerbeds down along the garden fence. Through the porch floor of the big house, a gramophone grew.

Everything else was as his memory had left it. His own shack—he still thought of it as his shack, did not think of the others who had thought of it as their own—was blackened along one wall, but inside there was the stove and the little cast-iron pot, there were the three silver spoons, there were the two spindle chairs, there was the zinc tub, there was the rusted cot with the bare corn-shuck mattress. On the table, Sterling had laid out all he'd brought with him: a starched shirt, a pair of denim trousers, a pair of black army boots, the olive

army coat. A Buffalo nickel, a corncob pipe, a tin of Granger pipe tobacco, two cigarettes. A book of matches. A wax bag of sawdusty peanuts. The King James Bible given to him by Parthenia Wilson. He did
not have a hat. He did not have a gun.

He'd asked George Wilson for one, but George Wilson had seen
no need. After the hearing, after the warden had delivered Freddie
home to his grandmother and Juke home to the farm, Mr. Wilson had
brought Sterling to the mill. Upstairs in his office, he poured Sterling
a whiskey. Sterling told himself he ought to stay clearheaded if this
white man was going to try to kill him. Then he told himself that, if
this white man was going to kill him, he might as well die with a little
whiskey in his belly.

"Reckon you wondering why I turned you loose, Sterling." Mr.
Wilson sat down across from him. Mr. Wilson sat in the chair and
Sterling sat on the couch, between them a coffee table the size of a
flatbed on top of not one but two rugs, stacked like flapjacks.

"Not as much as I'm wondering why you turn Jesup loose."

Mr. Wilson smiled as he plucked a cigar stub from an ashtray and
lit it. He didn't have good teeth. They were like the little stones you'd
find in the river, dog yellow, pearl white, gunmetal gray.

"You ain't take kindly to him, do you, Sterling."

Sterling crossed his legs. "No, sir." The couch was as warm and
plush as a live cow beneath him. He was ready for it to buck.

"Never did."

"No, sir."

"I thought you might make friendly company together back then,
the way your women did. Instead you were like neighbor dogs growling through a fence. Cost that cotton a lot of time, that quarreling."

"I'm sorry, sir."

"It was a long time ago."

"You take kindly to him, sir?"

"No, Sterling, I don't."

"But you did."

"Once. That's right." He puffed on the cigar but did not offer one to Sterling. "Once I took to him with a father's heart. Here. In this room." He waved his cigar around the room. "He kept my son's heart alive and so I gave him everything I would have given my own son. I gave him a house. I gave him a farm. I gave him freedom. I saw his face and I saw my son's face. I saw his hands and I saw my son's hands. What does a man build anything for, if not for a son?"

Sterling sat with the cold drink in his hand.

"He took what I gave him and then he tried to take more. He tried to take my own blood. My own son's son. He infected my grandson. It's the way a disease works, Sterling. That's what I didn't understand. I thought I could cure him of his poverty, of his filth. But he's a disease. He's a cancer on that land. Only way to cure it is to do what your woman did to your child, to cut it out at the root."

Sterling clamped his teeth across his own tongue until he tasted the iron tang of blood. "She didn't mean no harm. She had a disease in her own mind."

Mr. Wilson clucked his tongue. "She had wildness in her blood. I saw it here in this room."

The glass slipped in Sterling's hand. He caught it just before it dropped.

"It's the white clay them colored gals eat. Makes them crazy for white men. It was my mistake, Sterling. I shouldn't have let Juke bring no women here, but as I say, I indulged him. I wanted him to have the whiskey, the women. Same thing I'd want for my own son." He plugged his mouth with the cigar and for a moment let the smoke carry him back. "They might have carried it out on the farm, but she liked it here, I reckon. The privacy of it. The secrecy of it. Some nights it was other women with her and some nights it was just her. You could think of her as a prostitute, Sterling, if it helps. I never paid her a penny, but if I gave her a scarf or a little jewelry, it was because I liked her and wanted Juke's lady to take home something fine. She was a beautiful woman, with a wildness in her."

Sterling lowered the glass to the table. He pressed his thumbs to the bridge of his nose. His thumbs were cold from the glass. They numbed his mind.

"I know why you left, Sterling. Any man with any dignity would have done the same. Woman running around on you like that. I ain't sore with you for running off all them years back. You don't owe me nothing. It's just something to tell the judge. It's Jesup owes me something."

Mr. Wilson leaned over and added a drop to Sterling's glass, though he hadn't had but a sip. "You ain't thirsty?"

"I drink slow, sir."

"All right, now. Listen. Weren't nothing you could have done back then but run, Sterling. Short a killing the man. You had reason enough to kill him then, Sterling."

"Sir, I couldn't do no such thing. You seen what they did to—"

"I understand, I understand. You was in a bind, Sterling. You saw you wasn't wanted."

"I had no gun, sir. He took my gun."

"I understand. Now, listen. You had enough reason to kill him then, Sterling. After knowing what he been up to with your woman. Now. Now, come to find out what he been up to with your own child."

Now Sterling did take a sip. Since that morning in the courtroom when Jesup had made his claim, Sterling had been keeping back from it, keeping it out in front of him so he wouldn't fall over the ledge. If he fell off the ledge and looked at the truth, then he would kill the man with his bare hands and he'd be back on the chain gang and out of his daughter's reach by the end of the day.

"It weren't your fault, Sterling. No mother or father to protect her. You had to go."

"I tried," Sterling said, his voice rough with whiskey. "I tried to get back."

"Ain't you want to kill him, Sterling?"

"Course I want to kill him."

Mr. Wilson shrugged. "Then kill him."

"Sir, I kill him and I'm good as dead myself."

"Only if it looks like you killed him. If it don't look like you killed him, well, that's a whole other hog. I got something in mind to help you with that, Sterling. I aim to put you both back on that farm, same as old times. But it ain't gone be no old-time farming, not this year. I got a surprise for you and Johnny Jesup. Gone help with the planting and a whole lot more. And if you can do that for me, Sterling, if you can help me with that, then I'll help you." George Wilson pointed the cigar at him. "I'll put you in the big house, son. It'll be yours. The mules, the cows, the cotton. You'll work for me and I'll treat you as well as I treated any man on any farm. You can work that land all the days of your life."

Sterling wished he hadn't taken that sip. His head felt like it was on crooked.

"What about my daughter? And her child?"

"Why, they can live there with you. It's what a family should do. Keep with their kind."

Sterling felt himself walk up to the ledge. He looked over it.

"I'll keep it out of the law, now. I'll see to it. Just wait for my signal. Don't get ahead of yourself."

"What signal?"

"Wait for my word. I'll tell you when and where and how."

"When will you tell me?"

"You'll know it. You just do what you're called to do. It's your calling, Sterling. Ain't need no gun." George Wilson sat back under the curtain of smoke and admired him. "Look at those shoulders. Look at those hands. They were made for killing."

Again the two men were neighbor dogs growling through the fence. Jesup stayed in the north field and Sterling stayed in the west. They readied the land for planting.

His hands remembered what to do, his feet found tread in the rows, but his head wasn't in it. His head was somewhere else. He had already fancied the ways Jesup and Ketty had betrayed him. Now, worse. Was there anything worse? Now every acre of the farm, the cotton house, sugarhouse, smokehouse, every room, was where Juke Jesup had climbed on top of Sterling's daughter.

And so now every tool hanging in the barn was a weapon. He watched Jesup's distant figure and he spoke low to Clarence and thought of all the ways he could do it. Since he'd become a man he'd wanted to kill Juke Jesup but he'd had to keep his desire deep in his pocket and forget it was there. Now an old white man had pulled it out like a magic handkerchief. He couldn't help but look at its bright colors, imagine it out into the light, for fear it might be hidden again. It was the truth. It was him, his desire, his calling. There was the machete. The sickle. The scythe. Any of these could open the white fishbelly of his neck. There were a great many hoes, some sharp, some dull, that could sever a wrist, stump a leg. The point of a hoe, even a sharp one, was that it was duller than any manner of sickle, it would require repetition, chopping away at a bone like you chopped at a cotton stalk, that was what a hoe was for. There was the ax. What use was there for a gun when God had made the ax? A gun you dispatched from across a room like you'd mail someone a letter. There were shovels. Pointed shovels, flat shovels. That was the kind of thing you made a beating with, starting across the back. Then you could knock out a person's lights with one, one blow to the head, like putting out a candle. Spades you could hold in the palm of your hand, almost like a knife. That was for the white fishbelly of the belly.

There were ropes. Ropes he steered clear of.

He was going to have to wait. George Wilson would decide what he killed him with and where and when because it was to look like he was not killed at all. But what Sterling wanted was for Juke Jesup to know he was going to die and that Sterling was the one who was going to kill him.

He didn't let himself think of Nan. It was as though she still lived on the other side of the world, as though they were both still shackled from each other, because if he believed that, then he could hold her there safely in his mind until he did what he had to do. Then their life together could begin.

So he thought of the wood logs that lay in ashes, good for clubbing behind the knees. He thought of the rakes and pitchforks, the way they would stripe a whole body like a field.

He didn't let himself think of Ketty, either. But one night in the shack his heel stepped on a loose floorboard and it swung up and slapped his leg. He knelt down. In the space between the floor and the dirt beneath it was a coffee tin with its label worn away and inside were several pounds of white Georgia clay. It was still soft and damp. He smeared two fingers with it and smelled them. He smeared himself a mustache where his mustache used to be. Still kneeling, he painted his face with it. He smeared it into his mouth. It tasted like Ketty. Cold as the creek.

Although if Jesup had forced himself on Sterling's own daughter, then he was capable, wasn't he, of forcing himself on Ketty. Perhaps she hadn't betrayed him after all. The thought brought up tears, and the clay on his face ran muddy and got in his eyes.

He wiped his face on his shirt, put the lid back on the tin, and put the tin back in the floor. Then he saw that the board next to it was loose too, and he pulled it up, nails and all. Under the floor, behind the coffee tin, was a sealed pint of Cotton Gin. And behind that, when he reached his hand into the dark under the house, was a hat. A golden corn-shuck hat. He reached around for more but couldn't find anything but cobwebs.

He blew the dust off the hat. It was snug on him but it fit. He thought it was Juke Jesup's hat. He thought it was Juke Jesup's gin. He wore it and he drank it, and for now that helped him to wait.

THIRTY-ONE

THE DAY ELMA LEARNED THAT KETTY WAS NOT HER MOTHER, UN-cle Sterling called her out to the sandhill behind the cotton house. Her father was in town; Ketty had taken Nan on a call. Under a clutch of wiregrass, a baby gopher tortoise was emerging from the only egg that had not been gotten by rattlers or foxes or raccoons. A few steps away, the mother stuck her head out of her burrow and watched along with them. This was Pretty, and her baby, Elma decided, was Tiny. Tiny was a girl, and when she was fully hatched Sterling showed her again how to tell, flipping her over into his palm, her little elephant legs swimming. Elma ran her finger over the rough length of her belly: it was flat. Females had flat bellies; males had a dip. Sterling righted the turtle into Elma's hand. They were crouching in the sand, Pretty restless at their feet. Pretty was Pretty because years ago they had painted her carapace with su-mac paste, marking her. The red paint had faded to a pink watercolor wash, but still she was Pretty, prettier than any of the armadillo-gray turtles that burrowed through the field, turtles her father kicked and cussed at.

"Can we paint this one too?" she asked Uncle Sterling.

"When she's bigger," Sterling said. "She's got to grow some. Put her down, so she can meet her momma."

Elma did. She must have been five. She asked him, "How come people don't come from eggs?"

"They do," Sterling said, thinking it was Ketty who should be teaching her about such ways. She might have told about donkeys and horses. "They in a egg inside their momma. In their momma's belly."

She remembered Ketty's belly swollen with baby Nan inside, and remembered what it was to be outside that belly. Maybe it was watching Pretty come to meet her baby, who had hatched all on her own, who had escaped the rattlers. She had a feeling there was some knowledge outside of her that would soon be inside. She said, "Was I in a egg inside Ketty's belly?" Because she couldn't imagine who else she might have been in an egg inside.

Sterling sat crouched beside her. The sun was warm on their necks. It was coming on fall. Hatching season.

"You ain't know about your momma?" Elma could tell he regretted it. He would have taken it back, or made it kinder. "Honey," he said—Elma remembered his shoes in the dirt, great black boots with brass eyelets and the shine gone out of them—"Ketty raise you up, just like Miss Pretty gone raise up Tiny here. But your momma was Miss Jessa," and he told Elma about her, what he could.

It wasn't that anyone had lied. No one had told her that Ketty was her mother. But there had been a way of stepping over it, walking around it, like you'd steer clear of a rattler under a peanut stack. The woman in her father's wedding picture had been Jessa, but Jessa had not been her mother—she might as well have been her dead grandmother, so distant was she. When Ketty had soothed her fever with a warm sackcloth, smacked her bottom with a wooden spoon, picked the lice from her hair, wasn't she saying she was her mother? Wasn't your mother the one who was there?

Elma was angry at her mother for dying and at Ketty for lying

and at Sterling for telling the truth. She was angry at Nan for being
Ketty's daughter.

She threw rocks into the creek. She made mud pies and ate them.
She climbed the gourd tree until the insides of her thighs were rubbed
raw. And every day she went out to the sandhill to look for Tiny
and Pretty. She picked wiregrass and laid it out on the diamond-
shaped rock behind the cotton house. She skimmed her hand over
Pretty's pink shell. She turned Tiny over in her palm and watched
the desperate swim of her legs. She felt calmer knowing that, if she
wanted to, she could crush the little tortoise under her bare feet.

Then Ketty cut out Nan's tongue and buried it under the gourd
tree and for a time Elma's jealousy was confused by a dark, near-blind
and righteous love.

For her own good, said Ketty.

But what Elma saw was the near-black blood dribbling from the
baby's mouth, and she held Nan on her little lap and found that her
own little mouth knew how to shush her crying, knew how to say, because she had heard Ketty say it when Elma herself was a baby, *There
there, there there.* That was it. Elma would be the little mother. She
stopped leaving wiregrass for Tiny. Instead she fed Nan the warm
milky grits with a spoon. She did not hate Nan anymore, or Sterling.
All her rage she saved for Ketty.

How was it, she wondered later, that her father had escaped her
hate? He should have been the one she hated. Even that fall night
when she saw with her eyes what he did with Ketty, to Ketty—
when she was older she would wonder if he did it with her or to
her, though it seemed to her then it was something they were doing
together—she didn't think to be angry at him. It was only that she
was confused, confused and curious and ashamed, as any child who
walks into her parents' room in the middle of the night, awoken
by sounds new to her ears, is confused by their moaning about in
their bed in the dark. Elma had woken from a nightmare, a mouth
full of broken, bloody teeth. She'd seen a light under her father's

door. The light was a candle burning at his bedside. Was she still dreaming? What was confusing was not what they were doing, not just that, but that it was Ketty. Ketty was not her mother. Sterling had said so. It was not Ketty's bed. But there was Ketty, where she did not belong, on her belly like a turtle, the long, naked slice of her side visible under her father. Her hair, which Elma had only seen wrapped in a cloth, was loose and dark and wild, and some of it was in her father's clenched mouth.

Elma closed the door and, unseen, slipped back down the hall.

She did not tell Sterling. She did not tell Nan, even when she was old enough to understand. Elma herself was not old enough to understand, only knew that she had seen her father climb upon Ketty the way the old gopher tortoise climbed upon Pretty. Later, she would doubt what she saw, thought maybe she had made it up.

The next afternoon she went out to the sandhill behind the cotton house. It had been days since she'd visited, and she was frantic, suddenly, that Tiny had starved. But there on the rock was the fistful of grass she'd left, and there were Tiny and Pretty, both of them, eating it!

She looked closer. It wasn't wiregrass but sawgrass. It wasn't the grass she'd left. It was fresh. Uncle Sterling must have left it, she thought. Uncle Sterling—at least he was there. He would not forget to feed the tortoises. He would not cut out her tongue. (There it was. She was afraid of Ketty. Ketty and her scalpel. Who was to say it wasn't her own tongue she'd come after next, when she leaned down to kiss her good night?) She looked closer still, and saw that Pretty's shell was darker, redder. She touched a finger to one of the tiles on her back, and her fingerprint came back stained with berry juice. Staghorn sumac.

She went and found Sterling in the barn. Yes, ma'am, he'd given her a new coat of paste. He thought she was due. Elma was disappointed. She'd wanted to help. He said they could paint Tiny's shell instead, and that afternoon they did. She got sumac juice down the front of her dress and all day long she sucked her red fingers. She liked that feeling, the taste. Ketty said quit, but she didn't listen.

Elma didn't remember much about the trip into town with her father early the next morning, but she remembered coming home and watching from the wagon as her father and Sterling stood in the driveway. She remembered Ketty stumbling out of the house, picking up Nan from her father's arms, and stumbling into the shack. She remembered her father telling her to go play in the house. What she had done was gone through the house to the back porch and hid behind the well, where she could hear the men's voices rising. They were talking about Ketty, that much she knew. When she saw Clarence galloping down the road, dragging the wagon behind him, she took off too, spooked as he was, into the cane field. She shot up the gourd tree, because it was closer than the house, making as though she'd been climbing it all along.

She'd been climbing that tree since she was old enough to get her legs around it. It was a pole; it was meant to be climbed. The gourds swayed above her, heavy in the blue sky. She never could get to them. But there was nothing like the feeling of climbing toward them, clinging there to rest, the sun-warmed pole pressed to her cheek and to her ribs and her pelvis, and if she inched up, ever so slowly, she could catch that warm, dizzy flutter between her legs like a tiger moth in her cupped hands, and she did not ever want to come back down.

She climbed the pole and thought of the old gopher tortoise climbing Pretty. Slowly, slowly. Slowly, she inched up toward the gourds, her head emerging above the sugarcane now so she could see as far as the farm went. She could see the barn and the shack and the outhouse and the far-flung fields. She could see the cotton house, where the day before, Sterling had stumbled upon Pretty on her back, her legs not swimming, her flat belly bleached white. For many years she did not know that he had found another gopher tortoise to paint red, a surrogate mother for Tiny, who by then would be full grown. Elma would be full grown, and a new mother herself, when she would turn over Pretty and find that, where her belly should have been flat, it was concave. By then, her hate had been turned on herself. She would not be angry with Sterling. She would know by then that you told children stories to protect them.

She had not known, that day her head emerged over the cane, that it would be the last she would see of Uncle Sterling for a long time. She saw him come out of the shack with a sack slung over his shoulder, and she started. She slid down the pole half a foot, then caught herself. He stood under the clothesline and raised a single hand to her. She did not dare let go of the pole, or she might fall. She held on tighter. Her heart beat against the wood. And when he left, and when he did not come back, she thought he must have seen what she had been doing there, climbing the gourd tree, just as she had seen her father and Ketty in his bed, when they thought there were no eyes around. He saw her, and he did not come back. Sterling, of all of them.

When she finally came down, she slid fast and fell hard. She stood and dusted off her hands. Her fingers were stained red, and splintered.

THIRTY-TWO

OLIVER MIGHT NOT HAVE SEEN IT THAT MORNING HAD HE NOT been waiting for the paper. He'd made a habit of waking early, before the rest of the house and before the sun, so he could fetch the paper from the porch steps where the newsboy thunked it, sit at the table with a cup of coffee, and slip out any news he deemed unsuitable for his wife. There was trouble in Scottsboro, Alabama, where a mob was set to lynch nine Negro youths for raping two white girls on a train. He didn't need Elma reading that aloud over breakfast, nor any word about her father. But that morning the news was painted across 52 Main, in tar black letters ten inches tall, one word on each step:

NIGGER
LOVING
DOCTOR

Oliver's legs didn't like stairs. He had to hobble down, clinging to the railing, to reach the sidewalk. He raised himself on his legs and read the words, the dew on the pear blossoms above him glowing blue in the early light. Then he took his cane around back to the shed and found a stiff brush and a gallon of white house paint. He had to sit on the steps in order to paint them, and he got some paint on the cuffs of his pajama pants. By the time he'd dressed and left for work, his good leg was as tired as it was at the end of the day.

It was a Wednesday and not a wash day, and the pajamas lay in the wicker wash basket on the bedroom floor and Winna Jean crawled around it in the way she'd taken to, not on her knees but on her hands and feet, like a baby bear with her rump in the air. Her mother powdered her face, though she had no plans to leave the house or to answer the door to anyone. When the doorbell rang, the breakfast dishes still in the sink, the purged paper still on the table, she ignored it. She had taken to imagining it was a church bell, ringing on the hour as it seemed to, a distant sound from the street. In the back room, Wilson still slept through it. He was tired these days, like a warm, heavy doll, and some mornings he slept until his mother woke him. His mother was awake and dressed and reading the purged page of the newspaper, which Oliver hadn't burned but simply stacked with the old newspapers on the hearth. She read standing up, with the page flat on the nightstand, so that if someone passed through the backyard and looked through the window she might appear not to be reading but to be giving the paper a passing look. That was what she was doing when Frank Colfax came around to the back door and knocked on it.

That was the sound that woke the baby, because the door was her door, the porch door, and because the crib was right there next to it. Frank's face hung there behind the glass, his hands cupped around it, his breath steaming his spectacles. Nan went to the door and opened it. He looked as surprised as she was.

"Morning, miss. You remember me?"

Nan nodded.

"I'm Frank. Mrs. Wilson's driver. You remember?"

Again she nodded.

"Excuse me for troubling you." He had not stepped into the room but he looked at Wilson, who lay on his back in the crib, now crying. "You need to pick him up, miss?"

Nan shook her head. She didn't know why. Did everyone now know he was her child? Did Frank know? If he did, what did it matter?

"I got Mrs. Wilson around front a the house, miss. No one answer the doorbell. She want to talk to Mrs. Rawls."

Now Nan did pick up the baby. She nodded and closed the back door and went to find Elma, who couldn't seem to understand what Nan was trying to tell her. Nan found a pencil in the kitchen and wrote on an edge of the newspaper, *MRS WILSON*. And then erased it. Elma stood up straight and touched both of her own cheeks, as though to see how hot or cold they were. Then she picked up Winna Jean, set her on her hip, and walked to the front door.

Frank was where Nan had left him, behind the closed back door, and when she opened it he began to talk again, as though he'd only been waiting for her to return. "Baby sound like he got something," he said. "My cousin got her a son name February. Got a baby name August, a baby name July. Every baby named after the month it was born in. February had him a bad case of gas. His gut just crushed up like a fist. That baby cry all day long, even when he asleep. I got me a fiddle at home. Back on the farm. My people are farm people. My fiddle the only thing make February stop crying. Got me a fiddle. Made me a couple cigar-box banjos. Made me a lute from a gourd. My uncle taught me. He can make him about anything. That fiddle the only thing calm February down." But in fact Wilson's cries had quieted at the sound of Frank's voice, and now when Frank lowered his face to his, Wilson got ahold of his glasses and lifted them right off his nose. Frank laughed and Nan laughed and Wilson gave a weak gasp of a laugh.

"My grandmomma had one a them porch swings," Frank said, hitching a thumb over his shoulder. "Maybe the baby like the fresh air. Maybe the three of us ought to swing some."

Parthenia Wilson came bearing a Bundt cake, the center stuffed with a milkweed bouquet. The front door wasn't all the way open before Elma said, "So, now we live in the First Ward, you come to meet Winna Jean?"

Mrs. Wilson was wearing a spring hat, lavender trimmed with rhinestones and pearls and little sprays of baby's breath. It looked not unlike the cake she was holding. Her spectacles hung from a beaded chain around her neck. Though it was April and the sun shone behind her, she wore her beaver coat, a white ribbon pinned to its breast.

"I'm here on behalf of the Florence women of temperance, to welcome you in Christ."

Elma smiled. She started to stand back and hold the door open, but she stopped. Behind Parthenia Wilson, the morning was coming to life, automobiles passing by in the street, a crossing guard with his whistle on the corner down the block, schoolchildren with their books under their arms. For weeks Elma had been living behind drawn curtains, and out here the branches were thick with blossoms, the air sun heavy and honey sweet.

"Well, it's a fine morning," Elma said. "Why don't you welcome me in Christ out here on the porch."

Mrs. Wilson looked about in confusion, as though she'd never sat on a porch before. She counted two rockers, dusted in pear blossoms but otherwise empty, waiting. "It's a fine morning," she agreed.

Elma brought the cake into the house and returned with two glasses of sweet tea, tumbling with ice cubes. "We're clean out a lemonade," she said. "I suppose this will have to do."

Mrs. Wilson thanked her. The women sat and took their first long, quiet sips. A rust-breasted robin chirped in the pear tree. The crossing guard's whistle chirped back. The grand ferns on their pedestals had gone brittle and brown at the edges, and Elma wished she had swept the porch ceiling for cobwebs. She had been waiting, with anticipation and with dread, she had been making up her face each morning, for Parthenia Wilson. She had not really believed she would come. And now she was here and Elma's hair was unpinned and the baby's fingernails were dirty, but she had a porch to sit on, a respectable house, Carlotta Rawls's white house with the green shutters, and Elma sat as tall and proud as the pear tree in the front yard.

"Well, we had Frederick fitted for an eye patch," Parthenia said, looking out at the road. "It's made by a gentleman in Atlanta. Navy blue silk, very fine, very hardy." She rubbed some invisible fabric between her frail fingers. "The gentleman makes them out of handkerchiefs. He sends each eye patch in a little package with a matching handkerchief."

Elma had not one idea how to reply to this. As though Freddie was just a mutual acquaintance, or as though Elma was another member of the WCTU, with a grandson of her own to report on. Parthenia Wilson was nervous.

"He looks almost dapper in it, I must say. It hasn't harmed his looks any. He looks even more like his daddy."

"Mrs. Wilson, are you chatting with me?"

Mrs. Wilson waved her arm at the street. Elma watched her swallow. "That's what we're doing. We're having us a chat."

"You know who Freddie looks like?" Winna made happy sounds as her mother bounced her. "This child. His daughter."

Mrs. Wilson tilted her head, studying the baby. Winna was in a dust-colored dress, but her hair was buttercup yellow, curling now in a tuft atop her head. "Oh, I don't know about that. She's a comely child. But it's not for me to say who she takes after."

In the street, a gray car passed, gleaming silver under the sun. It was Mrs. Nightingale Highland, the grocer's wife, a colored man driving her. She squinted up at the porch, her eyes trying to read their faces, and then she was gone.

"Here. Hold her."

"No, no."

"Go ahead." Elma stood and dangled the child by the armpits in front of the old woman. "Get her on your knee. See if you can't tell who she takes after."

"No, thank you! I won't! Thank you! I can see her quite well from here."

Elma waited for another car to pass in the street before she rested Winna on her hip. From around the other side of the house came another baby's cry, Wilson's jagged little moan. Mrs. Wilson looked about, confused.

"You think she might get your nice coat dirty?"

Mrs. Wilson dusted off her lap.

"Think she's got colored on her? From sharing a crib with a colored child?" Elma kissed Winna's ear. "Don't worry. Colored don't rub off."

Mrs. Wilson clucked her tongue. "I have no worries. That child is no more related to that colored child than she's related to me."

"She *is* related to you! She's a Wilson!"

"It's not for me to say. It's not for you to say, either, the way you keep changing the story. First they were twins! Raped by a colored man! Poor girl! they said. That's the way your story went." She was wagging her finger. "Now come to say the child is your own father's. Shameful! He's been trouble since he was a barefooted boy. Both of you ought to be ashamed. Both of you ought to pray for forgiveness."

"It wasn't what I wanted. It wasn't my story to change."

"I knew you weren't to be trusted, even before. Now, how my ever to believe that's Freddie's child? How my to believe she isn't your husband's?"

"She's a Wilson. Her name is Winnafred Jean. After Freddie."

Mrs. Wilson looked pained, the ropy muscles in her neck tensing, as though the strain of sitting up straight in her chair were going to break her.

"You're a smart girl. You have a lying tongue, but you're clever. You must know a name doesn't make kin."

Elma was kissing Winna's ear repeatedly; she was standing and swaying and kissing her daughter's ear. She said, "What makes kin, then?"

"Blood. Blood makes kin, child. I will tell you something. The truth will come out. Not your version of it. God's truth. I will tell you something. Somewhere in your house there are three vials of blood. Blood. Your husband took the blood. He took it from your father and from Freddie and from that Negro, the father of your house girl, in your husband's office, telling them it was part of the bond, and the fools believed it! My own grandson among them. I know this because my husband asked for my perfume bottles, three of them, itty-bitty, no bigger than an ounce"—she spread her finger and thumb an inch apart—"and when I wouldn't give them to him, because I want no part in it, understand, no part, he emptied them in the sink. Perfume he bought me himself! One from Paris, France. A full bottle. He emptied them and rinsed them and he gave them to your husband. They were in my house and now they're in your house, and now they have blood in them. And they will tell the truth."

"What in Heaven."

"Do you want to know why you can afford to live in Carlotta Rawls's house another month, child? On a cripple's paycheck? Because my husband paid your husband to take blood. Blood money." She laughed. "That's what they call it."

"My husband hasn't killed anyone! My husband is a good man! It's your kin with blood on they hands."

"My husband is no killer. I don't aim for him to become one. A woman has got to do what she can to stop bloodshed."

"The bloodshed's already happened, Mrs. Wilson. It's not what I wanted. If y'all had just opened your home to us. To Winna. It didn't have to happen."

"I'm talking about the blood that's yet to be shed, child. I'm talking about your father."

"What about my father?"

"I have no love for him. He's a killer himself. Some might say an eye for an eye—that he should be killed for his crime. But I don't intend on any more bloodshed. God doesn't want it. I don't intend for your kind to drag my kind down with you."

"What about my father?" she repeated.

"Something's fixing to happen on that farm. Men talk. When my husband has whiskey, he talks. He's sent that Negro to do harm to your father."

Elma sat down on the edge of her rocker. "Sterling wouldn't harm my father. He wouldn't harm anyone."

"I don't know who that man is. But I don't aim for my husband to be involved in it. I want nothing more to do with it."

"With what? What's going to happen?"

"I've come to tell you that you must put an end to it, child. There isn't much a woman can do in this world. But if there's one thing she was made to do, it's to keep men from shedding each other's blood."

Elma's arms prickled. She thought of Ketty's phrase: the all-overs. All over. She held the baby close.

"Why is it for me to do? He's your husband. Tell him to call it off!"

Parthenia Wilson sat with her iced tea cradled in her hand, all but untouched. When she lifted her wrist, Elma could see that she had a tremor.

"Don't you love your father, child?"

The old woman's ice cubes rattled in her glass. From around the side of the house, from the other side of the world, came another weak cry.

"I pity you, raised with a father like that. But kin is kin. You could have stopped the killing before. Now you're here sitting on this porch, wearing Carlotta Rawls's ring on your finger. You should be ashamed of yourself. You must go to the farm and pray for God's forgiveness. You must pray for Him to bring peace."

———

Oliver was at the office. A scrim of white paint ridged the print of his right thumb. He rubbed his thumb and forefinger together. It was nearly five o'clock and his waiting room was empty but he did not want to go home. Before him on the desk sat the telephone, a box of wood and chrome, which he had unplugged from the wall; three dollars and fourteen cents; and a ledger, on which he had written "$3.14." He understood that there were other numbers he should be writing—expenses, estimates, projections—but he did not know what those numbers were. They were abstractions, as inconceivable as outer space. The maths he had taken at Emory had been the maths one took to learn the optimal angle of an incision. Concrete math, the math of the physical world. Not economics, not accounting, not the math of running a business, of keeping the water flowing in the pipes and electricity flowing in the wires. What was electricity? An abstraction. His father had kept meticulous records, every patient, every visit, every dollar, but they were indecipherable to Oliver. At moments he wished his father alive so that he might ask him the difference between an amortizing mortgage and a balloon mortgage—there was something almost heartening, aortic, about the words, something buoyant—and what happened to each when the name of the bank on the envelope changed, and how to budget, how to balance, in a time when his dwindling patients paid in coins rummaged from their linty pockets, or with IOUs, or not at all. He extended credit to them because he himself had been extended credit, which was in turn an extension of his father's credit. It was the credit which in fact kept his father alive, corporeal. What was credit? It was a helium balloon that you held in your hand like a child. Then you added another balloon, and another, and your feet lifted off the ground, and the more balloons you added, the higher you rose in the sky, and the farther you had to fall.

It was more house than they could manage, and more than they needed. What use did they have for two fireplaces, two staircases? How might a man in his condition manage to fill all those bedrooms with children?

He opened the desk drawer, and his father's little leather apothe-cary case inside it. He had never not known the case, its brass corners and worn leather strap, the little corked vials of powdered camphor and codeine—it had been the toy box, the treasure chest, of his youth, though he was not to open any of the bottles, ever, and he didn't, he had a reverence for them, they were powerful, and pinching them be-tween his fingers was enough.

A colleague from Atlanta, he had done his dental residency at Emory, he had filled a tooth for Oliver once, he had lost all his sav-ings through a thrift, he owed money for his tuition, he had sat back in his hydraulic dental chair one day and sifted two hundred mil-ligrams of camphor down his throat. A patient had found him there the next day.

He lifted the vial of camphor now. It was ancient, the label yel-lowed; it might have been filled with dust. He unscrewed the cap. He drew it up to his nose. It would be like eating dust, dirt. He smelled, to his horror, the herbal burn of Pears soap.

He closed his eyes. He saw Elma's wedding dress falling to the floor. He saw his own legs lying helplessly before him. He saw the mask of regret on her face.

Parsnip, shrink, rot.

He wasn't man enough. Was he man enough? He dipped his fin-gers into the empty slots of the case, leaving the camphor uncapped. He had not been a man here in his office the other day. He had not used the perfume bottles, they were contaminated, ignorant; he had sterilized three new glass vials and taken the men's blood with a lancet, from their fingertips, one, two, three of them, and applied the glucose solution to keep it from coagulating, and labeled the vi-als himself, meticulously. The men had not protested. They had not flinched. They were men. What was a little blood? It was a small pay-ment for their freedom, a deposit to the state. They did not believe that their blood was theirs, that anything in it told it was theirs apart from the label on the vial. And yet there was the unavoidable intimacy,

Oliver's hands holding each of their hands loosely, by the wrist, the knuckles resting on his own wrist, their blood beating there together, both of them concentrating for a moment on the same silent task. The Negro, Nan's father, had thanked him. Jesup had said, "Your daddy wanted to stick me. I guess he got me after all." He said, "Tell Elma not to worry. Tell her not to be a stranger."

When it was Freddie Wilson's turn, he said, "That wife of yours more clever than I thought. She done lied all the way to the doctor's house."

Oliver gripped Freddie's wrist tighter, so his own wouldn't shake.

"Reckon you got you two babies now."

He imagined these hands on his wife. His wife letting him put these hands on her. His wife liking these hands on her. He gripped harder.

"Ain't you able to make your own, Doc?"

He could have opened one of the man's veins. He was a cripple but he held a blood lancet; he could have let the man's blood out on the floor.

Perhaps if he had been a man, if he had not already been a disappointment to his wife, he would have. But he had seen the look on his bride's face the night of their wedding, a resignation that did not ease, no matter how many packages she brought home from Cantor's. And there in the corner of the office sat Freddie Wilson's grandfather, watching to see that he was thorough. He wanted it done right this time. It was too late to recover his manhood, and so he would do the next best thing. He would pay the mortgage.

After George Wilson dismissed the three men to their waiting rooms, he handed Oliver the fifty-dollar bill. Nearly half of that money would pay for the transportation of the samples to the lab in Atlanta. The other half Oliver would mail to the mortgage company, hoping it was the right address on the envelope, that indeed it would hold them off another month.

"I can't test it here myself, you understand," he'd told George

Wilson. The samples would have to be driven to the city directly, and tested by Mercer, his mentor at Emory, who would do it as a favor to Oliver, to ease his own guilt for letting him go, but only when he got around to it. The results could take weeks.

A funny little country mystery, Mercer seemed to think. "What you up to with all this blood?" he asked when Oliver rang him up. "You bloodletting all the farmers in that jerkwater town?"

Oliver laughed it off. "Just tell me the types," he said. He told Mercer he didn't know why the tests were necessary, and it was true. He'd told Mr. Wilson in this office that blood typing was in its infancy, that it was inconclusive. Mr. Wilson had answered by sitting down across from Oliver, leaning his elbow on the desk, and as if readying to arm wrestle, proferring his own hand. "Whyn't you go on and stick me too, then."

Oliver pushed away from the desk. The old man was more desperate than he'd thought. "Why?"

"Go on. You said we needed more samples," Mr. Wilson said. "Now we have the samples. I want you to have all the blood you need. No mistakes this time."

"Yes, but as a method of identifying paternity," Oliver said, readying the lancet again, despite himself, "it can only prove impossibility, not possibility. It's an imperfect process. It's guesswork." There was math involved. Probabilities. Nothing more concrete than blood, its platelets and cells clearly outlined under a slide, and yet the story the blood told—that was still a human abstraction.

"Then guess," Mr. Wilson said. "That's what a doctor does, isn't it? Diagnose. No one knows what goes on in a woman's womb but God. But you can guess."

Oliver took the lancet and eased it into the soft flesh of the old man's forefinger. He would do what the man asked for. Like his father, he would do what he had to do to take care of his family. But that didn't mean he wouldn't ask questions. "Why do you need to know?"

He removed the needle and Mr. Wilson put the pricked finger in his mouth. Oliver handed him a bandage, but he waved his hand. He said, "An old man wants to sleep."

For the life of him, he still didn't understand. Why did he need George Wilson's blood? "Even if I can tell you, if I can make a guess—what would it matter? Jesup's gone and claimed the Negro child as his own, in a court of law. Isn't that all you wanted to prove?"

"I got no interest in what the courts say. The courts don't say what father a child belongs to. A Wilson takes care of his own, but only if they blood."

"Is it Winnafred? You want to know if she's a Wilson? You want me to stick that baby because you can't take her mother's word?"

George Wilson stood and pulled his business card out of his billfold and handed it to Oliver, spotted with his blood. "A word is nothing, son. What's a word? Tell me what the blood says. All of it. Make it talk."

He'd tried to explain it to the girls this way. He told them, drawing their samples at the kitchen table that night, that it would keep them safe. It would help to prove, if it came to it, that their children were their own. It would help to make sure that no one could take them away. Each sat her own child in her lap and lowered her head, and he took the babies' blood next, siphoning it from their earlobes. They cried. He did not tell them that George Wilson had ordered it, that he had paid for it. He did not tell them that he had taken the fathers' blood, and George Wilson's own blood, that he would add their vials to the others. He would lay them flat in an egg crate and pack it in ice, and together the bottles of blood would make the journey by courier to Atlanta. And part of him, the part that was still a child pinching the medicine vials between his little fingers, believed that they might in fact reveal some answers, that they would speak the truth. And because he knew the truth was nothing to fear, they could put all of this behind them.

He screwed the cap back on the vial of camphor. He closed the apothecary case. The child's reverence for the treasure chest of medicines—was that what kept him from doing it? Was it the same innocence and ineptitude that kept him clinging helplessly to the tail of the balloon? Or was it just that he too was out of choices?

He thought of something. He wheeled his chair around and over to the far-right file cabinet. In the drawer marked *W-Z*, in between Freddie and Parthenia, he found a folder—he would have bet his life on that folder being there—for George Wilson I. It was thick with a healthy man's lifetime of checkups, so thick Oliver felt a touch of tenderness flipping through them. His vaccinations—he had no fear of needles; a case of scarlet fever as a child; a fractured wrist in 1908. Oliver had thought he might find some clue to the man's mystery, but there was nothing at all of note until the final page in the file, October 5, 1930. In his father's barely legible scrawl: "Brown Lung Disease. Prognosis 6–12 months."

Oliver looked up. George Wilson was sick. He had been sick when he'd paid a visit to his father's deathbed, and his father had known. And now it was April.

Then came the sound of the bell on the outer waiting room door. It was past five o'clock, after his office hours, but he was grateful, momentarily, for the distraction, another patient to delay his return home. Oliver returned the folder to the drawer and wheeled himself into the waiting room, where a man stood in a fedora and tidy suit, his overcoat already over his arm. The way he held his briefcase at his side, with finality, fatality, the way a police officer comes to the door with his hat over his heart, made Oliver understand that it was heavy with papers bearing empty lines, where Oliver would be made, at long last, to sign his name.

"Dr. Oliver Rawls," the man said. He too produced a business card, which in fact bore the name of the bank that owned the mortgage on his father's house, which he would be forced to empty by the end of the month. The business card sliced a paper cut in the bank man's middle finger, and he put it in his mouth. He looked at Oliver for a moment, as though expecting him to offer to bandage it. Then together they realized there was nothing to be done.

———————

He could smell dinner before he was all the way in the back door, Brunswick stew and cornbread, the air in the closed-up house dense with it. "Nan made a Bundt cake," Elma said. On any other occasion, it would have made for a sweet end to a long day, a soft place to land, but the smell made Oliver's stomach ache. "I got a stomachache," he told Elma. "And a headache." He was done with lying. He hung his jacket by the back door and wheeled himself to the refrigerator. He opened it and sat before it for a moment, his forehead resting on a cold bottle of milk. Then he closed the icebox and wheeled to the telephone on the wall. He had to prop himself up on his good leg in order to reach the coat hanger hanging from the hook. He tugged on Elma's overcoat. It tumbled down to the floor. He replaced the receiver on its cradle.

"What you do that for?" Elma asked, picking up the coat.

"No more need to hide."

"That phone's gone be ringing any minute."

And it did. A long, dissenting wail of a tone, and then a short, surprised one. There were two more long rings coming and Oliver could not bear to hear them. He lifted the phone from the wall.

"Oliver."

It was his mother's voice. She sounded surprised, as though he had been the one to call her.

"Darling, I've been ringing you and ringing you."

"Hello, Momma. How you feeling?"

"For days and days! I thought the line might be disconnected."

"No, no. The line still works. I've paid for the line." He closed his eyes. "But we've lost the house."

He opened them. Elma stood looking at him, the coat on its

hanger folded over her arm. Nan stood at the kitchen sink. The babies sat in their new high chairs.

"What do you mean, you've lost the house?"

"The bank's taking it, Momma. I'm sorry."

"Oliver. It's that woman."

"Who?"

"That wife of yours. She has charged up all my accounts. Every account in town. She is the problem, Oliver."

"No, no. Daddy was behind on the house. He had two mortgages on the place."

"You've been married two months and already she has driven you to this."

"Momma—"

"You've got to leave, Oliver. Get out of there. Come to Savannah."

From where he sat he could see one of Irene's notes on his father's prescription pad taped to the wall beside the phone. He could not read the words—his eyes felt loose and bleary in their sockets—but he saw the constancy of her handwriting, her always-there, never-gone shape in this room. He had a sick, sorry feeling he knew to be true. She had not abandoned them. It was she who'd been betrayed. His father had let her go, after thirty years, because he could no longer afford to pay her. He wondered if his mother even knew.

"I ain't coming to Savannah, Momma. I got to hang up. I got a headache. I'll call you later."

"Oliver!"

He half-stood in his wheelchair and returned the phone to its cradle.

Elma and Nan stood looking at him.

"Oliver," Elma said.

Oliver clapped his hands. "All right. We gone talk about this. But we gone wait till tomorrow. My head can't hold another word today."

His head felt like a balloon. One of those Chinese paper lanterns let loose in the sky.

He excused himself to lie down. He was halfway to the bedroom when the doorbell rang. Oliver leaned over and laughed into his lap. He sat up and rubbed the top of his head.

"Open it," he said to Elma.

Elma did. At the door was a mustached man in a suit. He stood back on the porch, turned to the street and puffing on a pipe, as though he didn't expect anyone to answer the door. It took a moment for Elma to recognize him; she hadn't seen him up close since that day in August, when they'd sat at the table in front of the crossroads store. But Oliver knew Q. L. Boothby before he turned around; he'd smelled that pipe tobacco the last three summers in Warm Springs, and seeing him there was enough to make Oliver relax his shoulders, take a breath; he smelled the magnesium waters and the pines, the fresh-cut grass.

"Mr. Boothby," Elma greeted him. "We have nothing to put in the papers, thank you kindly."

"Mrs. Rawls." Mr. Boothby tipped his hat. "Good evening to you. Dr. Rawls."

"Quincy! Glad to see you."

"I haven't come on behalf of the *Testament*. This is a friendly visit."

And then suddenly it was. Q. L. Boothby was Uncle Quincy come to visit, Uncle Quincy who smelled of pipe tobacco, who talked like the city. Oliver introduced him to Nan, who waved from the sink— there were no shadows for her to hide in here, the kitchen bright with electric lights—and when Mr. Boothby stepped forward and extended his hand for her to shake, she looked the most surprised of any of them. He did the same to the babies, kneeling down to the floor and putting out his large hand to them, and Wilson clapped both his around it and Winna put it in her mouth, and they all laughed. Nan made coffee and Oliver wheeled himself over the threshold and out to the porch, and the two men drank it, Oliver in his wheelchair, Mr. Boothby in the rocker where Parthenia Wilson had sat that morning. The mild day had given way to a mild evening, the sky going quietly pink over the neat brick houses across the street, the robins and spar-rows chattering in the pear trees. It was the moment the sky seemed most alive, most in need of attention, just before the sun sank behind the trees. For a few breaths Oliver sat in the kind of peace that grows from enervation, every cell of his body aching for rest but his mind dizzyingly, glowingly awake. He felt the gas in his head slowly begin to release, the door shutting on the long and terrible day.

"Night like this brings my mind around to Warm Springs," Mr. Boothby said.

But already Oliver's mind was there, the tall pines and the long, sloping lawn—

"You know your father was on the board at the institute."

"I do."

"Valued member. A trusted physician, and the medical knowledge he brought. Kept up with the latest in polio research."

"He did."

"You've taken his place here at his practice." Mr. Boothby puffed on his pipe. "I come to ask—being as you aren't inclined to answer your mail or your telephone—if you'd take his place on the board."

Well, of course he would, Oliver said. He'd be honored.

"Marvelous," said Mr. Boothby. He started to tell him about the meetings, the research, the fund-raising, but Oliver was think-ing about the waters, about lowering himself into them, and floating, weightless, under the clouds.

"When can I get up there, Quincy?"

Well, he was welcome anytime, Mr. Boothby said.

He had a need to get away for a while, Oliver told him.

Mr. Boothby said he understood. When you were married as long as he was, he said, there came a need to get away from the Mrs.

Oh, no, Oliver said. He would bring the Mrs. with him. Just a little retreat with his family. He did not tell him about the foreclosure. That would find its way to the papers in time.

Well, of course, Mr. Boothby said. They'd all been through a trying time. Of course they had need to escape. Mr. Boothby himself was heading there on Saturday to spend Easter weekend with the Roosevelts before returning home to Macon. Would Oliver like to join them?

Oliver laughed. He laughed his thanks.

Mr. Boothby extended his hand, and again they shook.

THIRTY-THREE

A GAIN NAN RODE IN THE BACKSEAT OF THE BLACK PLYMOUTH
Phaeton with Wilson in her lap, Florence disappearing behind her. This time Oliver was sitting in Dr. Rawls's seat.
She might have felt the noose of the place loosening, the air returning
to her lungs as the white clay gave way to red, but this time Wilson
was sick, not cold as a block of ice but warm and feverish and limp,
a spineless cut of fatback. Out the window, the road signs swept by:
Meredith, Rebecca, Leslie. In Americus, Oliver stopped at a filling
station to let Nan nurse, not wanting to repeat what had happened
in Atlanta, though the secret was a secret no longer. Nan did not
know that just down the road was the colored hospital; if she had,
she might have taken Wilson then and there. She did not know that it
was where Dr. Rawls had overseen the autopsy of Genus Jackson, and
where he had taken and tested the dead man's blood, the blood that
had revealed such malformed red cells that he had neglected to pay
attention to the blood type—B—which was rare enough but not so
rare as a disappeared spleen. She did not know—God barely knew—
that down the road a bit farther was a place called Archery, which
was not on a road sign but where a five-year-old boy, one of the only

white children in the town, ran the fields of his family's peanut farm
with the children of the colored field hands. In many years, when the
boy would grow up to live in the White House in Washington, D.C.,
Nan would feel the same restored pride she'd felt when listening to
the governor of New York, who would himself, very soon, live in the
White House in Washington, D.C., and who would soon name his
retreat in Warm Springs, where the Plymouth traveled now some sev-
enty miles north from Americus, the Little White House, where he
would die at the end of a long and bitter war.

She had not expected to make the trip without Elma. It had been
a long and bitter argument, conducted in Elma and Oliver's bedroom
after the babies had fallen asleep. Nan did not want to listen to it, but
even with her bedroom door closed, she could hear every word. Elma
did not want to go to Warm Springs, of course she didn't, and how
could Oliver run off on a vacation with a trial coming up and a house
going under?

"That's exactly why we're leaving. We don't have any other place,
Elma. Where else we going to go? The farm?"

Elma didn't answer.

"Elma. No."

"I have to, Oliver. Else he's going to kill my daddy." She had lowered her voice, but Nan could hear.

"Who is?"

"Sterling."

Here Nan had rushed on tiptoe to her bedroom door and pressed
herself to it. What was she talking about, and how did she know, and
would she slow down? It was Oliver asking Nan's questions now.
Why else, Elma said, would George Wilson have put them both on
the farm? She had made up her mind: she was going back. "Going
home" was how she put it.

"For goodness' sake, Elma. I'm not letting you. You're not going.
If that man's as dangerous as you say, then it's all the more reason for
you to stay away!"

"Oliver, you been my husband for two months. He's been my daddy all my life."

Nan heard somebody throw something, like a shoe against a wall.

"Well, why'd you bother marrying me if you're going back there? Huh?"

"Oliver—"

"Go on, if you got your mind made up! But you're not taking Nan. I won't let you put her back in harm's way."

Nan ran to her bed and pulled the covers to her chin. She wrapped the pillow over her ears. She thought of her father sleeping in Genus's bed. The shack door didn't even have a lock.

She heard Genus's voice: "If I end up dead, it's by that man's hand. And if he ends up dead, it's by mine."

She could go back. Look after her father, despite Oliver's wishes. Return to her pallet in the pantry, or drag it into her father's shack. That had been what she'd wanted, hadn't it?

But she remembered the bottle of gin between her thighs, the clothesline lighting up the night. She had not been able to save Genus. Now she had to take up for her son.

She could only sleep once she'd taken Wilson, still sleeping, into her own bed, pressing him to her shoulder as Winna held her rag doll.

The next morning, the morning they both readied to leave the doctor's house, she wrote a note and handed it to Elma. *Look after him.*

Elma read the note and Nan watched the confusion pass over her face. She was wondering who *him* was. She caught herself before she asked. Nan wanted to add, *He won't hurt anyone.* She was angry with Elma for believing he would. But what did Nan know of her father? If she were cornered again on that farm, she couldn't promise that she wouldn't hurt Juke herself.

Elma nodded, fanned her watering eyes with the note, and then tore it into pieces in her apron pocket.

"It's the twins being apart," she said. She picked up Wilson and kissed him. She didn't finish. For months the girls had strained against calling the babies twins, but now they clung to the word. Elma tickled Wilson's fat thigh above the knee, but he didn't laugh as he usually did. He gave a low mew. In his ear she whispered, "You'll be all right, little sheep."

Nan lifted Winna Jean and breathed in the pink sugar smell of her hair. For a few minutes, they each stood on either side of the crib, hips rocking. It was the first night Elma would spend apart from her husband in their short marriage, and, aside from the nights Nan had caught a few hours' sleep in Rocky Bottom cabins, it was the first night Nan would spend apart from Elma in all her life. The silence was painful enough that Nan wished Elma would say something more, something to reassure her that the silence was the kind of complicit, companionable silence they'd lived in for so long, not the silence that would divide them. Then they heard Oliver start the engine in the driveway. He would drive them all out to the farm to drop off Elma and Winna and Pollux before going on to Warm Springs. Without speaking they traded babies, as they'd done a hundred times before.

Now every mile took her farther from the farm. "Don't be nervous," Oliver said from the driver's seat, finding her eye in the rearview. "I'll be with you, just like Elma. You can trust me. Do you trust me?" Nan hesitated only a moment before she nodded at the mirror. She did trust him, didn't she? Anyway, there was no one she trusted more. "You need something, I'll get it for you." She looked down at Wilson, who was breathing shallowly. His eyelids fluttered open and closed. "You miss her," Oliver guessed.

Nan looked up. Did she miss her? It wasn't quite right, but she nodded again. It was true that she was nervous. On calls, alone, she had walked into unfamiliar houses, she had found a way to communicate what she had to, but Elma had never been far away. "She ain't acting like herself," Oliver said. At first Nan thought he meant *he*, meant Wilson. Wilson wasn't acting like himself. "Or maybe she is. Maybe I just don't know her. Is she acting like herself?" he asked.

Nan tilted her head. Then she shook it. She meant no, Elma wasn't acting like herself, but also no, Nan didn't know her, either.

"How she can go back to that farm, after all I did to get her off it, is beyond me."

All he did. Nan thought about this.

"What is she doing out there? What loyalty does she have to him? After what he did to you, to both of you . . ."

Nan shifted in her seat.

"What's the sense in going out here now? I don't know. I've been sitting here driving and thinking about it. What's the sense?"

Was he ashamed? she wondered. He had given up much for Elma and for Nan, it was true. And yet he seemed to need others to see what he had given. Was he disappointed that he should return to this place of his youth, to meet the governor of New York, the man whose every word he'd hung on, without his wife—his young, long-legged, beautiful wife—by his side, but instead with Nan and a sickly, sallow-skinned baby? He'd never been at Warm Springs when the governor was there. Now his picture of that meeting had a hole in it. "Maybe he won't be there," he said. "Maybe he'll be called away." Nan could tell he was shielding himself from his own hopes, and she felt sorry for him again. "But you'll love it here, Nan. Either way. You'll see. It'll be just what we need." That was the way it was, when you couldn't talk back—the person who was talking ended up coming to the conclusion he wanted all by himself. "It's just—peaceful. So peaceful that people come from all over the country to be there. Ever had a place like that?"

Nan thought. There was her family's shack, when she was small. There was the creek, for those few nights with Genus. There was the first cabin with Elma and the second. But always they were little rooms of light in the midst of the darkness around it. Always there was something just outside the door. But maybe that was true of the place they were going too. Maybe there was no safety without wilderness on the other side of it.

"I wanted her to see it," he said, turning off the road down the long, wooded drive. "That's all. I just wanted her to see it." He drove on, slowing the car, perhaps out of duty to Nan and her son but also, she thought, out of spite—he would not change his plans. He had changed enough of his plans for Elma.

Quietly the buildings came into view. They were neat and tall, the green grounds lying compliantly before them. It was like the campus at Emory, all of the bushes squared by some invisible gardener, and despite herself Nan felt her heart rise up seeing it. If they would be safe anywhere, if someone knew how to help Wilson, it would be here in this place of order and abundance. In front of the building that was not yet the Little White House, Oliver eased the car into park. Beside it was a convertible with its top down, and as Nan stepped out she could see that it had the same funny hand controls as the Plymouth. Still holding Wilson, she helped Oliver out of the car and into his wheelchair. Passing the convertible, he gave it a pat on its haunches, like a dog he'd met a long time before. She gave his shoulder a pat, and he looked up at her and gave her a smile that was first confused, then grateful. I see it, she was saying, and she thought he understood.

It would be a memory, more than a lived moment, following Oliver's wheelchair up the paved path to the grandest house she had seen, the grass shorn as clean as a haircut, the clouds still as a held breath overhead. On the porch of the house, in a wicker wheelchair just like Oliver's, sat the governor. The sun glared off his eyeglasses like two bright coins. With him were Q. L. Boothby, who had traveled on ahead of the Plymouth, and two other white men, one of them also in a wheelchair, a card game Nan did not recognize spread on the table between them. She was not entirely in her body, she was not entirely herself, not just because she was visiting on the governor of New York, not just because she didn't have Elma by her side, but because her son was sick and he was crying, and because she didn't want him to call attention to him or to herself. A cloud shifted and she stood in the sunlight behind Oliver on the flagstone path, and

Oliver offered his greetings to Q. L. Boothby and to the other two men and then—she could see his shoulders shaking—to the governor. He wheeled his chair up the ramp and as the two men shook hands, their knees nearly kissed. And then, calling her his nurse, he introduced Nan.

Franklin Roosevelt looked up to see her there, shielding his face from the sun, and then she saw his eyes. She took a step up to the porch and nodded at him. Did she nod at him? Later she would wonder if she had nodded or only meant to nod. Oliver reached over his shoulder and, introducing the baby now, gave Wilson's socked foot a tug.

The sun and the drive and Wilson's fever had put Nan in a loose mind. She had a kind of fever herself. In later years, when she remembered this day, when she wrote it down, she'd recall that it was Franklin Roosevelt who had tugged on Wilson's foot. But Franklin Roosevelt did not touch the baby, only nodded hello at him with a smile from his wheelchair on the porch. It was a smile of concern, Nan thought. It was because the baby looked so sick. The governor of New York was used to seeing sick babies. The concern was because Wilson was sick, she thought. Franklin Roosevelt leaned over and spoke a few words into Q. L. Boothby's ear, and Q. L. Boothby stood and walked into the house. What Oliver hoped was that he would return with Mrs. Boothby and Mrs. Roosevelt, who would offer them some of the tea that was sweating in the men's glasses. What Nan hoped, allowed herself to hope, her hope rising perilously high in her throat, was that he would return with a real nurse, another doctor— someone who would take Wilson into their arms and say, "This child needs help."

Instead he returned with a colored woman, tall and old and gaunt, in sunhat and apron. This was Miss Aubie, Mr. Boothby said, and she would help them settle in. It took Nan a moment to understand that he meant Nan and Wilson, and she saw the understanding come late to Oliver's face too. She saw the panic follow, and then the remorse, and then he gave them a limp wave and said good-bye, he would see them in a while.

Mrs. Roosevelt, Nan heard Miss Aubie say to another of the maids when they reached the colored dormitory, was home in Albany. Miss Aubie pronounced it the way they pronounced the town in Georgia. She heard her own mother say it: "All-benny." It took Nan some thinking to understand it was another city, far to the north. Perhaps there were many Albanys, a country of them. Foolish girl, her mother would say. Foolish, foolish girl. Oliver would stay with the men and play cards all afternoon, his left cheek turning pink when the sun came in at a certain angle under the porch, and Nan would not see him until the next day. He would look like he'd been slapped on that cheek.

THIRTY-FOUR

BETSY RICHARD, AS SHE WAS KNOWN SINCE SHE WAS AN ORPHAN boarding with the Richards at the mill, did go on to find a husband. She and her baby lived through the day after they boarded the Ponce de Leon in Florence, and the day after that, through Atlanta, Chattanooga, Knoxville, Lexington. That she made it all the way to Cincinnati, Ohio, the last stop on the Southern Railway, was due in no small part to the Pullman porter, whose name was Phillip, and who produced without the notice of other passengers orange juice and chicken legs from the dining car, and a blanket to cover her nursing breast, and from Betsy's own suitcase, a clean dress to change into when her bleeding soaked the train seat. While she made her way to the hopper, he held the baby girl, who was named, halfway through the trip, Tennessee, and when the mother and daughter got off in Ohio, Phillip scrubbed the seat with the girl's discarded dress and sent them to his mother, who owned a rooming house in Over-the-Rhine. It was there that the pair lived, first next door to Phillip, when the train brought him home, and then, when they married, in the two rooms together, the wall between them sledgehammered. She did not return to Florence, because her colored husband could not provide the disguise George Wilson expected. That was only one of the reasons she married him. He was kind and, mostly, he was gone. She had not realized it was his mother she would be marrying. On days when she knocked on the door at all hours, saying do this, try this, baby won't grow if you feed her that, Betsy missed the Richards, their cold, quiet ways, her neat little bed in the mill village. The Richards left her bed untouched. They mourned her like a lost daughter. Her spite for George Wilson became theirs.

The baby did not sleep in Betsy's open suitcase, as Nan had imagined, but it was Betsy Nan thought of her first night in Warm Springs, when she opened her own suitcase in the colored dormitory and made a nest of it for Wilson. Well, it was Carlotta Rawls's suitcase, leather, with brass clasps, too large for all of Nan's things. She lined one side of it with sackcloth diapers, stacked her clothes in the other side so it would lie flat on the floor. She slept lightly, as she always did, and woke with a start from a dream that the jaws of the suitcase had snapped shut, trapping Wilson inside. She was sleeping on the bottom of a bunk and slammed her head on the bed above as she sat up.

A light went on. A girl's bare legs swung over the edge of the top bunk. "You all right, little momma?"

The girl was as little as Nan, a daughter or granddaughter or niece of Aubie's, but she talked like she'd never not known everything there was to know. She hopped down from the bunk, landing easily on her two feet. She wore two swinging braids on either side of her lollipop neck. Her name was Elvie.

Nan nodded and leaned down to the suitcase, where Wilson was breathing roughly in his sleep. As he slept, his hands and feet floated and then fell, as though he were trying to keep from swimming up to the ceiling. He winced and stirred. Was it the light that was bothering him? She looked closer. Elvie knelt beside her. His hands were swollen hugely, two purple rubber mittens. Nan peeled off his socks—his feet too. His feet were swollen too.

She scooped him up and shuttled him to her bed, and as soon as he was in her lap he was awake, howling. His eyes opened and locked on to hers. He looked at her and he howled and his hot little body twisted in her lap and she had to struggle to hold him still, to keep him from slipping to the floor like a bar of soap. In waking he had remembered how to cry. He had remembered he was in pain. She shouldn't have moved him. She shouldn't have woken him.

"Poor baby," Elvie said. "He's got colic."

Nan shook her head firmly. No. No, he did not have colic. His forehead was clammy, his whole body hot except his hands and feet, which were cold to the touch.

Holding Wilson to her shoulder, she nodded toward the door. Elvie looked at her blankly.

"You want me to leave?"

Nan pointed at the door, more fiercely. She made a loop—pointing, then returning her finger to the room.

"You want me to come back?"

Nan stomped. She walked her fingers, two racing legs, through the air. She leapt up and began to scribble with an invisible pen against the door, her eyes darting about for a real pen, some paper.

"You want me to get help and come back," Elvie somehow managed. Proudly she got up and left the room. While she was gone Nan tried to quiet the baby with her breast, and though he latched on hungrily at first he began to cry again as soon as her milk was down, as though he'd forgotten how foul it tasted. Elvie came back with Aubie, stooped in a night bonnet, struggling to put on her eyeglasses. Once she had them on she took a long look at Wilson in Nan's arms. She didn't touch him.

She said over his howling, "This child got hand and mouth."

Nan opened her eyes wide, asking for more.

"Hand, foot, and mouth?" Aubie wondered, looking at the fat bottom of Wilson's foot. "One a them. Look at them feet. It's a childhood illness."

Nan nodded. Hand, foot, and mouth. A childhood illness.

"It'll pass with the fever."

Nan nodded. A fever. But Wilson was writhing in her arms. She couldn't seem to get him still. He needed a doctor. He needed Oliver.

She nodded toward the door again. She scrawled more words on an imaginary pad. Did nobody read or write in this place? She knelt down to a seated position and wheeled an imaginary chair.

Elvie said, "You want a wheelchair?"

Nan spun her free hand encouragingly. The door opened, and behind it, two other maids, their heads wrapped, their robes tied, peeked in.

"Who's crying?"

"It's the nurse's baby," Elvie said. "Little momma."

"She a nurse?"

"She don't know we ain't have no colored nurses here."

"If she a nurse," Aubie said, "she know it's hand and mouth. Baby's got a fever is all."

"Close that door. Gone wake the whole house."

"What time is it?"

"Time for that baby to quiet down."

"He needs an ice bath."

"Whose nurse is she?"

"Ain't the time for no midnight ice bath."

"Can't she talk?"

"Nuh-uh."

"She want a wheelchair," Elvie told them.

Nan shook her head no.

"She want the governor?"

Nan stood still, considering. The governor would do.

Aubie laughed a tired laugh. "He won't be keen on getting woke in the middle of the night by no sick colored child."

"I ain't keen on it, either," another woman said, appearing in the door and opening it wider.

"He's just a baby," Elvie said.

"What's he got?"

"Hand foot mouth," Aubie said. "Just a fever. Y'all go back to bed." The women left, Aubie the last of them. "Try to keep that baby quiet now. Ply him with milk. We ain't need no attention called on us." When the door was nearly closed, she put her head back in and said, "Don't be getting no ideas about going to no crippled white folks' hotel."

Elvie swung herself up to the top bunk and turned out the light. "Good night, little momma. Good night, little man."

For a moment the darkness seemed to startle Wilson's cries quiet. His body stilled. Perhaps it had been the light after all that had set him off. Nan felt her heart slow and realized how madly it had been pounding. It was quiet enough to hear Elvie's nose whistling like a child's toy.

Carefully she slid back on the bed to the concrete wall and rested against it, not daring to move Wilson from her arms. For what might have been a few minutes, the two dozed together in peaceful exhaustion. But all the while her mind did the restless math it did through her dreams—where was Wilson, where was Winna, where was Elma, where was Juke, the distance to the closest bed, the closest door.

Then she woke suddenly in the darkness, understanding her mistake. The room was too quiet. Wilson lay still in her arms, too still. His body was boiling.

Without stopping to think it through, to question, to take a blanket, she leapt out of bed and stalked barefoot through the door and, closing it quietly behind her, through the hall. The hall was long and concrete and featureless and lit by a trail of high bulbs against which her eyes strained. She did not know her way. She turned to the left, tiptoeing fast, and when she couldn't find a door, turned right. She tiptoed as though the concrete floor burned her feet. Finally she found the exit and went out into the night. There was a sidewalk under her feet and she followed it. There was a moon and she found it. In the shadowy distance, couched in a horizon of pines, she could see the shape of a house, large, dark, hulking. It wasn't the governor's house, but she went to it. Was it the crippled folks' hotel? Was it where she would find Oliver? And was that a porch light on? The sky was swarming with stars, and she cranked her head back to drink them in. Orion, Cassiopeia, Castor and Pollux. She might have been walking the farm. She was under the same stars. She remembered the night she and Genus hid behind the bedsheet. And now she half-expected a clothesline to take off her head. Wilson lay hot and limp against her breast. He was sleeping. He was just sleeping. It seemed a mile between the dormitory and the inn, to the dim porch light swarmed with mosquitoes, and it seemed that was where she was going.

She must have been quiet as a shadow. She paused before the first porch step. In the white light, she thought she could make out a porch swing, and someone on it. She could hear the creaking of the chains. And then she must have made a sound, or Wilson did—was it Wilson?—because the someone moved, startled. The dark shape on the swing pulled apart and became two dark shapes. "Someone there?"

It was Q. L. Boothby's voice. In answer, Nan took two steps up the stairs and there they could see each other clearly. He wore a bath-robe, his pipe peeking out of its pocket, and without his hat she could see his hair was thinning. The someone next to him was a young man. She thought he was one of the men who had been playing cards the day before. Now he wore a pair of pinstripe pajamas. His dark wet hair was combed neatly, his hands were on his knees, his Adam's apple was trembling, and it was the first time Nan had seen a white man afraid. Beside the swing sat a black, empty wheelchair.

"Heaven's sake," said Mr. Boothby, standing up from the swing and coming down a step. "What in Heaven are you doing, girl, roaming about here in the middle of the night?"

He stood over her, hands on his hips, and she could see that his hands too were trembling.

By way of explanation, she shifted Wilson in her arms, showing him.

"What have you there?" he whispered, as though he had not seen a human child before. He did not understand because he was looking about, over her head, worried that someone else had heard, was coming. "Come inside," he said. "Get the hell out of the dark."

The young man had shifted himself into the wheelchair. "It's all right," Mr. Boothby told him, holding a finger to his lips. "It's all right. Better take care of this. Time to turn in. I'm sorry," he said. "Get some sleep."

Without a word, the man bowed his head and wheeled himself through the door Mr. Boothby held open for him, and then he wheeled himself across the black-and-white tiled lobby and disappeared down the hall. Nan stood looking after him. She found she wondered what it was his voice sounded like.

Mr. Boothby settled himself behind the great fortress of the front desk and lit his pipe. He picked up a pen and the pad of paper in front of him and pulled the telephone close, as though he'd been in the middle of a story and that was what she'd interrupted.

"I have a call to make."

She looked from the telephone to his face, and he looked away.

"It's three in the afternoon in Tokyo." Then: "I was interviewing that young man." He started to say more, then stopped. "What is it?" he asked her. "What are you looking for in the middle of the night? You'll get us both in hot water!"

Again she showed him the baby.

"You can't speak a word, can you?"

She gave her head a single shake.

"Not a word?"

She put her hand to Wilson's cheek, his feverish forehead, but Q. L. Boothby was now looking past her, down the hall, and a smile came to his face. "I'm not the one who should be worried. Why should I be worried? You can't say a word."

She would not waste another minute. She leaned over the desk, spun the pad of paper around, and took the pen from the man's hand.

Flipping to a new sheet, she wrote in clear and tall letters, *NEED DR. RAWLS.*

He removed the pipe from his mouth. Slowly the smile fell from his face.

"Well, I'll be damned."

She did not have time for his admiration.

On a new line, she wrote, *MY SON IS DYING.*

———————

He was a doctor, and so it was his job to solve. To find a solution.

From the Latin *solutionem*—a loosening or unfastening. And from the Old French *solucion*—division, dissolving. It was the kind of division he could understand. Solving for *x*. Dissolving the tablets. Resolving. But also: the termination of a disease by a crisis. There were cases where crisis was the only cure.

He loved a crisis. He loved an emergency. When he was six, his sister had fallen from the roof, where she had climbed to rescue a lodged kite, and he had run to his father's office to fetch him, bare feet slapping the sidewalk, the adrenaline ballooning his lungs. He had never been happier. There was no high higher than saving someone, than solving.

Before a crisis could be solved, it had to be identified as a crisis. For Oliver, this was normally no difficulty. He would declare a sprain a crisis if it meant he could solve it. But when Quincy Boothby roused him from his bed with the note, he refused to accept the emergency.

"It's from the girl. Nancy. Did you know she writes?"

Maybe it was that shame of not knowing—he couldn't accept Nan's message because he couldn't believe that she'd written it. "No, no," he said without thinking. There had to be another explanation. He fumbled for his glasses. Then, as his bearings came to him, reading the note a third time, he said, "Yes, of course I knew. But it can't be so dire." He had just seen Wilson yesterday—he was feverish, but not dying. "Let's see the child."

It wouldn't do to bring him into Oliver's room. It was strange enough that both men were there in their pajamas. "Bring him into the exam room," Oliver said.

"Oliver. You know you can't do a thing like that."

Oliver shifted his legs over the edge of the bed, the good one and then the bad. "Is there no colored exam room?"

"I'm afraid not."

"Well, do they see no colored children here?" He reached for his wheelchair, his mind paging back through his summers, and dropped his arm. Of course he could not remember a single colored child in the waters.

"I'm afraid not."

Only now did he adopt the necessary outrage. "Quincy, my God. This is an emergency! It's the middle of the night! I will see him in the lobby."

In Nan's arms, Wilson looked smaller, like Winna Jean's rag doll. He was sleeping. Nan looked relieved and terrified all at once. She sat down in the chair across from the desk and Oliver wheeled over to her, his satchel in his lap, Wilson in hers. Quincy stood over his shoulder, puffing furiously on his pipe. Oliver took the baby's temperature; even the thermometer hung limply from his mouth. While they watched the mercury rise, Oliver counted his pulse. Listened to his heart. His lungs. He handled his poor swollen hands, his feet. He had the strange feeling that he was holding Daisy's hand—her hands too had been swollen, had been cold. His mind paged through the solutions. His own pulse raced. He knew nothing, he was a fraud—it was what he thought every time he fitted the stethoscope to his ears—but he knew enough to know that a quiet baby was worse than a crying one.

For many breaths they all waited in the cloud of pipe smoke, in the light of the tea-colored bulb. Nan sat in the wooden chair that was like the chair where he had first seen her with Wilson in her lap. He had thought he had known her then, that first day. He had thought he could save her. He had thought he could speak for her. And look—all this time she could speak for herself.

He reached out a hand and placed it on hers, which lay over Wilson's gently rising ribs. Then he slipped the thermometer from the baby's mouth and shook it. "He's not dying."

He felt her exhale.

"But he's sick. He's got an infection. What we call hand-foot syndrome. That's why he's so swelled up. The oxygen isn't getting to his extremities."

Nan nodded steadily.

"He needs fluids. When did he last eat?"

She weaved her head ambiguously.

Quincy tapped his shoulder. He handed him the pad of paper and a pen. Oliver considered. Then he rested the pad on his knees and fit the pen into her hand. She looked at him, as though to ask if he was sure. She wasn't so desperate now. She took her time to make the letters straight. On a clean sheet, she wrote, *Wont take my milk.*

Oliver swallowed. "All right, then. We'll see if he won't take some sugar water from a spoon. And we'll give him something to make him more comfortable." He zipped his bag. "Mr. Boothby, will you help me in the kitchen?"

Nan closed her hand around Oliver's wrist, keeping him there. With her pen, she wrote something else, and then she turned the pad toward him.

THANK YOU.

Oliver closed his eyes. He found he couldn't look at her. He nodded.

The kitchen reeked of boiled eggs. They fumbled along the wall until they found the light switch. They fumbled in the pantry until they found the sugar. Quincy warmed a kettle of water on the stove and Oliver tested the temperature on his wrist. Too hot. They added more cold water until Oliver was satisfied.

"Is he going to make it?" Quincy asked.

Oliver measured out a teaspoon of the morphine powder, its crystals feathery in the low kitchen light. "I believe so."

"What is it? What kind of infection?"

He released the powder into the water and stirred. "Splenic."

Quincy stared. Oliver turned to him.

"An infection of the spleen."

Quincy nodded. It meant nothing to him. Oliver's mind too still hadn't caught up. It was focused on performing the steps. He dried the spoon on his robe. He lowered it into the sugar. His mind was dosing out the word to him: *crisis crisis crisis*.

He plunged the sugar into the tumbler and stirred. He watched the cloud evaporate and the water clear.

"Splenic crisis," he said.

Quincy did not understand. He turned away and lifted the piece of paper he had brought to Oliver's room. He held it to the light. *MY SON*.

"What are we to believe here, Oliver? She's the child's mother all along?" Even at three o'clock in the morning, he was a newspaper reporter first.

Oliver stared through the tumbler on the counter.

"And Jesup is the father? Is that what we're to believe?"

Quincy studied the words as though they contained some kind of code. Oliver was as misguided as he was. For years he had studied the cells under slides, for years they had wallpapered his dreams. But never since Daisy had he seen the signs in a child in his care. Now he allowed it to settle over him, the satisfaction of the solution, the great dissolving relief of diagnosis, even with its deathly new weight.

No. Oliver thought the word but didn't say it. No, they weren't to believe it.

The next day is Easter. The maids are up early to dye the eggs. The eggs are blue and yellow and cotton-candy pink, but the kitchen still smells of them, of boiled eggs, which is to say rotten eggs, and will smell rotten for three more days, so that on Wednesday Aubie will go looking under the sink, in the cupboards, to be sure that a possum has not gone and died. By that time they will be gone from this place, Oliver and Wilson and Nan. Now the maids prepare coffee and grapefruit and bacon and eggs and, in small crystal bowls, grits, which Aubie says the governor enjoys with brown sugar. The maids laugh wickedly at this. One by one the trays disappear from the kitchen. Nan listens from her room for the kitchen to empty, and then she takes Wilson and tiptoes down the hall. Oliver has said he will meet her there. He will check on Wilson at eight o'clock. She will wait for him.

In the kitchen the dozen dozen eggs are drying on racks, and the breeze coming in the open window seems to make the smell not better but worse. The smell of the eggs makes Nan feel restless and crazed. Is she the only one who smells the smell of a dozen dozen boiled eggs? Wilson has slept a few hours that morning—he took the sugar water the night before; perhaps the medicine is working—but now he begins to cry again. Nan believes he is in pain and she is right, but he is also crying over the insult of the eggs in his nostrils, eggs which in another hour will be hidden by the maids under jutting rocks, in mounds of grass, at the webbed feet of pines, to be discovered another hour later by white children too lame to reach them: with this too the maids will help. There will be a child Elvie's age, twelve and a half, with two braids just like hers, who will sit perched in the throne of her wheelchair and point to an egg Elvie herself has hidden, clever girl, in a metal rainspout, and Elvie will clap her hands gamely for the child until she finds she can't get the egg out of the gutter, can't coax it out with a stick, can't shake it out, until she does, and the egg rolls out and falls to the ground and, to Elvie's disappointment, does not break. She will place it in the girl's basket on a cloud of Easter grass.

While Wilson sleeps in his suitcase and Nan in her bunk, Oliver has been lying in his room down the hall from the kitchen, not sleeping. The rotten smell hangs over his bed. At seven he is awake and dressed and on the telephone at the front desk of the lobby. The receiver tastes of Quincy Boothby's pipe tobacco. He is dialing Charles Mercer. It is a Sunday morning at seven o'clock, Easter Sunday. Charles Mercer does not answer the telephone at the office. He does not answer the telephone at his home. Charles Mercer is most likely eating Easter brunch in his mother's dining room. Oliver returns to his room and rolls his chair back and forth across its length. He is pacing. He returns to the front desk, places two more calls, returns to his room. What has kept Oliver awake, what keeps him pacing now, is not Wilson's illness—the baby will live, of that much he is sure—but his face. He tries to piece it together. Are his eyes hazel or green? His brow narrow or wide? He wants to know how a baby who has sickle cell disease could have the face of Juke Jesup. Because it is Juke Jesup's face that the baby has.

It is Elma's face. He closes his eyes. He tries for a moment to piece her face together. He can only see pieces at a time. He knows nothing at all.

Does she know? Elma? Does Nan know? Have they known all this time, and it's he who's been in the dark? Has his wife kept him—cruelly, unforgivably—in the dark?

He opens his eyes. He's getting ahead of himself: he needs more facts. He needs the blood.

There are seventeen Mercers in the Atlanta telephone directory he finds in a drawer of the desk. He has apologized to six of them by seven fifty in the morning, at which point he reaches a *Mercer, Mrs. Harold,* of Crescent Avenue, and is connected to Charles Mercer, his mentor and friend, who sounds as tired as Oliver is awake.

"Mercer!" he laughs. "I've found you!"

It's such a relief, such a victory, he forgets for a moment his reason for calling. He clears his throat.

"Mercer, the samples I sent you."

"Did you get them?"

"Did I get the samples?"

"Did you get the results."

"You tested them?"

"Sure I did. I've got the results here in my briefcase. I mailed them days ago. You didn't get them?"

He pictures the mail slot back on Main Street, the letters piling up on the mat.

"I'll be damned," says Oliver. "I've left that address, Mercer." Only as he says it does he understand it's true: he has left.

"I've been trying to reach you, Oliver. I called and called."

He had expected Mercer to be short-tempered, reluctant. "I'm sorry, Mercer."

"Listen. You want me to read them to you?"

"Please. Please, Mercer, if you don't mind."

Oliver can hear stirring on the other end of the line. "Hold on a minute." The sounds seem like kitchen sounds, and then he realizes he is hearing the sounds from the dining hall. The guests are coming down the stairs for their breakfast. Oliver looks at his watch. Nearly eight o'clock.

"All right," says Charles Mercer, "I've got them here."

"I'm ready," says Oliver.

Mercer reads the results with a level voice. Eight types, all told. Oliver records them on the notepad, hand trembling, ink pen bleeding, a column of letters down the right side—

ELMA JESUP:	O
NANCY SMITH:	O
JUKE JESUP:	A

WINNAFRED JESUP:	O
WILSON JESUP:	B
STERLING SMITH:	AB
FREDERICK WILSON:	O
GEORGE WILSON:	A

For several moments, the letters are as meaningless to Oliver as they are to Mercer. A report card of sorts. The characters might as well be numbers, or another language. Oliver cups his hand around them, to protect them from view. "All right," he says. He must focus. He must eliminate. He circles three of the names:

NANCY SMITH:	O
JUKE JESUP:	A
WILSON JESUP:	B

He draws a chart, arrows; he underlines. Nobody, including Oliver himself, could be asked to make any sense of them. He adds a final name and a final letter, which he has memorized from the autopsy report:

GENUS JACKSON:	B

"Mercer, I don't have my books with me. I'm a little foggy on the types. The child. Wilson Jesup."

"He's a B."

"Which means . . ." He doesn't want to say it out loud, but he feels he must make certain. "Which means he can't be son to an A."

"That's right," says Mercer.

"But a B."

"He could be son to a B."

"All right," says Oliver. He swallows. "All right, then. You're sure, Mercer?"

"We ran all the slides twice. We were slow around the lab, needed something for the new technician to get her hands on."

"You got a new technician? A woman?"

"Don't be sore, Oliver. We ain't paying her much. She's just a kid, needed the hours."

"I'll be damned," says Oliver.

"Don't be sore. It's a good thing we did. I had a feeling. We ran the child's sample."

"Wilson?"

"Never seen sickles sharp as that, Oliver. Telltale." Mercer can hardly keep the excitement out of his voice. "Poor pickaninny's inherited more than a blood type."

"I suspected," Oliver says.

"I was calling and calling. He's going to need care."

"He'll get care."

"I'm glad you reached me, Oliver."

"Mercer, you'll keep it confidential. I don't have to ask you—"

"Of course, of course."

He sits for a moment, looking at the pad. From the dining hall comes the ringing of forks and spoons. The letters merge and part like cells under a slide. He is happening on something, something frightful. His mind is working against it as hard as it is working toward it.

"Oliver."

When he looks up, Quincy Boothby is standing beside the front desk, wearing a fresh gray suit with a red handkerchief blooming from its pocket. He stands with his hands behind his back, his mouth around an unlit pipe, waiting.

"All right then," Oliver says into the phone. "Thank you kindly."

He hangs up, folds the paper into quarters, and places it in the breast pocket of his own suit.

"What you got there?"

He stands. "Nothing of worldly concern." What is recorded in his pocket will not be printed in a newspaper. He will not burn it. He is too afraid he'll forget it. But he will keep it hidden, a code only he can discern.

"We all want to know the truth, Oliver."

"Why? Why do we? What good does it do us?"

"It doesn't. It doesn't do us any good."

"Stop being a reporter, Quincy. For Heaven's sake, for five minutes, stop being a reporter."

Quincy removes his pipe and smiles. "What shall I be?"

Oliver says, "Be a man."

———

So for the hour after breakfast, while the children inch their chairs across the green lawn and the maids follow behind them, their white aprons feather-dusting the grass, the baskets filling contentedly with eggs, the sky above them all a fragile Easter-egg blue, the distant radio singing "The Old Rugged Cross," Q. L. Boothby stands guard outside the white walls of the springs and Aubie stands guard inside them. They each know something about sneaking into the springs at night, and they don't ask questions. Oliver once daydreamt about doing the same with his wife. Or they'd slip out to the lawn, and Elma would lay out a blanket and undress with him under the stars and at last they'd be husband and wife to each other. That was the kind of place it was, he thought. He was a man of medicine, and yet he had seen lame children stand from their wheelchairs and walk. What might it have done for him, had his wife been there?

Now Nan helps him slide out of his chair and into the water. There might be an hour left of its magic, he hopes, before it turns cold and bitter, drained of its healing powers. He wears the bathing suit he's packed in his suitcase, the one he's worn season after season, when he was a man young enough to believe that this place was any better than any other. Nan wears an old suit borrowed from the young maid named Elvie, though the only occasion Elvie ever has to wear it is to a swimming hole carved out of the woods not far off, where she likes to slip away to meet the boy who shoes horses on the neighboring farm, lying on the flat rock like a lizard drying in the sun. It's a white suit with a full flounced skirt, and in it Nan's long, thin arms and legs look darker, and in his black suit, Oliver's thin arms and legs look lighter. His left leg is as thin as Nan's. He watches her watch him. They slip their slim bodies into the pool. And then Aubie slips Wilson, naked, into his mother's arms.

At first, he braces. His little back buckles. He cries out, and Nan tenses, and he tenses too. The water is warm, heavenly warm to Nan—she understands all at once its allure, understands how chilly the air was—but how does it feel against the baby's feverish skin? Too hot? Too cold? She holds him at chest height, one arm behind his head, trying to help him float on his back. He squirms, then stills, his eyes rolling back, and then he pisses, startled, legs churning, into the holy water. They laugh with relief because his body is doing the most ordinary thing it knows how to do.

"The water will regulate his temperature," Oliver tells her.

She nods. She can see what the water does to Oliver too—how steady he is, how straight.

"It will help with the circulation. The swelling."

She nods.

"Inflammation. The pain."

She nods.

"It's the magnesium. It's not like bathwater," he says, as though she has objected. Too often her silence is mistaken for objection. Too often her silence is mistaken for assent. She is assenting. What other choice does she have? She is wondering what her mother would do if she were here. What herbs she would stuff into a poultice for Wilson's hands and feet. Why not believe in the magic waters? She senses Oliver is stalling, and he is. The truth is, there is not yet much to be done. Even at the colored hospital in Americus, where they will find themselves by the end of the day, where Wilson will be admitted to his own room, where they will not need anyone to stand guard at the door, they will only be able to administer the morphine Oliver has already given him, and pump his little body full of fluids. It will be years before transfusions will become common for sickle cell, but already Oliver is thinking, *I would give him my blood if I could*, imagines it coursing, oxygen-blue, through the little boy's veins, though he knows very well that his blood would not take, that Wilson is a B—how will he tell her?—and that he, like Juke Jesup, like George Wilson—curse his blood—is an A.

He cannot save him. Wilson has his own blood, with its own curse.

"Nan," he begins.

Nan is cupping her hands with the silky water and letting it slide over the boy's belly. The boy likes this. It calms him. In another time, in another country, they might have been a family. They might have been lovers. Aubie, indeed, watching from afar, believes that Oliver is the child's father. She sees the child's light skin, his green eyes, his red hair, sees the way the doctor is studying the child's face, reading it, as though looking for his own. But it's another man's face the doctor is looking for. Problem is, he doesn't know what that man's face looks like. Only Nan knows for sure anymore. Aubie cannot hear the words that pass between them. She watches from the deck, folding the white towels that are warm from the line. The radio floats over the wall and ripples on the water. She believes they're the words of star-crossed lovers stealing a few minutes together with their sick child, and who is she to deprive them of their privacy? She doesn't know that his words are bringing her the greatest sadness and the greatest joy of her life—the name of the child's illness, and the name of his father.

She sees the girl cry. She hears her. It is a hard sound to hear, the sound of a mute girl crying. Even if the girl did not have such a hard time making sounds, it would be hard to know what pain brought them. If Aubie had to bet, and she makes a bet with herself, folding a towel over her arm, she'd bet that the crying is the crying of a girl who must leave her lover.

Oliver puts his arm on Nan's shoulder. Her tears bring him pain, but also relief: She did not know. She did not lie. Elma did not lie. Together they help to hold Wilson in the water. For a moment he seems to float between them, a turtle on his back. His eyes shine up at the sky, glass-bottle green. Jesup eyes. Looking at the child, his wife's face finally takes form in front of him.

There is something else he must tell Nan. Something else the letters have spelled. Sitting at the front desk, after Quincy had left, he took a final look at the notepaper, unfolding it from his jacket pocket, to be certain.

STERLING SMITH: AB

It was the rarest of the types, rare enough that he knew no man of that type could be father to a child of O.

There at the desk, he let the force of the fact come to him. From the kitchen, the smell of the hard-boiled eggs turned his stomach.

"Good God," he said aloud.

Now, in the water, he watches Nan watch her child.

Must he tell her? That the father she has loved, who has returned to her, isn't her father at all? That the reason her baby has Juke Jesup's face is that he isn't her baby's father, but hers?

In the coming years, as her face fills out to its womanly proportions, the possibility will cross her mind—skate over it, never landing on its feet. She will look at her own face in the mirror and see Juke. She will see George Wilson. She will see the face of the mule breeder, whose name, she does not know, is Early Bledsoe, whose face she doesn't know, either. She will see in her face the face of old white men. By then, she'll be old enough, she'll have loved enough, to imagine what sins might have driven her mother mad enough to take her own child's voice. She'll think of her not with judgment but sympathy as she looks at the men in the market, at the swimming pool, at the many doctors' offices she will visit with Wilson, in cities in the South and cities in the North, colored men, white men, Indian men, men from distant continents. In them she will see her face. She will think that, if you go deep enough into history, anybody could be your father, and each time she is surprised when the thought brings her not just despair but comfort.

She will not see her face in Sterling's face, but she will see Sterling's face in Sterling's face, for he won't be just a memory to her, not for a long time. She will have him there with her, his face, his own face, and that is enough.

But she will never again doubt that Genus is her child's father. What Oliver tells her in Warm Springs will settle in her like clay. Of course: of course he is. Despite the shape of the cells in his blood, Wilson will grow up to live longer than his blood-cursed father, longer than his grandmother with her poisoned tongue. He will eat grapefruit, travel across the ocean, read English and Latin and Greek, play baseball, build a house, watch a movie in a darkened theater with a white girl he loves. He will be tall like his father, with his father's soft voice and deep laugh and large hands, and he will become a father himself. He will walk his father's walk, long, loping steps, bending his back like a sickle to ease the pain in his gut, though he will try not to, because it makes his mother close her eyes. He will try not to drink alcohol, because that makes his mother close her eyes too. It will be the morphine, then, he comes to depend on, the morphine fed to him since he was a baby, mixed with a sugar spoon, morphine he can find all too easily from the doctor who for a short time is a kind of father to him. The doctor will spend many years shaking his head sadly. More than once he will have to close the door to the boy, when he is not a boy any longer. More than once the mother will have to find a new hiding place for her coin purse. The mother too will have to send the boy away. She will always open the door again, because she will always be sorry that, when he was born, when she saw his face emerge from her, she did not have the faith to believe his father was his father. And because of these things she will love him too much.

Now the mother and the doctor hold the boy in the water. He is breathing in the sky. The boy is hers, and he is his father's. Why deny her what blessing there is to find in this moment? Why must blood be thicker than water?

So he doesn't tell her the rest. No one else will know what Oliver knows—not Nan or Elma or, he must believe, Juke himself. Even a beast as great as he could not know his own beastliness.

Oliver has already told one lie that morning, and now it will be two. After he hung up with Mercer, after he was free of Quincy, and after he looked once more at the folded paper, he sat for a moment in the front lobby, the plates and glasses still clattering down the hall. He steadied his breath. He thought about what George Wilson had told him in his office. He'd said, "A Wilson takes care of his own, but only if they blood." He thought about the way his own father had tried and failed to leave something for his children. Oliver had thought George was talking about Freddie, but now he understood the only thing that would drive a dying man to such lengths, why he'd insisted on Oliver taking his own blood: he was talking about himself.

Before he lost his nerve, he picked up the telephone again and dialed the number on George Wilson's card. When he answered, Oliver said, "You told me to guess. This is me guessing." He said, "You want to know if Nancy Smith is your daughter." George was silent. Was he pleased? Fearful? He told the old man what he thought he wanted, despite himself, to hear. There were two men who could have been father to Nan, and though he believed with all he knew that it wasn't George Wilson, he gave her the father who might do her more good than harm. "You aren't to tell her. She already has a father she loves. But if you don't see that she's provided for, I will see that every paper in Georgia knows what God knows."

The springs are more like blood than water anyway, placental, plasmic, magnesium rich. The three of them are bathing in it, Oliver, Nan, and Wilson, this fluid their bodies are not supposed to share. Over the white wall, the Easter egg hunt goes on. The children shriek happily. The radio asks, *Are you washed in the blood of the lamb?* They are washed. They are washing Wilson, making him new. A verse comes to Oliver, a bit of Scripture Irene has written for him to find in his memory right now: *This is He who came by water and blood.* He finds the rest of the words, speaks them out loud: *"And this is the testimony, that God gave us eternal life, and this life is in His Son."*

Nan isn't thinking of Scripture. She is thinking of Genus, standing in the cool creek with him, the water up to their ribs—like this—the stones under their feet.

She is thinking of Wilson, his baptism in that creek. He was in another mother's arms then. He was given another man's name.

Now she lifts the slippery baby and asks his forgiveness. She will not allow that to happen again. She will give him a new name. She does not wait for the doctor to anoint them. She holds Wilson to her breast and together they go under.

They are safe. They are underwater. They are washed in the warm womb of the springs. She opens her eyes. She speaks his name to him through the water: *Wilson Jackson. Wilson Jackson. Wilson Jackson.* His eyes are open too. The walls of the pool are the smooth white inside of an eggshell. The blue sky is very far away.

And then they rise.

THIRTY-FIVE

KETTY WOKE TO A MOUTH FULL OF ASHES AND KNEW SHE WAS pregnant. She didn't tell anyone, not right away. She weighed one breast, then the other.

One of the cows was pregnant too. A couple months before, George Wilson had brought over a big brown bull and turned it loose with them a few hours. It was Maggie he liked. She'd calved June the summer before and still gave good milk, and now her udders were as full as Ketty's, and like Ketty she vomited and trembled and refused to eat. Maggie's breath smelled like spoiled fruit. Ketty thought it was just the pregnancy.

But then the men became sick. Juke and Sterling. They spent most of three days in the privy together. She didn't like that. What might they talk about, for three days? When they were well enough to eat again, she made them grits with milk. Then they were sick all over again. She thought they might die, both of them, together in the privy. Did she want them to die? Ketty thought about it. She hadn't been able to tolerate milk since her first week of pregnancy, and at nearly four years old, Elma would still drink only Ida's. It was only the men who'd drunk Maggie's milk, and it was the north field Maggie had been in when that bull had found her. The thought came to Ketty in the early hours of the morning and wouldn't let her go back to sleep. After breakfast she went out to the north field and discovered the white snakeroot growing along the fence, innocent as baby's breath. She thought about going back for the machete and chopping it down. Then Elma came running through the tall grass and asked what was she looking at.

"Don't touch them flowers. See the little white ones? They'll poison you, you eat those. Tell me you won't touch them."

Elma told her she wouldn't.

Maggie was a black and white cow, more freckled than spotted, and she was sick. Ketty kept her out of the north field. She kept her milk in the bucket and the bucket in the creek, which was still cold. When the men didn't die, and could eat again, she gave them Ida's milk. She even put June on Ida's tit, and even June liked it.

She waited three months to tell them she was carrying. George first. He told her he'd have the doctor take care of it. She told him no doctor would touch her, and besides, didn't he know she knew her body, knew the times to keep to her husband's bed? It was the same thing she told Juke. You sure? they both asked her, George one night, Juke the next. The next night, Sterling lifted her up into his arms, tried to get her back into the bed right there. Men believed what they wanted to believe, and didn't believe what they didn't want to. At least, with Sterling, she could plead her sickness. And at least, she told herself, her child would grow up with Jessa's child. That was something. She weighed her breasts.

She thought Maggie might get better, like the men. She had thought she would let nature take its course. That was what a midwife did: she didn't interfere with what the body wanted; she helped it along. She said to herself that her body, like Maggie's, must want a baby.

The two of them had talked of babies, Ketty and Jessa, fussing over their needles in lamplight, over their new husbands' socks: what their faces would look like, what their names would be. When Jessa died, Ketty darned both men's socks. And she let out the hem of Jessa's dresses. Ketty's hips and shoulders were wider, so she slit them down their spines and sewed panels in them. She had been wearing the green one when Juke had taken her for himself the night three months before, the night she was certain it was him and no one else. Usually he asked, usually he was nice, but that night he had not asked, he was not nice. She would not have been so foolish as to find herself in his bed, knowing she was ripe. "It's that dress," he said, accusation and apology. He'd put her on her knees and ripped the panel out of the back. And the next evening she had sewed it back again.

Well, she had wanted to live Jessa's life, in Jessa's house, with Jessa's man, mother to Jessa's child—this was what she had asked for.

Would she serve the milk cold, in a glass? Would she make buttermilk out of it, and bake it into biscuits?

It hadn't killed them yet. Would it kill them now? Perhaps if they had enough. But what if they didn't have enough? Was it Sterling she wanted to kill, for loving her? Or Juke, for taking her for himself, even if some nights she could crawl deep enough inside Jessa's dress she thought she could see through to loving him? Well, this is what she'd asked for. Maybe it was she who should drink the poisoned milk. Would her child be poisoned too? Was that what she wanted—to do herself what she'd refused the doctor to do?

Maggie grew as Ketty did. She wondered which of them would give birth first. She let nature take its course.

And then Maggie lay down on her side and died. Ketty cut the calf out, but it was too late. June went on suckling from Ida.

Ketty had a funny thought: that cow had been mother to them. All motherless, they had drunk Maggie's milk. And now Ketty would be a mother. She kicked the milk bucket into the creek and it was a white cloud in the water, and too late Ketty thought of the fish, and then she thought: Yes. It was right, that some creature should die, and that it should be the fish.

———————

Years later, it was the same ashy taste of death in her mouth, a tin spoon she couldn't spit out. She might have thought she was pregnant again, but even Juke wouldn't come near her, so foul was her breath. All the men who had taken her over and over, all the men she had spared, and now she was dying.

She wasn't alone. She had a daughter. What a daughter was good for was to wash you before you died. "Wash me like it's Sunday, honey," she said, and Nan did, in the zinc tub in the shack, evening light coming in the window. She washed and dried her mother's feet, and under her low-slung breasts, and kneaded almond oil into her hair. When she was clean, Ketty might have put on the green dress, but she asked Nan to bring her her own blue one instead, the one she'd worn the day she met Sterling Smith in church, the one she'd worn in that church on their wedding. Alone she wore the blue dress into the north field, picked a bouquet of the white snakeroot, and ate it. She did not mean to punish herself. (She had done that long ago, when she'd taken her daughter's tongue. For the fish hadn't been enough. The cow hadn't been enough. She'd had to do something else she couldn't undo.) She was just putting herself to sleep.

"I'm just gone close my eyes," she told Nan, coming in from the field. Already she could feel death stealing through her body like the milk cloud in the water. She kissed her daughter on the forehead, lay down on her cot, and crossed her hands over her belly. She was not brave, and she was sorry for it.

THIRTY-SIX

FTER OLIVER AND NAN AND WILSON HAD LEFT HER AT THE farm, Elma drew some water from the well, found some splinters of lightered wood for the stove, and started a stew. She felt the kitchen rise up around her. She took off her shoes and felt the wood floor find the shape of her feet. She sighed. "Okay, Winna girl. Winna Jean Bean." She put the baby down alone on the rag rug, gave her two wooden spoons to play with. The pantry was all but empty, but she found some gnarled potatoes and went about sawing off their eyes. The kitchen filled with the damp earthy smell of potato skins. Under it was lye soap and cinnamon and lamp oil and Nan. She'd been home for five minutes and she was crying over the potatoes. The paring knife shook in her hands. Winna beat the floor with the spoons. *El-ma. El-ma.*

"Little drummer girl," Juke said, coming in the door.

Elma jumped. She let the knife clang onto the hunt-board slab.

"Scared me, Daddy."

Juke wiped his boots on the mat and hung his straw hat by the door. He looked thinner, his shoulders narrow, his cheeks sunken.

Glory's cooking had fattened him up last spring and now it was spring again and there was no one to keep him fat.

"You staying?"

"For a while."

"How long?"

She wiped her face on her apron. "Till the trial, I guess. Till all this passes."

He came into the kitchen and knelt down next to Winna Jean. "She likes them spoons. Got her a good ear." He worked one of the spoons out of her hand and tickled her under the chin with it, then handed it back to her. "Tell you what," he said to Elma. "I don't like Nan running off with that husband of yours."

"They ain't running off," she said, though she could think of no better way of putting it. "Oliver goes there sometimes, to get well. Wilson's awful sick. Oliver can keep a watch on him."

"And why ain't you go with them?"

Elma turned back to the slab and picked up the knife and resumed her peeling. "Someone's got to cook for you. You look like skin and bones."

"I been eating poor," he admitted.

"Besides," she said, working up her nerve, "he ain't my child. You made sure everyone in that courthouse knows it."

He stood up, but she couldn't see him. She was chopping the potatoes, her left hand planted on her right, her body rocking with each chop. He went for the tobacco tin in his chest pocket.

"Why'd you tell, Daddy?"

When he didn't answer, she turned around and looked at him over her shoulder. His eyes were a rheumy river green, the crow's-feet etched deeply around them. When she'd last seen him, at the courthouse, it had been winter, and now the skin between his cheeks and his ears was red and raw, like side meat.

"All that time you made me tell a lie, Daddy. And then you went and told. You made a liar out of me."

"Aw, girl. You ain't proud of your daddy, talking himself out of jail? Look at me. I'm standing here before you, ain't I?"

Elma shook her head. "'Proud' ain't the word."

He stuffed his mouth with chaw and said around it, "Well, you do what you do to get out of trouble."

She turned her back again. Through the kitchen window, Uncle Sterling was leading April and Anna out to pasture. She thought: Tell him. Warn him.

She went on chopping. Winna went on drumming. She hoped her father would say something else. When he didn't, she said, "Neither one of us out a trouble yet."

For two days it went on like that, the three of them in silent orbit around the farm. On Saturday, Juke trapped a possum—he had no gun anymore to hunt with—and Elma made a potpie of it. Easter Sunday, Sterling caught some trout and Elma fried them. They shared the meals but took them under separate roofs, Elma delivering them out to Sterling in the shack, Sterling saying, "Thank you kindly." Each time she knocked on his door she was fixed on saying, "Sterling, I come to talk some sense into you." Or "I know what Mr. Wilson put on you, Sterling. But I know you wouldn't hurt a fly." That was the way to do it, she reasoned—appeal to his good nature.

Then she'd remember the note Nan had left her with. *Look after him.* Look after Sterling. Elma had nodded, hadn't she? Wasn't that a promise? Wasn't that her word?

But now she was on the farm and she saw how powerless she was to stop either one of them from harming the other. What was she to do? Raise a white flag? Throw herself between them? She couldn't be everywhere. There was a baby to care for. There were meals to cook. That was what she could do, after all. Feed them, keep them alive.

And watch them. Through the kitchen window, she tracked their figures across the field, her father to the outhouse, Sterling to the barn. She cut herself twice, looking out that window when she should have been looking at what she was cutting. The second time, cleaning the last of Sterling's fish late Monday morning, she cut a deep gash in the web between her finger and thumb. She tore off a strip of her apron and bandaged it, but still her hand shook. Her vision went white and she held tight to the table's edge. The paring knife lay on the cutting board, red with her blood. How easily she had opened up the poor fish! She would leave it its head, the little gems of its eyes, its frowning mouth. Suddenly her eyes found all the sharp things, all the things in the kitchen that might make someone bleed—the knives, the cleaver, the corkscrew. She gathered them all up in what was left of her apron, left Winna Jean on the floor, and went out to the well. She dumped it all like scrap metal, the blades flashing as they sliced the surface. She watched the water ripple and then go smooth again. Very far below, she could see her reflection, and the blue sky above her.

Someone might fall down that well and drown. Her father had warned her about it when she was a child.

She whipped her head about the farm. Someone might get trampled by a mule, or fall from a hayloft, or get hanged from a tree.

What was she to do? Throw every blade on the farm down the well? The hacksaw? The hoes? How was she to cook without a knife?

She could see Sterling in the west field, plowing away from her. She went to the shack and let herself in. In the drawer, she found a single knife, a carving knife Ketty had once used. It was rusty but its blade was sharp.

Back in the kitchen in the big house, Winna sat perfectly still on the rug.

"I know," Elma said. "That was dumb."

Winna said, "Da da da."

Then she heard an engine out on the road. It didn't sound like a regular automobile engine. It was puttering. It was more than one engine, then a lot more. A horn sounded, then another. She put the knife down, picked up Winna, and went out to the front porch.

A chain of vehicles was making its slow way west down the newly paved Straight. Elma might have thought it was a parade, or a funeral procession, but what was holding up the traffic, at the head of the line, and turning now into the driveway of the crossroads farm, was George Wilson. He was riding a denim blue Caterpillar tractor. Pulling in behind him, his arm hanging out the window of his green Chevy truck, was Freddie.

"Oh, good Lord," she said.

They had seen her already. There was no hiding in the kitchen. She stood there frozen on the porch while they pulled around the house into the scrubgrass yard. By the time it occurred to her to go through to the back porch and ring the dinner bell for her father, two other trucks had pulled in behind them. Jeb Simmons and Bill Cousins stepped out, a son tagging along with each. How long had it been since George Wilson had been to the farm? Now he was climbing off a tractor in a pair of Sears, Roebuck overalls—overalls!—that looked like they'd been ironed and starched, or else come straight out of the mail. Elma had never before seen him in anything but his white suit and vest and tie, which might have been the only thing more preposterous to ride a tractor in. She might have laughed about it with Nan, if Nan had been there.

Freddie stepped out of the truck and ashed his cigarette into the dirt. He was wearing the blue silk eye patch his grandmother had bought him. With his other eye he squinted up at her on the back porch. "Morning, Mrs. Rawls."

She was surprised at her own relief. Get it over with, she thought. "Freddie."

"What'd you do to your hand?"

She looked at the bandage across her left palm. It had pretty well soaked through with blood.

"Fish got me. What'd you do to your eye?"

Freddie took a pull from his cigarette and looked off. "Rooster got me."

"Morning, Mrs. Rawls," his grandfather said. "Freddie come to drive me home once I leave this tractor here." The other men chimed in with their greetings. They'd seen George Wilson on that tractor and they had to put their hands on it themselves. Well, she knew how to be in front of men, didn't she? She knew how to hold their attention. But they were looking at her differently now. Drink Simmons did not look her up and down, she thought, so much as through her. She set her jaw.

"My daddy's coming." She didn't mean it as a warning, but it sounded like one. They could look at her all they wanted. She'd stand there all day as long as someone else was there on the farm with her to break up the deathly silence she'd been living in. The sun beat down on them. Juke and Sterling came in from their separate fields and they all shook hands as though all was forgotten, and Elma thought maybe it was.

"Morning, Juke."

"Mr. Wilson."

"Fine morning."

"Jeb. Bill. Morning to you."

"Sterling."

"What you got there, Mr. Wilson?"

"L15." He patted its rump. "1929 model. Four cylinders. Come all the way from Illinois." He put the *s* on the end. Then the men gathered around the tractor like women gathered around a newborn. All the attention that had once been paid to the twins now turned to the Caterpillar tractor. So this was how it would be: not Parthenia Wilson's empty porch chatter but the men's version of it, grunts and whistles and well-I'll-be's. Elma cared not a lick about that tractor, but her whole body filled with gratitude for it, its dull hulk, its dumb distraction. "Nearly three tons of metal in there, boys." George Wilson bragged that he couldn't find a truck big enough to haul it. In fact, the tractor was powerful enough to do the hauling. The only time they'd had a tractor out to the farm before, one they'd borrowed from

Ben Hill County—remember?—was when they'd had to haul some drunk's wrecked truck out of the creek, and that tractor didn't have half the horsepower of this one. Bill Cousins had a rusted-out Case C back on his farm that was older than the war, and home to a family of uppity squirrels. A tractor that plowed and tilled, that did the work of mules and horses—that was something new. Elma slipped back into the house and made a pitcher of tea and left it on the porch—they could help themselves—and then went back inside to the fish she was cleaning. For a long while the men stood scattered in the yard, the chickens clucking, the guineas honking, more neighbors arriving, the men taking turns squatting to gaze up into the machine's private parts. They spent some time hitching the disk harrow to its rear. Once they got that accomplished, the engine groaned and sputtered and died. Bill Cousins sent his son back to his farm for some tool or another. Elma hummed as she watched them through the window. She didn't sing but she hummed. The knife was too large to bone the fish properly—her perfectly good boning knife was at the bottom of the well—but she let herself hum. Stupid girl, throwing away a perfectly good knife. It was a regular day, the sun was beating down, the men's voices pleasant in the yard.

"That's your daddy out there," she said to Winna Jean. "Wonder if he'll come in and see you." It was a pleasant sort of worry, that old worry about Freddie. "He's a dog," she said. "I'm sorry to say it." There it was. That was all there was to it.

"Da da da," said Winna.

The tractor roared to life again, its engine full-throated now. Even Elma looked up to admire it. The men clapped. She couldn't hear what they said after that. The tractor was too loud. But she remembered something. The drunk who'd wrecked his truck in the creek? It wasn't a truck. George Wilson hadn't even been there. It was a tractor he'd wrecked, and it had crushed his legs underneath. That was the way the story went. Elma had been a little girl. After that, her father had said you couldn't catch him near a tractor.

Now she watched her father climb onto it. He looked like a boy on a horse too big for him. It bucked out ahead of him once, and he held on to his hat and went off into the field, the disk harrow scraping its comb of rusty teeth behind him. The fields had been plowed but not yet tilled.

She remembered sitting in her father's lap over that harrow, in the seat that rode high on a pole over the disks. She remembered her surprise when her father had taught her that a round thing could be sharp. He'd drawn the tip of his thumb across one of the blades, showing her the bead of blood.

"Sterling," George Wilson said after he sent Juke off, after the other men had gone home, "let's have us a hunt."

"I want to go hunting," the white boy complained.

"Not this time, Freddie."

"What am I supposed to do?"

"Set in the truck. You can carry me home in an hour."

Freddie kicked one of the tires, then got in. From a locked box in the truck bed, Mr. Wilson removed two guns. One of them was a Savage 99 hammerless rifle. The other, a Winchester twelve-gauge shotgun, he handed to Sterling. The wood was worn, the metal barrel oily with fingerprints. Sterling had to turn it over a few times before he believed it was his.

"Told you I'd get it back for you." He gave Sterling a small smile. "Just took me a fair while."

It was a good feeling, setting off into the piney woods with the gun his father had taught him to hunt with, the handsome black dog bounding along at their side. He saw his little brothers, whose names were Thaddeus and William, running ahead of him in the woods with their walking sticks. He felt his father's arms around his arms, his father's cheek against his cheek, showing him how to draw up along the stock. Mr. Wilson had convinced him that he didn't need it, and so he'd convinced himself that he didn't want it, that a gun was im-personal. But a gun was personal, he thought, now that it was in his hands. Nothing was more personal than this gun.

"You said I didn't need no gun," he said, looping the strap around his neck.

"What you aim to kill supper with, then?"

Sterling followed Mr. Wilson into the woods along the road. Their boots crunched over the needles. From behind them, in the north field, they could hear the distant drone of the tractor.

"We really aim to kill supper?"

"Sure." Without taking his eyes off Sterling, Mr. Wilson aimed his rifle into the head of a slash pine and pulled the trigger. A skittish flock scattered out of the treetops, but nothing fell to the ground. The dog barked, pleased. "Go ahead, Sterling."

Sterling aimed his gun up into the tree and squinted along the sight. But between Mr. Wilson's shot and the dog's bark they'd scared off anything around. "Ain't nothing to shoot at."

"That's all right. Shoot anyway."

Sterling looked to the old man. The old man nodded. Then Sterling looked back to the sight and shot up into the tree. He forgot what a kick it had. It nearly knocked him off his feet.

"Very good. You're a good shot, Sterling."

Sterling lowered his gun.

"You want to talk more, Mr. Wilson? Without anyone about?"

Mr. Wilson held his gun loosely, as though he might decide to shoot up into a tree at any time. "You're a clever one too, aren't you. Clever and strong." He began walking again, and Sterling and the dog followed, and they were walking together side by side, like they were out for a Sunday stroll. The woods were dark, but the light came down through the leaves onto their shoulders, and George Wilson told Sterling that he was to kill Juke Jesup with the Caterpillar tractor.

"With the tractor?" Sterling stopped.

"That's right."

"How my to do that?"

George Wilson spun his hands. "A Caterpillar is a dangerous machine. All those moving parts. The tracks. All manner of accidents happen with a tractor. Specially a tractor unbroken by an unschooled field hand."

"You want me to—to ram him with it?"

"Three tons of metal. It won't take much more than a bump, I reckon. That thing can lay a body flat. I've seen it happen myself."

Sterling closed his eyes. He tried to picture it. He felt the rumble of the machine and the skeletal crunch of Jesup's body under the steel tracks.

It was possible. But maybe he'd jump out of the way. Maybe the tractor would be too slow to catch him. It was so slow it had held up traffic all the way down the Straight, and then they couldn't even keep the thing running. It might conk clean out. It was about as probable as killing someone with a mule.

"A tractor?" He couldn't mask his disappointment. He looked down at his useless gun. "Ain't a gun more particular?"

Mr. Wilson smiled. "You want to try to explain that to the sheriff, go on and shoot him." He resumed walking, and Sterling followed. "I want to show you the land you fixing to come into, Sterling. I don't aim to turn it loose, mind you. The profits we'll divide. But in all respects it will be yours to work as you like. There's a mighty creek down that bank," he said, pointing, as though Sterling had not bathed in that creek for years of his life. "The soil's fine as you're like to find in Cotton County, not too rocky. Juke's let that west field run over with ragweed. Put all his time in the gin. I gave him too much control. I confused him." He shook his head, disappointed. "I let it happen."

"Ain't your fault," Sterling said, because he thought it was what he wanted to hear.

"Ain't no one's fault," said Mr. Wilson.

Sterling paused, because Mr. Wilson was panting and he thought he needed a rest. "Well, it's Jesup's fault, ain't it?"

Mr. Wilson looked up into the trees. A triangle of sunlight came to rest on the bridge of his nose. "I suppose so. If it's anyone's fault, it's his. It's all his fault, is one way to see it. Not just back to the Negro he killed." He hooked a thumb over his shoulder in the direction of the gourd tree. "From the time he was a boy, he was bringing trouble to this land. See that sandhill that way?" He pointed. "That big flat rock across it? Come here." He led Sterling to it and they stood over it and looked. "My boy String, I came across him once, he was watching a little baby gopher tortoise burn alive on this rock. I said, what in Hades you doing, child? John taught me, he says. John Jesup—he was John then—liked to come out here and turn the turtles on their backs. When they were little enough and it was hot enough, they'd fry on that rock in ten minutes. I turned the poor thing over. A tortoise gets stuck on its back, another tortoise'll come and right it. Flip it over. You seen that? Tortoises. But a boy, a certain kind of boy sees a creature in trouble and he doesn't right it. He just goes on and lets it burn." George Wilson could see his son there on the sandhill. Barefoot, sunburned, towheaded. "The devil was in Jesup even then. And he introduced the devil to my boy. String got it in his head to go off to the war. Lord knows he didn't have to. Got it in his head he was gone make his own path. Should have been Juke that went. I should have run that family off the farm." He shook his head. "Instead I tried to right him. I thought I could save him."

Sterling was crouching, peering into the burrow, and now he stood and looked at George with sympathetic eyes. "You got your hands dirty," he said, sounding as though he meant to agree.

"I never get my hands dirty," said George.

Sterling looked at him for more. Below and just out of their view, the creek trickled on.

"That's your job here, Sterling. Are we agreeing now? I'm a man of my word. I trust you are too."

They didn't shake on it. George saw no need. Sterling nodded, and that was good enough.

"What's the other way of looking at it, Mr. Wilson?"

"Beg your pardon?"

"You said it was one way of looking at it, that it was all Jesup's fault."

George paused, short of breath again. Leaned over with his hands on his knees. He hadn't worn overalls since he was a boy, and he felt like a child now. And yet he liked them, he liked Sterling, and though he'd pretended he'd had no partiality to it, he loved this farm where his children had grown tall. He should have been content to be a farmer. String had resented moving to town. They should have stayed and worked the land, the way George's father had. But his brothers had shamed him with their talk of railroads, turpentine, sawmills. The cotton mill had been his life's work and now it would be his death.

"I ain't got many more breaths in me, Sterling. Doc Rawls, before he died, said it's brown lung disease. What do you think of that?"

"Mr. Wilson." Sterling put out his hand and for a moment it grazed George's shoulder. "I'm awful sorry."

"Couldn't be pneumonia, cancer, no. Something respectable. Brown lung. Ain't nothing to be done for it. Ain't that something." That he was afflicted with the same disease that struck down his lintheads, a disease he'd brought on himself, breathing in his own toxic cotton dust, was a cosmic affront to his dignity—as great as losing String and Freddie to the devil. If that wasn't God's work, he didn't know what was.

"I reckon it's God's fault. God's joke. I reckon He's got Him a wicked sense of humor."

He had done his best to play God. He had never, unlike his grandson, deigned to kill a man by his own hand, though he had hired, arranged, seduced, dispatched, and dispensed with them—men and women—and had given orders to Doc Rawls to end more than one life before it began, which his wife would find more godless certainly than the decades of petty indiscretions, which she excused, and perhaps more godless even than killing a man who'd already lived part of his life. That the unlived lives belonged to his own offspring—well, if he could control that, if he could save a child from the vagaries of God, then he might also save himself from suffering their loss.

"Look," said Sterling Smith. He was crouching again, and slowly George Wilson lowered himself to the sandy ground and was crouching beside him. Through a fan of wiregrass, a gopher tortoise came lumbering out of its burrow. "Hey there," Sterling said, keeping his voice low. "You Tiny? You ain't so tiny anymore." Carefully he lifted the animal with two hands, inspected its belly, and returned it to the ground. "Maybe you Tiny's brother. Or her son." What did it matter? It was a tortoise; they were all tortoises. He gave the animal a stroke under its chin, like he might pet a dog's snout, and George saw that his own hand was reaching out to do the same, and he was filled with the slow, easy burn of love for the tortoise, and bitterness and awe, that this creature should live so many long years of contentment on this land, that it should survive from the hundreds of eggs its mother laid, that it had outlived its neverborn siblings and would outlive him.

"Your daughter," George said to Sterling. "Nancy."

Sterling looked up but didn't stop his petting.

"Where is she?" He had been hoping to see her. He had been hoping she, God help him, would see him, an old man in overalls. He had been hoping in some way to confirm with his own eyes what the doctor had called to tell him the day before.

"She on a trip to the polio springs with Dr. Oliver."

"She's with him there?"

"Yes, sir. Baby Wilson was sick. She wanted to stay with the doctor, I reckon."

Baby Wilson. George understood that the child was his grandson, but the name knocked out what air was left in his lungs. He'd raised three daughters—he didn't need any others—and had produced a dozen grandchildren, none of whom had ever set foot on any of his farms. But here on this farm, there would be not just Nancy but her children, and their children, and their children.

"She'll stay on the farm with you?"

"Yes, sir. I hope she will."

"She's a good little nurse."

"Midwife," said Sterling.

"Like her mother. Ketty," George reminded him.

He had not ended the girl's life before it began. No number of scarves and jewels could convince Ketty to submit to the doctor's knife. So the girl was born and Ketty had taken her own knife to her, and goddamn if George hadn't had a feeling about that child, and didn't have a feeling toward her now, a daughter he would never know. He had wanted to know what God knew so that he might leave her something, a roof over her head, crops in the field, so that he could go to his grave knowing the farm would be carried on by his kin, and so that he might take Juke Jesup's last piece of pride—not just removing him from the big house but putting a Negro in it, the Negro whose wife they had both thrashed about with. (He did not count Winnafred among his grandchildren. He had discovered her existence too late to cut down that tree at the root. If she was a Wilson, she was also a Jesup, and for that reason she would inherit no love from him. She would be Freddie's blood to bear.)

But now, looking at the big Negro, at his empty, ignorant face, this man who thought his daughter was his, his pity for him only grew. It made not a lick of sense—Ketty had belonged to Sterling, not to Juke; it should have been Sterling he tried to hate. And yet it was easier, wasn't it, to hate the man who'd done the same sin he had, taken Ketty from her husband's bed. One man he'd provide for and he was the one who'd kill the other. There would be no waiting for the court to settle its verdict, no allowing for the comfort of a jail cell. As long as he breathed, George Wilson would do God's business himself.

"I trust you'll take good care of this land, Sterling."

"Like it was my own, sir."

They left the tortoise to its burrow and began to walk again. The dog went ahead of them. Where the woods thinned into the west field, George took one more shot into the trees. Still nothing fell.

"That's all right, sir," Sterling said, because it seemed to him that Mr. Wilson had been trying this time, and that he was disappointed. Again Pollux barked, now disappointed too.

"Not *like* it was your own, Sterling. It will be yours."

"Sir?"

"I've changed my mind. What good will profits do me when I'm gone? The farm will be yours, Sterling, and Nancy and Wilson's, if you get this business done."

Sterling did not know how to answer. They traced the edge of the west field, heading toward the house, and Sterling thought, this could have been cane, this could have been peanuts, five acres for tobacco.

––––––––

Freddie Wilson heard the first two shots and he knew that he had time. His ears were not tuned enough to recognize that the shots came from two different guns, but they could tell that whoever fired them was in the woods, far off, far enough. Juke Jesup was far off too. Through the windshield of the Chevy, through his one good eye, Freddie could see him on the tractor floating along the distant edge of the north field. Months ago when Freddie was on the run, under the railroad trestle where he abandoned the truck, he had splintered the windshield handsomely with the Savage 99, making like the Meredith police had done it after he robbed the cotton bank. Later, after his grandfather drove him out to reclaim the truck, he'd tell folks in the mill village that that gunshot was how he'd lost sight in his eye, and though the truth was out, he did still like the sight of that shattered spiderweb, a bull's-eye big enough to put his finger through, which he did now. His grandmother had said to get the windshield fixed, but he didn't want to.

With his left foot, he eased open the truck door and stepped into the dirt. He put out his cigarette under his shoe. He didn't close the door. It was late afternoon, the shadows lengthening across the yard, the chickens and guineas giving him hungry looks. He might have cussed at them or thrown rocks, but he needed to be quiet. He needed to get back around the front of the house without Elma seeing him. The kitchen window faced the yard and the north field beyond it. Silently he went up the porch steps and through the screen door and into the kitchen. Her back was to him. She was facing the window, humming, stirring something in a bowl, her hand still bandaged. On the slab he could see flour, sugar, two broken eggshells. She was wearing a dress and an apron and no shoes. Her hair was in a long red braid down her back and Freddie's thought was that it would be easy to grab.

He was so intent on her that it took him a few moments to see the baby on the floor. It sat on the rag rug, looking back at him. In its mouth was a wooden spoon, sticky with what looked like cake batter. He made up his mind in the time it took to take four steps toward it that he would pick it up, and then he did. He had never picked up a baby before. His thought was that she—it was a she—was heavy and soft and warm.

"Pretty baby."

Elma turned, her braid whipping over her shoulder.

"She smells like cake."

Elma left the bowl she was stirring and marched over. She had a smudge of flour on her forehead. "Put her down."

"You making me a cake, little wife?"

"Put her down, Freddie."

"Why? I'm just saying hello." The baby's eyes were wide but she didn't cry. "Ain't you want me to come meet her? Say how do you do?"

Elma reached for the baby, trying to pull her from his arms. He stepped back, turned around, did a little dance.

"Give her to me!"

"I'm just having a little dance with my daughter. She's my daughter, ain't she?"

Elma stood with her hands on her hips. "What if I said she ain't?"

Freddie laughed. "Whose is she, then? The darky's?"

"What if she's my husband's? I ain't your little wife, you know."

He went on laughing. "Your husband's? The cripple?"

"He's father to her. More than you could be if you tried."

"So you changing your story again, are you? Just making up lies to suit you?"

"Freddie, please."

"That's my daughter you lying about. Saying she was a nigger twin. That's low, Elma. That's real low."

She stood still, breathing heavily. He could see her mind turning over.

"I wouldn't have done it, if it hadn't been for you." He nodded toward the rocking chair in the front room. "You sat right there in that chair and said you was raped by that nigger, Elma."

She opened her mouth to speak, then closed it. Her hands were on her hips but they were trembling.

"I'm sorry," she tried. "I'm sorry, Freddie."

"Oh, you playing nice now!"

"I'm sorry," she whispered. "Please give her to me."

"She ought to be ashamed, this poor child. Her momma being a lying whore." He made a sweet face at the baby. She still had the spoon in her hands. Freddie's thought was to take it from her and put it in his own mouth and lick it, and he did. "Mmmm. That's good. That's sweet." Then, her hands free, the baby reached up and grabbed his eye patch and popped it like a slingshot. It snapped against his eye.

"Ow!" It didn't hurt, but it startled him so much he dropped the spoon and nearly dropped the baby. Elma went to catch her but he whisked her away. He took four steps to the rocking chair and put the baby in it, roughly.

"Don't hurt her!"

He turned back to Elma and blocked her path. Then he reached around and grabbed her by the braid, hard. With his hand on the base of her neck, he pushed her toward the kitchen table. He bent her over at the waist and pressed her face to the surface. "You wanted to be nigger-raped, did you?" He leaned down and spoke low so that he could feel his hot breath wet in her ear. He needed to be quiet still. "You lying whore. No one's going to believe a word you say. Not this time."

"Please, Freddie."

"Don't holler. Don't you holler. Don't you even talk," he whispered, lifting her dress. "Or I'll take her. I'll kidnap me that baby."

Winnafred sat in the rocking chair, her feet in her hands. She tasted the sweet batter in her mouth. She heard the unfamiliar motor of the tractor outside. She felt the chair rocking and sensed that if she moved forward or back she would spill out, so she sat still. She watched with concern as her father raped her mother, though she would not know the word for what she was seeing for many years, and by the time she did, she would have no memory of what she saw, would have no memory of ever having seen her father at all. Her parents' eyes were closed. Her mother was quiet, as told, making only the low sounds people make when trying not to sound as though they've hurt themselves. Her father was louder, making the same sound but without restraint or regard, which was perhaps why he didn't seem to hear the tractor motor come to a shudder and stop, and a few moments later, the third gunshot from the woods. He struggled against her, the table moving, inching, bucking across the kitchen floor, pushing the rag rug along with it, nearing the west wall of the room that faced away from the window, away from the door. When her grandfather entered the house, her father had worked the table, and her mother over it, into the corner. In one silent stride, her grandfather saw what was happening. In five more he was across the kitchen, and her father, blind as he was in his right eye, didn't see him. She watched Juke's eyes find the carving knife on the tabletop where it lay beside the boned, watchful trout. Winna watched and the fish watched as Juke approached Freddie from behind, trying to find the best angle for the knife. He would have to be careful. He plunged it between Freddie's shoulder blades, Freddie still pressed to Elma, Elma still pressed to the table. He dragged the knife down Freddie's spine, gutting him, and then he pulled it out. Freddie's body went slack. It fell forward onto Elma like a flour sack. Then she did scream.

A number of things happened one after another. Elma slid herself out from under Freddie. She stood, stumbled. Her skirt fell. Freddie's body clung to the table, his upper half lying across it where hers had been. The knife had gone clean through him and the blood poured both ways, out his front and out his back, pooling under him and onto the table, flooding the back of his shirt. It had darkened the back of Elma's dress. Her braid was wet with it. Her hands were red with it, the bandage soaked through. Seeing all the blood, she began to cry, and only then did Winnafred, in the rocking chair, cry herself. Elma ran to her and lifted her and held her, and then the blood was on the baby's dress too.

Juke was breathing heavily, leaning over, his hand on one of the chairs. "Tractor died," he said. The knife was slick with blood but still in his hand. He expected Freddie to stand up and come at him any second, but he just lay there with his arms outstretched on the table, his cheek and patched eye pressed to it, his good eye, round and blue and unseeing, staring up at him. His pants lay around his boots; his white ass pointed toward the door.

That was the scene the dog came upon. Pollux was there first, her wet nose on the screen door, scratching. She had not barked, or if she'd barked, the people in the big house had not heard her. She barked now, the smell of blood strong in her nose. Juke took a step toward the door, the knife still in his hand, then stopped. What was there to be done now? He looked at Elma and said, "Ain't nothing else to be done."

"Daddy," she said. "Daddy."

"It's all right. Ain't nothing else to be done."

They listened to the footsteps come up the porch stairs. It was George Wilson who came up next. He pushed open the screen door and Pollux bolted in. George's eyes went from Freddie's body to Juke with the knife to Elma and Winna to Freddie again. Frantically the dog sniffed Freddie's boots, his pants, his bare behind. The blood dribbled from the table to the floor. Then Sterling came up and looked in through the door. "Holy Lord," he said.

"Come in here and get this dog away!" George Wilson said.

Sterling came in and slipped in the blood and took the dog by the scruff of the neck and dragged her out, saying, "Holy Lord, come on, girl, oh holy Lord." Sterling stayed on the porch with her. He and the dog looked back in.

George stood inside the door. The hunting rifle was still slung over his shoulder. They all were still for perhaps half a minute, listening to the blood drip to the floor. Then he took a few shuffling steps toward the table, went down on one knee, and put his face close to Freddie's. Freddie's eyes did not blink. Blood leaked out of his mouth.

"You done this," he said to Juke. He sounded as though he hoped for some other explanation, but there was the knife in his hand, the blade red with his grandson's blood.

"He was raping her."

George stood up. He looked to Elma. If he doubted this, his face didn't show it.

"You knifed him. You done it."

"Son of a bitch was raping my daughter. You would have done the same. Anyone would."

Sterling's eyes and the dog's eyes looked in on them through the screen.

"For pity's sake, honey." His voice broke. "You went and done it."

Juke swallowed. His hand had seized around the knife and a pain shot through his wrist but still he held on.

"Don't come closer," Juke said, his voice low.

"Juke. For pity's sake, Juke."

Juke's eyes flew from George's to Elma's and back. "Ain't nothing else to be done."

George shook his head. He looked up to the ceiling. He called for Sterling.

"Yes, sir," said Sterling through the screen door. It was coming on evening and the day had darkened behind Sterling and they could see little more than his silhouette and that of the shotgun crossed in front of him.

"Come in here, Sterling."

"Sir?"

"Come back in here and do what I asked you, Sterling."

A moment passed. The screen door didn't open. "I don't want to let that dog in, sir."

"Come in and leave the dog out, Sterling. Come on and get it over with. You can use your gun."

George was watching him and Juke was watching him and Elma was watching him. Winna was crying and at Sterling's feet Pollux was whining. Sterling looked in at the brightly framed room, the pond of blood under the table, Juke with his knife and George Wilson with his gun. He saw the frightened child in her mother's arms and he saw his own baby daughter, the last time he'd seen her before he left, choking on a pearl from her mother's necklace.

"I ain't coming back in, sir."

Elma watched him disappear into the shadows of the breezeway. He was there, and then he was leaving, and then he was gone.

You could just leave, she thought. You could just go.

"For pity's sake," George Wilson said. "All right. All right, then." He shook his head with disappointment. "Make me get my own hands dirty. I will if I have to."

Juke did not beg. Elma did not beg. She thought about begging. She thought about stepping in front of her father. He wouldn't kill her too. He wouldn't kill a baby.

Grimly, George Wilson cocked his gun. "Go on," he said to Elma. "Take that baby out of here."

Elma closed her eyes. Parthenia Wilson had told her that it was a woman's job to keep men from shedding each other's blood. But Elma was too late. Freddie's blood was already drying on her back. Men would shed each other's blood, and it was a woman's job to slip out from under it, to step out of the way.

She opened her eyes. She looked at her father. She did not take her eyes off of his as she put one foot closer to the door, then another. Slowly, another step, another, she carried Winna across the room. She cupped her hand to the back of the baby's head. She might have closed her eyes and made a run for it, but she went slowly, eyes open, so she might have to remember the fright on her father's face. She backed out of the kitchen, leaned back into the screen door. It swung open. She took one more look at her father. She nodded at him. He nodded back. And then she was outside in the evening.

Sterling was standing in the doorway of the shack. Once she saw him she did close her eyes and she did run. As she ran she pressed one of Winna's ears to her chest and covered the other with her hand. They were halfway across the yard to the shack when the shot came.

Elma stopped. She turned and looked back at the big house.

Another shot.

In the doorway of the shack, Pollux stood, alert. She barked twice.

Then Elma went to Sterling. The dog went back to eating the dried fish Sterling had given her. The shack did not have a lock, but when they were all inside Sterling closed the door and pushed one of the spindle chairs under the knob. He held a hand out to her and she took it. They did not know what to pray for, but together they dropped to their knees.

They did not know who the second bullet was meant for. But after some time the screen door did open and George Wilson came out of the big house carrying a large bundle in his arms like a groom carrying a bride. It was his grandson, swaddled in the blood-soaked rag rug. His legs were in his pants now and they dangled crookedly from the rug. Slowly George came down the porch stairs, taking feeble, uncertain steps. From the window of the shack, Elma and Sterling watched him lay Freddie in the bed of the Chevy truck like a sleeping child. The driver's door still hung open. George Wilson got into it, started the engine, turned on the headlights, and in no hurry to get to town, drove off the farm.

EPILOGUE

FOR FIVE MORE YEARS THE TWELVE-MILE STRAIGHT LAY FLAT and trim as a yardstick between the town and the pines. More tractors came across it. Some mules still came across it. Some mules left in trucks. The chain gang kept its ditches clear. Along it grew rabbit tobacco and wiregrass and black-eyed Susan. Groundhogs and gopher tortoises lived along it and sometimes tried to cross. One moonless night in 1933, just east of String Wilson Road, a Dodge Victory Six veered to miss a wild boar standing in the middle of the Straight and ended up in the creek. The driver broke his collarbone. For weeks folks talked about it at the crossroads store. For a long while nothing else of note happened along that stretch of road.

But when the twins were going on six years old, the weather in Georgia began to change. The whole of their lives had aligned with the greatest drought to touch that region in a hundred years, so that they knew nothing but rain-starved fields and cotton leaves that crumbled to dust between their fingers. To keep the soil from getting gullied and rilled, the state paid them eight dollars to plant an acre of kudzu, but what the kudzu did was bring rain. The vines grew wet and green where the sorghum had been the season before, and it climbed the gourd tree as tall as the twins. They made a tent of it, and capes; they fancied the gourd tree their beanstalk. When the thunderstorms came, the twins stripped naked and played in the mud puddles in the yard, and their mothers let them. In one of the storms, a bolt of lightning struck the gourd tree, blasting the top cross into splinters, rattling most of the gourds to the ground. Later the twins collected them and set them under the porch, and they found that all manner of animals liked to nest there, not just birds but squirrels and field mice and lizards, and once a pine snake they named Ugly. The kudzu grew even there, under the porch. If they let it, Winna's momma said, it might cover the whole farm, it might grow right over the house, and Winna's momma said she might let it.

But soon the gourd tree wasn't so tall. Trucks brought telephone poles and raised them up along the road. They strung up electric lines, and the purple martins found them to be a fine place to roost. The whiskey still had been abandoned shortly after George Wilson died, and when Georgia finally went wet in 1935, long after most other states did, no one even went out there to drink in their trucks. The county camp out west of town packed up and moved its tents, but the road had already been paved. The land was level, the soil was rich, rich enough that they built a new community out there, not on George Wilson's dollar but on Washington's.

Soon it wouldn't be the Twelve-Mile Straight any longer. When Cotton Acres was finished, they would extend the Straight to the state road, and the chain gang would pave it. It wouldn't be far from there to Albany, Macon, Atlanta. Some would still call it the Twelve-Mile Straight, or Twelve-Mile Road, or Twelve-Mile Pass, now that it passed through to someplace else. Some would call it the crossroad, or the number the state gave it. The twins would no longer be young

when the county renamed it Genus Jackson Road. In later years, most
folks shortened it to Jackson.

Before that, in the days before Winna left the farm for Cotton
Acres, that spring she was going on six, her daddy tried to talk up
their leaving. The sow had just farrowed and Winna had spent the
morning playing with the piglets, saying good-bye to them one by
one. She'd given each of them a name, but she got them mixed up.
Her dress was dirty with them, but her daddy parked his wheelchair
on the front porch and patted his lap and Winna climbed onto it.
He put on his radio voice. Did she know what a utopia was? It was
a community where folks homesteaded together, cooperated, grew
crops, lived happy lives. Did she know what homesteading was? It was
building a new home. It was lighting out for new territory. He pointed
west down the road, in the direction of the pines. It was starting over.
It was sharing.

Like sharecroppers? Winna asked.

No. Real sharing.

He told her about the president, whose voice she knew from the
radio, whom he had known when he was governor of New York,
who had chosen to build one of the farm projects in Cotton County.
He told her about the governor of Georgia, who was gunning to be
president himself, who didn't want help from outsiders, didn't want
a handout.

Why not? Winna asked him.

Her father thought about it. Because he's proud, he said.

But Cotton Acres would have its own school, a pool she could
swim in. A cotton gin. And he would have his own clinic. Wasn't that
wonderful? Weren't they lucky? He wouldn't have to travel the countryside anymore, or pretend he knew how to plow a field. It was all too
hard on his legs. He would leave that work to others. Now that Aunt
Nan had a car—when Parthenia Wilson died, she'd left Uncle Frank
the Buick—she was traveling as far as Valdosta to deliver babies.

Momma says she don't want ladies telling her what to plant and how, Winna said. And she don't want to have to wear shoes in the yard.

Her daddy laughed. You won't have to wear shoes in the yard, he said.

Winna could see herself in her father's glasses. She knew he wasn't her real father, but she loved him like one. Winna's real daddy was a bad man who had been killed by her granddaddy, who had good and bad in him. That was why her granddaddy was in Milledgeville. He had a bullet in his spine that made his legs frozen like her father's and another in his neck that made his mouth frozen like Aunt Nan's. That was because her great-granddaddy was a bad shot. (Or good, some folks said, depending.) Her granddaddy was in a wheelchair too. Winna had visited him twice. He drooled and moaned but he could hug her. Her momma didn't know how much he could understand, even how much he could see. He should have been in jail but the judge said jail wasn't the place for him because he was crippled, so he sent him to Milledgeville instead. But now he'd been there five years and even the sanitarium wouldn't keep him. He was being sent home. Her momma had agreed to take care of him. That was why they were moving to Cotton Acres.

How come he can't come back to the farm? Winna wanted to know.

Her father smoothed her hair with his hand. Because he doesn't belong here anymore, Winna Jean Bean. There ain't room for all of us. Specially with Nan and Frank's baby on the way.

Well, why can't they come with us?

Her father gave her the kind of smile that meant he was buying time to think. Because they belong here, Bean.

What about the piglets?

They belong here too.

Momma says it's her job to look at her daddy's face every day.

Her daddy stopped smiling. His face looked stern, then sad. He said, I suppose she thinks it is.

———————

They would be leaving the first of May, and Winna wanted a May Day party. It was her idea to use the gourd tree as the maypole. What did they need it for anymore, now that the gourds had fallen?

Her mother and Nan stood over bowls in the kitchen. Her mother looked at Nan and then at Winna. I don't think that's a good idea, she said.

Why not? said Winna. We're gone pretty it up. We can have watermelon and lemonade and fried chicken. She told all the people they'd invite: Lucy Cousins and her brothers and sisters, Al and Cecilia and their grandchildren, Uncle Quincy from Macon.

Her momma said, I don't know about all that.

But Nan gave her momma a look that said: Let her.

So at the five and dime in town, Elma bought spools of ribbon, yellow and green and blue and pink. Nan made a wreath of catalpa pods, and together they sewed the ends of the streamers to it. It took an hour to ax the kudzu vine from the base of the gourd tree, and to clear a circle big enough to walk around it. Then Sterling held the ladder and Frank shimmied up it and placed the wreath over the top like a crown.

There were all the things Winna wanted. Women brought hardboiled eggs and biscuits and chicken legs. Men brought their instruments and flasks of corn liquor. Sterling showed the children how to throw horseshoes, and Oliver gave them rides in his wheelchair. There were the field hands and the neighbors, Aunt Mag and her man and her daughter, her daddy's country patients, babies he or Nan or both had delivered. (The families who were not pleased to be left with Negro neighbors, the undeserving heirs of a fickle benefactor, did not accept the invitation. They had made their opinion known. The twins' first birthday, Sterling opened the mailbox where he'd once left a bouquet of blue hound's tongue to find that it was packed with cow flap.)

But the first day of May, a Friday, Frank led the fiddling band in "The Old Hen Cackled and the Rooster's Going to Crow" as the children took up their streamers and danced around the maypole, Winna chasing Wilson, Wilson looking over his shoulder, laughing, their bare feet kicking up dust, their arms raised above their heads, circling till they were dizzy. When they'd run out of streamers, Elma helped pin them to the foot of the pole. Then all the children collapsed in the yard to see the braid they'd made of the gourd tree. It stood with its crooked cross and one dangling gourd, its trunk wrapped in ribbons.

Nan stood a ways off, watching. She cocked her head. Something was wrong. It looked like a scarecrow dressed in Sunday clothes. What if she just loosened it a bit? And a bit more? She saw the ax lying in the dirt, clean and ready.

———

It's time, Wilson's papaw said after the cars had gone. He found Wilson in the barn, talking to the mules.

I know, Wilson said.

You say good-bye to them pigs?

Yeah, he said.

All right, bud. I'm gone need your help. You got to be brave, hear?

Papaw?

Yeah?

We got to do it? How come we can't keep em?

His papaw came over and swung Wilson up onto Clarence's bare back. It was Wilson's favorite thing, to be taller than his grandfather. He liked to take his hat and play cowboy, but he didn't do it now. His papaw did it for him, taking off the corn-shuck hat and resting it on his head. He looked up at him.

There's too many of them, Sterling said.

But you said they good eating.

Government say we got to. Everybody's got to. Won't no one buy ten grown pigs from us this year.

We can take care of em.

It don't make sense, I know. Times are getting better. That's the price we pay, I reckon. But ain't feel right to have so much for once and do away with it.

The barn was darkening into shadow, the late-day sun slicing through the cracks in the roof. Already the farm seemed quiet, emptied. Sterling remembered the day many years ago when he'd roamed this farm in a fever, looking for some ghost he couldn't name who might take something from him. For a long time, he'd had so little that he'd been afraid of losing it. Now he smoothed his hand over Clarence's snout and gave Wilson's bare ankle a jiggle. All he'd lost, all they'd lost, and still: look at what they had. Too much, too much.

We gone do some work on this farm, Wilson. You and Frank and me.

Yessir, Wilson said. He knew Frank wasn't his real father but he loved him like one. He made his mother laugh and shake her head and make a face that said: Don't you dare. He was teaching her to play the fiddle and she was teaching him to cook. Sometimes, after a good meal, he would push back his chair, fall to the floor, and say he'd died and gone through the gates of Heaven.

We gone work it right into shape, his papaw said. But first—

I know. First I got to go to school.

That's right. But first—

He stopped.

We got to do it now?

He helped Wilson down from the mule.

Tell you what, Sterling said. I got it. You go on.

So many things he wanted the boy to learn, so many ways he wanted him to be ready for the world. But there was time yet for him to learn this one.

I can do it, Wilson said. I can be brave.

I know you can, bud.

Wilson started to take off Sterling's hat and return it to him, but Sterling said, Keep it. It's yours.

Then he said, Go help your momma instead.

When he'd disappeared into the woods, Sterling gathered up all but two of the piglets. He didn't think too much about which ones to leave, just grabbed the ones who didn't squirm away. Some of them were still suckling when he pulled them off and put them in the zinc tub, and the momma was squealing. He carried the tub down to the creek. It was Lizard Creek, and before that it was Creek Creek, and before that it was Muskogee Creek, and before that it was water passing over rocks.

He was aware of each of his steps. He was aware of the feeling that he couldn't get out from under God's eye. It was the feeling he'd had when he'd gone hunting with George Wilson, that there was some evil calling him. This time he didn't see a way out of it. If he had to sacrifice something, he could think of nothing so innocent, so precious, as a pig. The pines were thick and nobody else saw him as he eased down the bank, rested the tub in the stony creek bed, and one by one, held the animals under the water.

When her mother had died, years ago now, it was spring. All the joy the winds brought, the peach blossoms angling to be adored— she hadn't wanted any of it. She had wrapped her feet in the winter's newspaper so she might not feel the warm divine blades of grass. She had sat on the porch with a basket of field peas between her knees, not looking up to see what bird was calling.

Now it was spring again and she sat in the same rocker. The gourd tree stood before her, gagged with streamers. In her lap, wedged against her belly, was her mother's coffee tin of white clay. From time to time she fed herself a cake of it. She wasn't quite twenty but deep in her bones was the dread of the seasons. She did not like them to change. She did not like what they asked of her. She did not like to say good-bye.

Good-bye! Wilson had called from the porch, watching the cars back out of the drive. Frank had followed the Plymouth in the Buick to help carry the last of their things.

Good-bye! they'd all called back. Oliver blew the horn. Even Winna's little dark-skinned doll waved. Elma blew a kiss out the window, and then pulled the pins from her hair so it fell in a wing over her face. Nan had taken off her own head rag and wiped her eyes with it.

Good-bye!

Good-bye!

Good-bye!

They'd be six miles down the road, she told herself, and yet she felt as though she and Elma had just been torn from the same warm body. It was all this birth she was grieving, because birth was a death of what had come before.

All the joy of spring, all the new life, and now her father was drowning God's pigs in the creek. Too much innocence, too much beauty—it was as unbearable as hate. She thought of her mother's knife, of her tongue buried out there under the gourd tree, and for a dizzy moment she understood it: that when you had been harmed, there were times you had to harm those you loved, so you could bear your love for them. That their innocence—that was what was unbearable.

She sat and she rocked. She sat with it for a while, her love and grief and forgiveness.

Then Wilson came up from the pines and across the yard and up the porch steps. She gave him a questioning look.

Just in the barn, he said. Papaw said come help.

No. She pointed to his hat.

Oh. Papaw gave it to me.

She closed the coffee tin and placed it on the floor and slapped her empty lap. He had to sit sideways on her knees, so big were they both getting. There were leaves crumbled on the back of his overalls. She brushed them off and rubbed his back and he let her. With his dirty little hands he polished the egg of her belly. She stroked the silky edge of the corn-shuck hat. Soon, when he learned to read, she would tell him about it.

For now, they had work to do and an hour of daylight. She tapped his back and he hopped off her lap and followed her to the yard.

You wanted to get them streamers down, Frank would say when he got home and for a long time after, you could have waited for me to get the ladder.

There was no more waiting. They had made the wretched thing beautiful. For a few hours, it was innocent again. She'd thought that might be enough, but even its beauty was unbearable. Now it was time to bring it down.

They took turns with the ax. Nan showed her son how to start, how to make a knee-high notch on one side, so it would fall away from the house. She showed him how to swing the ax, to put his shoulder into it, to aim low. The ax was heavy, and Wilson was proud. They turned and made a notch on the other side. The pole creaked in the breeze. They chipped at it, and rested, and watched the sun go down. Nan returned to the first notch, gave it one more swing, and looked up to see the last gourd shuddering. A lone purple martin leaped from it, dipped down over the yard, and went for the treetops.

When the gourd tree finally came down, it fell slow and regretful. It shook the ground beneath their feet. The birds fluttered in the trees. Down at the creek, Sterling felt it.

What was left was a stump, like the stub of a tongue. In time it was grown over. The gourd tree was good yellow pine, and they built two little mule-ear chairs from it, child's size, and they put them on the front porch. The wreath of colored streamers they hung from the porch too, the ribbons reaching almost to the ground, on some days lifting loose in the wind. From either direction, coming down the road, it was the first sign you'd see of the farm.

Acknowledgments

I'm indebted to a great many people, places, and books for their help in shaping this one.

Many thanks to the Atlanta History Center; the Georgia Historical Society; the Georgia Museum of Agriculture; the New Georgia Encyclopedia; the Digital Library of Georgia; Georgia Southern University; the Stuart A. Rose Manuscript, Archives, and Rare Book Library at Emory University, which provided me with an invaluable research fellowship, especially curators Kevin Young and Randall K. Burkett; Clayton McGahee, Archives Coordinator for the Woodruff Health Sciences Library at Emory; the family of Aaron Bernd, especially Gus B. Kaufman, and the family of Viola Andrews, whose papers in the Rose archives were indispensable; Brian Brown, historian, photographer, and curator of Vanishing South Georgia, for his warm expertise; Sherri Butler of the *Fitzgerald Herald-Leader* for her insight and generosity; Janisse Ray for inspiration; and Rebecca Makkai for that 1929 Sears catalog.

My research brought me to many books, but I'm especially

grateful for *The Tragedy of Lynching* by Arthur F. Raper; *The Warmth of Other Suns* by Isabel Wilkerson; *Georgia Nigger* by John L. Spivak; *Cotton Tenants* by James Agee and Walker Evans; *Hard Times* by Studs Turkel; *Trouble in July* by Erskine Caldwell; *Momma Learned Us to Work* by Lu Ann Jones; *Like a Family: The Making of a Southern Cotton Mill World* by Lu Ann Jones et al.; and *Moonshiner's Daughter* by Mary Judith Messer, all of which were essential to imagining life in the South in the 1920s and 30s.

Ithaca College has offered me critical support for this project, from a summer research grant that enabled an early trip to Georgia to a faculty leave that enabled me to finish it. Many thanks to my wonderful students and colleagues in the Department of Writing. Thank you also to the Saltonstall Arts Colony, the Shop Café, and Philippa Matusiak, for quiet desks around Ithaca; and Chris Holmes, for the encouragement. Thank you to Katie Marks and Jaime Warburton for their support and friendship. Thanks also to Andrew Clark of the Department of Molecular Biology and Genetics at Cornell.

Thank you to my tireless, talented readers: Derek Adams, Anna Solomon, Callie Wright, Ursula Villarreal-Moura, Jack Wang, Jacob White, Justin Quarry, and especially Mary Beth Keane, who was with this book from the first hopeless draft, and who never lets me off the hook.

Bottomless thanks to my magical agent, Jim Rutman, and my visionary editor, Megan Lynch, who understood this book from the inside out, even when I didn't. Thank you to Brian Egan at Sterling Lord Literistic, and to my amazing team at Ecco: Dan Halpern, Miriam Parker, Sonya Cheuse, Meghan Deans, Emma Dries, Eleanor Kriseman, Sara Wood, Suet Chong, Victoria Mathews, and Dale Rohrbaugh.

Thank you to my high school English teachers Robin Wright and, in fond memory, Rhonda Wilson, a daughter of Georgia, who assigned *Absalom, Absalom!* and *Beloved* the same year.

My love and gratitude to my family, who shared their stories with me graciously and housed, hosted, and otherwise supported me, in particular Bob and Gretchen Babcock and Allen and Ann Stephens Henderson.

My love and gratitude to my mother, Ann Babcock Henderson, whom we lost during the writing of this book, but who was with me on every page.

My love and gratitude to my sons, Nicolas and Henry, and to their father, Aaron Squadrilli, who every day released me into another world and then welcomed me back into theirs.

This book is dedicated to my wise and generous father, William Cecil Henderson, born in Ben Hill County in 1932 and still the best reader I know. More power to your elbow.